The Silent Child

MJ White is the pseudonym of bestselling author Miranda Dickinson, author of twelve books, including six Sunday Times bestsellers. Her books have been translated into ten languages, selling over a million copies worldwide. A long time lover of crime fiction, the Cora Lael Mysteries is her debut crime series. She is a singer-songwriter, host of weekly Facebook Live show, Fab Night In Chatty Thing.

Also by MJ White

A Cora Lael Mystery

The Secret Voices
The Silent Child

MIRANDA DICKINSON WRITING AS

MJ WHITE

THE

SILENT CHILD

hera

First published in the United Kingdom in 2022 by

Hera Books
Unit 9 (Canelo), 5th Floor
Cargo Works, 1-2 Hatfields
London SE1 9PG
United Kingdom

A CIP catalogue record for this book is available from the British Library.

Print ISBN 978 1 80436 084 2
Ebook ISBN 978 1 80436 079 8

Look for more great books at www.herabooks.com

Printed and bound in Great Britain by Clays Ltd, Elcograf S.p.A.

1

For Al Smith

Thank you for the many, <u>many</u> chats

that helped bring Cora to the page.

And for believing in her from the beginning.

x

'In some causes, silence is dangerous.'

Saint Ambrose (339AD-397AD)

'The realm of silence is large enough beyond the grave.'

George Eliot (1819-1880)

Lottie

I'm not dumb.

Whatever they say.

I'm *not*.

I just choose not to speak.

They want me to talk, to prove I'm not dumb. They don't realise what they're asking. What could happen if I talk again.

Nobody understands. Nobody knows the truth. But I do.

If I could smuggle you inside my head, you'd know I wasn't dumb. You'd hear my thoughts screaming. Because behind the silence everyone sees, I *am* screaming. I've been screaming for eleven months.

It isn't a fad, or something I'll grow out of. This is my life now.

If you were inside my head, you'd know why I don't speak.

Why I can't speak again…

Chapter One

Minshull

The body was badly concealed amid piles of old clothing in the former hay barn, one pale arm clearly visible, hanging between the grubby jumpers and jeans too ripped for anyone to wear. Tossed into a corner, forgotten. There was no dignity in death here: there never was for bodies like these.

What a lonely place to die.

The farm where they stood lay twelve miles northwest of Ipswich, set back from the narrow country lane that twisted around low-hedged patchwork fields. It was far enough from other farms and buildings to appear remote, yet only a mile away from the nearest village. The twists of the road and the broad fields surrounding it gave it the feeling of being completely cut off from the world. Abbot's Farm was abandoned now, not yet grabbed by developers greedy to sell the dream of rural living to wealthy ex-Londoners. The farmhouse was far from derelict, its roof still good, but its darkened windows were cracked and flaky-framed, the first beginnings of grasses appearing at the edges where nature had begun to reclaim it.

The old barn beside the farmhouse reeked of neglect, mildew and death, mingled with ancient straw. It hung in the air like the dust, a thick cloud that clogged your lungs and clung to your clothes. DS Rob Minshull gritted his teeth and pressed forward, the ghostly pale face of DC Dave Wheeler a pace behind him.

'I wouldn't bring my gran to this jumble sale,' Wheeler joked.

'I don't blame you,' Minshull smirked. At times like these humour was the only weapon against creeping dread. He was glad Dave

Wheeler was here. Minshull crouched by the body, following the line of the arm from dirt-blackened fingernails up along its deeply scratched bare forearm and over the contour of the clothing pile, trying to make out the rest of its position.

'What do you reckon, Sarge? Drugs?'

'Could be. Who called it in?'

'Dog-walker.' Wheeler grinned when Minshull looked up at him. 'Improbable as that sounds.'

'Out here?'

'Farmer from the next farm along, walking his dog the long way. His dog suddenly dashed off and when he managed to catch up with it, it was here, licking the deceased's arm. The farmer has called us before, apparently. Three months ago. Lights and vehicles and noise here late at night. He thought it was a rave.'

'Shit rave.'

Wheeler's chuckle was a tiny gift of warmth to hold on to. There was precious little else to warm the soul here. Scattered around the floor amid the straw and ancient animal dung was the tell-tale paraphernalia of drugs: spent needles, burned foil and discarded dirty swabs. Lately, more sites like these had come to light, a spiralling problem of the drug trade in desolate, rural areas. South Suffolk Police were about to launch a widespread investigation following a damning exposé in the national press: once again they were on the back foot, battling accusations of bumbling rural police being trampled over by intelligent drug gangs crossing the county border from Essex and London beyond.

The body could be yet another victim, another statistic. But something about its position bothered Minshull. It was half hidden under the piles of clothing, but it couldn't have perished there. It had been dumped deliberately and hastily covered with garments in an attempt to conceal it. A stark statement of the person's worthlessness and someone's hurry to be rid of the problem.

'So, did the dog smell blood?' Minshull asked, looking around.

'There's none around that I can see. And our friend here would have been long dead by the time our doggy chum found him. The farmer thinks it might have been the smell.'

3

'That would make sense.' Minshull nodded, mentally blocking the scent of death that you never got used to in this job, no matter how many times you encountered it.

The edge of a coloured shape where the arm disappeared into the clothing mountain caught his eye. Minshull peered closer, tilting his head. 'What do you reckon this is, Dave?'

The DC leaned in. 'Tattoo of some sort?'

'That's what I thought. I don't want to move the fabric covering it till SOCOs get here. Can you work out what it is?'

'Can't see from here. Hang on, if I grab hold of your shoulder I reckon I can lean in closer than you can. Shall I give it a go?'

'Be my guest,' Minshull replied, dropping one knee to the dirt floor and keeping his shoulder steady as Wheeler braced against it and leaned towards the body.

'Steady... Hold it there, Minsh...'

'Anything?'

'I'm just trying to get a bit closer... Ah! It's a top hat.'

Minshull frowned. 'A what?'

'A brown shiny top hat. Like magicians pull bunnies out of.'

'Really? Weird.' He waited as Wheeler pushed back upright, then rose to his feet, brushing a dank brown stain from the knee of his suit trousers.

'This could be a magic trick gone horribly wrong,' Wheeler suggested. 'Maybe our pal was trying to do a Houdini water tank trick with bags of clothes instead?'

'Best of luck selling that theory to Anderson,' Minshull grinned. 'How long before the SOCOs arrive?'

'About forty minutes, they reckon. They got delayed by that job across the border.'

'How come Norfolk are nicking our bods?'

Wheeler shrugged. 'Budgets, Sarge. It's always budgets.'

'Right. You okay to wait for them? I need to get back to Anderson.'

'Sure. I don't envy you the task.' Wheeler's grimace said it all.

'Me neither, Dave.' Minshull slapped a hand on Dave Wheeler's shoulder as he passed. 'Make sure you mention that tattoo to them as soon as they get here. And call me when they've moved our friend, yeah?'

The blast of fresh air met his lungs like an elixir, as Minshull stalked away from the barn towards the pool car. If the deceased was a victim of a drugs gang, it could be a significant lead in their fledgling investigation into organised drug activity crossing over into Suffolk. DI Joel Anderson would be grimly delighted when Minshull briefed him of the details – not about the death but about the step forward it might offer them. But the body bothered Minshull. It didn't feel like a simple death. Anderson, wishing for a clear-cut lead, would not be delighted to hear that…

Chapter Two

Cora

CASE LLM462/LMA – BRIEFING

Subject: LOTTIE MAY ARUNDEL
Age: 15 years, 2 months
Address: Fourwinds, Upper Branstoft Road, Woodsham
St Mary
Issue: Has not spoken for eleven months

Notes
Initial interviews conducted with family, friends and
teachers have largely drawn a blank. While Lottie is
willing to communicate via written notes and her adapted
iPad, she refuses to be drawn on her reasons for not
speaking.

Lottie has received two courses of speech therapy
and has been under the care of a consultant neurologist.
Neither the speech therapists nor consultant have been
able to identify any physiological or neurological reason
for her lack of speech. Current conclusion is that she is
displaying indicators of Elective Mutism.

Family interviews have so far revealed no reason for
trauma or significant events that could have triggered the
condition. School interviews suggested the same. Close
friends will only confirm that she ceased speaking eleven
months ago. They offer no reason why.

Dr Cora Lael frowned at the case file and wondered what on earth she could find in common with an electively mute fifteen-year-old. Her new boss was watching her like a hopeful puppy. In her three months of working with him in the South Suffolk Education Authority's Educational Psychology Unit, Cora had already learned the danger of this expression. It was endearing, but it ultimately signalled more work for her.

'Why do you think I can find a different outcome?'

Dr Tristram Noakes shrugged and pushed a tin of biscuits across his desk towards her. Another warning sign – not everyone in the department got offered biscuits. 'Honestly? I'm not sure you can. But we've reached an impasse and the kid's parents are threatening legal action.'

'So much for my show-stopping expertise, then.'

'It isn't like that.'

Cora raised an eyebrow.

'Seriously, Cora, it isn't. You see things others miss. I think we need that here. Standard approaches just haven't worked and the longer we go on relentlessly pursuing the same old things, the more we'll hit brick walls…'

'…And litigation.'

Tris gave a sigh as heavy as the invisible weight on his shoulders. 'That too. We're underfunded as it is: expensive legal bills could close us down.'

'I don't know, Tris.'

'Just meet her at least? Get a sense of where she's at.' He dipped his head a little. 'See what you can *hear*.'

Cora smiled. His carefulness was sweet. Telling people about her emotional synaesthesia – the ability to sense emotional echoes from discarded objects – still felt like a risk, but since she'd returned to Suffolk from the wilds of Devon's South Hams it was part of her new life. The study she'd helped research and write with the University of South Suffolk was published and now her condition was known, if

7

not yet widely. As it turned out, Tris Noakes had met her in the pages of the study before she'd joined the team as consultant psychologist. When Cora had mentioned during her interview for the job that she was the quoted SUBJECT A in the study, she'd been surprised by Tris's reaction. It was the first time anyone had met the news of her condition with unbridled admiration. Tris was a safe place when it came to Cora's ability and that calmed the rush of nerves that always followed any mention of it.

'When are you next seeing her?'

Tris offered a sheepish smile. 'I'm due over there at eleven today.'

Cora stared at him. 'Tris!'

'I know...'

'Talk about putting me on the spot!'

'You wouldn't have to come today if you didn't feel ready. But it could be a good opportunity to meet her.'

She should have seen it coming. But Tris Noakes was offering her his most pleading smile and it was hard to resist. 'So tell me what you know already.'

'She seems like a good kid, apart from the silence. Not overly timid, carries herself well, is reportedly bright and a good student. I think that's why it doesn't make sense. If she found social situations awkward, or suffered from anxiety or low self-esteem, her lack of speech would be more logical.'

'How does she communicate?'

'She has an iPad with a text-to-speech function. It's strange: after a while you forget she isn't physically speaking the words.'

'And she's given no indication of what stopped her speaking?'

'No.' He risked a smile. 'Admit it: you're intrigued.'

'There has to be something else going on there.' She smiled at her own admission. 'Okay, yes. It could be interesting. A bit of warning would have been preferable, of course.'

'Best to strike while the iron's hot,' Tris grinned. 'Or before you think better of it. I think you might be the difference, Cora. Give us a different perspective, not a typical medical professional approach that investigates, labels and leaves. I don't know, maybe Lottie might respond to that.'

Cora leaned back, feeling the chair back sturdy and strong against her spine. The shoulder injury she'd sustained from two gunshots over a year ago could make sitting for long periods of time uncomfortable. Tris Noakes's high-backed office chair provided welcome relief. 'I can't promise I'll get her to speak. But I'll meet her with you today. See how we get on.'

Tris clapped his hands and helped himself to a celebratory biscuit. 'That's all I'm asking. Who knows? Maybe you and Lottie will hit it off.'

Why would a fifteen-year-old refuse to speak? Cora had to admit it was a puzzle that appealed to her. Back at her desk with the case notes open, she picked up a photograph. A dark-haired, hazel-eyed girl stared out, surrounded by laughing friends at what looked like a party, her face strangely unmoved as her eyes bore into the camera.

A chill passed through her as Cora recalled photographs of herself in her late teens. Pages upon pages in her mother's photograph album, the backdrops shifting through family celebrations, holidays and college graduation, but her wild, staring expression unchanged in all of them. The unmistakable mark of someone who felt they were an outsider.

What had stolen Lottie Arundel's words? Or who?

Chapter Three

Anderson

It was a PR nightmare.

Another one.

DCI Sue Taylor was doing her nut, sweeping around the corridors of South Suffolk Constabulary HQ like a raging, screeching Northern banshee. Maybe if she'd listened to DI Joel Anderson six months ago, they wouldn't be on the back foot with this now.

But Sue Taylor chose not to, because Sue Taylor would never admit Anderson was right.

An internal investigation following the high profile missing child case in St Just a year ago had ruled that Anderson and his CID team had been justified in their recruitment of a civilian consultant. His superior officer, anticipating the book being thrown at him, had been shocked by the verdict and now was hell-bent on wreaking her revenge on Anderson in any way she could. Had he been closer to the correct age for early retirement she would have pensioned him off immediately. But until that was an option, she had resorted to thwarting him at every turn.

Anderson understood personal vendettas as much as anyone in the force. He'd seen them in action too many times during his career. But DCI Taylor's obsession with dismissing him had bit her in the behind this time. Six months ago he'd raised the issue of drug gangs heading to the wilds of rural Suffolk to bring their unwanted trade into the county. He'd seen increasing reports from the public of suspected drug houses and wanted the force to nip the issue in the bud, before it spiralled out of control. But DCI Taylor had dismissed it out of turn:

'That might be a problem for the city forces, Joel, but we're small fry. There's not enough potential trade in Suffolk to warrant any major gang's attention. I'm not committing valuable time and resources to a minor problem. We've far more pressing issues to attend to.'

She was eating those words now, wasn't she?

The special report in *The Sentinel*, published a week ago and now flooding every news outlet, claimed that dangerous drug gangs, keen to avoid the increased scrutiny of the police in London and Essex, were heading into Suffolk to trade under the radar. *The last place anyone expects to be a haven for the drug trade is sleepy, picturesque Suffolk*, the report stated. *But now the county most likely to appeal to OAP coach tours and holidaying families is the destination du jour for organised drug crime. And all of it is happening without any concerted effort from South Suffolk Police. Local residents have seen warning signs for years but it appears the county's law enforcers have turned a blind eye. With Suffolk now reliant on the tourist trade for survival, could this wilful negligence by police threaten the very lifeblood of the county?*

It was the first piece of adverse publicity the force had encountered for a year, arriving just at the moment when Anderson was congratulating himself on a pretty decent run of avoiding the headlines. Compared with other constabularies in the country, that was an achievement indeed.

He still didn't like to think of the last time South Suffolk CID had faced the wrath of the media, even though in the end they had emerged, phoenix-like, from the ashes of slander. He'd recommenced counselling at his wife's insistence and while he grumbled every week about going, privately he valued each session. Lately, he'd felt a return to his old self, a recalibration of his sharp mind that had served him so faithfully before.

Smugness wasn't part of the therapy, but today it was a reward.

Rural drug dealers aren't a priority, Joel. Our budgets only stretch so far.

They'll be a priority now though, won't they, Sue?

Anderson relaxed back in his chair, enjoying the warm rays of sunlight sneaking in between the slats of his office window blinds.

Today was going to be a good day.

'Guv?' DC Kate Bennett knocked against the wooden architrave of Anderson's open office doorway.

'Ah, Kate. Lovely day, don't you think?'

Bennett hovered uncertainly by the open door. 'Sure, Guv.'

He smiled broad and wide, resisting the urge to laugh at his earnest colleague. Bennett was a great DC – by rights she should have been DS now instead of Rob Minshull – but Anderson worried a little for her. She'd not been her usual self of late. Anderson would hold his hands up to say he was the least perceptive when it came to his colleagues: that he'd noticed it was definite cause for concern. All of the team had times when they kept their heads down and it was understood to give space where needed. But he hadn't seen Bennett as guarded as she had been this week, not even with the nightmare she'd endured a year ago buying a new house. Come to think of it, that was the only pertinent piece of information he knew about Kate Bennett. Did she have a life beyond policing? He hoped she did and that she was protecting it with her silence.

'Come in. Forgive my rare good humour today. I can assure you it won't last.'

The slightest glimmer of mischief flashed in her smile. 'That's a relief, Guv. Although I might be the one to end it.'

'Ah well, I had my moment. Sit, please.'

'I just got word from Dave Wheeler. A body's been found in what looks like an illegal drug den.'

'Where?'

'Middle of nowhere. Abbot's Farm on the Semer Road near What-field, about twelve miles out of Ipswich? It's been abandoned for twenty years, according to locals. But there have been several reports of loud music, lights and vehicles coming in and out, for the last few months.'

'Were those investigated?'

Bennett's expression said more than she needed to.

'Wonderful. Are SOCOs there?'

'On their way. It's been assigned the operational name Feldspar. DS Minshull should be back here shortly. He can tell you more.'

'Okay. Thanks for the heads-up. Can you start preliminary enquiries into the location? Previous history, last occupants of the farm, any reports into suspicious activity and so on?'

Bennett rose from her chair. 'On it, Guv.'

'Excellent. Er, Kate?'

His young DC turned in the doorway. 'Yes, Guv?'

'Is everything okay?'

Bennett's steady smile tightened. 'Yes, Guv.'

'I don't mean between you and I – although if I've offended you in any way...'

'You haven't, Guv.'

'Good. Good, well, if you have any concerns or issues you would like to talk over, I hope you know my door's always open.' Beneath his desk, Anderson's feet balled in his shoes. If his attempts to encourage Bennett to speak were this excruciating for him, how bad must it be for Kate?

'I know that, Guv.' She shuffled a little. 'Is there anything else?'

Briefly, her eyes dipped. Anderson caught it immediately.

'That's all,' he said, dropping his voice to a low burr. 'I value your work, Kate. But I also watch out for my team. It's important you know that. If you need anything...'

'Guv.' She nodded, gaze averted. Anderson sensed a door firmly closing.

'Okay. Thank you.'

Watching his DC hurry out into the open-plan office, Anderson clocked DS Rob Minshull arriving.

'Ah, Minshull, bring us a brew and step in my office,' he barked happily. Minshull's eye-roll was another unexpected reward. He'd hate having to make coffee and Anderson knew it. Might as well use his advantage while he was still in charge of the unit...

Five minutes later, surprisingly drinkable coffee delivered and a flush-faced detective sergeant seated on the other side of his desk, Anderson faced Minshull.

'So, we have a body?'

'Yes, Guv.'

'Any word on ID yet?'

'It's too early to say. The body was still in situ when I left. It's been dumped in the middle of a large pile of old clothes and rubbish, most of it hidden. We believe it's a male: beyond that we won't know until the body can be retrieved.'

'What's your initial impression? Overdose? Rough sleeper?'

'Murder.'

Anderson sat back in his seat, all traces of humour obliterated. 'Because?'

Minshull placed his mug slowly back on the desk as if the action would order his thoughts. 'It's been dumped. No way the deceased could have died where we found them – half-buried by piles of clothing. Someone would have had to put the body there. They tried to cover it up but failed. And I feel like the death was no accident, either. It feels intentional, planned, although the method of the body's disposal was more an act of panic than planning.'

'In what way?'

'They made a pig's ear of concealing the body. One arm was hanging out of the clothing pile – the farmer from a neighbouring farm who alerted us said he'd found his dog licking it.'

Anderson shuddered. 'So whoever dumped it there was in a hurry to get away. It doesn't prove murder. Perhaps they discovered the body and wanted to hide it. Like you say, they panicked. No evidence that the person who dumped the body also killed the deceased.'

'No evidence that they *didn't* yet.' Minshull was clearly not ready to let go of his theory. 'We'll know more when we get the body moved.'

'Fair enough. When's Dave due back?'

'He was just waiting to brief SOCOs when they arrive and then he was coming back here. Should be in the next hour or so?'

Anderson nodded. 'Right. Soon as he's back we'll do a team briefing. You okay to sort it out?'

'Sure, Guv.'

Anderson waved for his DS to leave but just as Minshull reached the door, he called him back. 'And Rob?'

Thinly veiled consternation flashed across Minshull's expression. 'Guv?'

Grinning, Anderson lifted his mug. 'Excellent coffee. Must have you make it more often.'

Minshull's thin-lipped smile brightened Anderson's mood no end.

Chapter Four

Bennett

Kate Bennett breathed a silent sigh of relief as she left Anderson's office. His question had come out of nowhere and she'd barely managed to answer calmly. Had he noticed? Joel Anderson was a great boss most of the time, but he didn't always notice nuances like the change in emotions of his team. This new development was worrying.

She busied herself at her desk while the banter of the CID office played out around her. Since the media broke the story about drug gangs from London and Essex crossing the border into Suffolk, she had been tasked with trying to establish which gangs were currently operational in the area. In many ways South Suffolk Police were flying blind. But Bennett relished the challenge. She loved a puzzle and the reward that came from untangling a seemingly impossible problem. It was why she'd been first choice when DS Minshull had assigned tasks for Operation Collegiate, the hastily commissioned investigation into the gangs plying their trade within the county.

He appeared at her desk now, his face bearing a flush she only ever saw after his meetings with Anderson.

'Kate, how's it going?'

She stared at her screen. 'It's a needle in a haystack.'

'Yeah, sorry.' He bowed his head and pulled a chair up to sit beside her. 'It's going to be a bastard to unravel.'

She offered a smile. 'That's why you've got me.'

'I appreciate it. What do you have so far?'

She turned back to her screen. 'I've been going over drug-related arrests over the last nine months as a starting point, seeing if any names reappear.'

'Good.'

'Trouble is, all of these guys are small fry. They either no-commented in interview or pleaded guilty in court because they knew a custodial sentence would be preferable to ratting out their bosses. We've had phones that auto-delete information or lock before we can decipher them, which suggest more organised groups but so far that's all I've found in common.'

Minshull sank back into his chair. 'It's all good stuff, Kate. We knew it wasn't going to be easy. Any links, however unimportant, could be key to bringing cases together. It's going to be a ton of work.'

'I don't mind,' Bennett replied truthfully. Right now she welcomed the distraction.

'Okay, put this on hold for now and make the checks DI Anderson has asked for on Abbot's Farm. Then as soon as you can, get back to it.'

It was a lot of work. But work meant fewer awkward conversations to navigate. This morning, that was a gift.

–

An hour later, the history of Abbot's Farm was slowly emerging in the notes on Bennett's notepad as she searched methodically for mentions of the farm. She'd been vaguely aware of DC Dave Wheeler arriving back in the CID office but had quickly pushed the conversation of her colleagues to the back of her mind as she focused on her work. When she reached a natural break, she emerged into the middle of their conversation, a little dazed from her concentration.

'He's a bloody nightmare,' DC Dave Wheeler was saying. 'I always know when he's been here on nights because I can never find anything.'

'Old Bruce been stealing your Post-its again, Dave?' DC Les Evans smirked, enjoying the joke.

Bennett saw DC Drew Ellis suppress a grin as he delivered mugs of tea to the team. Ordinarily, she would be in the thick of the CID office banter, but not today. She sent Ellis a brief smile as he placed her *Line of Duty* mug on her desk, a surprise bourbon biscuit carefully laid beside it.

Bless him.

He gave her a nod of solidarity before he moved away.

Small gestures like that meant the world, even if right now Bennett couldn't fully process them. Nobody seemed unduly concerned about her, though, and that was a blessing in itself. The rest of the team carried on as usual around her and Bennett was glad of the familiar ordinariness of it all.

'It's not about sticky notes, Les, it's about him always choosing my desk to spread his gubbins over on night duty. Why doesn't he choose Drew's, hmm? Or Kate's? Or yours?'

'He doesn't choose Les's desk because he'd have to excavate it first to find a flat surface,' Ellis replied, causing Wheeler to choke on his tea. Ellis had done more of that lately; returning fire on Evans' incessant mocking with whip-smart replies that floored his colleagues.

Bennett remembered the lanky, beetroot-blushing youngster Ellis had been when he'd first joined as a probationary DC over a year ago. How much had changed since then…

Inevitably, her mind strayed beyond the four walls of South Suffolk CID, dragging her heart to her heels.

Too many things had changed…

No, she scolded herself, forcing her attention back to the list of Abbot's Farm mentions on her screen. *I am not thinking of that today.*

Around her the team continued their jokes and moans about DC Bruce Ovenden, the detective who covered the CID office during the night. Bennett had only worked with him a handful of times, but she knew his reputation well. Everyone in the station did. By rights, he should have retired years ago, but as he was the only one happy to regularly cover the graveyard shift, he'd so far escaped every attempt by DCI Sue Taylor to coax him away.

'Leave him a note,' Evans suggested, clearly enjoying himself. '*Hands off my desk, Brucey!* That ought to work.'

Wheeler harrumphed into his tea.

The sudden opening of Anderson's door sent every head dipping back to their screens as their superior appeared in the CID office.

'Okay everyone, briefing in five minutes please.'

'Guv.'

'Yes, Guv.'

Work was halted, notebooks grabbed and chairs shifted, the team quickly taking their seats around the large whiteboard on the wall beside Minshull's desk. Minshull had already pinned up initial photos of the abandoned farm where the body had been found, together with a map of the immediate area and the first image of the body in situ amid piles of clothing.

When all were assembled, he turned to face them, snapping the lid back onto his whiteboard pen. Anderson perched on the spare desk alongside Bennett's and motioned for Minshull to begin.

'Thanks everyone. So, we have a body, discovered at seven a.m. this morning, Wednesday 19th April, by Mr William Carter, who owns a neighbouring farm. His dog found the body...'

'A dog-walker? Seriously?' Evans chuckled, his mirth subsiding when Minshull shot him a look.

'Dave and I have already done that joke, Les,' Minshull replied, with no hint of a smile but a note of fun in his tone. 'Keep up, yeah?'

Evans slumped into disgruntled silence.

Minshull turned back to the board. Bennett strongly suspected this move was to mask a smile. She thanked her stars again for the safe predictability of her colleagues. It helped, especially today.

'So, the body was located here, in the old barn at Abbot's Farm, on the Semer Road near Whatfield. Kate, what do you have for us on that so far?'

Bennett consulted her notes, 'It's been disused as a farm since 1997, but I did find a record that Mr Carter had previously contacted us regarding unusual activity on the site. Lights, noise, vehicles coming and going at strange times. There was a cash-for-clothes business that operated from that address about two years ago, but no mention of ownership of the site. I found a mention of it on a flyer posted on a community Facebook page. It seems it operated for about six months before it was abandoned.'

'That explains the discarded bags of clothes.' Minshull observed. 'But you say whoever operated that wasn't listed as owner or tenant?'

'No, Sarge. My best guess is that someone set up there as a business squatter, abandoning it when they were discovered. I checked the land registry but it appears the most recent owner died with no record of family to pass the farm on to.'

'Could a drug gang have operated it? Or taken over the site when the clothes business left?' Les asked.

'Either are possible,' Minshull began, silenced when Anderson held up a hand.

'I don't think we can make that link at this stage,' he said. Bennett could tell from Minshull's expression that the DS may have already been working on that theory.

'There are signs of drug activity there, Guv,' Minshull replied. 'Recent, by the looks of it. And that, added to Mr Carter's reports, could suggest it could have been a viable location for drug operations. The report in the *Sentinel*...'

'...was sensationalist, inconclusive speculation,' Anderson snapped back. 'The drug stuff could be local kids, rough sleepers...'

'Bit far out for rough sleepers, Guv,' Wheeler interjected.

'Our DOA could be a rough sleeper. The drug litter could be his.'

'With respect, Guv, our bloke didn't put himself there.' Minshull tapped the blurred phone camera photo with his pen. 'Whoever he was, someone else shoved his body into that bank of clothes.'

Anderson reddened but had to concede. Even from the blurry image it was plain to see. The position of the body indicated someone had tried to conceal it within the layers of old clothing. Badly, as it transpired.

'So are Op Collegiate and Op Feldspar linked?' Bennett asked, aware that her question could simultaneously win favour with one party and lose it with the other.

'No. Not yet.' Anderson answered before Minshull could reply. 'We don't rule it out, but for the time being we treat Operation Feldspar as wholly separate from Operation Collegiate. Op Feldspar has to be our priority until we have all the details of our victim, cause of death and history.'

Minshull observed his superior for an uncomfortable moment. Not taking his eyes off Anderson, he replied, 'Kate, stay on the Abbot's

Farm info search until we get a positive ID, but then I'll need you to go out with Drew for interviews.'

Bennett knew it was inevitable, but that didn't make it any more palatable. Being out of the office, in a car with one of her colleagues, meant a greater possibility of fielding awkward questions. It was the last thing she needed.

Turning from Anderson at last, Minshull addressed the team. 'Dave, any update from the SOCOs?'

'They arrived about ten minutes after you left. Got away from the Norfolk job earlier than expected.'

'Bet they were happy about that,' Minshull smiled.

'Happy to be back on the right side of the border,' Wheeler grinned. 'Initial observations are being made now and when the pathologist arrives and is happy they'll move him.'

'Who's the duty pathologist today?' Anderson asked.

'Dr Amara,' Wheeler replied, frowning at a snigger from Evans.

'Spooky Morticia!'

'*Les.*'

'I'm just saying, she's a scary woman.'

'So you're volunteering to attend the full post mortem, are you?' Minshull cut across his colleague. That was enough to silence Evans. 'Thought not. Dave, as soon as you have anything from the pathologist on site, let me know.'

Wheeler nodded. 'Sarge.'

'Okay, until we hear from the SOCOs we focus on missing person's reports for the last six months initially. Any males aged eighteen to forty reported missing in the county. Let's see if we can get a heads-up on our victim as soon as possible.'

Minshull surveyed the team. Bennett noticed that he didn't quite make eye contact with Anderson. It was unusual to see Minshull rattled by anything. When he looked back at her, Bennett busied herself with her notes.

'Okay, thanks all. Be ready for when developments happen. As soon as they do we'll move fast.'

The team headed back to their desks, Bennett quick to get her head down as soon as she could to avoid being caught in one of the whispered conversations going on around her. A murder case was big news here and she could sense the itch of impatience amongst her colleagues. She understood it: being given the news and then told to wait to get cracking on it was the worst. She left them to their hushed exchanges as she returned to her work.

Lottie

They're sending a new person to see me. A doctor, apparently.

They're coming today, Mum says. I could tell by the way she said it that she's getting her hopes up again.

I hate that.

It reminds me how powerless I am; how this *thing* can hurt everyone I love without a second thought.

I've made the right decision to stay quiet, but I don't like hurting Mum. She's tried everything to help me, and with every new shot I see hope dying in her a little more. I hear her crying in the bedroom when she thinks I'm not listening. She locks herself in there pretending to dust, forgetting our house is one big glass echo chamber for her sobs. I'm not stupid – I know what she's doing. I hear everything.

Dad's hurt too, probably, although it's impossible to see behind his short temper and ridiculous flounces out to the workshop. He's been barking about legal action lately, as if suing all the therapists, doctors and caseworkers who have tried to cure me is going to bring back my voice, or make everything else go away.

I don't like denying them what they want, but it's better than the alternative.

If they knew the truth, it would end them.

So I'll be a good girl when they arrive and I'll smile and nod and type answers for the New One, but I won't budge. I can't. Dr Cora Lael can do what she wants, but she'll leave as all the others have done: with nothing.

Chapter Five

Cora

Tris Noakes was waiting by his car when Cora arrived at the address of her latest case. He gave a self-conscious wave, stepping back as Cora parked.

'Well, what do you think?'

'It's – very different.'

The approach to the house had been grand enough, its wide gravel drive sweeping up from the road, but the glass and steel building that greeted them at its end was something else. Its expansive glass exterior reflected the sky so that it was almost as if the building didn't exist, a barely perceptible ghost gazing across an uninterrupted view of the tidal estuary and out to the sea.

'Imagine living with that view every day,' Tris said, his words almost stolen by the bracing blast of wind rushing over the lip of the manicured front garden towards them from the river valley below. 'Gorgeous, but you'd never get anything done.'

It was beautiful, but Cora tried to imagine how a fifteen-year-old might feel here, so far from other houses and seemingly on the edge of the world. It was a mile and a half outside the sprawling estuary village of Woodsham St Mary and six miles from Lottie Arundel's school. Did friends ever visit? Were the family involved in village life? Could isolation have contributed to Lottie's silence?

'The view is remarkable,' she replied, turning back to the house.

'Wait till you see inside. It's one of those upside-down houses, built specifically to take in the view. Bedrooms and bathrooms on the ground floor, living spaces on the first floor. Windows on all four sides up there, so you get a 360-degree view. It's the kind of place that would have George Clarke in raptures.'

Cora chuckled. 'You know, if you ever retire from the Ed-Psych team you've got a ready-made career as an estate agent.'

'A guy can dream.' His usual smile tightened a little. 'You all set?'

'As I'll ever be.' She had gone over Lottie's case file since Tris had handed it to her earlier that morning, noting any potential areas that previous professional investigations might have missed. But even though she went over every detail again she found nothing. Lottie Arundel had no enemies of note, no professed fears relating to school, no previous history of anxiety or low self-esteem, nothing to explain why she didn't speak. 'Have you told Lottie's parents about my ability?'

Tris reddened. 'Not yet. My plan is to see how we get on today and provided you and Lottie get on well, we'll address your methods moving forward.'

Cora wasn't sure whether it was an advantage to withhold the particulars of her condition or not. She'd wondered last night how they might approach the subject. She had formal training and quali-fications identical to those held by Tris and the three other educational psychologists in the local authority-run unit, so there was weight to the argument that this was all Lottie's parents needed to know. But purposefully not sharing the advantage Cora's ability gave her over the rest of the team sat uneasily with her. 'If Lottie and I are going to work together, it's important her parents know.'

'Of course. Leave that to me. So, any theories yet?'

'I can't see a general cause and until I've spoken with her and the family it's too early to say.'

'But? Come on, Cora I know you. You never go into any case without a working theory.'

She had to concede that point. It was both a source of significant comfort and undeniable irritation that Tris Noakes understood her so well after such a short time working together. She glanced up at the drifting clouds reflected in the upper storey of the house. 'I think we're looking to identify an event, rather than an issue. In every other respect, on paper at least, Lottie is a standard fifteen-year-old with a pretty regular kind of life. Something must have happened to make her fall silent. One event, or perhaps a few that are linked.'

'Such as?'

She gave a shrug, willing the sense of unease to leave her. Whatever had caused Lottie Arundel to choose silence over words must have been significant. Cora had been only a year older when her ability had first manifested, the memory of it still raw despite the years that had passed. Nobody should have to face trauma like that, let alone a fifteen-year-old. 'I don't know.'

'Interesting.' Tris nodded, but his half-smile revealed satisfaction that he'd made the right choice to bring Cora here. 'Let's get started, shall we?'

The woman who greeted them at the door didn't smile, despite her words of welcome. She was dressed in the kind of easy casual wear that cost a small fortune – cream cashmere sweater, soft grey leggings and a large shawl scarf the colour of the first pink of dawn. But it was her eyes that Cora was immediately drawn to: haunted, far-gazing, without focus. She had seen eyes like that before, in a young mother terrified for the safety of her eldest child. The difference here was that Monica Arundel was facing the disappearance of her daughter while the child remained in full sight.

A sudden rush of heavy sighs rose up to meet Cora as she and Tris followed Lottie's mother up the glass staircase to the first floor. The jarring sound came from everywhere, despite the space being completely free of clutter. It was as if the deepest emotions of those who lived in the glass house on the hill had seeped into the very fabric of the building, disturbed by her arrival.

Cora shuddered. Beside her she felt the weight of Tris's stare.

'Thank you for coming,' Monica Arundel said, pausing by an opaque blue glass floating wall at the head of the staircase. 'Lottie is waiting for you. Please try to help her?'

The dashed hopes of eleven months hung on her words.

'I'll do all I can,' Cora replied, the briefest glimpse of life flickering in the woman's stare in reply.

Tris had been right about the breathtaking interior. The entire top floor was glass, light flooding in from all sides. The expanse of cream

26

carpeted space incorporated a pale grey kitchen, a dining area with a glass table and transparent acrylic 'ghost' chairs, and a wide seating area filled with a collection of white linen interlinked sofas. Seated at the farthest edge of them was the girl Cora recognised from the photographs in her case file.

Dressed in black, with long dark hair, Lottie Arundel was a stark shadow in the space filled with light. She looked impossibly small, dwarfed by the furniture and windows around her, so that it appeared she was caught amid clouds. She was watching them from behind a veil of fringe, head high despite the uniform of a disgruntled teen. The walk across the open floor seemed to take an eternity, Cora aware of whispers of Lottie's parents from every flat surface and the stark absence of the girl's voice.

Cora had spent her adult life sensing emotional echoes from objects, her ability now diagnosed as emotional synaesthesia. But the voices were always attached to specific things: waste paper and empty takeaway detritus, old newspapers left on café tables, belongings that had recently been used, or worn, or held. It was as if the act of a person touching an object left not just physical fingerprints but also emotional ones. Recently, Cora had trained her mind to search for the sounds around objects, giving her a multi-dimensional soundscape from which she could sense the setting of the last place an object had been held, external sounds to suggest the location and sensations of temperature, air and emotion. She was aware that the more she utilised her ability, the more she discovered.

But the sense of sound surrounding the Arundel house was new, and unsettling. Cora could guess at the direction from which the voices came, but in the ultra-neat, supremely controlled environment, it was impossible to tell exactly. Nothing was out of place here. No discarded newspapers, empty mugs, or half-read books set aside on the arms of the couches.

As she neared Lottie Arundel, a new sound emerged. But it wasn't the girl's voice, as she had expected. It was an intake of breath, repeating endlessly, the volume increasing the closer Cora moved to the teenager. A myriad of inhales with no exhale following. Cora felt it, tight at the centre of her own chest, as real as if she were holding her own breath.

'Cora?'

Tris touched her arm and Cora became aware of three pairs of eyes observing her.

'Yes?'

'I was just telling Lottie that you're our consultant psychologist.'

Mentally muting the sound of the breaths, Cora forced a smile. 'I am. Hi, Lottie. I'm Dr Cora Lael. Good to meet you.'

Lottie observed her for a moment, then looked down at an iPad resting in her lap. Her nails squeaked a little as they tapped the screen. A synthesised voice cut sharply into the room as the girl raised her eyes back to stare at Cora.

Thank you for coming to see me.

'You're welcome. Mind if we sit with you?'

Lottie blinked, fingers moving across the glass.

Be my guest.

'We were recommended the app Lottie is using by the last neuro-logist we saw,' Monica said, her flat tone indicating the many experts who had been where Cora was now. 'It's been a godsend. Lottie's found it so helpful, haven't you, love?'

Yes.

The generated voice sounded sarcastic, the delivery jarring. Cora felt Tris fidgeting self-consciously beside her.

Monica glanced between them, her carefully manicured fingers twisting and untwisting the fabric of her scarf. 'She has a tablet at school but was using a notebook at home, or sometimes WhatsApp for messages to us. But the delay – it made everything take much longer than speaking norm—' The sudden closure of her mouth severed the end of her sentence.

Lottie's gaze slid to her mother. Without looking away, she typed another message.

It feels more natural this way. Like I'm just talking normally. You like it better, don't you, Mum?

Cora caught the instinctive clench of Monica's jaw, felt the air constrict around Lottie's mother for an instant. 'That's right,' she rushed, her tone as flat as the computer voice.

Her daughter sent a shy smile to her mother before looking back at Tris.

So what do you want to do this time?

'I thought you could chat with Dr Lael. See if you get on.'

Here?

Tris looked at Lottie's mother. 'Anywhere you feel comfortable. A walk outside, maybe? It's a lovely morning.'

'It's better we stay here for their first meeting,' Monica replied, her expression flint. 'I want to hear what Dr Lael has to say.'

I'd like a walk, Mum.

'Maybe next time. *If* you get on.' The bristle at her daughter's words was impossible to conceal.

Lottie betrayed no outward signs of frustration, but the unspoken breaths grew louder around her. Cora decided to step in.

'I'll level with you both before we begin: I don't know if I can help. But I can listen. And maybe come up with some strategies...'

No offence, but that's what every other person Dr Noakes brings here says.

'Lottie!'

No, Mum. You know it's true. I don't want to upset you and I don't want to let anyone down. But endless questions and breathing exercises and fake friendly chats aren't going to bring my voice back.

The slap of the synthesised words was absolute.

Watching her colleague sag and Lottie's mother tense, Cora felt her heart drop. Why did she think she could do this? Tris meant well but bringing her into this case had been a mistake. Lottie clearly didn't want to speak – if eminently qualified speech therapists and consultant neurologists had failed to find a solution, what hope did Cora have?

'Tea,' Tris rushed, a hint of hysteria in his cheeriness. 'We should make some tea, Monica, don't you think?'

'I'm not sure tea will help...'

'Monica, in all the time I've been coming here, you've kept promising to show me your wonderful kitchen but I've yet to have the tour. I would love to see what you've done with it.'

He really was grasping at straws now.

Lottie's gaze drifted back to the window.

Torn between supporting her daughter and the chance to talk about something other than the issue dominating their lives, Monica hesitated. 'But Lottie…'

'I'll sit with her,' Cora replied quickly, the grateful smile she received from Tris proof that this was what he'd hoped she'd say. 'The view is very special from here.'

Monica Arundel's frown softened a little. 'It is, isn't it? Best view in Suffolk, I think.' She rearranged the dawn-pink scarf around her neck. 'So. Tea and a tour, Dr Noakes.'

The held breaths around the teenager remained but the volume began to reduce as her mother and Tris walked away to the far side of the upper floor. Cora said nothing, taking time to breathe and think. It was how she dealt with every instance of heard voices – affording herself space to calmly work out her response. This was unlike anything she had experienced before and the challenge was immediately outfacing. In order to find a way to deal with it, she needed to identify the elements that this occurrence shared with previous heard voices.

I'm sensing sound that audibly represents emotion. I can mute each sound in turn as it arrives. It may be a breathing sound instead of audible words or phrases, but they come from the same place…

As she noted each aspect of the new sound, the hushed breath intakes coming from the young girl slowly fell under Cora's control.

Opposite, Lottie shifted self-consciously. In a standard interaction, this would be where Cora's client would give in to the impulse to talk to fill the awkward gap, often sharing more information than they had originally intended. It was a method she had discussed with Rob Minshull during one of their walks along the Suffolk coast, Rob admitting he used it to great effect during police interviews. Here, in the glass house, in the absence of words, it had a disquieting effect for both Cora and Lottie. She allowed the silence to stretch further before she spoke, keeping her voice low.

'I don't want to make you talk,' she said, careful to keep her eyes on the wide expanse of Suffolk countryside beyond the glass. 'I'm not here to judge your reasons for staying silent, or trick you into speaking. I just think maybe nobody has listened to you yet. Really listened to you.'

Lottie didn't turn her head, but in the periphery of her vision Cora saw her fingers return to the screen.

Nobody listens.

'So try me.'

A glance, then, fast and quickly over, the fringe veil parted for just a moment.

Why does it matter to you?

Why did it? In many ways it would be easier to admit she was the wrong fit for this case and walk away. But the repeated inhales and visceral sense of constriction surrounding Lottie made Cora think of all the years she had felt locked in by her own mind. Being on the periphery was something Cora knew only too well.

'Because I think it should matter. I think you deserve to be heard.'

When she turned to face the girl, Lottie was staring at her.

'That kitchen is something else,' Tris was back, his forced cheeriness breaking the moment. Cora glanced at Lottie, but she had turned back to the window. 'We made tea. Cora?'

Despairing of her colleague, Cora accepted the cup and saucer he held out to her. Monica Arundel resumed her seat beside her daughter and Tris wittered on for a while, filling the space with unwanted words. When he paused long enough to draw breath, he finally caught Cora's eye and didn't speak again.

'Were you all right while we were gone?' Monica asked the air between her daughter and Cora, not quite looking at either of them.

'We were just looking at the view,' Cora said, as Lottie's fingers began to traverse the tablet screen.

I want Cora to come back.

'Do you?' Monica's voice cracked, her teacup gripped in her hands.

By herself next time. Please.

Tris flushed beside Cora. 'Yes. Of course. That's perfectly fine.'

Thank you.

Lottie sent Cora a brief nod before turning back to the window. Cora sensed the constriction lessen for just a moment, heard the breaths skip a beat.

It would have been so easy to miss. But it was there.

A tiny crack in the wall.

An invitation.

Chapter Six

Wheeler

The waiting was the worst.

Around him, the detectives of South Suffolk CID busied themselves as best they could but restlessness prowled between the desks like a stalking lion. He kept vigil at his desk, one eye trained on his phone. Brian Hinds, the chief Scene of Crime Officer, had promised to call him as soon as they had moved the body. The pathologist had been held up on her journey there and everything was now on hold until her arrival.

Meanwhile, twiddling his thumbs on the other end of the line while he waited for news felt like a special kind of purgatory.

'Tenner says they're linked,' Evans whispered, leaning towards Wheeler's desk.

Wheeler replied with an eye roll.

'I'm just saying, drug stuff found near the body, in an abandoned barn with previous reports of suspicious activity. And we know it would be a gift to drug gangs wanting out-of-the-way locations...'

'Give it a rest, eh?'

Evans gave a loud tut and slunk back to his work.

Wheeler bristled. He understood the jokes – everyone in CID cracked them to compensate for the frustrations of the job. But he'd been to the crime scene today, had seen the senseless end of a life and was still trying to shake the smell of death from his clothes. This one felt personal. He'd seen the tattoo on the blueing skin and been within touching distance of the deceased. You didn't forget near contact like that. You certainly didn't try to make a fast buck out of it.

'Dave, any news?' Minshull paused by Wheeler's desk on the way to the small office kitchen area, empty mug in hand.

'Not yet.'

Minshull nodded and carried on walking.

The first hours of the investigation were critical, everyone knew, making any delay seem gratuitous. The proper processes had to be observed, of course, everything done in the correct manner to gather as much evidence while the body was in situ, to help bring those responsible to justice and some comfort to the loved ones of the victim. But until the ball started rolling, everything seemed to take an age.

The farmer had alerted the police at seven a.m.; Wheeler and Minshull attending by eight. SOCOs arrived at ten a.m. just as Dave was getting restless waiting, and he'd passed Dr Amara's car on her way to the scene as he was driving back to the CID office in Ipswich around ten thirty a.m.. Now it was approaching noon and already the day seemed the longest he'd endured for some time.

He almost jumped out of his skin when his desk phone rang, every head at the desks around him lifting as one. Every ear attuned to the conversation.

'DC Wheeler?' he answered.

'Dave, it's Brian Hinds over at the crime scene. We've just moved the body, with Dr Amara leading. So, we have a white male, approximately twenty-five to thirty-five years old. He has the tattoo you mentioned – a brown velvet top hat. He also has a bloody big hole in the back of his head.'

'What?'

'Whole of the back of his head bashed in, poor beggar. He's been slammed with tremendous force. He wouldn't have stood a chance against that.'

It was a shock to hear. There had been no visible sign of any such injury when Wheeler and Minshull had attended the scene, but the victim's head had been obscured beneath the layers of old clothing and rubbish bags.

'No prizes for guessing cause of death then,' Wheeler said, grimacing at his colleagues who were heading over to his desk. 'Any idea how long he's been there?'

'Hard to say, although judging by the state of the body I reckon a few weeks at least. Dr Amara's pretty sure the fatal blow wasn't administered in the barn. We've only found traces of blood in the vicinity of the body so far and nowhere near the amount we'd expect to see on the stack of clothing that was covering him. Reckon he was attacked and brought here to be dumped.'

'That's what DS Minshull and I wondered when we saw him. Can you get us some updated photos ASAP, Bri?'

'Just sent them over, Dave.'

'Cheers, mate.' Ending the call, Wheeler addressed his colleagues. 'Right. We've got a white male, twenty-five to thirty-five. Suspected fatal head injury, but it looks like he might have been attacked somewhere else and dumped there. Might have been there for a while, Brian reckons, although that's just his guess on sight.'

Minshull made notes as Wheeler spoke. 'Okay. So, we treat this as a murder investigation, separate from Op Collegiate for the time being. But I want to know what the link is between our body and the drug litter found nearby. Kate, Les, step up those mispers searches, please. Dave, do we have the latest photos?'

'Downloading them now.'

'Good work. Drew, do a sweep of social media, see if there have been any references to local men gone missing who fit our body's description. Also check for speculation or mentions regarding the farm. People say stuff online that they don't report. You might find something we've missed.'

'No problem, Sarge.'

Wheeler found the email just arrived from Brian Hinds and printed out the photos attached to it. The images slowly appeared at the mouth of his printer, his stomach churning as the full extent of the victim's head injury glared into sight. He had to look away until the whirring of the machine fell silent, scooping up the sheets and taking them straight to Minshull's desk.

Minshull didn't flinch when he accepted them, pinning them straight to the board and standing back to quietly observe the lurid display.

'Not drugs, then,' Wheeler ventured, keen to put conversation between himself and the crime scene images.

'Drugs didn't kill him, no. But I wonder...' His voice trailed away as he scanned the images.

'If he was involved?'

'Hm.'

'As what? Drug runner? Someone higher up?'

'I doubt someone higher up would be dumped like our guy.'

'Although it's a heck of a message to send to the rest of the gang if one of the commanders stepped out of line.'

'Maybe.' Minshull let out a long sigh. 'I mean, it could be a coincidence. The guy could be a rough sleeper in the wrong place at the wrong time, like Anderson thinks.'

'But that's not your gut?'

'I think there might be a link, that's all.' He peered closer at the side view of the body, tapping the visible top hat tattoo with his pen. 'That's our best hope for the time being. I can't imagine too many mispers in our files have a tattoo like that.' He looked over to the rest of the team. 'Les, can you search specifically for a mention of a top hat tattoo in the mispers files?'

'I can narrow it down to tattoos but after that it's a case of going through every one on the list.'

'Well, that's better than nothing. How about checking to see if the design is a symbol of any groups or organisations, too? It might lead us closer to finding out his identity. Kate, are you okay to help? We need an ID as soon as we can. Everything hangs on that.'

'Sarge.'

Wheeler watched Bennett hurry to Evans' desk. 'You think someone reported him missing?'

Minshull's eyes were wide as he looked back at the board. 'I bloody hope so.'

Chapter Seven

Anderson's good mood from earlier had now vanished completely. The arrival of the updated crime scene photographs had temporarily lifted his spirits but now, three hours later, he had regressed to a brooding, muttering Caledonian boar.

'No word on ID. No word from the path lab. What the hell is taking everyone so long?'

Seated on the other side of Anderson's desk, Minshull kept his voice calm and steady to counteract his superior's mood. 'The team are moving as fast as they can. I've put Drew on it as well as Les and Kate. If our man is in there, they'll find him.'

'I know that. I do. It's just frustrating.'

Minshull held up his hands. 'I am with you on that, Guv. But we have everything in place to find out who he is. And Dr Amara is the best – if she's taking her time it's a good thing.'

Anderson gave a long groan, stretching the stubborn knots from his shoulders. 'You're right. Forgive me. Any news on Op Collegiate?'

'Nothing yet. Kate's done some sterling work already; as soon as we have an ID for our body she'll go back to the search.'

'You still think they're linked?'

It was a leading question, Minshull knew, but the chance to distract Anderson for a while was too tempting. 'We're treating the two investigations as separate concerns, as you suggested…'

'That's not what I asked.'

Minshull observed his superior. 'If the drug litter found in the barn is a coincidence, it's a pretty interesting one. Right now, that's all I have.'

'Bollocks, Rob. I know how your mind works. What are your theories?'

So much for toeing the party line. 'He could be a user who owed too much. But why go to all the trouble of stashing the body where it was for someone at the bottom of the food chain? If he were higher up in command, perhaps he overstepped the mark and was taken out as a warning to others? It seems extreme but these gangs aren't anything like those we've dealt with in Suffolk before. They're ruthless because they can be: they're running professional organisations with significant profits and reputations to uphold. They can afford to use whatever methods necessary to ensure everyone knows how powerful they are.'

Anderson rubbed his chin, a little of the consternation smoothed from his expression. 'So who's our guy? Middleman? Dealer? Runner? Rich kid trying to run with the big dogs?'

None of the suggestions seemed to fit. 'Could be any of them. Could be none. We need to know who operated there, whether it was a temporary, convenient location for a few nights or part of something bigger. I just think there's more to discover.'

He was interrupted by a sharp knock at the door, followed swiftly by a flush-faced DC Evans.

'Guv. We've got an ID.'

–

The CID team had gathered around Bennett's computer, the buzz in the office that had been missing for the last two days magnificently returned. They parted as Anderson reached them, all eyes on him and Minshull.

'Right. What do we have?'

Bennett pointed to a photograph on screen of a young man wearing a suit and tie, surrounded by a class of teenage students in a formal class photo. 'Oliver James O'Sullivan, thirty-four years old. He's an English teacher at St Audrey High School in Woodbridge.'

'And we definitely know it's him?' Anderson looked at Minshull. 'You saw the body. Does that look like him?'

'From the little I could make out. The tattoo will be the clincher.'

38

Bennett tapped the screen with the end of her pen. 'His former partner, a Ms Raphael, reported him missing three weeks ago. She mentioned the top hat tattoo and the exact location of it in her description.'

'Promising.'

'But here's the odd thing, Guv: it appears he hadn't been seen by anyone for about four weeks before Ms Raphael last had contact with him.'

'He'd not been at school?'

Bennett shook her head. 'Uniform checked with the school at the time of Ms Raphael's report. According to them he was on sabbatical following the death of his mother. The school said he'd been granted two months off and they were expecting him to contact them soon about coming back.'

Evans leaned in, a laptop in his hand. 'I checked his socials. His last post on Facebook was seven weeks ago; before that he was a regular post-a-day bloke.'

The laptop screen revealed a profile picture of O'Sullivan dressed in shorts and a T-shirt with a sunny beach behind him and as Evans scrolled down, the page revealed a set of photos of the young teacher, playing rugby, grinning with friends over drinks in a beer garden and standing next to a newly built wall of bookshelves. One head-and-shoulders photo offered a blurry glimpse of the top hat tattoo just above his left elbow as he posed in a bookshop, smiling next to an older man, a book being held between them.

'Who's that?' Minshull asked, vaguely recognising the other man.

'Seth Naseby, the thriller writer,' Ellis cut in. 'His books are amazing.'

'My wife reads him,' Wheeler said. 'Great big bricks of books, they are, but she whips through them in about three days. It's all car chases and spies and conspiracy theories.'

'I would have thought being married to you was excitement enough for your missus, Dave.'

'It is, thank you, Les. Sana reads for the *respite*.'

'He lives over near Aldeburgh,' Ellis continued, ignoring the jibes between his colleagues. 'Only ever appears in public when he has a new book out.'

'Well now we've established *that*,' Anderson said sharply to dissuade any further discussion, 'we need to talk to the people who saw Oliver O'Sullivan most recently.'

Minshull checked his watch. 'I know it's getting on but we need to talk to Ms Raphael today. Kate and Drew, are you okay to do that?'

'Of course.'

'Thanks. Call first, then try to get over there to see her in person. Find out everything you can – the last time O'Sullivan was in touch, people he would have been in regular contact with, and anyone that might have had cause to harm him.'

'Sarge.'

'Dave, come with me. We'll head over to St Audrey's and chat to the Head. We should get there before the end of the school day. We'll call the school on the way; make sure they stay open for us. Les, keep looking into the history of Abbot's Farm – any previous reports of activity there, former official use, previous owners or tenants if you can track them down.'

'Sure, Sarge.'

Minshull turned back to Anderson. 'Anything to add, Guv?'

'No, that all sounds good. I'm waiting for a call from Dr Amara and as soon as that comes in I'll head straight over to the path lab. Good work, team.'

Chapter Eight

Bennett

It was good to finally be out of the office. The mountain of mispers reports Kate Bennett had sifted through in the company of South Suffolk CID's grumpiest detective constable had seemed an endless, painful purgatory. It didn't help that Les Evans had decided he was being deliberately sidelined in the investigation. His snide remarks trying to invite Bennett to share his grievances about Minshull and Anderson had tested her patience to its limit. Why did everyone in the office assume she was the go-to sounding board for all of their gripes? Being the sole female detective was a test in itself, although she had done her best to resist being seen in a different light to her colleagues. And she had succeeded, in all but two areas: counselling and tea. She didn't seek out other people's problems, neither did she request tea when she was out on calls: but her fellow detectives and the general public deemed her a willing receptor for both.

Temporary lights on the road out of Ipswich brought the pool car to a premature halt. She rested both hands on the steering wheel as she waited, willing the knots to leave her shoulders. In the passenger seat beside her, DC Drew Ellis was preoccupied with his phone.

Good.

Opting to drive from Ipswich to the home of Oliver O'Sullivan's former partner had been a calculated move on Bennett's part, a reason to keep her eyes on the road and conversation to a minimum. It wasn't that she disliked Ellis, or found his company tiring, but he liked to chat and she didn't have the words for it today.

Exhaustion pulled at her body as she tried her best to relax into the unforgiving car seat. Three hours' sleep and endless laps of her empty living room in a vain attempt to lure it back in the early hours were now taking their toll. She'd managed to hide her yawns in the office but would Ellis notice as they worked at close quarters this afternoon? Ellis noticed everything, it seemed, the DC's ability to spot and recall pertinent details unnervingly sharp.

He wasn't watching her now, though.

A quick glance at his phone screen revealed a *Men's Health* article on interval training. During the last few months, Bennett had caught snippets of conversation between Ellis and Minshull in the CID office about running and training programmes. Dave Wheeler reckoned Ellis was on a mission to beef his lanky frame out.

Bless him.

Smiling, she turned her attention back to the road as the lights ahead changed.

It was only when they drove along the high street of the village where Sonja Raphael lived that Ellis lifted his head, staring out of the window in disbelief.

'Here?'

'I know.'

'Why didn't you tell me?'

'Because it's just a village, Drew.'

He squared to face her. 'It's not *just* a village, Kate. It will never be normal to come here again. Why do you think I moved?'

'I still live here, thank you.' she laughed, a stab of reality killing her humour on contact. Quick to cover it up, she added: 'At least we aren't going to the Parkhall Estate. Ms Raphael lives on the other side of the village.'

Ellis muttered something indecipherable and slouched defensively in his seat.

In the dim afternoon light, St Just looked exactly as it had on the day their missing child investigation began last year. Dank, brooding, with an ominous air hanging over its busy streets. DI Anderson still lived with his wife in the village, DC Wheeler just outside: Ellis had spent most of his life in St Just, but had recently moved to nearby Evernam. Last year had changed a lot of things for the people closest to the case. Bennett didn't want to think of her own link with the village, planning a circuitous route to avoid a street she never wished to revisit…

Sonja Raphael's house was at the furthest corner of St Just, a new development built on the site of a former farm. It was in half of a converted barn, joining three other similarly partitioned buildings set around a vivid green square of lawn to create a courtyard. The turf had been recently and carelessly laid, the edges beginning to curl.

'My dad would be disgusted by that,' Ellis said as they walked alongside the edge of the grass. 'I once had a lecture for an hour on the principles of a well-laid lawn.'

Bennett wasn't really in the mood to ask but she did regardless. 'Bit of a fan, is he?'

'He's worked as a gardener alongside the running the farm since he was sixteen,' her colleague replied, his smile tardy in its appearance. Was he offended by her remark? Or annoyed that she didn't already know his father's occupation? Just as Bennett was considering this, Ellis added, 'So if you ever need any gardening jobs doing, I know a man.'

Of course he was okay. Ellis always was.

I'm too tired for this, Bennett scolded herself. There was nothing to analyse here. Tonight she would treat herself to a long bath, a book and no screens past seven. Prepare for bed properly, instead of staring blankly at Netflix into the early hours as she had done every night for the last three weeks.

They headed for the middle barn in the courtyard, knocking on the large oak door on the left side of the building. A tall woman opened it immediately. Her hair was swept up into an artfully messy bun on the top of her head, the kind of thing designed to look spontaneous that probably took an hour to achieve. Despite the chill in the air, she was dressed for summer: a soft grey wide-necked sweatshirt revealing a slender, sun-kissed shoulder, worn over the tiniest pair of denim shorts Bennett had ever seen.

'Finally,' she stated, turning before they could reply and stalking inside.

Stranded by the open door, Bennett shrugged at her colleague as they walked in.

43

By the time they arrived in the double-height living space illuminated by an enormous arched window where once a barn door would have been, Sonja Raphael was already settled in the centre of a large sage-green sofa, her legs tucked up beneath her. Bennett caught Drew Ellis's wide-eyed stare at the woman's lowered lashes and sudden appearance of more bare skin above the draping neckline of her sweatshirt. Suppressing a groan, Bennett followed him across a thickly woven, brightly coloured rug to sit on a pair of armchairs opposite the sofa.

'Ms Raphael, I'm DC Kate Bennett and this is DC Drew Ellis. We need to ask you some questions about Oliver O'Sullivan.'

'Have you found him?'

Ellis dropped his gaze to his knees. Bennett steeled herself. Delivering bad news was never easy, no matter how many times you had to do it. Sonja Raphael didn't seem unduly concerned about the presence of the two detectives, but appearances could be deceptive. Bennett had seen stonier faces than hers crumble the instant their worst fears were confirmed.

'We think so.'

'You *think*?'

'A body of a man fitting Mr O'Sullivan's description was discovered this morning in a disused barn, about eight miles from here. We're awaiting a formal identification, but we believe it's him. He had a tattoo of a dark brown velvet top hat on his left arm, just above the elbow.'

The extended lashes dipped for a moment.

'I'm sorry to have to bring you this news,' Bennett began, softening her tone in preparation for the woman's shock to take hold. 'We need to ask you a few questions about Mr—'

'A barn?'

'Sorry?'

'You found him in a barn?'

'The body we believe to be him…'

'Why was he in a barn?'

'We're trying to find that out. Can you tell me what made you call us regarding Mr O'Sullivan?'

'He wasn't online. His mates at the rugby club hadn't seen him for weeks, not since he finished at the school.' Sonja began to pick at the fringed hem of a cushion beside her. 'I tried his house a few times but no reply. I figured he'd taken off for a few days, to sort his head out. His bike was gone.'

'Okay.' Bennett flipped a page of her notebook as Ellis reached for his. 'What kind of bike?'

'Motorbike. A Triumph, I think. It's black, red inside the wheels.'

There had been no mention of a motorbike found at the farm that Bennett was aware of. Could it have been stolen? Might that have been the reason he was attacked?

'Did he often go away?'

Sonja gave an empty snort of laughter. 'Only when he'd been found out. He doesn't do apologies.'

'Found out?'

Sonja's eyes slid to Ellis. 'He's my ex for a reason.'

'Can I ask what that was?'

Bennett bristled at the question. Ellis should know better than to ask this until they had established more details of O'Sullivan's life.

Sonja smoothed the cushion fabric with slow, deliberate strokes. 'Let's just say his priorities had stopped being me.'

'I see.' Ellis fumbled with his pen, blushing fiercely as he made a note.

'But you were still in contact?'

'Sometimes. We were together four years, so it wasn't easy to cut him off. We have the same friends, go to the same places. St Just isn't somewhere you can avoid people.'

Bennett knew that only too well. It was only a matter of time before someone she knew saw her going into a house that wasn't hers… Pushing aside the knot in her stomach, she pressed on. 'When did you last see him? Or speak to him?'

'He phoned me two weeks before I called your lot. It was a pretty rubbish line but I just assumed he was out on his bike somewhere.'

'And how did he seem?'

'He sounded excited. Said something about a project nearing completion.'

'Any idea what that was?'

Sonja shrugged a perfect shoulder. Ellis's eyes followed its upward and downward journeys. Bennett breathed against the irritation.

'I understand he had taken some time off school?'

'Yeah, the cheeky sod. Managed to get eight weeks off on full pay. I thought he might have been job-hunting but he didn't mention having any interviews lined up.'

'So he was unhappy in his job?'

'No, it was just time to go. His five-year rule.' When Bennett and Ellis waited for more, Sonja groaned. 'He never stays in any place longer than five years. Reckons it's healthy for him to be on the move.'

Beckett made a note and sent a subtle nod to Ellis for him to take over. It was a tag-team approach they were close to perfecting, ensuring a steady flow of questions.

'Did Mr O'Sullivan take drugs of any kind? Recreational or prescription?'

'Why do you ask that?'

'It's pertinent to our enquiries.'

The woman's manicured nails settled on the edge of the fringed cushion, pulling it slowly across her lap. Bennett looked up from her notes. Was Sonja Raphael protecting herself?

'He did a lot of stuff I didn't know about.'

'Did he ever mention drugs? Or offer them to you?'

'No...'

'Did you see him taking anything?'

'I said no.'

'Did any of his friends have links to drugs? The rugby team, maybe? Other teachers from his school?'

The woman's discomfort was tangible now, as if the air in the vaulted space had become shards of shattered glass ready to fall. 'What does this have to do with me?'

Ellis pressed in. 'Do you think it might be of concern to you?'

'I don't... What is that supposed to mean?'

'You seem rather defensive about the subject. If there's something you know...'

'*Defensive?* You come to my home, tell me my ex is dead, that someone killed him, and then you dare to insinuate that I might be involved with drugs? That I helped cause his death?'

Bennett inwardly groaned. This was not the gentle interview she thought she'd made clear it should be. What was Ellis doing? She moved quickly to calm the exchange. 'Ms Raphael, we're only asking if you were aware of Mr O'Sullivan having any interest in, or history with, drugs.'

'I know what you're asking. But he's saying I was involved...'

'What my colleague was trying to say,' Bennett continued, hoping her emphasis was a verbal kick to Ellis's shins, 'was that we think the person who killed Oliver was most likely involved with a drug gang. As one of the people closest to him for four years you might have been aware of a drug link that others weren't. That's all.'

This appeared to have the desired effect, the fire slowly retreating from Sonja's voice when she replied. 'He did some, yeah. Not with me – I'm not into that shit. But he smoked some weed, did some E. He said stuff at school was getting heavy, pressure to perform and that. But towards the end I found he'd moved on. Cocaine. I found a bag of it in his bike jacket. Told him to get out – and he did.'

'How long ago was this?'

'Four months. Told him we were over and I wouldn't change my mind.'

Bennett checked the notes she'd taken. 'You mentioned he said things were "heavy" at school. Do you think that influenced his decision to take a sabbatical?'

Sonja gave a derisory snort. 'I reckon he just wanted a long holiday. Didn't do well with responsibility, you see. He acted more like one of his students than a teacher. That's why they all loved him. Knowing him, he probably planned to get off his head for eight weeks straight while the school paid him for the pleasure.'

Ellis gave a small cough – a request to join in. Bennett ignored it. 'One more question, Ms Raphael: can you tell us when Mr O'Sullivan lost his mum?'

'What?'

Oh shit... Bennett's heart hit the expensive rug at her feet. Had she unwittingly delivered another piece of bad news?

'Forgive me, I thought you knew.'

'Janet's dead?'

The sooner they could get out of here, the better. Bennett's head had begun to throb, her body now loudly bemoaning its lack of sleep. 'It was the reason Mr O'Sullivan requested time away from St Audrey's. He said he wasn't coping well with her loss.'

Sonja blinked at them both and for a horrible moment Bennett thought the hard-edged woman was going to cry. Instead, she shifted to the edge of the sofa, fixing them both with a thunderous frown. 'Then he's a bloody liar as well as a shit boyfriend.'

'Sorry, are you saying...?'

'Janet O'Sullivan isn't dead.'

'How do you know?'

The woman fixed Bennett with a stare. 'Because unless I spoke to a ghost this morning, I chatted with her for an hour on the phone...'

—

'I never saw that coming,' Ellis said as he dropped into the pool car's passenger seat. It was the first chance he'd had to say anything; Bennett had stormed from the house without giving him a moment to speak. 'So what was O'Sullivan up to that he needed eight weeks off for? Minsh is going to love this...'

Bennett said nothing, starting the engine and reversing sharply, the back wheels of the car sending an angry spray of gravel flying.

'He's got to be involved with the gang,' Ellis continued, blithely unaware of the building storm beside him. 'I mean, it adds up: access to drugs, a change in his attitude to work, lying to his missus. Totally makes sense.'

Bennett was aware of his eyes on her as she drove. She stared resolutely at the road ahead.

'Don't you think? Kate? I said—'

'I heard what you said.' The snap of her reply split the air between them.

'But it's got to be the gang, right? Right?'

Bennett gripped the steering wheel. 'You were completely out of order in there.'

'Sorry?'

'You had no right berating the woman like that.'

'But she clammed up when we mentioned drugs. You saw that as well as I did. It made sense to call her out on it. There's no way she didn't know what her ex was up to. And I was right about it, wasn't I? Because look at what she told us…'

Bennett had heard enough. Checking the rear view mirror, she braked hard, swinging the car to a spine-shuddering halt in a small dirt lay-by beside the gated entrance to a field.

'What the…?'

She twisted in her seat to face her startled colleague. 'You *never* berate a witness like that. Especially not in their own home and absolutely not on a call where we've just informed them of a loss of a loved one. We needed Ms Raphael to talk to us, to trust us. You basically just accused her of hiding a drug involvement.'

'But her body language—'

'I don't care!' It was louder than she intended, but Bennett was all out of compassion today. 'You can't do that, Drew. It doesn't work like that. You almost ruined any chance of us getting the information we've just walked away with.'

'Oh come on, Kate…'

'You might be a great DC, Drew. You might have a lot of potential. But errors like that can cost us investigations.'

'Yeah, that's right, patronise the kid.' Ellis glared back. 'I'm not a rookie anymore, *DC Bennett*. I've been in CID for over a year. And you have no right—'

'I have every right. Because when we're out together, I am the senior officer. *My* call. Not yours. Clear?'

'Clear.' He was shaking his head now, possibly the worst thing he could have done today. Because his expression mirrored another. One she'd faced four weeks ago. One her colleagues knew nothing about. Bennett swallowed her anger and looked back at the country road stretching ahead of them.

'Call the Sarge. We need to tell him O'Sullivan lied to the school.' Without another word, she started the car.

Chapter Nine

Minshull

'Oliver O'Sullivan lied, Sarge. His mum's still alive.'

'You are kidding.'

'She lives up in Birmingham but they were in regular contact. Phone calls every week, regular visits to each other. Whatever he wanted eight weeks' compassionate leave for, it wasn't mourning his mum.'

Drew Ellis's voice was shaky on the other end of the call, breathless as if he'd been running. The excitement was impossible to conceal. It was what kept you going in the job; the breakthroughs and missing pieces clicking into place that made all the rest of the drudge worthwhile. Minshull remembered being bowled over by it in his early days as a DC. The power of the adrenaline hit was intoxicating, addictive. No matter how cynical you became, how disillusioned with the job, a shot of that feeling could summon your heart right back.

'Great work. Is Kate driving?'

A definite pause, then: 'Of course.'

Reception must be patchy where they were. It was an occupational hazard when so much of your beat was rural. 'Okay, get back to the station and contact the mother. We need to arrange an in-person visit to break the news. We'll work out who goes up when Dave and I get back.'

'No problem, Sarge.'

'What about Ms Raphael? Would she do a formal ID if O'Sullivan's mother can't?'

'I got the impression she'd rather Mrs O'Sullivan did it. She and Oliver had been separated for some time.'

'Okay. Thanks, both.' Minshull ended the call as Wheeler parked in a visitor's space in the packed car park of St Audrey High School, his mind racing.

'All good?' Wheeler asked.

'Turns out our teacher was playing hooky from school. On full pay.'

'Jammy git.' Wheeler chuckled as they headed towards the glass-fronted entrance. 'Always thought teachers were just big kids with money. Do we tell the school now?'

Minshull paused before ringing the bell on the entry intercom. 'Not yet. Let's see what they can tell us first.'

St Audrey High School was an eclectic mix of buildings, from the 1920s original carved stone schoolhouse to fading 1970s additions and a brand new wing that looked like it had been dropped onto the site from an alien craft, all steel and glass and futuristic lines. On the drive over, Wheeler had brought Minshull up to speed on the recent history of the school. An independent school established by a heritage trust, it entered into joint local educational authority control in the early 1990s and still funded a percentage of its operations from private donations – hence the new building, markedly at odds with the other schools in Woodbridge. What attracted parents to it were its consistently excellent exam results and access to facilities its links with business sponsors provided.

'It's a regular secondary school that thinks like a private one,' Wheeler had observed, drily. 'I imagine some of the parents like the idea of that. Heck of a sight cheaper than sending your kid to a private school, too.'

The head teacher's office was in the oldest part of the school, the corridors leading to the staffrooms and offices complete with satisfactorily creaking floorboards and rooms panelled in light oak.

When Minshull had spoken to the Head, Tom Dillinger, on the phone earlier, he'd pictured the owner of the deep, considered voice as middle-aged, possibly a few years from retirement. So when a much younger man with an impressive sweep of blond hair bounded out to meet him, it took Minshull a moment to marry the two.

'DS Minshull, hello. Thank you for coming. This is such a terrible shock for everyone.'

'I can imagine. This is my colleague, DC Dave Wheeler.' Minshull waited while Wheeler and the Head shook hands. 'Thanks for hanging back for us.'

'Not a problem. And it's better that we talk now without students in the school.'

Minshull nodded. 'We have some questions we need to ask you.'

'Of course. Come into my office, please.'

Tom Dillinger led them into a startlingly modern office, with a large floor-to-ceiling window looking down to a lush green quad below. Minshull and Wheeler sat on comfortable leather chairs by the glass desk, accepting freshly brewed coffee from an efficient school secretary. When it was served and the office door closed respectfully, the Head took a breath and fixed Minshull with his earnest stare.

'You told me on the phone a body has been found. Are you sure it's Olly?'

'Our enquiries are ongoing but we've good reason to believe it is Mr O'Sullivan.'

Tom Dillinger swore loudly, raising a hand in apology to the detectives. 'He was three years younger than me. What a bloody waste. Tragic. You hear of this sort of thing going on in other places but you never think it could happen in Suffolk. How did he die?'

'Again, we're still investigating. Were you and Mr O'Sullivan close?'

'Not best friends, but we played rugby on the same team. I've known him socially for a couple of years.'

'And how long has he taught at St Audrey's?'

'Five years. He's our English teacher. *Was…*' He shook his head. 'Sorry. I can't think of him as *not* present. Heaven only knows what we'll tell his students. They all love him.'

'Who does he teach?'

'English for years nine, ten and eleven, plus year ten Drama. Thirteen-year-olds to sixteen-year-olds. This is going to hit them all so hard. He's by far our most popular teacher in Arts and Humanities.'

Wheeler made notes beside Minshull, his expression impassive. Minshull knew he would be thinking of his own kids at home, the driving force of Dave Wheeler's life.

'I understand he'd been on sabbatical this term?'

'That's right,' Tom Dillinger confirmed. 'On compassionate grounds. He's just lost his mother. And now this…'

'Did Mr O'Sullivan say how his mother died?'

'Car accident.' He gave a long sigh. 'Head-on collision, apparently. The only blessing is that she would have known little about it. Tragic, though.'

Minshull was careful to make no reaction but O'Sullivan's choice of fictional death for his mother was telling – and hugely convenient. No lie about ill health, no need to construct an elaborate back story to cover the months leading up to her supposed demise. It was a very dramatic choice of death that would shock sufficiently to negate any further questions being asked.

'How had Mr O'Sullivan been in the months leading up to his request for time off?'

'Before his mother died he'd been working on a raft of after-school programmes for us. His baby: he wanted to bolster our arts provision to attract new students. We've been chasing Arts Academy status for several years with no success, despite solid support from our private donors. Olly thought we could argue for an Arts specialism if our extra-curricular activity programme was extended.'

Wheeler looked up from his notes. 'What kind of activities?'

The Head blew out his cheeks. 'Everything you can think of. A drama club, a music society, a theatre arts stream with set design, prop-making and loads of backstage stuff. Also playwriting, direction, a puppet workshop – Olly was ambitious, if slightly naïve.'

'Naïve?'

'Taking on too much. Relying on his energy alone to keep it going. He was here at all hours – early mornings, lunchtimes, after school. Had it been anyone else, they might have admitted defeat. Not Olly. He stuck to his guns and inspired everyone around him to do the same. That was why he had such a committed group of students helping him. Volunteers were never a problem to find for his afterschool clubs.'

'We may need to talk to the volunteers at some point,' Minshull ventured.

Tom Dillinger paled. 'Yes. Of course. As long as their parents give their consent.'

'Naturally. Did Mr O'Sullivan have any concerns outside of school that you were aware of? You said you saw him socially with the rugby team?'

'Beyond being exhausted and distracted? Nothing.'

'He was distracted?'

'By the work. I kept telling him to pare things back but he wouldn't hear of it. I think he needed the attention, you know? Needed to be liked by the kids. Olly is the kind of teacher who prefers being on a level with his students. Not preaching at them. *Was* – sorry.'

It was an interesting observation. Minshull noted it. 'Did this – distraction – impair his work at all?'

The Head's eyes widened. 'Oh, no, you misunderstand, I wasn't suggesting...'

'But being tired all the time, distracted by the extra-curricular projects; that must have had a detrimental effect on his work?'

'Well yes, but...' Dillinger licked his lips, eyes flicking to the side. Nerves or a fast rewriting of his testimony? 'Okay, I will admit it was somewhat of a relief when Olly asked for time off. He was devastated when his mother died, obviously. Wasn't sleeping at night, his doctor was talking about prescribing antidepressants – he was in a bad way. As a friend, I was concerned. As his boss, I'd begun to see slips, errors of judgment, a lack of focus—'

'Errors of judgment?' Wheeler cut in, the startled response of the head teacher another note on Minshull's list.

'In his work.'

'I see. Did Mr O'Sullivan say what he planned to do during his leave? Knowing him socially as you said, did you discuss it outside of school?'

Minshull hid his smile. Dave Wheeler missed nothing – sharper than anyone ever expected from the seemingly easy-going detective.

'I – I hadn't seen him much before he took his leave.'

'But the rugby club?'

'I had an injury. And work was *insane*.' He ran a hand through his hair. 'So, what happens now? Has the body been formally identified? I suppose you have someone to do it, but if not I can volunteer?'

Wheeler looked at Minshull, who accepted the baton. 'We think we have someone, but we'll get back to you if not.'

'Fine. Was there anything else?'

'Just one more thing for now; did Mr O'Sullivan mention anyone he might have an issue with? A disagreement, or a grudge? Someone who might have wished him harm?'

Tom Dillinger considered this as he took a long sip of coffee. Minshull and Wheeler waited, careful to keep their expressions neutral. When the mug met the desk again, the head teacher's eyes flicked between them as he replied. 'I really couldn't say. Olly sometimes assumed people were against him, more so in the weeks leading up to his leave being granted. It was all nonsense, of course, but I think the mental exhaustion and the grief for his mother had heightened his insecurities.'

'Was he concerned about anyone in particular?'

'Not that he mentioned. It was more a general feeling that he wasn't liked or trusted by some sectors of the staff. Sorry I can't be more specific.'

'Okay, thanks. I think that's everything for now. Unless you have any questions?'

'Do the media know the body is his?'

It wasn't the question Minshull had expected. 'We won't make a statement until we have a formal identification. Is there a reason you ask?'

Dillinger clasped his hands together on the glass desk. 'The school. I know we can't stop St Audrey's being mentioned, but I'd like to be sufficiently prepared when it is. We rely substantially on our sponsors and financial donations from parents for our position in the league tables. They fund everything the education authority won't. Any bad press has a direct effect on our good standing. As I'm sure you appreciate, damage limitation is paramount now.'

'Odd thing to say,' Wheeler observed as they drove out of the school grounds. 'O'Sullivan was meant to be his mate. I'm not sure *damage limitation* would be first on my mind if one of my football buddies was murdered.'

'He was being very careful with his replies,' Minshull said, watching the sun breaking through the stubborn clouds that had claimed the sky all afternoon, rays of pale light falling down over the passing fields.

'Clocked that, too. And the Wimbledon eyes.'

'Wimbledon eyes?'

'Yeah, you know…' Wheeler's eyes flicked from left to right, like a spectator at a tennis tournament, 'Murray, Nadal, Murray, Nadal…'

'I'll have to remember that.'

'You're welcome,' Wheeler grinned, a brownie point scored for making Minshull laugh. 'What he said – about O'Sullivan being distracted, thinking everyone was against him, behaving erratically – that could be drugs, couldn't it?'

Minshull had reached the same conclusion, tempered only by Anderson's insistence that Operation Feldspar remain separate from Operation Collegiate. 'I have to say, it's looking increasingly plausible.'

'But a drugs gang?'

Minshull groaned. 'That kind of behaviour suggests O'Sullivan was using rather than running. Unless he was in hock to a gang and had to run for them as payment. But I just don't see it. He had a good job; money clearly wasn't an issue for him. There's something we're not seeing yet.'

–

Back in the South Suffolk Constabulary CID office the team had reassembled, all quietly working when Minshull and Wheeler returned. Anderson was just out of his meeting with DCI Taylor and appeared to be surprisingly calm, considering.

'O'Sullivan lied?' he said, meeting Minshull at the door.

'He said his mother was killed in a car accident.'

57

'Charming son.'

'It would have made the lie easier. Shock tactics and no need to elaborate on the details.'

'Sarge.' Drew Ellis appeared behind Anderson, his face ashen. 'Mrs Janet O'Sullivan is on the line.'

'What?'

'Sonja Raphael called her after Kate and I left. She wants to talk to you.'

Minshull had been bracing himself for visiting Janet O'Sullivan or arranging for local officers in Birmingham to deliver the news. This was completely out of his comfort zone. 'Transfer it to my desk, please.'

Anderson stared at the ceiling as Minshull skirted him to hurry to his desk. Accepting the call from Ellis, he answered, aware of the eyes of his team watching him. 'Mrs O'Sullivan? I'm Detective Sergeant Rob Minshull from South Suffolk CID.'

'You've found my son.' Her voice was quiet, controlled, but pain threaded through her words.

'I believe we have. I'm so sorry. We can come and see you, tell you everything we know? I can make the journey now.'

There was a long pause. Minshull caught a whisper of a shuddering breath. 'No, I'd like to come down. For the identification.'

'Are you sure? The Head at Oliver's school has offered to do it if you would prefer.'

'I want to see my son.'

Minshull bowed his head. 'Of course. I'll make the arrangements. When would you like to see him?'

Janet O'Sullivan murmured something away from the phone, another muffled voice replying. 'We'll drive down tomorrow. I have friends in Ipswich who've offered to put us up. So Friday morning?'

'That's fine with us.' He hesitated before asking his next question. 'Is there anything you'd like to know? Some things are being investigated, so we don't have all the answers yet, but I can do my best to tell you what we know so far.'

'Did he take his own life?'

Thrown by the question, Minshull looked over at his team. Their willed support was more welcome than any of them would have realised. 'No, we don't believe he did.'

'Well, at least that's something. Who will be there at the – when we see him?'

'I will be, together with Dr Rachael Amara who is the lead pathologist on this case, and my colleague, DC Drew Ellis.' Minshull nodded across the room to the startled DC. 'You just spoke to him.'

'He was kind. So what happens now?'

'I'll arrange everything here and I'll get DC Ellis to call you in the morning with all the details, if that's okay? What time do you think you'll be leaving tomorrow?'

'About ten. We want to miss the morning traffic—' She broke off at the exact moment Minshull felt the jarring of such a mundane conversation in the stark shadow of Mrs O'Sullivan's loss.

'I'll ask Drew to call you at nine.'

'Thank you.'

'Do you have someone with you now? Would you like me to call anyone?'

'My partner is here.' Her voice cracked. 'We'll be okay. I'll see you on Friday, detective sergeant. And thank you – for telling me the truth.'

That was the kicker: the mother of the man who had claimed her death as reason to skip work, thanking him for his honesty.

Ending the call, Minshull dropped his head into his hands.

Chapter Ten

Cora

It had been a long day. As Cora unlocked her front door, she breathed in the silence of her apartment, the soft rush of the sea beyond the window and the blessed relief of no other intrusive voices.

She had arrived home as the sun was setting across the sea to find a neighbour's wheelie bin had been upended, its contents blown by the wind across the car park. For her fellow residents it would be an inconvenience: for Cora it was as if a huge crowd had assembled between her and the door, each scrap of rubbish bearing a voice, an emotion, a presence demanding her attention. Usually she was prepared, but this had been a shock as soon as she had got out of her car, a sudden rush of noise she'd had no time to brace her mind against.

It had taken all of her resolve to push through the wall of noise and get into her building.

Here, on the third floor of the former hotel building on the cliff overlooking Felixstowe's North Beach, all was still. It was heaven. Dumping her bag on the kitchen counter, she crossed the open-plan living room to flop into her favourite chair facing towards the window. The sunset this evening was a balm to her soul.

Work had been intense to say the least: in addition to Lottie Arundel, she had four more cases she was involved with monitoring. Today had been endless paper trails and countless minutes spent on hold while the various relevant departments and professionals did their best to avoid her calls. She loved her new position but it differed so greatly from the university department where she had previously worked. Being employed by a local education authority meant being tied to the labyrinthine organisational structures of local government, with each invested party seemingly speaking a different language to everyone else. Most of her work entailed trying to catch all the loose ends of conversation and bring them together.

Even the usually sunny Dr Tris, who generally took red-tape-jumping and interdepartmental spat-navigation in his stride, had spent most of the day with a phone in one hand and his head in the other. His precious tin of biscuits had taken a serious battering as he had apologetically handed them around to everyone in his team, which was never a good sign.

He'd brightened a little when they'd grabbed ten minutes for a much-needed wander down to the brightly painted coffee truck parked alongside the council building where their department had a small cramped pair of offices tucked away on the lower ground floor. Cora knew good coffee and the chance to talk about her latest case were just what Tris needed.

Taking advantage of a sunny break in the cloud-ridden sky, they had found a bench and settled down to enjoy their coffee.

'So ask me,' Cora had said, when his fidgeting silence became too much.

'Thank you,' he'd breathed. 'What was going on at the Arundel house?'

Cora had been formulating her own response to it and still wasn't certain she had everything settled in her mind. But as she spoke, she found a clarity that surprised her. 'It's unlike anything I've encountered before. Lottie has no discernible voice from any of her belongings. The house is too tidy for any discarded objects I might sense emotional echoes from.'

Tris turned to her. 'But? There has to be a *but*, right?'

'But,' Cora smiled, touched by Tris's faith in her ability, 'the house itself carries emotion. Almost as if it's locked inside. The stairs to the first floor – walking up them is like wading through a tide of audible sighs.'

'Fascinating.'

'That's one word for it. It's troubling – emotionally. There is a great deal of pain in that place and I've never sensed that in a building so strongly before.'

'And Lottie?'

'It sounds like a sharp intake of breath repeated on a constant loop. The sound increases whenever Lottie feels vulnerable.'

'There are no words?' Tris frowned. 'So she's imprisoning her thoughts as well as her spoken voice?'

'Exactly.' She knew it wasn't the news he had wanted.

'So it's pointless...'

'No, Tris. It's different. And I can't promise I'll hear anything. Not in the way I always have. But I've been thinking about it and this is exactly the kind of development I've wanted to explore with my ability.'

'Meaning?'

'There are words trapped behind the held breaths. I sense them.'

'Not in Lottie's belongings?'

It was hard to explain, even to an ally as predisposed to believe her as Tris Noakes. 'I've been pushing my ability for over a year. Not just listening to the immediate emotional echoes from someone's belongings, but also where they were when the emotion was transferred. The air around it, the space beyond it, building up a three-dimensional picture of the moment to better understand the circumstances where it occurred. I think... I'm certain I can take that and push into the breaths around Lottie. Into her mind.'

'I don't understand.'

She hadn't expected him to. But her gut told her she was on the right track. 'Okay, imagine this: until now, I've sensed emotional fingerprints on objects that have been relinquished – picked up and put down. Imagine now that Lottie has all those objects, but instead of putting them down or letting them go, she's still hanging onto them. I think I can sense the fingerprints being left without the objects leaving her. Only she's holding them in her mind, not her hands.'

Even now, in the blessed peace of her home, Cora wasn't sure if Tris had grasped what she'd been trying to say. But, while everything ached after a long day, she felt exhilarated by the prospect of pushing her gift.

She considered cooking but then decided a takeaway was more than deserved. Scrolling through the options on her phone she chose a handful of dishes from her favourite Chinese restaurant and sat back to watch the sun dip slowly towards the sea as she waited for her meal to arrive.

Life felt good here.

Cora hadn't expected to return to Suffolk after the trauma of her involvement with the police last year. The search for the missing girl and all the associated turmoil of her own life had taken its toll, marking her home county with emotion and memories she didn't want constant reminders of. Devon had been the sanctuary she needed – until Rob Minshull found her there. It had been his words – an apology first and his surprising insistence that they had unfinished business together – that had coaxed her back east. The job with Tris had arrived a week after her decision to move home, confirmation of a place for her in her home county. Things, as her mother Sheila loved to say these days, had a habit of working themselves out if you let them.

She smiled, thinking of her mum. Sheila was a woman transformed. Her re-emergence from a dark, heavy shroud of grief had been nothing short of remarkable. Now she was out exploring her world, newfound friends from her local WI whisking her away on trips across the country. She'd just returned from a long weekend in Derbyshire and was off again on a painting retreat in the Cotswolds. The gleefully written postcards she sent Cora from each new adventure had pride of place across the mantelpiece in Cora's apartment, a joyful parade of possibility and renewed hope. Cora glanced at them now, spotlit by pink-golden light spilling across the room from the wide window.

The apartment was a world away from the last place she'd lived in the coastal town. It felt as if it had been built just for her – a haven of peace with a view of the sea. Any way she looked at it, Rob Minshull's intervention had made all this possible.

Her phone rang and Minshull's name appeared on the screen. Smiling at his timing given her train of thought, she answered the call.

'Evening, DS Minshull.'

'Dr Lael.' His smile sounded down the line. 'How's every little thing?'

'Busy. You?'

'Hell of a day. I've only just got in. The whole team were working late – I had to drag Dave Wheeler from his desk. He didn't even get a chance to tidy it like he usually does. He wasn't happy.'

'Poor Dave. Is it a big case?'

'Possible murder.'

'No! Are you okay?'

There was a pause. Cora tracked a flock of seagulls flying in v-formation across the red, gold and pink sky. Her question had felt natural to ask but was it the right thing to say? She heard a soft sigh draw out at the other end of the call.

'You're the first person who's asked me that.'

Cora sensed more behind his words. 'Do you want to talk about it?'

'I can't… That's not why I called.'

'Okay. Why did you call?'

'I've missed our chats. Work's been crazy…'

'For me, too. But now the weather's getting better we could do those evening runs you were talking about?'

'I'd like that.' Another pause.

Cora sensed there was another reason for his call, one he didn't quite know how to broach. When the silence on the line began to feel uncomfortable she opted to prompt him.

'Are you sure you're okay?'

'Honestly, I'm not sure. I had to confirm to a mother that we believe the body we found is her son.'

'Oh Rob. That's horrible.'

'It's part of the job but it never gets any easier. And this one's been playing on my mind, more than I thought it would.'

Cora's heart went out to her friend. 'I can't imagine how difficult that must have been.'

'And the worst of it was that we just found out he told his employer his mum had died, weeks before he went missing. She doesn't know that and I won't tell her, but the knowledge of it makes everything I said to her this evening a little bit of a lie, you know?'

'Were they close?'

'Apparently, according to his ex-girlfriend. Despite what he'd told his boss.'

'Then that's what matters.'

'Do you think she knew, though? From my voice? And will she see it in my body language when she meets us for the formal identification on Friday?'

Now it made sense. Minshull had been careful not to ask her anything in a professional capacity since his apology for the events of last year. This was new – and Cora was surprised to feel touched that he had asked, rather than cornered by his question. She kept her tone soft as she replied. 'Are you asking me as a psychologist?'

'Yeah, I think I am. Sorry.'

'Don't apologise. I can see why you would think that. So much of our communication as humans is non-verbal, and when you know more than you can say, I can see how you'd worry about revealing it. You just have to focus on her when you meet, Rob. On what she needs to hear. Compassion communicates far more strongly than anything else in situations like that. She'll be seeking reassurance first and foremost. In such awful circumstances, our basic needs override everything else.'

'But the adverse stuff we're finding out about him – my gut tells me there will be more.' Emotion pinched the edge of his question. 'If it's in the back of my mind, won't it pass into my tone of voice, my actions?'

'Not if you set your focus. Whatever else he might have been or done or said, he was her son first. Remember that and it will guide everything else.'

'Thank you. I knew you'd know what to say.'

'Any time.'

'I'm glad you came back, Cora.'

Surprised, she smiled out at the sunset beyond her window. 'I'm glad you persuaded me.'

'So you're saying I was right?' The mischief was back in his tone.

'If you think I'm ever going to give you that much ammunition, you're sadly mistaken.'

'So I *was* right.'

'You made a valid point.'

His laugh was warm against her ear. 'I'll take that. And sorry, again, for the professional liberty tonight.'

'It's okay. You buy the meal next time we meet.'

'A fair price to pay. We'll make it soon, yeah? Look, I'd better let you go. But thanks.'

'My pleasure. Call me if you need to tomorrow, okay?'

'You're a star. G'night Cora.'

Making her way into the kitchen to prepare for her food delivery, Cora felt the warmth of her smile as it lingered. When she talked to Minshull or spent time in his company, she always left with the same sense of quiet satisfaction, even if there remained many unanswered questions between them.

Rob Minshull was a strange one.

Since he'd come to find her on the Devon coast, the detective had been startlingly present in Cora's life, albeit from a respectful distance. They'd shared meals in the pubs and restaurants of Cora's hometown of Felixstowe and walked miles along the Suffolk coast deep in conversation, but if she tried to quantify what their friendship was, nothing quite fit. Certainly they were engaged in a dance of sorts around one another. Cora liked Minshull's company, even if a part of her suspected his eagerness to meet was still driven by lingering guilt from the case that had drawn them into one another's worlds.

The conversation this evening had been different, though. Deeper. More vulnerable. Minshull had broken his own cardinal rule of never seeking her professional opinion. That was new.

Had she said the right thing?

And would more questions follow?

Chapter Eleven

Anderson

Path labs scared the sweet shite out of every other copper he knew, but Anderson quite liked them. They were calm, methodical places, where answers were found and irrefutable evidence uncovered. No posturing, no pointless point-scoring. His cast-iron constitution helped, of course. Bodies didn't trouble him, whatever state they were in. There had been exceptions over the years – not least the ten-year-old boy in St Just whose murder had sent Anderson's world into freefall. But once they were here they were cared for, respected. There was a sense of relief to see them at rest on the pathologist's table after the chaos and horror they had endured at their lives' sudden end.

Dr Rachael Amara smiled at him as he strolled into her room. 'Joel. This is a pleasure.'

'Likewise, Rach. You wanted me to see something?'

'I did. Apologies for the early call.'

'No apology necessary.' Anderson's head was still protesting its lack of caffeine at the early hour but the rest of him buzzed. Waiting for news late into the night had been purgatory: this was the movement he'd yearned for.

'Excellent. Right this way.' She strolled across the floor, the soles of her pale green surgical clogs squeaking on the vinyl tiles with every step.

Oliver O'Sullivan's body lay on the table, a green sheet draped respectfully across his chest, his left arm resting over the top of it. As he neared the body, Anderson could clearly see the tattoo Minshull and Wheeler had described, nestled between a cluster of freckles an inch above his elbow. A glossy brown top hat, the kind worn by Victorian gentlemen in the old photographs that lined one wall of his local pub, the Miller's Arms.

'Cool tattoo,' Dr Amara observed, following the line of Anderson's sight. 'Been thinking of getting one for my fiftieth.'

'Victorian top hat a candidate?' Anderson grinned.

'I was thinking more a high-colour skull and roses.'

'Ah. Old school.'

'Always. Any idea why this one was significant?'

'Not yet.'

'He doesn't have any others. Makes you wonder why he chose to be inked with that one. If you find out, let me know? Mysteries like that are the perks of my job.' She moved to the top of the table. 'Intriguing tattoos aside, this is what I wanted you to see.'

In the pool of bright light from the inspection lamp above the body, the large head wound was a deep shadow against O'Sullivan's pale skin. The back of his skull had collapsed, a devastating injury.

'Did the blow kill him?'

'It's a huge blunt force trauma to the occipital area, which shattered the bone. I found fragments lodged in the brain. But this is what I want to show you: there's no significant bleeding. With an injury as devastating as this I would expect to see far more blood loss. But the condition of his brain and the area around the wound suggests to me that he was hit some considerable time after he died.'

'But bodies still bleed, don't they?'

Dr Amara's eyes twinkled. Not all of the duty pathologists welcomed questions from police officers: some seemed to consider them a personal affront. But Anderson knew her well enough to know she relished being asked.

'You would think. After all, the body still contains blood after the heart has stopped. But time is our key consideration here. Examining the body, we can see that livor mortis had already begun – it starts typically twenty to thirty minutes after death, but we don't see real evidence of it until about two hours after death. Patches appear on the body where the blood begins to settle to the lowest point. It clots and thickens after death so it doesn't flow as it would with a heart pumping it. Think of it like setting melted chocolate,' she grinned at Anderson's grimace. 'I found some movement of blood around the wound but it was well on the way to full coagulation. Hence my conclusion that it occurred at least two to three hours after he died.'

Anderson let the news sink in, mulling over what he already knew about the body. 'When we found him, we did a sweep for blood and found very little. A few drops here and there that may yet prove to belong to someone else who used the barn. If he was struck after he was dead, that might explain why.'

'Certainly, if this blow had been delivered while he was alive you would expect a huge amount of blood loss, either in the place where he was struck or seeped into the clothing bags directly surrounding the body.'

Anderson looked across Oliver O'Sullivan's corpse as if other clues might be waiting for his attention, his mind ablaze with questions. 'But why smash the back of his skull if he were already dead?'

'A blow to make sure the job was done?'

'Hell of a blow.'

'I agree. I suppose it could be a statement.'

Anderson stared at her. 'Of what?'

Dr Amara shrugged. 'Power? Control?'

'A warning to anyone who saw it.'

'Hell of a warning.'

'Touché.'

She smiled and bowed her head in reply.

'So, if the blow didn't kill him, what did?'

Dr Amara's smile grew wide. 'That was the *other* thing I wanted to show you.' She beckoned Anderson to the other side of the table. 'Look here.'

Halfway between O'Sullivan's collarbone and jaw was a tiny blueing bruise, a purplish-red dot at its centre. Had the pathologist not drawn his attention to it, Anderson wouldn't have noticed it at all. 'A needle?' he asked.

'Top marks, DI Anderson!'

'He was killed by an injection. Of what? An overdose of drugs?'

'That's what I assumed at first. But the cocaine I found in his system was negligible, certainly not enough to kill him. So I tested for other substances – prescription drugs, morphine, methadone, heroin; the usual suspects. Nothing. But then I remembered a case I'd read about years ago, tested the theory and *bam*!'

When Anderson didn't reply, she held her hands out like a magician at the end of an impressive trick. 'Bleach!'

'Bleach?'

She nodded happily. 'Ordinary, everyday, easily obtainable household bleach. Injected here it would travel quickly into the body, slowly shutting down every major organ. Ingenious, really. Not a very nice way to go: slow, unbearably painful and designed to create maximum suffering. Acute kidney failure, thrombosis caused by inflammation of the veins, severe pain, internal burns – the whole gamut. Bleach ruptures the red blood cells, you see, interrupting the oxygen supply to the body. So his vital organs would likely have failed, one by one, as they were starved of oxygen. The worst of it is that he would have been well aware of what was happening and yet powerless to stop it.'

If he were conscious while all of that was happening, would he have seen his murderer? Someone he had known well; someone who betrayed him?

Dr Amara was still enjoying the thrill of a mystery solved as Anderson wrested his thoughts back to the darkened lab. 'And the best part is, whoever did this expected us not to go looking for it. They thought we'd buy the head injury as cause of death. But they left it too long to hit the body. That was their mistake.'

'Brilliant, Rach. Bloody brilliant.'

'My pleasure. I do enjoy outwitting people who underestimate pathologists. So do you have any idea who he was, yet? We found nothing in his clothing: no wallet, no phone.'

'My team believe he's a local teacher from a high school in Wood-bridge, Oliver O'Sullivan. Reported missing three weeks ago by his former partner who also mentioned this,' he indicated the top hat tattoo. 'Turns out it tells us more about him than any form of ID he might have carried in his pockets.'

'And they say the dead don't speak.' The pathologist lowered her voice to a spectral whisper. 'But they speak to me.'

It was the strangest place to laugh in, but Anderson couldn't help it. He was well aware of the many other police personnel Rachael Amara had creeped out with her morbid humour. She had gained something of a fearsome reputation among his colleagues for being strange and seemed more than happy to feed the rumours.

As Anderson drove back to the station in Ipswich more questions presented themselves. Had O'Sullivan been killed and sustained the head injury elsewhere, and then brought to the barn at Abbot's Farm? Could he have been injected in the barn, his murderer leaving him to die, returning later to damage the body and stash it in the bank of clothes? Or had they waited at the barn for two hours after he was dead to do it? Did the same person who administered the fatal dose of bleach return to break his skull, or did someone else finish the job?

Why had they covered the murder method with another?

What did they have to hide?

Chapter Twelve

Cora

Cora was better prepared for entering the glass house for her second visit to Lottie, but the anguished sighs on the staircase still threw her off-guard. She paused for a moment to steady herself, then hurried up the remaining stairs to the sunlit first floor. Monica Arundel didn't wait at the top for her as before, instead sweeping into the space in a blur of pale grey and baby blue.

Today, Lottie was sitting at the large glass dining table, books spread out across its surface. Her appearance was as before – resolutely black – but this time her hair had been pulled into a high ponytail, her fringe a little less severe without the stark frame of the rest.

'Home school sessions,' Monica explained, her grimace revealing her opinion as clearly as the dining table beside her revealed everything beneath it. 'She's just finishing up. You can sit here if you like. Coffee?'

'Please.'

Monica headed for the kitchen without a word.

'Hi.' Cora smiled, pulling out one of the transparent chairs and shrugging off her coat.

Lottie offered the briefest grin, the voice sounding from her tablet.
Hey. Glad you came back.

'Glad you asked me to. How's home school?'
Riveting.

Cora laughed. 'I can imagine. Do you have a favourite subject?'
Home time.

'Nice.'

She met Lottie's gaze and was surprised to find a glint of mischief.

English. And Drama…

The many-voiced sharp intakes of breath suddenly crashed into the space between them when the tablet spoke the second subject. The sharp constriction in Cora's chest returned.

'I guess it's hard to take part in a drama class without your voice.'

Lottie blinked, a moment of stillness settling between them amid the sharp tides of breath. Then:

I slay them with mime.

As a comeback it was perfect, arriving at the best time.

Last night, as she had prepared for her first real session with Lottie, Cora had battled doubts. There had been a spark of recognition during their introductory meeting in the midst of Tris's overblown positivity and Monica's prickliness, but was that enough of a foundation to build a meaningful connection on? Cora had told Lottie she didn't want to make her speak, but if that were the case, what was she aiming to achieve?

Tris had called around nine p.m., just as Cora was settling in for an evening of reading, clearly as on edge as she felt.

'You'll be fine,' he assured her, sounding anything but confident of his assertion. 'Lottie likes you. It's more than we've had with anyone else who's seen her.'

'That's reassuring. So she might remain silent but at least I'll have a new buddy to hang out with.'

'That's not what I meant. You can make a difference here, Cora. Find a way behind the fortress she's built around herself. You don't think like I do, or like any of our colleagues in other disciplines. And you listen. In more ways than one.'

But what did hopeless sighs from the walls and withheld breaths surrounding Lottie Arundel really tell Cora? And what if they were the only voices she heard?

Now, with the surprise of Lottie's joke still sparkling between them, Cora allowed herself to relax. Tris didn't need overnight results. What mattered to Lottie was being listened to. If Cora did that consistently, investing time in gaining the girl's trust, maybe something meaningful could be founded.

Monica returned with coffee, the breaths around Lottie swelling a little before settling to an insistent murmur.

'What were you talking about?' she asked Cora, the slightest hint of accusation in her voice.

'Home school,' Cora smiled, accepting a pale pink mug. 'Lottie tells me she enjoys English.' She was careful not to mention Drama, not wishing to summon the staccato breaths back.

'She's top of her class for it.'

Can't help being a genius.

Monica bristled at her daughter's words. 'She works incredibly hard.'

'Can I ask, why are you home schooling? I understood Lottie was still attending her classes.'

'She has home classes one day a week,' Monica replied. 'Not my idea. The school thought it might be beneficial for her to have extra attention, particularly in the more participatory subjects. We're trialling it at present: if it works we might move to a fifty-fifty time split between physical and virtual lessons.'

I don't want that.

'I am aware of your thoughts on the matter, thank you. You have your GCSEs next year. I'm not allowing your excellent grades to slip because you can't...' Monica checked herself. 'Because you choose not to speak.'

I would rather be in school.

'It isn't the time for that discussion.' Pointedly, she turned to Cora. 'Dr Lael, you may begin.'

'Here?'

Lottie's mother frowned. 'Where else did you have in mind?'

'I thought we might go out. Walk down the estuary path a little.'

'Not today.'

Mum. You said we could go outside this time.

'*Not* today.'

Cora back-pedalled, not wishing to upset either mother or daughter. 'Over on the sofas, then? It's important our meetings are as relaxed as possible.'

74

'I prefer to stay here. It's easier for Lottie to type at the table.'

I'm fine.

'I said, we are staying here.'

Then this whole thing is pointless.

It wasn't what Cora had imagined. Being seated at the dining table with Monica Arundel presiding over their exchanges would be too formal. Already, an indignant flush was rising in Lottie's cheeks, the rumble of breaths beginning to swell. Before the argument could escalate further, Cora jumped in.

'Mrs Arundel, the key here is that Lottie feels as comfortable as possible. Lottie, I'm not going to put you under any pressure to talk. I want to listen to you, but only if you are ready to do this.' She turned back to Lottie's mother, who was glaring at her hands. The strain was clear to see, etched into the line of every muscle in her body. 'I think we maybe stop now and try again another time. In a few days, perhaps?'

No. 'No.'

Both voices sounded at once, the audible and the synthesised. Cora felt her pulse skip.

'So what do we do?'

Monica didn't lift her head. Instead, she spoke to her outstretched palms, as if her precious daughter were cradled there. 'Where would you go?'

'Not far. I noticed a footpath opposite the entrance to your drive? The sign was pointing to the estuary.'

It's where I go with Mr Draycott.

'Mr Draycott?' Cora asked.

Slowly, Lottie's mother raised her eyes. 'Lottie's form teacher. He visits sometimes, after school. He's been a good friend to the family.'

We wouldn't be out long, Mum. I can text you from the bench.

Mother and daughter observed one another. The tension at the centre of Cora's chest eased.

'All right. But no more than an hour.'

75

Down at water level all was still, beneath the wind that constantly buffeted the glass house on the hill. Wading birds paddled in the sandy shallows; the taste of salt was fresh on the air. An egret passed overhead, the beating of its wings a ghostly white motion, and Cora watched it follow the tidal river out towards the coast.

It's better out here.

'Good.' Cora smiled at the teenager beside her. Out of the house she looked younger, less severe, a gentle smudge of pink across her pale cheeks as she walked.

Sorry about Mum.

'No need to apologise.'

She's intense.

'She's concerned. And probably feeling a little helpless.'

She should try being me.

The breaths around Lottie swelled, then subsided. Cora sensed doors immediately slam – the glimpse of truth hastily barred from view. It should have felt like an opportunity missed, but instead Cora was encouraged. A candid moment this early in their acquaintance was a hopeful sign, however fleeting. Did Lottie want to let her in?

She changed tack, not wishing to push the teenager. 'What a gorgeous place. Do you come here a lot?'

I used to. Before. Now Mum won't let me unless someone is with me.

'Your friends?'

Lottie nodded.

'And your teacher?'

Mr Draycott. Andrew, when we're not in the house. He listens to me.

'Do you find that helpful?'

Yes. Most people aren't interested in listening. Only talking at me.

They had reached a bench on a hummock of grassy bank. Its weathered wood had witnessed many winters and summers, the edges of its wooden struts cracked and gnarled by salt air and time. Lottie sat down and Cora followed, feeling the warmth of the old wood where the sun had fallen across it.

I'll just message Mum.

Cora waited while Lottie sent the message, taking the opportunity to inspect the breaths ebbing and flowing around them. During the last year she had begun to push deeper into the voices she heard, searching around them, through them, feeling the space around them and seeking out hidden sound they may be masking. The more time she invested in this practice, the greater the definition she sensed between the layers of sound.

But she had never encountered anything like Lottie Arundel's secret voices before. The complete absence of words, coupled with the magnified physical manifestation of emotion she experienced was unfamiliar territory to navigate.

Lottie sent the message and quickly became distracted by a social media app. Cora closed her eyes and began to nudge aside the outer layers of the audible breaths surrounding her young charge. They resisted at first, but then she sensed a slackening of their hold. More layers reluctantly conceded to Cora's mind until the shadow of a word began to form. Cora sensed it as a figure on a stage concealed by drapes of chiffon, the edges of the form blurred and shifting. The breaths obliterated its sound but it was there. Mentally Cora reached for the next layer obscuring it from view...

Have I bored you already?

The emotionless synthetic voice broke in, and Cora jumped back through the layers of breath as she opened her eyes. Lottie was staring at her, a mixture of amusement and concern playing across her face.

'Breathing exercises,' Cora rushed, forcing a smile. 'Sorry.'

Don't be. I thought...

Lottie's brow creased and she glared at the tablet in her hands.

You have to breathe. Right?

Cora laughed. 'It's kind of important.'

So what do we do now?

'What would you like to do?'

Sit here and look at the view.

'Fine by me,' Cora replied, settling back. If she was going to help Lottie, she had to demonstrate that she was willing to let the teenager lead. The glimpse of something beyond the breaths Lottie was cloaked in was enough to keep Cora there. If she gained Lottie's trust, could she reach further behind the sound to decipher the hidden word?

As shadows from the passing clouds dipped and rose over the banks and shallows of the estuary beside them, she was aware she was being watched.

That's it? You're not going to ask me anything? Or lecture me?

'You want to sit, so that's what we'll do.'

And if I want to talk to you – on this? She lifted her tablet.

'You can do that, too. Your call, Lottie, not mine.'

She risked a smile, which was slowly returned.

It was a start.

Lottie

I like her.

I wasn't expecting that.

Everybody else they've sent to see me has made me feel like an inconvenience, like they were furious I wasn't a solvable problem the moment they arrived.

Dr Lael wasn't like them. She listened – not just to the voice coming from my tablet, but to *me*. She watched my face like she was lip-reading even though my lips weren't moving. She didn't do The List, either: the same twenty-five tasks and questions every other idiot has turned up clutching. She just talked to me. And sat in silence for ages when I asked her to.

That's new.

I'm not sure what to think.

Mum says she reckons I've just been waiting for the right person to connect with. I figured she was grasping at straws again, but what if she was right?

I like Dr Lael. Cora, she said to call her. She has a cool name. She isn't one of those people who push me for answers all the time. She's a lot younger than the others, too. Way older than me, of course, but not Mum and Dad's generation. Maybe that's why she relaxed more with me, talked about stuff I might understand.

Of course, I haven't told Mum and Dad yet. I have to be sure we have a connection worth working on. But I'm intrigued. Could Cora Lael turn out to be the one I've been waiting for?

Chapter Thirteen

Ellis

'Okay, everyone, team briefing in five, please,' DS Minshull announced, walking across the CID office towards DI Anderson's door. 'Let's find out where we are with this.'

Drew Ellis saved the work he'd been compiling, scribbled a note to himself of what needed to be looked at next, then grabbed his notebook and chair as the team assembled in the centre of the office, facing the large whiteboard on the wall. He had dreamed of sitting in briefings like this when he was going through his detective exam preparation. He'd watched so many TV crime dramas where the gathered detectives would bring pertinent pieces of evidence to share, the solution to the mystery slowing forming on the board before them. The reality was nowhere near as charged as the dramatised versions, but he still felt a thrill at even having a seat in the room.

There was a definite change in the air since the revelation of Oliver O'Sullivan's lie and the gruesome photographic evidence of the body taken at Abbot's Farm. Instead of the tragic addict found forgotten in a deserted barn, the team now faced a far darker narrative. Now it was murder.

In his year as a DC, Ellis had encountered assaults, domestic abuse, intimidation rackets and the missing child case that had been his first serious investigation in CID. But this was his first murder case. The atmosphere was markedly different, a pace he'd not experienced before injected into everyone's work. This was what they had all become detectives for. This was the real deal.

He swung his chair beside Dave Wheeler, jumping when an angry voice hissed in his ear.

'Watch what you're doing!'

Kate Bennett was giving him evils from her seat behind him when he looked back.

'Sorry...' he began, but she was already staring past him.

Suit yourself.

Turning back, he dropped onto his chair, a flash of heat in his cheeks. What was her problem? She'd pretty much blanked him after her outburst in the pool car yesterday. It wasn't just Drew who had noticed, either. Raised eyebrows sent his way from Evans, Wheeler and even Rob Minshull confirmed that. It should have made him feel supported, but Bennett's stormy silence in the office was hard to take. It wasn't like her to go off like that.

It annoyed him. Fine that she mocked his age like every other bastard in the team – he expected that. He was fast learning that mockery was part of the deal: you gave it and you took it. But Bennett's silence was a shock. Ellis had no systems in place to deal with it, no practised comebacks or clever deflections.

His back protested as he slumped in his chair, the result of an angry session in the gym last night after the row with her. He'd taken out his indignation on a punchbag and pumped far bigger weights than his program specified. Good job his trainer Jess wasn't in last night – recklessness like that would have earned him a stern lecture on control and respecting his body. Instead, his body had assumed her role today, every ache a condemnation.

The chat in the office faded as Anderson and Minshull returned. DI Anderson had been like a gleeful Scottish mountain goat since his meeting with the pathologist first thing that morning, practically skipping around the office and being worryingly upbeat. He beamed at the team now, leaning on the edge of a desk as Minshull began the briefing.

'So, here's what we know. We believe our body to be Oliver James O'Sullivan, aged thirty-four, originally from Birmingham' He stuck a photo from the teacher's Facebook profile on the board next to the stark, bruised photo of the corpse. 'His most recent address was a flat in Woodbridge. He had sustained a large head wound here,' he tapped the back of his head, 'which would have been catastrophic had he been alive when it happened. But Dr Amara believes he was hit at least two to three hours after he'd been killed. Guv?'

Anderson's smile was incongruous given the subject matter. 'There would have been blood everywhere if O'Sullivan's heart was still pumping when he was attacked. No heartbeat means no significant movement of blood. Dr Amara confirmed livor mortis had begun, the dropping of the blood to the lowest part of the body. The blood would have already begun to coagulate. It certainly could explain why we found no significant blood evidence where we found the body.'

'If the blow didn't kill him, what did? Drugs?' Minshull asked.

'Bleach.' The DI's smile fit around the word. 'A significant amount. Injected into his neck. If it weren't for the delay in the body being struck we might never have spotted it.'

'Could it be residue from cleaning a syringe?' Bennett asked, careful to keep her sight trained on her superior. 'I've heard it happens sometimes with addicts reusing old syringes. They don't rinse them afterwards and accidentally inject themselves with bleach residue when shooting up.'

'The amount found in his system was too large and too neat for it to be that,' Anderson replied. 'But good question, Kate.'

Ellis wondered if Anderson was trying to encourage Kate after her uncharacteristic behaviour in the office. It was unnerving everyone, it seemed.

'What this means is that we now have firm evidence of intent to kill. Bleach injected into the body is a calculated act, designed to cause maximum pain and suffering. Every major organ shutting down, one by one, as red blood cells rupture and oxygen supply is stripped; the victim in horrific pain and fully aware. Whoever put that syringe into O'Sullivan's neck wanted him to die a slow, agonising death. We are looking for a murderer.'

Ellis felt the collective wince of his colleagues at hearing the method of death. A blow to the head would have been horrific enough but easier to imagine as a spontaneous act. But the thought of someone researching the murder method, measuring out the right amount, filling a syringe, made Ellis go cold.

'Do we know it's O'Sullivan for certain now?' Wheeler asked.

'We need an official ID to confirm it, but the unusual tattoo on his left arm is an exact match for the description his ex-girlfriend gave when she reported him missing. It isn't a recognised symbol of any group or organisation we could find: as far as we are aware, the tattoo was meaningful only to Mr O'Sullivan, making it pretty unique. Drew, did you speak to Janet O'Sullivan this morning?'

'I did, Sarge.' Ellis checked his notebook even though he had already rehearsed his answer. 'She and her partner should be on their way by now. I also called the path lab and I've arranged a viewing of the body for tomorrow morning at nine o'clock.'

Janet O'Sullivan had been oddly calm when Ellis had spoken to her first thing. Shock, he supposed. How were you meant to react to that sort of news?

'How did she seem?' Minshull asked now.

'Quiet,' he replied. 'Resigned. She wanted to know the practical details and didn't ask for any more information. But I've given her my work number and told her to call me whenever she needs to. I hope that's all right?'

He felt the eyes of the team upon him.

Minshull offered him a smile. 'Absolutely the right thing to do. I'll meet Mrs O'Sullivan tomorrow for the viewing. Are you still happy to come with me?'

'Yes, Sarge.' His heart began to thud within his chest. He'd thought about it all last night. The nod of Minshull's trust in him it represented was *huge*. Another first for his career. And even though the thought of the path lab made him queasy, he felt personally invested now, having spoken at length with O'Sullivan's mother. If he could make the horrendous experience easier for her, he was ready to be at her side.

He caught sight of DC Les Evans miming a happy puppy face, hands bent over like paws, tongue lolling out and pretending to pant. It was Evans's latest jibe chucked in his path at every opportunity. But like every other ham-fisted attempt to mock him, this was destined to fail. Ellis made a show of looking away, blanking his colleague. Let him mock: tomorrow he would be doing the important stuff and Les would still be chained to his desk by endless record searches.

'So, believing our deceased to be Oliver O'Sullivan,' Minshull continued, turning back to the evidence board, 'Dave and I visited St Audrey High School yesterday and spoke to the Head, Tom Dillinger. Now, we know O'Sullivan lied about his mother's death when he requested leave from work because of what his ex-partner told Kate and Drew. We didn't tell Mr Dillinger about O'Sullivan's lie – no point until we have official confirmation of ID – but things certainly weren't good for O'Sullivan in the months leading up to him leaving work. He'd been distracted, thinking people were against him and working ridiculous hours with little rest. Something was making him do that.'

'That wasn't ordinary for him?' Anderson asked.

'Apparently not. It sounds like he always had a lot of energy – I mean, you don't volunteer to run a ton of after-school drama and music clubs if you don't have stamina – but the paranoia and the distraction weren't part of his character.'

'Hmm.' Anderson turned to Wheeler. 'Dave, what was your impression of the Head?'

'He was very cagey when we started asking him about knowing O'Sullivan socially. Shifty body language, too. I mean, he answered all our questions, but he looked like a rabbit in headlights, eyes going left and right like he was dizzy. There's more he's not telling us.'

Wheeler didn't consult any notes as he spoke. Ellis was in awe of the perennially sunny, amiable DC's ability to recall every detail perfectly, without the need for any prompts. Maybe one day Ellis would learn this skill. For now he was bound to his notebook and endless lists by the fear of missing something vital.

'Did Mr Dillinger believe O'Sullivan's reason for requesting compassionate leave?' Anderson asked.

'He seemed to, Guv,' Wheeler replied. 'I mean, a sudden death caused by a tragic car accident is a bit hard to argue with. But he was definitely picking his words carefully when we asked about his friendship with O'Sullivan. And then he said "damage limitation" was his primary concern.'

'For him or the school?' Evans piped up.

'Good point well made, Les. Kate, Drew, anything to add from your meeting with O'Sullivan's ex?'

Ellis looked at Bennett who granted him the briefest of glances before replying. 'Only that she'd split up with him when she found cocaine in his jacket. They were obviously still in touch despite breaking up four months ago. Ms Raphael reported him missing because she said she'd been to his new address and had found his motorbike gone.'

'Did we find a motorbike at Abbot's Farm?' Anderson asked Minshull.

'No, Guv. That may be another indicator that O'Sullivan was murdered somewhere else and dumped in the barn.'

'Les, run a vehicle check for O'Sullivan's bike. If we can find that, we may find where he was killed.'

'Guv.'

'Sarge, there was one thing.' Ellis raised his hand, a brief check of his notes uncovering a detail he'd forgotten. 'Ms Raphael said she'd felt she was no longer O'Sullivan's priority. She didn't say why but it could be that he was becoming more involved in drugs.' He paused for breath, steadying himself before he aired his suspicion. 'So could that be the reason he lied to the school? He was involved with the drug gang?'

Minshull considered this. 'It's possible. Certainly the mention of his ex-partner discovering he had cocaine is significant, given what else we found near his body, the small amount Dr Amara found during the post mortem and what we know about O'Sullivan's most recent behaviour. For the time being we'll still keep the two investigations separate until a concrete link surfaces but let's keep noting coincidences like these. Excellent spot, Drew.'

Anderson clapped his hands. 'Right, great work, everyone. I have a meeting with DCI Taylor so let's stop there for now. We're making progress. Let's keep going.'

As the team dispersed to their desks, Ellis saw Bennett heading for the kitchen. Checking his colleagues were all working, he followed her.

'What are you having?' he asked, fetching their mugs from the sink drainer before Bennett could reach them.

'It's fine, I'll make my own.'

'Sod off,' Ellis said, the shock of his words having the desired effect as Bennett looked up. He fixed a smile. 'You know my coffee's way better than yours.'

Smile, he willed her. *Please smile.*

The stilted air between them had been there too long. Whatever Bennett's reasons for her distance today, there was no need for Ellis to return the attitude. They worked well together – everyone said so – and he couldn't go on nursing hurt feelings towards her. Maybe she needed someone not tiptoeing around her as the rest of the CID team currently were.

Bennett stared back, her hand gripping the edge of the small kitchen worktop. Ellis waited, only now questioning the wisdom of his attempt at humour.

'Then you'd better make this a bloody good one,' she returned, with the slightest smile.

Relief washed over him. 'Challenge accepted.'

'Fine. Milk, no sugar. And don't put half a cow in it like you usually do.'

He gave her a salute. 'Yes, ma'am.'

Bennett shook her head. 'Pillock.'

Ellis grinned as Bennett returned to her desk. It was good to have her back.

–

The afternoon passed stealthily, the list of tasks Ellis had carefully written in his notebook gradually rewarded with ticks in the boxes beside them. The team worked on their own, a joke from Evans or the delivery of a mug of coffee from Wheeler the only interruptions. The evidence board was incentive to keep going, even when the late afternoon sun streamed into the office and his aching body tried to railroad his concentration.

Going through older posts on Oliver O'Sullivan's Facebook and Twitter pages had brought nothing more than mentions of rugby and a few friends for Ellis to add to the list of acquaintances Wheeler and Bennett were working their way through. He was about to search for other social networks O'Sullivan might have joined when his phone buzzed on the desk beside him. He glanced down to see an email notification:

Google Alert – Suffolk drug gangs

He clicked on the notification to open the email.

And his jaw dropped.

Chapter Fourteen

Minshull

'Sarge, you have to see this.'

Minshull looked up from his desk to see Ellis. From this angle he appeared to tower over him, a smartphone in his outstretched hand inches from Minshull's nose.

'New phone?' he smiled.

Ellis didn't return it. That wasn't like him. 'No. What's on the screen.'

Minshull accepted the phone and took a closer look. '*The Bures Bowmen*,' he read, glancing at his young DC as Ellis moved to his side. 'You thinking of taking up archery?'

'This was just posted. I have a Google Alert set up for anything to do with the drug rings or the barn where we found O'Sullivan's body and it just flagged this post.'

New threat to local area, the headline stated, followed by a subheading: *Is now the time to act?*

'You get this kind of stuff a lot. People reacting to what they see on the news. You saw the articles we had when Hannah Perry went missing.'

Ellis was shaking his head, frustration flushing his cheeks. 'It isn't that, Sarge. These people aren't just having their say. Scroll down the page.'

Minshull did as he was told, eyes scanning the familiar, tabloid-style statements and breathless rage. He'd seen it all before. Not wanting to extinguish Drew's fire, he scrolled on, not really paying much attention to the text. And then, a set of photographs scrolled into view – and Minshull lost his breath.

'What the…? How did they get these?'

'I don't know, but they're all over the Internet. Starting here, then on the group's Facebook and Twitter feeds. It was posted an hour ago. Now it's been shared and copied hundreds of times.'

The headline accompanying every shared version of the story was the same:

DRUG GANGS IN SUFFOLK CLAIMED HIS LIFE.
THE POLICE ARE POWERLESS TO STOP THIS.
HOW MANY MORE WILL DIE?

Minshull stared at the crime scene photographs – including shots of the evidence markers and the gruesome close-up of the side of O'Sullivan's bruised and swollen head that was the central image on the evidence board in CID. 'Who are these people?'

Ellis shifted a little as if his size eleven shoes were pinching. 'Vigilantes.'

'What?'

'They're Suffolk-based, but they seem to draw support from across the country. I did a quick tour of their social media posts back over the last couple of years and most of the stuff seemed pretty harmless. Angry opinions, a bit of middle-aged sabre-rattling, that sort of thing. But this site is new and I haven't seen this rhetoric before. I think they're mobilising.'

'Vigilantes in Suffolk?' Anderson was beside them now, his stealthy progress from his office to Minshull's desk unnoticed. 'What are they? An army of angry tractor drivers?'

Any relief he might have felt about the good mood of his superior vanished in the pit of Minshull's churning stomach. 'They've posted crime scene photos, Guv.'

As Anderson snatched the phone, Ellis continued, flinching at the expletive-heavy explosion erupting from his DI.

'They call themselves the Bures Bowmen after a local legend. A dragon allegedly terrorised the villages around Bures, murdering livestock and burning everything in its path. In the end the villagers banded together and chased it out of the village, never to be seen again. The group believes it has a mandate to rid the county of drug gangs.'

'Chasing the dragon?' Minshull could hardly believe it. 'That's taking it literally.'

'And not just drugs, Sarge. Anyone they see as terrorising society. Paedophiles, gangs, thieves…'

'How serious do you think they are?'

'Up until now, it's all been hot air. But obtaining and sharing confidential crime photos – that's a warning shot.'

'It's bloody illegal,' Anderson growled, pushing the phone back at Ellis. 'Get it shut down. *Now*. I won't have these bastards thinking they can do this.'

'Guv. I'll get Tech on it immediately.'

'And any other idiots sharing those images,' Anderson called after him as he hurried out of the CID office. 'Press included.' He turned back to Minshull. 'That's the last thing we need. I want everything we can get on this group. Names, activity, any threats made in their stupid fury-posts. Bring them in, if we have to.'

'And the photos?'

Anderson's expression darkened. 'I want to know everyone in the building who had access to them. Find out who leaked them. And when you find them, send them to me.'

Behind Anderson, the team ducked as one.

–

Within an hour the main news agencies had located the story. *The Sentinel* quoted a tweet showing the images on their website, swiftly removed when a takedown order was issued, but it was up long enough to be seen and shared. The story was hastily rewritten to express outrage that South Suffolk Police had allowed sensitive images to be leaked. The story was a bombshell, feeding into the criticism already being levelled at them for a major drugs wave being missed.

The only comfort Minshull could draw from the debacle was that in the close-up image of O'Sullivan he was so bruised and contorted by his injuries that he wouldn't be identifiable. With his mother due to arrive in Suffolk today, the thought of her seeing the unprepared body of her son was unbearable. Tomorrow, he would be laid out respect-fully, the worst of his injuries masked from view, still a horrendous sight for a grieving mother, but far better than the alternative.

Any hopes of a normal finish time evaporated as Minshull, Anderson and the team worked to ensure no more photographs had been shared. DCI Taylor arrived at six, her fury meted out on the entire team the moment she entered the office.

'What is the point of everything the senior leadership team and I are doing to bolster the image of this force if highly sensitive photographic evidence can be stolen at whim?' she thundered. 'If I find that *anyone* in this office was responsible for this they will be arrested *immediately*. Understand?'

With that, she swept into Anderson's office, the door slamming behind her. The team exchanged glances as her muffled shouts continued from inside.

–

Minshull spent a fretful night monitoring the story as it spread from tabloids to broadsheets to the murkier, uncensored side of social media. The conversation quickly moved from the salacious details of the body at Abbot's Farm to condemnation of South Suffolk Police for not only missing the drug gang problem but also having so little security that crime scene images could be stolen.

> So much for keeping the community safe. If they can't even stop their own coppers nicking crime scene photos, what hope do we have of them protecting the public?

> Another scandal involving the amateurish South Suffolk police. Would taxpayers' money be better spent by outsourcing policing in Suffolk to a larger, more competent force?

> Someone is going to recognise that body. I hope the police bother to tell them before they see it splashed all over social media.

By the time Minshull arrived at work the next day, he was exhausted. Judging by the shadow-eyed, caffeine-fortified faces of his team, he wasn't the only one. Wheeler arrived at Minshull's desk with a surprisingly strong mug of coffee.

'I went for Les-strength,' he grinned grimly. 'I figured my usual wouldn't cut it today.'

'Cheers, Dave.' He looked across the office to the youngest member of the team who was furiously typing, head bowed. 'Drew, are you ready to go to Pathology? I want to get there early so we can talk to Dr Amara before Mrs O'Sullivan arrives.'

'Have fun with Dr Morticia, Drew,' Evans grinned over his half-eaten breakfast roll. 'She likes the young ones. Easier to devour.'

Ellis's laugh was decidedly shaky.

'Leave it out, Les,' Minshull said, but Evans was enjoying himself too much to listen.

'I heard she likes to sleep in the path lab. Snuggle up with the stiffs. You might need to leave the light on when you go to bed tonight, kid. Don't have nightmares now...'

Minshull drained his cup and headed across the CID office to rescue a fast-paling Ellis.

—

Bright sunlight after last night's rain made everything sparkle in Ipswich as Minshull and Ellis drove across town. Minshull thought of O'Sullivan's mother, getting ready this morning to see her son for the last time. Did sunshine help on such an occasion, he wondered? Or was it worse to see it, its hopefulness mocking the devastation a bereaved mother must feel? He hoped for the former: after the identification this morning there would be little comfort for Janet O'Sullivan.

An hour before the identification viewing was scheduled Minshull led Ellis down the empty pale grey corridors to Dr Amara's office. The pathologist was settled behind her desk, a newspaper spread out between stacks of files. She smiled as they entered.

'Good morning, gentlemen. I see you've brought some fresh blood to see me, DS Minshull.'

Minshull felt Ellis hang back a little behind him. He would have words with Les Evans about his humour when they returned to CID later. Jokes were expected, but terrifying junior colleagues was not part of the deal.

'This is DC Drew Ellis. And it's his first time in the building.'

Understanding his meaning, Dr Amara's smile softened as she rose from her chair and extended her hand to Ellis. 'Welcome, Drew. I'm Rachael. Forgive me; I know I have a rather fearsome reputation for my humour. When you have a job like mine you have to make your own amusement.'

Ellis relaxed the moment he accepted her handshake.

'Please, take a seat. Would you like coffee?'

'We're good, thanks,' Minshull replied. While more caffeine would be welcome this morning, he wanted an empty stomach for the viewing. He had only accompanied grieving relatives to the dark room with its large window and resting bed beyond twice before and both times the visceral punch of loss had twisted his guts.

'I saw the news,' Dr Amara said, tapping the copy of *The Sentinel* on her desk. 'Leaked crime scene photos?'

'Tell us about it. We've had all the ones we can find taken down but you know how fast images travel. It had been live for an hour before we discovered it, so you can imagine how many people it will have reached.'

'And the deceased's mother?'

Minshull grimaced. 'I'm hoping she hasn't seen it.'

'Nasty business. Any idea how they got out?'

'Not yet, but DI Anderson is after them.'

Dr Amara folded the newspaper. 'I bet Joel is spitting feathers.'

'Let's just say attending a murder victim viewing was more appealing than staying in the office today.'

'Crikey. I have a soft spot for your DI but I would hate to get on the wrong side of him.' She nodded at Drew. 'So, my company might be a lucky escape for you after all.'

Beside him, Ellis offered a tentative smile.

Forty minutes later Dr Amara's secretary Oisín knocked on the door to say that Janet O'Sullivan and her partner had arrived. Steeling themselves, Minshull and Ellis followed Dr Amara from her office to the viewing suite.

Minshull noticed that the pathologist's demeanour had dimmed, too, evident in the softer volume of her voice and her careful steps along the corridor. This was a moment nobody should have to witness, a stark intrusion into the private revelation of grief. O'Sullivan might have insisted his mother was dead to his employer, but Ellis said they'd been in regular contact and appeared to have an amicable relationship. He must have been loved as a son, even if not everything about his life had been easy to witness.

Janet O'Sullivan was seated at the farthest end of a line of chairs running along the wall opposite the viewing window, her handbag held tightly in her lap. Beside her a tall woman was standing, a careful arm laid around Janet's shoulders. They looked up together when Dr Amara, Minshull and Ellis approached.

'Hello, Mrs O'Sullivan. I'm Detective Sergeant Rob Minshull. This is Detective Constable Drew Ellis, who you've been speaking with, and this is Dr Rachael Amara, Chief Pathologist.'

Hands were shaken, tentative nods exchanged.

'I'm Janet. Please call me that. And this is my partner, Lindy Blaine. I know we're early, but…' Her voice ebbed away as her eyes drifted to the viewing window, a dark blue curtain drawn across it for respect.

'You're here at the right time,' Ellis assured her.

Minshull saw the soothing effect his familiar voice had on O'Sullivan's mother. These were the moments Ellis surprised him the most: the emotional maturity and compassion he displayed, far beyond his twenty-five years. Of all the team, Ellis had been the best suited to the delicate task of being the police contact for Mrs O'Sullivan.

'So what happens now with…?' Lindy asked, waving a hand in the general direction of the window.

'When you're ready, I will instruct my team to open the curtains,' Dr Amara said. 'You can sit or stand, whatever you feel most comfortable with. And we will leave the curtains open for as long as you like.'

'Is he...' Janet swallowed hard, Lindy's hand catching hers and holding it. 'Will he be covered with a sheet? I've seen that on TV...'

'He can be, if you prefer. Or we can have him ready for you to see him when the curtains are drawn back. He will look like he's sleeping.'

The pathologist's words were so gentle, so kind in the face of unimaginable horror, that Minshull felt a lump forming in his throat.

'No sheet,' Janet replied. 'But I might close my eyes until you tell me he's ready to look at.'

'Of course.'

'And – could I hold your hand, Drew?' O'Sullivan's mother gazed up at Ellis with fear-hollowed eyes. 'You on this side and Lindy on the other? I want to stand but I don't know if my legs will hold me.'

Minshull looked at Ellis, expecting to see fear.

'It would be my honour, Janet.' Ellis slipped respectfully past him and took her left hand. 'You just lean on me, okay? Squeeze as tight as you like.'

The silence Minshull had been dreading fell, then. The moment when polite conversation ceased and all that was left was the task at hand. Janet nodded at Dr Amara who gave a brief smile and left the room. Minshull stood by an intercom phone and waited until a small beep sounded to signify that everything was ready beyond the glass.

'Are you ready, Janet?'

A sob escaped her as she nodded and closed her eyes.

Minshull lifted the receiver. 'Okay, all good here.'

There was a low buzz as the blue curtains were drawn back. Lindy looked away almost immediately. Minshull saw Janet's hand grip Ellis's tightly.

'I can't...' she whispered, her body shaking.

'We're right here,' Ellis soothed. 'There's no rush. Take your time.'

O'Sullivan's mother nodded again, blowing air from her cheeks as she readied herself. Was she hoping the body beyond the window was a stranger, Minshull wondered? Or hoping her worst fears were confirmed so she wouldn't have to repeat this?

Slowly, she opened her eyes, a rush of air leaving her body as she sagged between the detective and her partner.

'Yes,' she managed, emotion snatching at her words. 'That's my son.'

–

Thirty minutes later, Minshull, Janet and Lindy were seated around a green melamine table in the small café opposite the pathology building. It had been Minshull's suggestion, some bland normality after such a life-altering event. It didn't seem right to just wave off O'Sullivan's bereaved mother at the door.

Janet looked up and managed a smile when Ellis returned from the counter with coffee for the detectives and a large teapot of strong tea for the women.

'Okay, here we go. I ordered some cake, too. The bloke's bringing it over. And if you don't fancy it now, Janet, he has some takeaway boxes for you to take it home.'

'You're a sweetheart, Drew. Thank you.'

She was calmer now, a surprising strength assuming the place where grief had been in the viewing gallery. There had been tears as she had approached the window, her hand slipping from Lindy's to rest against the glass. She had remained there for five minutes before asking Minshull to have the curtains drawn again. Ellis and Lindy had led her to the row of chairs to sit and she had hidden in her partner's embrace for almost twenty minutes while Minshull and Ellis averted their eyes. Now, pouring tea into two chintz cups, she had a poise and air of control Minshull hadn't witnessed in a relative of a deceased victim before.

'I suppose you have some questions to ask me,' she said to Minshull.

'I do, but it can wait if you…'

'I'm fine now,' she replied, passing a cup to Lindy. 'Now I know, I can start to move forward.'

'Okay. One moment.' Minshull's fingers fumbled as he retrieved his notebook from the pocket of his jacket. Finding the page, he offered Mrs O'Sullivan an apologetic smile. 'I wanted to ask how Oliver had seemed to you in the weeks leading up to his disappearance. Drew tells me you were in regular phone contact?'

'Regular for us, which could be a call a week for a month and then nothing for six weeks,' she replied, glancing at her partner. 'He sounded tired. Didn't want to be drawn on anything. I know he and Sonja were having problems but he wouldn't say why. I know now, of course.'

'Did he seem to have problems with concentration, anger?'

'Not that I noticed. I would probably have put that down to tiredness if I had.'

'Of course. Did Oliver mention about wanting to take time off work?'

Janet shook her head. 'The first I knew about it was when Sonja called me to ask if I'd heard from Olly. I wasn't surprised: my son has always been impetuous. If he got an idea in his head he would pursue it endlessly.'

'He's taken off before?'

'Six years back. I'd divorced his dad and Lindy was moving in. Olly didn't approve at first. He ended up moving from the school in Birmingham where he was teaching, going off for a month travelling before he moved to Suffolk and took the job at St Audrey's. We didn't speak for six months.'

Lindy placed a hand on her partner's arm. 'Janet was hurt by that, but we slowly got to know each other and the last time Olly visited, he and I were like old friends.'

Minshull checked his notes. 'And when was that?'

'Christmas. He surprised us with a two-night visit.'

'Would you say you were close in recent months?'

Janet bit her lip. 'More than ever.'

'And he didn't mention any concerns? Any disagreements with anyone?'

'Nothing specific.'

Minshull remembered the Head at St Audrey's saying something similar. 'But he did say something?'

Janet gave a long sigh. 'He didn't always keep the best company. Chased after approval from the wrong people, did stupid things some-times. He was young and a man – no offence to either of you, but I'm sure you know what I mean. His judgment wasn't always the sharpest. But he was a good boy at heart, DS Minshull. And I loved him.'

—

In the car driving back to the CID office, Minshull tried to make sense of what he'd heard. Oliver O'Sullivan had been close to his mum, had stayed in regular contact with her in recent months and even surprised her with a Christmas visit. The disagreements that may have come between them six years ago appeared to be long forgotten at the time he disappeared. Like Tom Dillinger at St Audrey's, Janet had heard some kind of vague mention of tension with others in her son's life but beyond that, all had apparently been well between them.

So why had Oliver O'Sullivan lied about his mother's death?

And what other lies might they yet uncover?

Chapter Fifteen

Cora

'Morning, Dr Lael.'

Cora smiled as she turned up the volume on her hands-free, driving along the country lane towards Woodsham St Mary.

'Morning, DS Minshull. Nice to hear from you.'

'I can't speak long, but I just wanted to thank you again for your words of wisdom on Wednesday night.'

'My pleasure. How did the ID thing go?'

'Better than I'd hoped. I mean, it was horrific to watch, you know, seeing the mother recognise her son. But you were right: focusing on her meant none of the other stuff came into play.'

'So do you know who your body is? Or is that confidential?'

'No, I can tell you. Joel gave a press statement at ten-fifteen, so it will be all over the news by now. His name was Oliver O'Sullivan and he was a teacher at a local high school.'

Cora pulled to a crossroads and waited for a tractor to rumble past. 'That's awful. Do you have any idea who might have attacked him?'

'Not yet, but we're working on it. How's everything with you?'

An angry driver in a Land Rover Evoque screeched to a halt behind the tractor, gesticulating furiously at the driver. Cora suppressed a grin as she indicated left and drove away from them both. 'I'm working with an interesting new case. A teenager with Elective Mutism.'

'Wow. How do you even begin to work with that?'

'Listening, mostly.'

She heard the rush of Minshull's self-conscious laugh on the other end of the call. 'Of course. Daft question. Look, I have to go, but I don't suppose you'd be up for brunch tomorrow? I'm in the office in the afternoon but was thinking of a beach run in the morning.'

Theirs was a strange new world, so different from their first experience of working together. Cora liked it: from Minshull's attitude he appeared to like it, too.

'How about I join you for the run?'

'Only if you think you can keep up.'

Cora laughed, indicating to take the sharp right-hand turn into a narrow lane that would take her to the glass house. 'I'll be waiting at the finish line with breakfast ready for when you catch up with me.'

'Ha! Deal! I'll text you the time and where I'm parking.'

'Great.' She hesitated, then added, 'I'm glad the viewing went okay.'

'What you said really helped. See you tomorrow.'

The call ended as Cora reached the entrance to the glass house's drive. As she reached the top, she saw another car pulling away, a young girl standing on the doorstep.

The teenager offered a brief smile when Cora arrived.

'Hey.'

'Hello.'

'Are you here to see Mrs Arundel?'

Cora shouldered her bag. 'No. Lottie.'

The young girl's eyes grew wide behind her long red fringe. 'You're the doctor, right?'

'That's right.' Cora smiled. 'I'm Cora.'

'Esme. Lottie's my best friend. She told me about you.'

'Did she?'

Esme nodded. 'She said you weren't a tedious nutter like the others.'

As endorsements went, it wasn't the most encouraging, but Cora would take it. 'Good to know.'

The door opened and Monica Arundel's face fell the moment she saw both visitors. 'Esme. Why aren't you at school?'

'School sent our year home, so I'm stuck doing rounds with Mum. She had a house call at the stables in the village, so she said I could come and see Lotts for a bit. Is that okay?'

'She has her session,' Monica snapped, relenting when she saw the effect of her tone on her daughter's friend. 'But you can come up and say hello before it begins.' With that, she turned and powered up the glass steps.

Head bowed, Esme hurried inside and Cora followed them, taking the time it took to close the door to mute the sighs from the entrance.

When she reached the living area, Cora saw Esme and Lottie hugging. It reminded her of Liz Allis, her oldest friend, who she had become firm friends with when she was fourteen, two years before her ability first manifested. She remembered the warm feeling of having a friend there just for her, even though in later years their friendship had become more of a habitual acquaintance. Now Liz was living Newcastle where her company had relocated six months ago, their phone conversations were sporadic. Cora didn't think they would ever return to the easy friendship she could see Lottie and Esme enjoying. She wasn't sure she would miss it. Now there was Rory from her former job at the University of South Suffolk, who had proved a better friend in the last eighteen months than Liz ever had. And Rob Minshull – although theirs was still a tentative acquaintance for now.

Can Esme come with us?

Lottie smiled at her across the room.

'I don't think that's a good idea,' Monica began, but her daughter ignored this, her attention solely on Cora.

Please?

'I don't have a problem with it,' Cora replied, sensing the storm brewing between mother and daughter. The held breaths around Lottie had begun to hiss like an army of snakes.

'It isn't the way it should be done.'

We're just walking.

'Lottie...'

Cora stepped between the warring Arundels. 'Monica, it would actually help me to get a real sense of what Lottie's everyday life is like. Observing interactions between friends often reveals things that discussion doesn't.'

There was a pause, Esme staring at Cora open-mouthed as Lottie and Monica continued their raised-chin stand-off either side of her.

Then Monica gave an aggravated sigh, wrestling the pashmina scarf from around her neck.

'*Fine*. But this is the only time, understand?'

Of course.

Monica turned her back on her daughter, sending a curt nod to Cora as she swept past into the kitchen, dropping her scarf on the glass dining table as she went.

This is a total waste of time. She doesn't want to get better, her subconscious voice snarled up from the tumbled chiffon. Cora acknowledged it and then dismissed it from her mind. She didn't need Monica's voice muscling in today.

Lottie picked up her jacket and the girls quickly headed down the stairs. Cora followed, a plan of action forming. She needed to break the wall of breaths Lottie had built around herself, to discover the word she'd had the sense of during her last visit. Perhaps if Lottie was occupied by conversation with her best friend, her guard would drop and Cora might be able to finally retrieve the word. Whatever Lottie was guarding, Cora felt certain it was key to unlocking her silence.

They crossed the road at the bottom of the drive and climbed over the stile that led to the estuary footpath. Cora stayed a pace behind the girls, partly to give Lottie the sense of space and encourage her to relax, and partly because the footpath was too narrow for them to walk three abreast. It suited Cora: the chance to have a wider view of both the physical landscape and the unseen sound dimension.

It was a decidedly dull day, the sunlight and fleeting shadows of their previous walk gone, replaced by a flat cloudbank of uninspiring greys. The estuary was at low tide, its wide expanse reduced to a narrow channel of water flanked by exposed banks of mud, sand and rock. But the closer they drew to the estuary edge the more the pale sandy mud seemed to glow. The water was a perfect mirror of the sky, as if it had turned into a stream of silver-grey mercury.

Ahead of Cora, the girls were in deep conversation, heads bowed towards each other despite only one of them talking. The staccato replies from Lottie's tablet sliced the quiet air, Esme's hushed answers taken by the gentle breeze.

Are you sure?

A murmured reply.

When?

A glance over Esme's shoulder. More hushed words.

Do they know about…?

A shake of Esme's head. A pause. Two hands meeting briefly for a squeeze.

Cora's foot twisted on a concealed rock at the edge of the footpath, causing her to stumble. The girls turned.

'Sorry. Missed that rock.'

It happens a lot. This path can be brutal.

'So, how are you going to help Lottie?' Esme asked.

'I'm going to listen first. And then we can think about developing other ways of communication that Lottie feels comfortable with.'

She's teaching me semaphore. The flags are in her car.

'Are you?'

Cora sent Lottie a rueful grin. 'No. Not yet at least. I was thinking interpretative dance first?'

Lottie's grin was immediate.

I'll dig out my leotard.

Esme was agog between them. 'Can you talk to a doctor like that?'

I can to this one.

It felt like the biggest victory. A moment of connection passed between her and the teenager. The breaths began to ebb away. Cora began to ease past them, the shadow of the concealed sound almost within her mind's reach…

G…

There. The start of the hidden word. A hard 'g' as in 'girl' or 'good'… Cora steadied her breathing as she pressed into the edge of the sound.

G…

Definitely a hard 'g'. Like a rock climber seeking out the next handhold, Cora stretched her mind forwards, reaching for the next sound. She could sense it coming into view, the layers of withheld breath guarding it beginning to shudder like wind through a voile curtain...

'Can we sit down? I've got a stone in my shoe,' Esme asked – and the moment was gone.

Cora quickly withdrew her mind as the breaths surrounding Lottie swelled once more.

They settled on a bench a little farther along the path from where Cora had sat with Lottie before. Esme apologised over and over as she took off her shoe and shook out a sprinkling of gravel. Lottie's gaze drifted out to sea, a strange stillness settling across her features.

'We weren't ignoring you, by the way,' Esme chattered, nervous of the silence on either side of her now.

'I didn't think you were.'

'It's just we had the worst news today.'

'Oh?'

'Our drama teacher's been murdered.'

Es. Cora doesn't want to know that.

'She'll see it on the news anyway. It was on TV this morning. They found Mr O'Sullivan's body abandoned in an old barn. And it's definitely murder.'

Mr O'Sullivan... The body Minshull's team had found at Abbot's Farm.

'That's horrible, I'm sorry.'

'It's so weird. He hasn't been at school this term because his mum died or something, but now everyone's thinking he might have been dead all this time. We only went in for an hour this morning and then the teachers sent us home. That's why I'm with Mum. She wasn't happy having me hanging around with her.'

'Did you know him well?'

'Everyone knew him. He was our form teacher and English teacher last year, our Drama teacher this year.' Esme looked at her friend. 'And then there were all the clubs he ran; drama, musical theatre, the props team, the directors' pod. I mean, he was everywhere.'

Cora looked at her charge, who was still staring out at the silver-grey water. 'Are you okay, Lottie? If you want to go back...'

I'm okay here.

'If you're sure? It's a big shock.'

Can we talk about something else, please?

'I think we should, too,' Esme said, staring at her hands. 'It'll be all anybody wants to talk about at school from now on.'

–

When she returned home, Cora left her car by her house and headed straight for the promenade. Felixstowe was glowing today, a haze of light skimming the calm waves on North Beach. The chill in the air hadn't dissuaded the hardy locals from heading down onto the beach and even a couple of the beach huts were open, giving the day the air of a weekend.

The chatter floating on the breeze swirled around Cora like the gentle lap of waves as she traced a route along the shoreline towards the pier. After her meeting with Lottie and Esme and the near miss of retrieving Lottie's concealed word, her mind was a tangle.

She needed to think.

Had Lottie relaxed her hold on the word because her best friend was there or had Cora's successful persuading of Monica to allow Esme to accompany them caused Lottie to momentarily drop her guard? Or was it the shock of receiving the news of her teacher's death?

Cora had been working to establish trust with Lottie, so that it might bring about a loosening of the breaths she cloaked the word in – hoping to establish a route where she might gain insight into Lottie's thoughts. Today it had suddenly been accessible, if only for a moment. But with so many factors potentially responsible for bringing it about, how could Cora hope to replicate the ideal circumstances again?

Her next thought was that she needed to alert Minshull to the link between her case and his investigation. Lottie and Esme would no doubt be contacted by the police for interview along with the rest of their classmates, but what if they could help provide insight now, before the routine interviews of the school began? At the same time, should she wait and talk to Lottie more before talking to Minshull?

Discover what other things she might share about O'Sullivan being her teacher?

Because there had been something else Cora had caught in Lottie's reaction, far beyond the natural shock of a familiar person's murder. Cora had seen it in Esme, too, had sensed it in their hurried whispers on the estuary path. Like the rest of the word held tight in Lottie's mind, the suggestion hung enticingly, just beyond her reach.

What did the teenagers know about Oliver O'Sullivan?

Lottie

Esme talks when she's scared. For the first time today I found myself wishing I could talk, too.

It's taken hours for it to sink in.

Mum is in bits: she liked Mr O'Sullivan. All the mums did.

At least she's let me go to my room to rest now. My head is banging from all of her words. I turned my phone off, too, because everyone is posting about it in our group chat.

I knew him better than most of them. I should feel something.

Right now I just feel tired.

I'm meant to be going to school on Monday but Dad is adamant I should stay off next week. His friend who lives across the road from St Audrey's said it's jammed up with TV news trucks, journalists swarming everywhere. They were turning up today as everybody in year ten was being sent home. Dad reckons they'll be hanging around for days. They're like vultures, he says, hunting out fresh meat.

There are vultures everywhere.

All the group chat want to talk about is about how he died. Like that's the only thing that matters. I don't want to think about it.

I should check on Amy. And Bindi. They're not in the group chat and I don't blame them. I know they'll be finding this hard. But I can't today. I just want to close my eyes and wish it all away.

I should feel *something*. Shouldn't I?

Chapter Sixteen

Minshull

'South Suffolk Police have today confirmed that a body discovered in a derelict Suffolk farm is that of local high school teacher, Oliver O'Sullivan. He was 34. His mother today thanked the police and the member of the public who found the teacher's body, but requested privacy at this time to grieve her son. We sent our reporter Ben McAra to the school where Mr O'Sullivan worked, in this exclusive report.

'St Audrey High in Woodbridge is a thriving, popular school attended by children from rural villages across the area. But today, it is a school in shock, as teachers, pupils and parents struggle to process the tragic loss of a much-loved teacher. I spoke to some of Oliver O'Sullivan's colleagues and asked them how the terrible news of his murder has been received...'

Tom Dillinger – Head Teacher

'Obviously, we are all in shock. We sent our Year 10s home today as a mark of respect and specially trained counsellors will be working with our students next week as we come to terms with our loss. Oliver was a popular, gifted English and Drama teacher who worked tire-lessly for the school. He was the driving force of St Audrey's excellent extra-curricular arts programme, and he inspired and touched the lives of so many pupils here. He will be terribly missed.'

Candice Loveridge – Governor

'It's a huge shock to everyone. He was such a larger-than-life character. So many parents and pupils loved him. The school won't be the same without him.'

Andrew Draycott – Teacher

'I can't believe it. Nobody can. Olly was someone who was a friend to anyone who needed it. Including me. He – forgive me – He was my good friend. I can't believe someone took his life away.'

'Do you know anyone who might have wanted to harm him?'

'No. No, everybody loved him. Everybody.'

'Police say enquiries into Oliver O'Sullivan's murder are ongoing, but they have appealed for anyone with information to contact them. One thing is certain: this shattered school community will not be able to heal until his murderer is found…'

—

'Have we spoken to any of the governors or that other teacher, yet?' Minshull asked the team gathered around his computer, as the news report ended.

'Not yet, Sarge.'

'Mr Dillinger sent over a list of staff contact numbers,' Bennett said, checking her notes. 'If we can't speak to them in school today, we can arrange phone interviews over the weekend.'

'Okay, good. Dave and Les, can you get over to the school now and see who you can chat to?'

'Sarge.'

'And be gentle, Les.'

Evans looked aghast. 'Why do you think I wouldn't be?'

'Because while Dave would win the title of Nicest Bloke on the Planet, your ideal role model is Gene Hunt.'

Evans harrumphed as the team laughed around him.

'Aw, don't worry, mate,' Wheeler said, clamping a hand to his shoulder. 'At least Minsh is letting you out of the office.'

'Kate, any movement on our missing motorbike?'

'Not yet, Sarge. We've put out an alert for local patrols to be on the lookout for it. And I'm waiting to hear back from Traffic about any sightings during the weeks either side of the time we think O'Sullivan travelled to the barn, working on the theory that the body might have been there for a month or so before it was discovered. Depending on which direction he travelled from, we might pick up something.'

Minshull made a note. 'While you're waiting for that can you give O'Sullivan's brother a call?'

Bennett frowned. 'He has a brother?'

'Apparently so. Janet O'Sullivan gave us his number. He lives up near Alnwick and runs a consulting business from home. He's happy to chat with us, according to her.'

'Sarge. Anything particular you want to know?'

'Find out if they were close. If he has any idea of who might have wished his brother harm. Anything that gives us more to build a picture of O'Sullivan. I feel like we're missing something about him, about his life. Check with Tech to see if they can track down any mobile phone records for him. I know his phone hasn't been found but maybe if we can locate his mobile provider we can access his records. We need bank details, too, so check with the school to see if we can access details of the account his salary was paid into.'

'No problem, I'll see what I can find out.'

'Thanks. Drew, what do you have?'

'I've been trawling through the Bures Bowmen's social media to try to work out who they are and what they stand for. They don't appear to have an official membership but their page on Facebook has one thousand and fifty likes and eight hundred followers. Couple of hundred on Twitter, eighty followers on the website.'

'Sounds like a ball,' Evans quipped, earning a stare from Ellis.

'Up until four months ago they mainly reposted other comment-ators' prejudiced guff. British jobs being taken by foreigners, police not being fit for purpose, government conspiracies, the usual. But then those stopped and they started posting as themselves. About paedophiles and drugs gangs. Just two subjects. And every single one is about how the ordinary man needs to "take back control".'

'Interesting.'

'They uploaded a new profile picture and banner on Facebook nine weeks ago – the change notification was still up. It's a shot of a crowd raising their fists. The posts have started talking about communities under fire with paedophiles being relocated to rural areas in the county and police ignoring serious drug crime. And the last four posts on their Facebook page before they shared the crime scene photos were hinting that something is about to happen. A call to arms.' He offered his phone to Minshull.

Enough is enough. It's time to act. Are you with us?

'Bloody hell.'

'And they've been signed,' Ellis said, pointing at the bottom of the most recent post. 'Two names – they're appearing everywhere: Garvey Maitland and Rhian Butler.'

'In plain sight?'

'Sarge. I think they're planning something.'

'What do we know about them? Are they even real names?'

'I've been looking into them this morning.' Ellis fumbled the pages in his notebook, covered with enthusiastic scrawl decipherable only to himself. 'Maitland was cautioned on public order offences in 2006 and again in 2015. Since then, nothing. Butler received a ninety-day court order for malicious damage to a former councillor's car and pleaded guilty to sending a string of abusive and threatening letters to the man's wife.'

Minshull grimaced. 'Sounds delightful. When was this?'

'Eighteen months ago.'

'Locally?'

'No, Sarge. This was in Plymouth. Butler moved to Felixstowe last year. Devon and Cornwall Police dealt with it. Want me to contact them for more information?'

'No need,' Minshull replied, a smile already growing at the thought. 'My brother's a DI on their CID team.'

Ellis seemed impressed. 'Bit of a family business, then?'

'You could say that.'

Ellis was too new in CID to have met his father, but Minshull wondered if retired DCI John Minshull's fearsome reputation had been passed to the young DC by osmosis. It was entirely possible. The spectre of John Minshull still hung ominously over everything Minshull did. A year under his belt as DS should have proved to everyone that Rob Minshull was his own man, but every conversation with DCI Taylor brought him right back to the small boy cowering in his father's fearsome shadow.

You're a credit to your father's legacy in South Suffolk. A worthy heir...

Minshull hated it. Worse, he knew John Minshull was only too aware of the comments swirling around his son, even from the distant vantage point of his restless retirement. Only where Rob found them stifling, John considered them a badge of honour.

Leaving the CID team to their work, he headed out to his car in the car park, placing a call to the eldest of the three Minshull boys.

'Robbie! Good to hear from you, man.'

'Forgive the Friday call. I know you're busy but I just need a bit of info.'

'I'm off today. Hang up, give me five mins to get to my desk and I'll FaceTime you.'

'No problem.' Reaching his car, Minshull settled in the driver's seat, the chance of a five-minute break a gift this morning.

Benjamin Minshull was nothing like his brothers. Always carving his own path through life since he was a kid, where Rob and eldest brother Joe tended to follow what was expected of them, even if neither of them liked it. Ben possessed more morals than their father, but he had an edge to his character that made him appear harder. He took less rubbish from John Minshull – living three hundred and fifty miles away made that far easier – and had taken a position with Devon and Cornwall Police despite his father's insistence he aim for a more prestigious force. He'd certainly had offers from across the UK and could have had his pick of positions. He maintained that his choice ensured he could make his mark on the department instead of being one brick in the establishment of the Met, West Mercia or Greater Manchester forces, but Rob Minshull knew the truth: the location had won his brother's heart over all other considerations. Ben loved his surfing more than anything: now he had kids, a home life that included a beach within easy reach was all that mattered. The job was a means to an end.

When the video call began, Minshull could see the sea through the window behind his brother. Judging by the faded T-shirt he wore and tight ringlets Ben's hair still hung in, he wasn't long off the beach.

'Robbo! How goes it in the Suffolk wilds?'

'Lovely as ever. Surf's not as good as your side of the sea, obviously.'

Ben grinned. 'I'm working hard.'

'On the board, yeah.'

'First day off in two weeks, thank you.'

'And making the most of it, I see.'

'Too bloody right. Mate, you should come down here. It's sweet right now. Lucy and the kids would love to see you.'

'I will. When this place gives me a second.'

'Now you sound like Dad.'

Minshull glared at the screen. '*Not* funny.' He glanced around the packed car park, with the warm sunshine bouncing off the roofs of the cars parked around him, and thought of his comfortable apartment across town. It was a good place to live, but small and uninspiring compared with his brother's fisherman's cottage in Looe overlooking the sea. 'We're investigating a local pressure group kicking off here and a name has come up I believe your lot know. Rhian Butler?'

'Yeah, I know Rhian Butler.' Ben stretched and straightened in his seat, the mention of work calling him finally to attention. 'Wish I didn't, to be honest with you. Bloody nightmare she was for us last year. Intimidation, publishing dodgy pamphlets and leaving them everywhere – there was even suspicion of her defacing property with red paint slogans, although we couldn't make it stick in court.'

'Property of the councillor she was intimidating?'

'Him and about five others. She claimed they were members of a paedophile ring, but we found no evidence to support that. One guy had to take his family into hiding for a while after an anonymous Facebook group posted his address and photos of his business online. A mob turned up at his house, damaged his car, threw his bins everywhere and like I say, red paint *Paedo* and *Evil Out* slogans daubed across the front of the house and garage.'

'How come she never faced charges for the slogans?'

'She had a good lawyer.' He shook his head. 'They always do.'

'Did she fund them herself?'

'Nope. A *generous sponsor*, according to her defence team. She didn't appear to have a job but she certainly had some wealthy friends.'

'Mmm.' Minshull consulted the notes he'd brought with him. 'Do you think the prosecution led to her relocating here?'

'It's possible. Although she was dating a property magnate for a while and I heard he had professional concerns on the Suffolk coast. She could have moved over with him.' He took a sip from a mug that had clearly been painted by one of his children. The word *Dad* sprawled over the glazed surface, surrounded by enthusiastic splodges of rainbow-hued colour. 'And you say she's causing trouble over your way?'

'She's put her name out on posts with stolen crime scene photos.'

'*Shit.*'

'Exactly. Not paedophiles this time: a murder in a potential drug gang location we're investigating.'

'Bloody hell. I didn't reckon South Suffolk had many of those to contend with.'

'We're the location *du jour*, it appears.'

'Need some help from us? I mean, resources must be tight.'

'No tighter than yours stretching across two counties.'

'Fair point. What's Dad said?'

The question was inevitable – in any conversation about work, John Minshull gatecrashed his way in, whether in person or hundreds of miles away. 'Dad doesn't know.'

'You sure about that?'

Minshull had to laugh. Ben knew him too well. 'I haven't asked him.'

'Best policy. Look, I'll get you everything we have on Butler. Just know what you're getting into.'

'What do you mean?'

'She may appear small fry, but that woman has very powerful friends. People who profit from scandal. Just – watch yourself, yeah?'

Ending the call, Minshull glanced at the arrest photo Ben had sent. Rhian Butler glared defiantly from beneath a severe black fringe, the tips of it dyed electric blue. If the Facebook posts had been a warning shot and her past history focussed on harassment, what might her next move be?

Chapter Seventeen

Cora

Rob Minshull was waiting by his car in the Convalescent Hill car park on Undercliff Road West, a wide grin appearing when he saw her walking towards him. Cora couldn't help but return it.

It had been a year since he had tracked her down to the seafront café in South Devon where she'd fled after the Hannah Perry case; that she was back in Felixstowe today was largely down to him.

She'd been taken aback when Minshull had arrived, but strangely not surprised to see him. He had brought apology and regret, but also a challenge.

'You shouldn't be the one to run,' he'd said, as they'd talked late into the night in the one-bedroom flat she'd been renting in Chillington, just up the road from her workplace. 'You might be happy here for a few months, a year maybe. But then what?'

'I'll figure it out.'

'Or maybe you won't. And maybe you'll find yourself stuck.'

'There are worse places to be stuck.'

'I don't think you're designed to be stuck. I think you were at the point of figuring out what you wanted...'

'That choice was taken from me,' she'd argued, the hurt of recent months still smarting.

'But you have a choice now,' he'd said. 'And a friend, if you want one.'

And that had been the truth Cora needed.

Minshull had been working hard to make amends for the mistakes he made before, when Cora had been brought in to assist on the missing child case, and while some resentment remained for Cora, the detective's efforts had not gone unnoticed. He showed up and kept showing up. In Cora's book that was better than hours of painful heart-to-hearts and apologies.

'Lovely morning,' Minshull said, locking his car and jogging over.

'It is. How's everything?'

'Let's just say I've earned this run. And breakfast. On me, of course.'

'Naturally. Shall we?'

'Okay. Which way, boss?'

'Let's head down to the pier and along South Beach then loop back here. Then we can grab breakfast at Al's.'

Minshull hit the timer on his watch. 'Sounds good. Let's go.'

They crossed the road and ran down to the promenade, the fresh sea air a perfect foil to the physical effort. With her heartbeat in her ears the voices of passers-by and the secret voices of discarded chip-papers and rubbish blowing across the promenade faded to a comfortable blur. It was good to be out in the early Saturday light, the satisfying stretch of muscles so welcome after the seemingly endless week she'd endured.

Having someone to run with was good, too. She hadn't had the pleasure of that before. Rory was a talker not a racer and when Liz had still been in Suffolk any idea of exercise beyond the four walls of the gym was an anathema to her. Rob Minshull was neither a chatter nor a gym fanatic, but he was excellent company. Cora liked spending time with him.

They ran in companionable quiet past the banks of beach huts as the familiar bulk of Felixstowe Pier rose into view.

Since her last session with Lottie, Cora had been debating whether to mention the Oliver O'Sullivan link to Minshull or not. But the growing number of news reports about the body in the barn at Abbot's Farm had convinced her. It could make a difference to the police investigation.

She waited until their final sprint back to the car park was done and they were walking up towards the small white café on the seafront to claim their reward before she shared what she knew.

'There's something I wanted to tell you,' she said, watching him carefully. 'I discovered a link between my client and your case yesterday.'

Minshull was mid-swig from his water bottle, his eye sliding to her as he swallowed. 'Oh?'

'Oliver O'Sullivan was Lottie's teacher.'

He stared at her. 'What?'

'Her friend came to visit during our session. She'd been sent home from St Audrey's with the rest of year ten and came to break the news to Lottie.'

'How did Lottie take it?'

'She was in shock. I haven't spoken to her since it happened but I'm due to do our next session on Tuesday.'

They had reached Al's seafront diner. Minshull held the door open for Cora to go inside, studying her as she passed him. The smell of cooking sausages and bacon replaced the tang of outdoor sea air. They found a table near the window, looking out at the sea through steam-obscured windows.

'Poor kid. Was her friend upset?'

'I think it was still gossip at the time she told Lottie. But their reaction was...' She summoned the memory of the girls' frantic whispers, the presence of the news that hung over everything else they talked about as they continued along the estuary walk. 'I don't know. I sensed something else going on there but I couldn't tell you what.'

Minshull leaned his elbows on the red melamine table. 'Something they didn't want you to know?'

'That's what it felt like.'

'That's interesting,' he replied, thanking the waitress who had arrived with the coffee jug. 'Two full English please.'

'Coming up, sweetheart.'

As the waitress walked away, Minshull appeared to be deep in thought. Cora sipped her black coffee as she watched him.

'You know, it's funny; I had the same impression when I talked to the Head at the school. And Kate Bennett said O'Sullivan's ex was cagey, too.'

'Do you think they're all hiding something? Lottie and her friend wouldn't be drawn on it but there was definitely more they weren't sharing.'

'I don't know. But I don't think it's a coincidence.'

I need a break...

Cora leaned back in her chair, muting the tired voice rising from the pile of empty sugar packets on the vacant table beside her. 'I'm sorry I can't tell you any more. I just thought you should know.'

'Thanks, I appreciate it.'

'I'm going to ask Lottie about her teacher when I see her on Tuesday. Having a few days to process everything might have stirred up some stuff and I want to check she's okay.'

'Could you let me know if she says anything? Only about this, obviously. I wouldn't ask you to break a confidence for me. We already know something else must have been going on for him to be found where he was. See what Lottie knew about him. Did he mention being stressed? Was there ever any suspicion of drugs? Anything he told her that could help us uncover what was really going on in his life.'

'Drugs? Do you think that's why he was killed?'

'I'm trying not to think that.' Minshull lifted a hand to rub his forehead. 'Joel thinks it's a mistake to link the murder with the drug gangs issue, but the more I see of this case, the more parallels appear. I'm just hoping something comes to light that gives us a definite answer either way.'

'If Lottie says anything, I'll let you know.'

'Thank you.' Minshull gave a rueful smile. 'And you said you'd never work with my lot again.'

'I meant it, too,' Cora returned, laughing at being so easily enticed back into South Suffolk CID's investigations. 'I totally blame you.'

Minshull acknowledged this with a raised fork of surrender. 'Happy to be to blame.'

'Just this one, though,' Cora warned him, wondering if this time it really would be. She hadn't chosen to enter this investigation as she had with the first, but the chance to use her ability for practical good was too tempting to resist. And now it seemed the investigation itself had its own agenda; the link with Lottie pulling her in completely. As Lottie's caseworker she was now involved, whether she wanted to be or not. The link to the murdered teacher made it unavoidable.

What would she find when she visited on Tuesday morning? An already emotionally vulnerable teen placed suddenly under the impossible weight of grief was a potentially volatile combination. And the suggestion that the girls – along with everyone else who had known O'Sullivan, it seemed – knew more than any of them would admit threw another unknown element into the mix.

Would Lottie retreat further?

Or could this be the catalyst for her way out of silence?

Chapter Eighteen

Anderson

'They need to be out of there tomorrow.'

Anderson squared up to DCI Taylor, his blood already on the boil. 'You can't be serious.'

'I never joke about man-hours, Joel. You of all people should know that.'

'But there are extenuating circumstances in this case. You can't expect them to sort and catalogue every item in that barn in two days,' he argued, knowing it was pointless but forging ahead regardless. Sue Taylor was out of her mind. She had been the one demanding answers, insisting that the giant wall of old clothes O'Sullivan's body had been hidden in be dismantled. How the hell did she expect that to happen quickly?

It didn't help that he'd already fielded several weary protests from Brian Hinds over at Abbot's Farm. His team were overwhelmed by the task, they were needed elsewhere and why did DCI Taylor think they would find anything of value there beyond the garments closest to the body? Anderson had no answers because he agreed with every point his colleague made. It was lunacy to continue.

And yet, here they were.

'I want it sorted as much as you do, Ma'am,' he tried, packing away his fury behind secretly gritted teeth, 'but we need more time if you want this done properly.'

'Time we can't afford. We need results, not excuses.'

'And with respect, we aren't going to find results in the rest of that barn. Dr Amara believes O'Sullivan was dumped there.'

'I want it done, Joel. And I want proof that Oliver O'Sullivan didn't die as a result of a drug gang. That rhetoric is already being spouted across the internet and I won't have it continue. We break the link with the two stories and we do it in two days. Understood?'

Anderson bristled as he watched his superior leave. What was the point of repeatedly insisting to the media that South Suffolk CID was up to the task of tackling drug gangs while also handling a murder investigation if behind the scenes every corner was being cut?

He was in an impossible situation, stuck between a DCI and his DS.

Sue Taylor wanted proof of no connection between the body in the barn and the elusive drug gangs running riot in the county, while Rob Minshull was being restrained from making the link. Where did Anderson fit into this? He wasn't sure. But the more he considered it, the more he could see Minshull had a point. Not that it mattered: without irrefutable proof either way, neither side could claim victory.

How was he ever going to make this work?

Beyond his office door the CID team were working in quiet determined fury, ducked beneath the media storm that raged on over their heads. They had agreed to work this Saturday split into two teams to pursue the various threads of the two cases: Evans, Wheeler and Bennett were working the morning shift from eight until one, when they would hand over to Ellis and Minshull, with Anderson joining them. After the run-in with DCI Taylor, the prospect of an afternoon's boots-on detective work was more than welcome. Anderson had never set out to be a career copper, had never desired the higher ranks where actual police work played second fiddle to paperwork and inter-departmental fire-fighting. How had he found himself so removed from the job he loved?

As one p.m. neared, Anderson was clock-watching, willing the hands round to the time when he could join his team. Ten minutes before the shift changeover, voices from the main CID office summoned him through. What met him was a strange mix of relief and anticipation, of camaraderie, a team briefly reunited and the grim task that overshadowed them all. Everyone had read the rolling news reports and social media damnations, however much they insisted they hadn't. Each detective took it personally, each one vowing to uncover the answers that had so far eluded their investigations.

Minshull offered him a smile as he handed him a takeaway cup printed with the logo of Anderson's favourite Ipswich coffee shop. 'Figured you might need this, Guv.'

Anderson grasped it as if it were a gift from the gods. 'If this is an attempt to curry favour with a superior, Minshull, I highly approve.'

Minshull grinned and handed another cup to Ellis. 'Couldn't leave you out, Drew.'

'You feeling all right, Sarge?' Ellis asked, his frown becoming a wide smile as he lifted the lid.

'Never better. Almond milk latte, right?'

'Perfect.'

'You realise this sets an irreversible precedent for future weekend working,' Anderson teased. 'Drew and I will settle for nothing less next time.'

'I thought you'd say that,' Minshull chuckled, depositing his rucksack and jacket on his chair before helping himself to the last cup in the cardboard carrier. 'Can I have a word before we begin, Guv?'

'You brought me the best coffee in Ipswich so how could I refuse?' Anderson gestured for Minshull to go into his office, following the DS inside.

Something had happened, Anderson knew immediately. It emanated from Rob Minshull like electricity. More than the coffee he'd brought in, more than his remarkably sunny disposition given the prospect of a six-hour Saturday shift. There was a fire to him.

'You know something,' he said, before his DS had chance to offer it.

Minshull's smile was instant. 'I saw Cora this morning. One of her clients is a student at St Audrey High.'

Cora Lael.

Anderson sensed the inevitable rush of guilt that accompanied that name. But he was listening, his coffee forgotten beside him. 'In O'Sullivan's classes?'

Minshull nodded. 'She's fifteen so would have had O'Sullivan for Drama this year, with English last year. He was her form teacher in Year 9, too.'

'How does Dr Lael know this?'

'While Cora was there for her client's counselling session one of the girl's school friends visited and passed on the news.'

'What did they say?'

Minshull hesitated, only for a moment but enough to make Anderson aware of far more of a story waiting to be delivered. 'It wasn't what they said, so much as their reaction. Cora said she felt the two teens were hiding something.'

'Such as?'

'She doesn't know yet. But she's promised to tell us anything she hears.'

It was a bombshell Anderson was unprepared to field. Not only the link between Cora Lael's young client and the Abbot's Farm murder victim but also that her assistance had been offered to Op Feldspar. After the missing child case, Anderson had vowed to never involve a civilian in an investigation again. Despite the internal inquiry that followed completely vindicating Anderson of any wrongdoing – much to DCI Taylor's consternation – he couldn't put anyone in that position again. Especially not Dr Lael.

'No.'

'Guv, it's a lead. One we don't otherwise have.'

'She'd be breaking a confidence. Passing on information without her client's knowledge. Everything about it is wrong.'

Suddenly battle lines were scored deep across the middle of Anderson's desk. Minshull faced him with infuriating defiance.

'Cora is the girl's caseworker. If she discloses anything during the course of their interaction Cora has a duty to report it to us.'

'And if she doesn't?'

'She thinks the girl and her friend know something. She could encourage them to talk to us.'

'Absolutely not.'

'We're going to interview the students at the school anyway. What's the difference?'

He wasn't letting this go, was he? Anderson squared up for a fight. 'The difference, *Detective Sergeant*, is that those interviews will be done in a monitored, strictly controlled manner within the school, with the express permission of parents acquired before we proceed. Not spying on confidential conversations with a vulnerable teen.'

'It's Cora, isn't it? That's the real objection here.'

'This has nothing to do with Dr Lael...'

'See?' Minshull gave a laugh of derision. 'You can't even say her name.'

He'd heard enough. 'Dr Lael has history with this department. History I have absolutely no intention of repeating. I am aware that you have a personal connection now and this may well be clouding your judgment...'

'No. That isn't what I'm saying.'

'Oh I think it is, Rob. I think you're looking for redemption by befriending her.'

'With respect, Guv, I—'

'You're acting out of guilt.'

That snatched the wind from Minshull's sails. He stared, open-mouthed, at Anderson.

Kicking himself for going there, Anderson hushed his voice to a gravelled burr. 'You think I don't share that? I can't think of Dr Lael without remembering what we did to her. What she almost lost because of us. I won't put her in that position again, however advantageous it might be for the investigation.'

Minshull looked away.

It wasn't the victory Anderson wanted.

'Look, I appreciate the gesture. I do.' He relented. 'But we are under the cosh with this. DCI Taylor is on the warpath already. She's pushing for results at Abbot's Farm, I've got Brian Hinds and the SOCOs threatening mutiny and we've already been branded failures by the media. I can't risk anything that could weaken our position further.'

'None of which has anything to do with Dr Lael. Why does DCI Taylor need to know? If Cora hears anything and she encourages the girl to talk to us, it would be in her professional capacity as a caseworker, nothing more.'

The fire had left both of them now; Anderson's head was aching in the wake of their verbal sparring. 'It isn't wise...'

'Just answer me this, Guv: if it wasn't Cora; if it was a classroom assistant, a student counsellor, a fellow teacher bringing us this news, would your response be the same?'

Damn him. Why did Rob Minshull have to be so bloody perceptive?

He didn't need to reply: Minshull caught the dip in his mood immediately.

'Why is Brian upset?'

Anderson observed his colleague. He shouldn't have to share any of it with Minshull, but the sudden ceasefire was a relief. Wearily, he offered the truth. 'DCI Taylor wants the SOCOs to process that mountain of clothing bags from the barn in two days.'

'What? That's insane.'

'Exactly. I don't know what she expects to find. Beyond the material in actual contact with the body, what can any of the other things tell us? They're not connected with O'Sullivan.' He risked a wry glance at his DS. 'Or any drug activity that we're aware of. We know they were stored in the barn when that short-lived clothes-for-cash business Kate found details of was operating there a couple of years back.'

'Unless that was a front.'

'A front?' Anderson sat back, surprised. 'For what?'

Minshull shrugged. 'I've been thinking about it and it might be coincidence or it might be hugely convenient. People arriving at all hours, packed bin bags being unloaded, money being exchanged... I mean, nobody would bat an eyelid at all of those things if it was a cash-for-clothes business.'

Cottoning onto his meaning, Anderson felt his spirits lift a little. 'So if other things were being exchanged instead...'

'It would explain why the clothes were left when they ceased operations.'

'But – no, hang on – the business was a few years ago. Our elusive drug gangs are a recent phenomenon.'

'Are they? Or have we only just learned about them?'

'What are you suggesting?'

Minshull blew out a sigh. 'I hate to agree with anything the media says, but we didn't know any of this was going on until the story broke. They could have been operating happily under our radar for years. The dealers from across the border could even have broken existing gangs in the county and muscled in on their business.'

'And we just didn't see it.'

His DS offered a small smile. 'You did, Guv.'

'Even that was too late. We have no advantage here, Rob. I wish we did.'

'Hm.' Minshull took a long, slow sip of coffee. The strange energy had returned to him. Anderson could feel it, like the prickle of skin heralding an approaching thunderstorm.

'What are you thinking?'

'Nothing.' Minshull shook his head, but Anderson was aware of cogs continuing to turn.

'Don't give me that. Just say it.'

'Maybe we could have an advantage.'

'How? We have no leads on Op Collegiate, no idea of anyone involved, and now no time to find any.'

'Not how. *Who.*'

Anderson's heart sank. Surely not, after the row they'd just had… Was Minshull daring to go there again? 'Don't even say it.'

'Dr Lael's ability – the mountain of discarded clothes – you have to see how it could work?'

'What part of *I won't have her involved* do you not understand? If I refuse to use her help in providing background information on Oliver O'Sullivan, what makes you think I would ever agree to taking her to a crime scene?'

'Because we have nothing else there, Guv. You said it yourself: no link, no advantage, and the clothing DCI Taylor wants fast-tracked through forensics is highly unlikely to reveal anything at all.'

'I said no.'

'Hear me out, okay? She might hear something there that no amount of forensic examination could detect. Emotional fingerprints left by the people using that barn before someone dumped a body there. Cora might sense voices, hear snippets of conversation, anything that could steer us down the right road.'

'And if she doesn't?'

'Then we haven't lost anything for trying. Cora walks away and nobody is any the wiser.'

'I can't allow it. If DCI Taylor got wind of this...'

'Who says she has to?'

Anderson couldn't reply. Dr Lael's ability had served them well before, her sense of voices hidden within the fabric of inanimate objects had been nothing short of remarkable. But any mention of her assisting the team again could have Sue Taylor braying for his head.

'It could be off the record. DCI Taylor wouldn't have to know. I could take Dr Lael over, let her walk the site. If she hears nothing, we leave and it's done. But if she picks up anything that might be a lead...' Minshull didn't finish the sentence. He didn't need to.

'Why would she agree to help us? After last time?'

'Because she's already involved. She came to me with the news about her young client: I didn't demand it. She could have withheld that information if she didn't want to help us again.' Minshull risked a careful smile. 'At the very least we could ask her.'

Anderson hated him for judging this so well. It was a huge risk, but they needed movement on Op Collegiate. Without it, Sue Taylor could well demand his resignation anyway. The only compensation for being so soundly wrong-footed by Minshull now would be the inevitable slump of his shoulders when Anderson stated his terms.

'Fine. But we ask her together. This afternoon.'

Chapter Nineteen

Cora

He was coming to meet her for coffee – and he wasn't alone.

Cora had been settling in for a quiet afternoon, the chance to read and maybe wander along the seafront, taking time to process everything she faced in the coming week, when the call arrived from Minshull.

Even now, as she saw the two men approaching the table she'd selected in Ipswich Town Hall's café, she wasn't certain why she had agreed.

Detective Inspector Joel Anderson approached with all the reluctance of a child summoned into the head teacher's office. He looked different; leaner, with more about him than the last time they'd been in a room together. Lighter, despite his obvious discomfort at being there. When she'd seen him last he had been facing the challenge of his career, a young girl's life hanging in the balance while a deadly game played out between her abductor and the police. He'd looked like a man haunted by a thousand iron ghosts. Today, he just looked mortified. It made for a positive change.

Cora stood as Anderson and Minshull reached her table.

'Ms Lael – *Dr*,' Anderson corrected himself, his embarrassment almost comical.

'What's this, a press gang?'

Behind his superior officer, Minshull hid a smile. 'DI Anderson wanted to come and play. I hope you don't mind?'

'Not at all.' She'd known Minshull long enough now to spot his humour but the presence of the man with whom there remained so much unfinished business made the joke bittersweet. Nevertheless, she extended her hand. Anderson's hesitant acceptance felt like a point scored. 'How are you, DI Anderson?'

The DI paled as he and Minshull took their seats opposite Cora. 'Good, thank you. And Joel, please.'

Cora didn't reply, giving a small nod of acknowledgement instead.

'Right. Coffee?' Minshull rushed, in the way a nervous host does, knowing two of their guests have recently had a row.

'Please.'

'And you, Guv?'

'Black Americano. Extra shot.'

Over Anderson's shoulder, Minshull pulled a comic grimace before hurrying over to the counter. The act broke the stalemate and Cora relented. On first sight she'd wanted to make the detective inspector sweat, but by the look of his visible nerves he was already doing her work for her. She decided to throw him a lifeline.

'So, how have you been?'

'Not bad. Considering.'

'Indeed.'

Anderson blinked as if momentarily wounded. 'Look, Dr Lael...'

'Cora.'

A smile, then. 'Cora, I hope you know how deeply I regret the course of my actions – and those of everyone in my team. I should never have doubted you.'

Cora observed Anderson for a moment. 'I appreciate that.'

'So, Rob tells me you're working in education now?'

'Yes. I'm a consultant psychologist on the Educational Psychology Team.'

'That's for the local education authority?'

'Yes.'

'And you enjoy it?'

Cora smiled. 'Probably as much as you enjoy your job.'

'Fair point. What kind of cases are you handling?'

'It varies. Everything from case work with excluded kids and helping schools provide specialist mental health services, to devising inclusive strategies and working with individual children in close study.'

'And your...' His brow furrowed as he auditioned potential words, '...*specialism* – does that come into play?'

She wanted to stay angry with Anderson, but his question summoned a smile. 'It helps, sometimes.'

'Are you two playing nicely?' Minshull beamed at them both as he delivered their coffee from a cracked melamine tray.

Cora caught the glare from Anderson as he accepted his cup. Minshull hadn't talked of his DI much during their conversations but the uneasy truce between the two of them was evident in every careful mention. She waited until Minshull had settled in his seat and everyone had taken self-conscious sips of their too-hot-to-drink coffee before she spoke.

'So, to what do I owe this pleasure?'

The way they both dropped their gaze from her was almost comical.

'Because, lovely as this is,' she continued, 'I'm guessing you didn't arrange to meet just to inspect the menu of the Town Hall café.'

Minshull was first to look at her. 'There's something we want you to see.'

Cora stared back. Whatever she'd thought the purpose of this meeting might be, this wasn't it.

'It would be totally off the record, not a formal involvement like last time... This is completely different.'

'In what way?'

Anderson reddened. 'I know you're aware of our current murder investigation. Rob has informed me of the possible link with your client. That's an issue in itself and we can discuss that later. But for now, there are certain items we would value your perusal of.'

'What items?'

'Old clothes. Stacks of them. The barn where our body was discovered had been used as a cash-for-clothes business, the excess clothing abandoned when it ceased trading. Whoever dumped the body tried to conceal it within the stacks of clothing bags. Unsuccessfully, as it turned out.'

Cora shifted uneasily, remembering the packed clothing bags at a jumble sale in her sixteenth year that had brought her gift to light when they were opened. The room filling with a cacophony of unseen voices, Cora's shock as they laid violent siege to her mind, and the horrified expressions of those around her who only heard the screams coming from the terrified, cowering teen. The moment when she was forever 'othered' from everyone she knew...

Even now she was working to understand her emotional synaesthesia and learning to use it rather than feel restricted by it, the memory of its first manifestation was forever shrouded in gut-wrenching fear.

Anderson pressed on, unaware of her struggle. 'I doubt any of the bags belonged to our deceased person but some looked as if they had been recently left there. I wondered...' Anderson glanced at Minshull for support. '*We* wondered if you might hear something from them. Anything that might give us a clue to the other people who visited the barn.'

Cora sat back in her seat. The sounds of the coffee shop swelled around the table as she observed the two policemen. By rights, she should tell them to take a running jump. The last time she'd assisted them it had almost cost her everything. She had every reason imaginable to say no.

'Why now?' she asked, the news throwing her growing friendship with Minshull suddenly into question. Had everything Rob done with her since she'd returned to Suffolk been a precursor to this?

Anderson couldn't meet her eye. Minshull fidgeted uneasily.

'Cora, we wouldn't be asking if it wasn't important.'

'And last time?' The words were out before she'd thought better of it.

'Last time we were unforgivably arrogant,' Joel Anderson cut in. Minshull's surprise couldn't be concealed. Whatever script they'd agreed before coming here was clearly being ripped up now. '*I* was unforgivably arrogant. And... not in my right mind. I never wanted to put you in danger, Dr Lael. Cora.'

'So this is reparation?'

'You could say that.' The DI lifted his gaze at last. 'Yes, it is. You would be well within your rights to give us our marching orders. And you are more than welcome to do so. But your – ability – could give us an edge we currently don't have.'

Cora fixed him with a stare. 'Go on.'

'We believe the barn was used as a location for criminal gang activity. Drugs, specifically. We're coming to this far too late, but there is a growing problem with rival drug gangs crossing the border into Suffolk and operating illegal hubs in rural locations, such as the barn where the body was found. We know little to nothing about them. Anything you could tell us might open a line of enquiry that takes us one step closer to apprehending the perpetrators.'

Cora said nothing, observing them both. Was this what she really wanted, after her life had finally returned to an even keel following so much upheaval last year? Her job, her new flat near Felixstowe's North Beach, the friendship she'd established with Rob – all this had granted her much-needed equilibrium in recent months. Was she ready to put it all on the line?

But possibility called to her. Could she use her ability, practised and honed now, to uncover details that might put Minshull and Anderson one step ahead of the drug gangs? She'd made a promise to herself upon her return that she would continue pressing into her ability, challenging it, broadening its scope. No more hiding. No more being held captive by her own mind.

'I'll see what I can hear,' she said, the surprise registering on the other side of the table almost making her laugh. 'But if there's nothing there, I walk away.'

'Yes – good – whatever you want,' Anderson rushed, scrambling to his feet as Cora stood. 'And you will be properly respected this time. You have my word.'

She turned to Minshull, not sure whether to be grateful to him or furious with him for pulling her into another investigation. 'So, do we go there now?'

He smiled – more apology than conviction – as he gestured for them to walk out of the café through the Town Hall's elegant lobby.

'No time like the present. Bring your car round to the station car park and you can follow me over. It's best if we don't arrive in the same vehicle.'

Bracing herself against a sudden rush of apprehension, Cora left Minshull and Anderson on the Town Hall steps and hurried to her car.

Chapter Twenty

Minshull

It was almost three p.m when Minshull arrived at the crime scene in heavy rain, bypassing a line of soggy photographers that had gathered at the entrance to Abbot's Farm and driving the pool car along the rutted track towards the run-down and derelict buildings. The SOCOs were still at work, doing their best to comply with DCI Taylor's demand that they catalogue the mountain of clothing that had surrounded O'Sullivan's body.

When Minshull neared the barn, he spotted a familiar face guarding the entrance.

'I hope you can fit these over *those*,' PC Steph Lanehan observed drily, handing him a pair of blue plastic shoe protectors and pointing at Minshull's mud-caked, ancient green wellingtons.

'Watch and be amazed,' Minshull grinned back, putting them on. 'Didn't think they'd send you out here, Steph.'

'Get all the plum jobs, me.'

'Lucky you. How's everything?'

'Can't complain. Except for the bloody rain. They sent you out here to help?'

'In a manner of speaking.'

The rumble of an approaching vehicle made Lanehan peer around Minshull's shoulder, her smile vanishing the moment she saw the identity of the driver.

'*Again?*'

'She's just here to observe.'

'I wasn't born yesterday, Sarge. Are you sure that's a good idea? After last time…?'

'DI Anderson asked for her,' Minshull returned, stretching the truth somewhat and hoping Lanehan wouldn't see how flimsy it was. 'She might hear something in there that gives us a lead. But not a word to DCI Taylor, okay? Or your sergeant.'

'No fear of that,' Lanehan snorted. 'As if either of them are likely to get their feet muddy out here.'

'Appreciate it. Buy you a pint next time I'm in St Just?'

'Too bloody right you will. Crisps, too. I hope you know what you're doing,' Lanehan muttered quickly, her smile returning as Cora reached them. 'Dr Lael, nice to see you.'

'PC Lanehan, it's been a while.'

'Just a bit. How's the… um…?' Lanehan patted her own shoulder.

'Better, thanks. Still aches but it's good.'

Aware this was the oddest small talk he'd ever encountered, Minshull cut in. 'Good to go in?'

'Ready when you are.'

'Great. You'll need to wear these.' He accepted another pair of shoe covers from Lanehan and handed them to Cora.

'It's what all the best dressed investigators are wearing this season,' Lanehan grinned. 'Wouldn't be seen dead without mine. No pun intended.'

The scene inside the barn was a stark contrast to the heavy rain and quagmire of mud outside. Here the sound was muted, hushed library-still, while the SOCOs continued their work. A row of trestle tables had been erected down the middle of the barn, a production line of processing well underway. The occasional click of a camera and burst of a flash punctuated the muted atmosphere, the team working in slow, methodical silence. The distant thrum of rain on the old wooden barn roof sounded high above them, an ominous soundtrack to the scene. The stench remained, less pungent than before due to the removal of the body, but enough to catch the back of Minshull's throat.

'We're pretty certain this place has been used as a drug hub for some time. SOCOs have found all the usual stuff to indicate this. There's some suggestion the clothing thing might have been a front for drug activity, but that's just a theory right now. But we've found other belongings here, too. Rucksacks, old coats, some discarded sleeping bags that could be connected to the drug gang or their customers.'

'So what do you want me to look at?'

'Everything?' Minshull looked at Cora. She was standing stiffly beside him, eyes wide. 'What is it? What can you hear?'

'A *lot* of voices,' she breathed. 'Give me a moment to navigate them.'

Minshull had seen her response to this phenomenon before, but it was still unnerving to watch, especially in this large, quiet building. She didn't display the terrified, ghost-faced shock that she had when Minshull had first seen her ability in action, but the effort of identifying and silencing the voices was visible in every muscle of her face.

'It's like every voice arrives at top volume,' she'd told him one evening over dinner, not long after she'd returned to Suffolk. 'Imagine a bank of TVs in a shop with each one playing a different programme. I have to manually turn down the volume on each one to navigate my way through them all.'

'Are you okay?' he asked now, unable to wait.

She smiled. 'I'm fine. It's just – *busy* in here. We can keep walking if you like.'

They moved slowly through the dimly lit space, keeping a respectful distance from the officers at work, following a designated path between yellow plastic markers. The barn had a solemn air, as if aware that a life had ended within its walls. Minshull wondered if the voices Cora was navigating her way through in the space bore witness to that, too.

'We'll start over there, okay?'

'Okay.'

He led her along the row to the end table, not far from where the body had been found. On it was a selection of dirty, battered items: an old parka coat, three rucksacks, one supermarket bag-for-life and the roll of an ancient-looking brown sleeping bag, its vivid orange lining visible through a broken zip. Better to start here than with the clothing mountain, he figured, not wanting to overwhelm his friend at the beginning.

He pulled a pair of latex gloves from his pocket and watched as she put them on. 'These items were found near the body. I wondered if one of them might have been his.'

Cora nodded. She placed a hand beside the first rucksack, a dark blue Fjällräven pack, the kind beloved by patrons of the new, hipster-style coffee shops springing up in Ipswich town centre. The curled fox logo was scratched and a dusty print on one corner revealed the partial markings of a moulded sole, perhaps from a trainer or a boot. It was empty inside, already inspected and catalogued.

'Anything?' Minshull asked.

'No. Nothing specific.' When she saw his confusion, Cora continued. 'There are voices around it, like in a space with lots of conversation, but the words are so low I can't make them out.'

'So what could that be? An echo of people in this space?'

'Possibly. There are several different tones, but beyond that I can't be specific.'

'Okay. Anything else?'

She closed her eyes for a moment and then reached for the middle rucksack, a black unlabelled bag with silver zips, the base scuffed and the tapered seams frayed from a great deal of use. 'A man's voice with this one.'

'Any words?'

'… "*Get this shit shifted*".' She gave Minshull a wry smile. 'Apologies.'

'I've heard worse.'

'Hang on.' Her smile vanished. 'There's a name.'

Minshull felt his pulse skip. 'What?'

'*McGann*.'

'First name?'

She listened again. 'Nothing, sorry. Just "*McGann's not happy*". Whoever said it was angry. It's a threat.'

It was more than he could have hoped for. A name – even just a surname – was enough to start a search, the first domino that could lead a tumble trail to the right person. That was what Op Collegiate had been missing: the loose thread that started the unravelling of everything else.

Beckoning the lead SOCO over, Minshull carefully handed him the bag.

'Was this empty when it was found?'

Brian Hinds frowned behind his mask. 'One moment.' He consulted a list on his tablet. 'There was a grey sweatshirt inside. We think it might have been wrapped around packets of drugs. It's been bagged up.'

'Great. Can we bag this as well, please? Thanks for letting us look at it.'

'Fingerprints and fibres?' Brian asked.

'Please.'

'No problem.' He nodded at the mountain of black sacks. 'Don't suppose you fancy going through that little lot for us while you're here, eh?'

'And deprive you of the pleasure, Bri? Wouldn't dream of it.'

The SOCO chuckled. 'Never mind. Reckon I could find myself a whole new look in those bags.'

'I always said you were a fashion icon.'

Hinds patted his white paper coveralls. 'Job requirement in my line of work. Have to possess inherent style to rock this look.'

Minshull turned back to Cora. 'Is there anything else?'

'There's an overriding emotion in here: hopelessness. The sadness is overwhelming. Visceral.'

He stared at her, startled by her words. 'I reckon if you asked everyone working in here they would say they feel that, too,' he replied, a shiver passing along his shoulders. Crime scenes often carried atmospheres, especially those in remote places like this, but you rarely acknowledged them. That way madness lay. 'Place like this, if it was used for what we think, there's very little hope involved. Can you make out any more words?'

'Not here. It's just a general burr. I think a lot of the items have been here for so long that they're just holding residual sound.'

'Like distant road noise?'

She appeared pleasantly surprised by this. 'Exactly.'

It was good to know he was beginning to understand more about the way Cora's ability worked, but it took them no closer to uncovering anything else to guide his colleagues in their enquiries.

'Okay. That's great, thank you. Cora?'

Her attention was no longer on him, her pale eyes scanning the barn's interior as if expecting to find something. 'Where was the body found?'

He hadn't expected that. The remit had been clear: the bags and items on the trestle tables only. But he was intrigued: why did Cora want to know?

'Over there, in the middle of a stack of bags.'

'Can I see?'

'Um, sure.' Minshull led the way to the now depleted wall of refuse sacks, standing only two rows deep now where before they had almost been stacked to the rafters. Cora stood for a while, listening. Minshull forced himself to wait this time, suppressing the impulse to push for answers.

'Hm. There's nothing here,' she said, scanning the remaining rows of sacks.

'Nothing at all?'

'No. I don't think he died here.' She turned to look around the space as if scanning for another sound she wasn't yet hearing.

'He'd suffered a head wound which we only saw once he was out of the clothing wall,' Minshull said, surprised by Cora's assertion. How could she have known that? 'We are now assuming he was killed somewhere else and his body was just dumped here.'

'Yeah, that would fit,' Cora nodded, walking slowly along the bank of clothes.

Minshull hesitated: should he follow her?

Opting to remain where he was for now, he watched her investigations. He still didn't completely understand her ability and maybe never would, but it was fascinating to witness. He remembered a conversation they'd had while walking along the coast path a few months before, about the changes she was experiencing now that she was actively exploring her ability.

If I imagine the sound as three-dimensional layers I can move through them, listening beyond the most immediate voices. I pay attention to the shape the air makes around the sound and notice any physical sensations I encounter on the way. It takes time and I'm still not where I think I can be with it, yet. But I think my brain is able to perceive emotional memory with far greater scope than someone without my condition could ever do.

Was that what she was doing now?

'Here,' she said, so suddenly that several SOCOs looked up from their work.

Minshull hurried over.

She was crouching in the corner of the building, at the end of the bank of clothes. In the decayed remains of straw and dung, Cora was pointing to a bare patch of earth. The ancient cobwebs strewn over the area around it had been torn, their dust-heavy strands hanging down like a ragged curtain.

When Minshull reached her side, he saw her wipe away a tear.

'What have you got?'

'This is where it happened.'

What did she mean? 'No, we know he wasn't attacked here. We've found no blood, his body was likely dumped here some considerable time after his death.'

She was shaking her head, eyes fixed to the spot. 'No, Rob. *This* is where he fell. I don't know if it's where the head injury occurred but it's where he realised what was happening. Not somewhere else: in this barn. I feel the shock of it, the revulsion—' she pressed her hand to her stomach, '—right in *here*. It's so strong...'

The change in her was remarkable, her distress shocking. Minshull almost reached out to touch her shoulder, to comfort her, but he drew back at the last moment.

'He felt betrayed.'

'How do you know?'

'I feel it. I hear it...' She stood quickly, as if suddenly repulsed by the unseen emotion. 'I hear *him.*'

'What can you hear? What is he saying?'

Cora didn't take her eyes from the space. '*It was a lie. You* lied *to me...*'

Chapter Twenty-One

Anderson

Anderson had been on high alert all afternoon. Now his ears rang with the stress of it all, his pulse insistent at his neck. He considered the bottle of Kalms and packet of grass-tasting chamomile tea in the top drawer of his desk – his wife's latest remedies for combating the mental pressure of the job. It was a kind thought but a pointless exercise: Ros Anderson had known her husband long enough to understand that. Joel Anderson ran solely on caffeine and adrenaline. No amount of herbal jiggery-pokery could replace it. Thank goodness DCI Taylor didn't do desk drawer inspections – one look at the selection from Ros would have her fast-tracking his backside to early retirement quicker than you could say 'stress relief'.

Knowing his DS was accompanying Dr Cora Lael around a highly sensitive crime scene had added more than one grey hair to the salt-and-pepper banks at his temples. He was doing the right thing, of that he was now convinced, but if his superior got wind of it…

'Guv.'

Anderson snapped to attention, only relaxing when he saw the hesitant smile of DC Ellis. 'News, Drew?'

'The Sarge is back.'

'Thank the Lord.' Anderson finally let the breath he'd seemingly held for hours escape as he slumped back into his chair. 'Send him in.'

From the moment Rob Minshull walked in, Anderson knew they'd found something. To give his young DS his due, Minshull waited until the door was shut and he was seated at Anderson's desk before sharing it. Even though they were safely enclosed in Anderson's office, they both lowered their voices, as if the walls themselves might betray them.

'Well?'

'We have a name.'

Anderson allowed himself a tentative breath as he took this in. 'Name of…?'

'Someone connected to the drug gang, we think. Cora heard the name being spoken by another person, which makes me think we're talking someone much higher up the food chain.'

'Who?'

'McGann. No first name. Whoever's voice or thoughts Cora picked up, they were using the name as a threat: *McGann's not happy.*'

'So check records for any McGann connected to drug activity. And I'll get onto Essex and the Met, ask them to check their databases as well. Great work. Please pass my thanks on to Dr Lael.'

'I will.'

'Who saw you there?' The question gave Anderson's nerves an extra twist.

'Steph Lanehan at the entrance, Brian and his team inside the barn.'

'And…?'

'They're cool. None of them batted an eyelid. And they won't tell anyone – they're all as keen to get things wrapped up there as we are.'

'Good. Let's hope it stays that way, eh?'

'Guv.'

Anderson expected Minshull to go back to the CID office to begin the search for McGanns in the records, but the detective sergeant remained seated, fiddling with his notebook.

'Was there something else?'

'Yes. Cora heard another voice.'

'Does she know whose voice it was?'

He watched Minshull do his best to remain objective, failing miserably. Rob Minshull might just as well have been dancing a polka around the office. 'She believes it's Oliver O'Sullivan.'

'What?' It was Anderson's turn to resist a dance. 'Is she sure?'

'As sure as I've seen her. It was – *weird*. Like before, only this time she experienced the emotion along with the words. As if the emotion was hers. It made her cry.'

'Oh, I bet Brian Hinds loved that. Quickest way to get him out of a building is to put him near a sobbing woman.'

'She wasn't sobbing,' Minshull returned, a little too defensively. 'It just moved her. And then the force of the words pushed her back – physically, like a shove.'

'Bloody hell. What did she hear?'

Minshull took his notebook from his pocket and slid it across the desk. Written in his annoyingly legible handwriting were words that sent Anderson's adrenaline pumping at levels his wife's calming remedies couldn't reach:

It was a lie. You lied to me.

Could he believe this? Was it a sound response? If it was real, the implications were huge.

'Could she be projecting? It would be easy to imagine the victim of an attack thinking this. Whoever he is, someone betrayed his trust to get him into that barn.'

'I believe her.' That fierce defiance Anderson had seen in his detective sergeant on the last case they'd worked with Dr Lael was back again. Could it be trusted, or were Minshull's personal feelings straying into his professional judgment? Anderson wanted to believe it but he couldn't allow himself to run away with the thrill. Last time it had almost ended him.

'Where did she – *sense* – this?'

'In the back corner of the barn, at the end of the stack of clothes. The floor there looked as if it had been recently cleared. I asked Brian to check it. If O'Sullivan was there, we'll know.'

Anderson flopped back in his seat. Minshull offered a smile. For a moment, neither spoke, the weight of events both experienced and relayed settling between them.

Finally, Anderson broke the silence. 'Is Cora okay?'

Minshull nodded. 'I made certain she was. That's the reason for the delay – I insisted on following her back to Felixstowe in the pool car to ensure she got home safely.'

Anderson tried to imagine the headstrong doctor's response to an unexpected police escort. It wouldn't have been positive. 'And she let you?'

'She didn't like it, but she didn't fight me. I learned my lesson last time, Guv: I won't take her ability for granted again.'

'So. McGann.'

'Guv.'

'You start the search now. I'll send info requests to Essex, the Met, Cambridgeshire and West Midlands, see what they have on their systems. Thank you, Rob.'

Once alone in his office, Anderson set to work. It was a relief to return to the task at hand after the unplanned events of the afternoon. He filed information requests with neighbouring forces, seeking any McGanns on their records, asking specifically for any connections with drug activity, past or present, connected with that surname. It could all prove to be a costly wild goose chase, he knew, but they had a name now, which was more than they'd had for Op Collegiate so far. If it turned up nothing, he could walk away from the voice Dr Lael had allegedly heard and the investigation would continue. But if it proved their elusive lead, it could be the advantage they so badly needed. Either way, Anderson was prepared to take the hit.

He was vaguely aware of the light changing beyond his office window, of shadows steadily lengthening across the carpeted floor. When the phone on his desk rang and he cast a cursory glance at his watch he was surprised to find it was almost six o'clock.

'DI Anderson.'

'Joel, hi. It's Lou Cairns from the Tech team. I've found the source of your crime scene photo leak.'

Anderson's mood instantly darkened. 'Who?'

There was a distinct pause before she answered. 'I think it's best you come to us. You need to see this in person.'

What was that supposed to mean? Swallowing his irritation, Anderson stood, scooping his suit jacket from the back of his chair. 'I'm on my way.'

Chapter Twenty-Two

Bennett

It had to be a mistake.

It *had* to be.

Kate Bennett rose from her seat as the arrest party entered the CID office. Across the room, Les Evans stood, too, stuffing his hands into his trouser pockets, unsure what else to do. Drew Ellis moved to Bennett's side, grim-faced.

'This is bollocks,' he whispered beneath his breath, his arm bumping lightly against Bennett's. The gesture was warmer than an embrace and just as welcome.

'Yes it is.' She inhaled sharply as the subdued figure between the uniformed coppers came into view.

Dave Wheeler couldn't look at any of them. He kept his head bowed, hands clasped tightly behind his back as the party swept through the room.

In the doorway to his office Anderson waited, stony-faced. He'd requested the entire team be present, the unplanned Sunday morning gathering feeling wrong in every sense. Bennett had just managed to drift to sleep in her stark surroundings when Anderson's call had rudely woken her.

He was watching now from the doorway of his office, daring any of the team to object, his sharp stare traversing the detectives like laser sights. Once the party were inside his office, he gave the CID team a long look before closing the door.

Evans swore as loud as he dared, stalking into the office kitchen. Bennett sagged and was surprised to feel the steadying touch of Ellis's hand on her shoulder. She looked up at him, seeking reassurance, but the young DC appeared as confused as she was.

'Where's Minsh?' she asked, careful to keep her voice low. 'He should be here.'

'On his way in.' Ellis kicked at a screwed up ball of paper on the CID office carpet. 'He was out running when Anderson called him.'

'I can't believe it's true. Dave wouldn't do something like this.'

'You don't know what he'd do,' hissed Evans from the kitchen. 'You don't know what any of us would do. Pressures of the job, frustration at the lack of progress – any one of us could have leaked those pictures.'

'Not me,' Bennett returned. 'Not Drew.'

'But you thought I did.'

Her cheeks burned with the accusation. Because she had suspected him, hadn't she? Pretty much everyone in CID had made that assumption. Les Evans was always the first port of call when something dodgy occurred.

'Les, I didn't mean—'

Her colleague dismissed it as he leaned against the sink. 'Point is, it could happen to anyone. Dave's no more of a saint than you, or Drew or me, Kate, so don't try making him into one. Especially not now.'

'They've made a mistake,' Ellis insisted. 'It can't be Dave.'

One by one they returned to their desks, the news an alien landscape between them. When Minshull appeared in the doorway, Bennett, Ellis and Evans stood again, rushing at him with questions.

'It can't be right, Sarge. Dave isn't capable of it.'

'Why are they pinning this on him?'

'Can you stop them?'

Minshull held up a hand. 'I'll sort it, okay?'

Helpless, they watched him enter Anderson's office.

Bennett dropped her head into her hands. It was the worst news. Wheeler was the steadying force in the team, the eminently fair voice of reason when frustrations and arguments rocked them. Anderson hadn't given much away when he'd summoned each of the detectives in this morning, only stating that the source of the leak had been found and it was Wheeler.

She was scared for him, but also for herself. With everything else in her world in freefall, this place was the single, unmovable sanctuary. She depended on its certainty, had been clinging to it for weeks now. No one else knew, but wasn't it the same for everyone, in their own way? The job anchored you; it gave you focus. Without that, what hope did any of them have?

'Do we know the full accusation?' Ellis asked. Questions were his coping strategy: it seemed the more he talked, the steadier he became. 'What did Anderson say to you two?'

'Just that Dave was the leak.'

'He told me they were investigating Dave's link with the Bures Bowmen,' Evans replied.

'The Bowmen? He isn't involved with them.'

'Obviously Tech disagrees.'

'Well, how would they know?'

Bennett closed her eyes. 'If he's accessed their site to share the photos there's likely to be a history of previous visits.'

'But their rhetoric isn't his.'

When Bennett looked over at her colleague she saw her own fears mirrored. 'I'm not saying it is, Drew. I'm saying they have to have found evidence to make a claim like that.'

'He's been pretty vocal on the drug thing. And you know how he feels about paedophiles…' Evans began, cut short by the glares of his colleagues. 'What? I'm just saying he's made no secret of his views. And those are two things the Bowmen are pushing for action on. He might not buy into the rest of their far-right guff, but on those two issues? Reasonable fears from concerned residents. That's how they drag people in.'

'Not Dave.'

'If you say so.' Evans slouched back to his desk. 'But nobody's immune. Everyone's furious about something.'

'You're throwing him under the bus?' Ellis squared up to Evans, who stared back. 'Really, Les? That's how fast you drop him?'

'Drew!' Sensing the danger, Bennett slapped a hand on her desk. 'Keep your voice down!'

'But he could lose everything! You heard DCI Taylor: she intends to throw the book at whoever leaked the photos. At Dave. She'll be out to get him. Anderson, too.'

'I know, mate. I know.'

It was hopeless.

Minshull returned almost an hour later, when heated whispers in the CID office had given way to numbed silence. His face was pale; his expression grim.

'Sarge?' Ellis began.

'Not here. Follow me.'

As one they hurried after him, down the corridor to one of the meeting rooms usually assigned for inter-departmental briefings. Checking it was empty, Minshull ushered them inside.

It was the smallest of the rooms, barely enough space for a table and four chairs. Nobody sat, all eyes on Minshull as he quietly closed the door and leaned his back against it.

'Right, we don't have long, so no questions and just listen, okay?'

Bennett folded her arms and glanced at Ellis who was staring at Minshull. 'It's such a mess.' Minshull pinched the bridge of his nose. 'It appears Dave accessed the photos via his computer and sent them using a proxy server to a Gmail address that Tech were able to link to one of the Bures Bowmen's administrators. When they went back through the access records they found multiple visits to the group's Facebook page going back a few months. Several of those visits – including the day he allegedly sent the photos – were around six thirty a.m.'

Ellis opened his mouth to reply but Minshull held up his hand for silence. Denied, the DC slumped back against the wall.

Everyone knew Dave Wheeler liked to be in early. He'd cycle in most mornings and make the most of the quiet office to catch up on paperwork he'd missed the previous day. Sometimes he would arrive at six a.m., especially in the summer. It was just a Wheeler thing, a fact accepted by everyone. Wheeler was usually first in, Minshull last out.

'The situation as it stands is that he is currently here voluntarily. He hasn't been charged but he will be questioned as soon as DCI Taylor arrives.'

Bennett's heart sank to the regulation grey carpet. Evans swore. Ellis shook his head as if it might dislodge the fever dream he found himself in.

'What does Dave say?' Bennett ventured.

'He isn't saying anything.' Minshull blew out his frustration, the weight of it all clearly as heavy on him as the rest of the team. At least that was something. If they could stay united, a spark of hope remained. 'I've got to hope he starts talking soon.'

'What can we do, Minsh?' Evans asked, his manner uncharacteristically subdued.

'Nothing. When the interview takes place it will be with me, DCI Taylor and DI Anderson. If it's found he did leak the photos, I'm afraid he will be arrested.'

'I want to vouch for him,' Ellis stated.

'You can't, Drew.'

'But I sit next to him. I can see his screen from my desk. If he accessed anything dodgy, I'd know.'

'And are you there at six thirty in the morning?'

Ellis bowed his head and fell silent.

Minshull sighed. 'We need to get back. Look, I know this is horrific, but we have to follow correct procedure. All of us are under scrutiny. The best way we can help Dave now is to keep our heads down and hope he does the right thing.'

He reached for the door handle, then stopped. 'But when we go down for the interview, get your heads together. Work out where we all were for the last three, four weeks. Note down anything Dave said regarding the drug gangs or divisive news articles. None of it is making sense right now: there has to be something we're missing.'

Chapter Twenty-Three

Minshull

Outside Interview Room One in the custody suite, Minshull made a final check of the evidence Tech had supplied. The IP addresses, sites visited and time logs merged into a bewildering fug in his mind that was still reeling from the revelation. Had Dave Wheeler become so disenchanted with the state of play that he'd taken matters into his own hands?

It just didn't fit.

Of all his colleagues in South Suffolk CID, Minshull would have said that he knew Wheeler the best. They had served together for years, Wheeler's steadiness a constant Minshull could depend upon. He loved his kids and his wife, his Sunday league football matches and his beloved Norwich City FC, despite continual mocking from those around him for supporting a non–Suffolk team. He cycled, he made terrible coffee with great generosity and he was the person you wanted on your side in any situation.

But did he have hidden beliefs, concealed frustrations, secret complaints? Before today Minshull would have sworn he knew everything about Dave. But now?

He hated this. He wanted to distance himself from what awaited him beyond the door of Interview One, but he was compelled to be there. For his friend. For his own peace of mind. For answers to questions he never wanted to ask.

Steeling himself, he walked in.

Wheeler was seated on the unfamiliar side of the interview desk, staring at the untouched tea in a plastic cup in front of him. He was diminished, a shell of the man Minshull knew. Was that guilt at play?

Opposite, DCI Sue Taylor sat perfectly still, hands folded on the desk, hawk-like stare aimed at Wheeler. Anderson sat beside her, hollow-eyed, jaw clenched. He had been scarily calm in his office, every word he spoke diamond-edged with accusation. Did he want to believe Wheeler guilty of the crime?

A duty solicitor sat beside Wheeler, there at Anderson's insistence rather than Wheeler's request. Minshull recognised him – Stuart York, a veteran of interviews in this building. He was a good man, decent and solid, not one of the briefs hell-bent on asserting authority. That was something, at least.

Although if Wheeler maintained the silence he'd fielded every question with in Anderson's office, his solicitor's character would be of little help.

Minshull took a chair in the corner of the room behind Taylor and Anderson. He opened his folder, spread out the evidence sheets across it, readied his pen. His role was to observe, not to question, but this meant he could watch for mistakes. Being on the periphery could sometimes be an advantage, he had discovered.

'Let's begin,' DCI Taylor said. A command, not an invitation.

Wheeler didn't look up.

'DC Wheeler, you are here because evidence exists indicating that you sent confidential crime scene photographs from our current Operation Feldspar investigation to a suspected vigilante group known as the Bures Bowmen. According to records assessed by our technical team, you emailed these photographs using a proxy server from your work computer early on the morning of Thursday 20th April. Those pictures were then, as we are all well aware, widely distributed online.'

She paused, her eyes fixed on Wheeler. He made no reply. Minshull felt the air constrict around them.

'That's correct, isn't it? You sent the photographs.'

Wheeler said nothing.

Minshull willed his colleague to speak. What hope did he have if he didn't even defend himself?

'Well?' When she received no response, DCI Taylor grabbed the evidence sheets from a startled Anderson and pushed them across the desk. 'Look at these, please, DC Wheeler. *Look at them.*'

Slowly, Wheeler complied. But his wide eyes appeared to focus through the paper.

'Thursday 20th April, six twenty-five a.m. That's when the photos were sent. Our CCTV has you arriving at the back entrance to the station on your bicycle at five past six. Plenty of time to get to your desk, compose the email and send it.'

'Dave, answer the question,' Anderson urged, his tone low.

'I wasn't aware I'd been asked one,' Wheeler muttered.

It was the worst thing he could have said.

Minshull braced himself as DCI Taylor stabbed the sheets with a furious finger.

'Don't be smart, DC Wheeler. The evidence is right there. You are in this up to your neck. May I remind you that this is not only a sackable offence but could also necessitate criminal proceedings and a custodial sentence?'

'With respect, DCI Taylor, DC Wheeler is here voluntarily,' Stuart York warned. 'Not to be tried and convicted.'

Taylor relented a little. Beside her, Anderson bristled.

'Perhaps this will jog DC Wheeler's memory, then,' she retorted. 'Monday 17th April, six twenty a.m., ten minutes spent looking at the Bures Bowmen's Facebook page. Tuesday 18th April, six twenty-five a.m., a direct link to the Bures Bowmen's website. Not through a browser or search engine facility, but an address typed straight in and accessed. From DC Wheeler's work PC. Wednesday 19th April, six twenty-five a.m. – the day the body was reported at the crime scene – another ten-minute visit to the Facebook page.'

Wheeler glared at DCI Taylor, his defiance startling.

'All these visits, most of them prior to the discovery of the body. A crime scene you were sent to, DC Wheeler, along with DS Minshull; a location you remained at until the SOCO team arrived. You were well aware of the theory that Abbot's Farm barn had been used by drug gangs. You were making regular visits to the vigilante group's website and social media and so would also be well aware of their stated response to those who perpetrate the drug trade in Suffolk.' She leaned closer. 'Tell me I've got this wrong, DC Wheeler.'

'What's the point?'

Anderson groaned. Minshull stared at his colleague. What was he playing at?

'Excuse me?'

'You've convicted me already, Ma'am. All of you have.'

'No, we are giving you the evidence we have and asking you to explain it.'

'No, you bloody well aren't. This isn't a voluntary chat. This is an ambush.'

'Dave,' Anderson began, but now Wheeler was ready to speak nobody could stop him.

'Years I've served South Suffolk Constabulary. I've never had so much as a rap on the knuckles for any of my service. Yet today, I've been wrenched away from my family on the only day I get to spend with them. I've been accused, frogmarched through the building and had all this shit levelled at me. And nobody, not anyone in this room,' his gaze travelled accusingly round them, 'has spoken up for me.'

'Maybe that's why you got involved with the Bures Bowmen,' DCI Taylor stated, oblivious to the shock of Minshull and Anderson. 'If you've resented your contribution not being recognised, maybe bypassing our authority made you feel vindicated—'

'DCI Taylor, I must protest,' York interjected.

'Arrest me if you want to, Ma'am. Because you've already decided that's what you want, haven't you? Maybe a jury will see what a catastrophic lapse of judgement you've made in accusing me.'

'The photographs were sent from your computer! The websites accessed from it, too! This is hardly an unsubstantiated allegation, DC Wheeler. This is irrefutable fact.'

'I didn't send them. I didn't look at those websites. I only found out the Bures Bowmen existed when DC Ellis found their posts online.'

'Then how did the photographs from *your* computer end up in *their* possession?'

'I don't know!'

An hour later, after the solicitor requested a break, Anderson and Minshull walked out into the corridor. Anderson motioned for Minshull to follow him as he strode towards the exit; slamming both double doors open with far more force than was necessary.

'What the hell is he playing at?' he growled, hauling open a fire exit door that led to the rear of the station where the squad cars were kept and stomping outside. Out here the air was fresh, a strengthening breeze greeting them.

Minshull sat on the edge of the concrete ramp that connected the fire exit to the car park. 'I have no idea.'

'If he didn't do it, why not say so?'

'He has, Guv, repeatedly. But DCI Taylor isn't listening: she wants him to confess and he isn't going to do that.'

Anderson stared at him, seeking answers. 'Do you think he did it?'

'Do you have to ask?' Minshull replied, wishing he wasn't battling the same question. 'It's *Dave*, Guv. Our Dave who doesn't even cheat at pub quizzes.'

Anderson rubbed the back of his neck. 'I know. But the photos came from his PC, at a time we know he was in the building.'

They fell into silence, the sounds of a lazy Ipswich Sunday morning drifting towards them from beyond the wall of the station.

Minshull had watched the interview from his vantage point, praying for a crack in the argument, willing Wheeler to fight back, feeling utterly helpless to change any of it. And behind it all lurked the spiky question of how much he really knew Dave Wheeler. Had he become so caught up in the everyday business of the CID office that he had missed the signs?

'You get the wrong day of the week, lads?'

They turned to see a squat, middle-aged man in a blue boiler suit heading up the ramp from the car park towards them.

'Morning, Oz,' Minshull smiled.

'Haven't seen your lot in on a Sunday for months,' Oz Synett grinned.

'Extenuating circumstances.'

'Say no more.' He offered a smile to Anderson who barely managed to return it; too preoccupied for small talk even with a colleague he'd known for years.

'How come you're in?' Minshull asked, glad of the distraction. 'I thought you were a strictly Monday to Friday man now?'

'Usually I am. But I wanted to give the pool cars a service 'afore your lot start hedge-jumping in 'em again, or whatever it is you do. In a right sorry state, most of them.' The mechanic wrinkled his nose as he shielded his eyes from the bright sunlight. 'Are all your crew in today?'

'Just for today,' Minshull nodded, praying Synett wouldn't question it further. The last thing anyone needed was to fuel station gossip before Wheeler's fate had been decided.

'You couldn't do me a favour, could you? I'd do it myself but I'm rushed off my trotters here.'

'We should get back,' Anderson snapped.

'This'll only take a mo, Joel,' Synett called, already on his way down the ramp to the garage bay.

Ignoring Anderson's groan, Minshull followed Synett. At the bottom of the ramp, he stopped dead.

Synett was wheeling out a royal blue wooden go-kart, a replica police chevron strip painted along its side. 'I should have finished it yesterday morning but that strip was a beggar to paint. Can you tell Davey Wheeler it's ready for him to pick up when he wants it?'

'Dave?' Minshull approached the wooden kart, his mind beginning to whirr. 'When did you make this?'

'Started three weeks ago. Davey brought in the bits ready-cut from home, I added all the pedals and steering from odds and sods we had lying around. I've had it hidden in the back of the workshop most of the time, in case my superior clocks it.'

'When have you been working on this?'

Synett's smile became a scowl. 'Oh now, you're not thinking of ratting on me are you, Minsh? I only did it as a favour and first thing in the morning before either of us clocked on. We used our own stuff, so it's all above board.'

Minshull felt the ground shift beneath him. 'When you say first thing, what time do you mean?'

'Six-ish. Gives us a good hour or so to work on it before we start work proper.' Synett narrowed his eyes. 'Everything okay, Minsh?'

Minshull resisted the urge to hug the mechanic. 'Oz, you're a bloody genius!'

—

'What is the meaning of this?' DCI Taylor demanded, as Minshull and Anderson lifted the go-kart onto the interview room desk, scattering papers and sending pencils and empty paper cups spinning.

'This is proof DC Wheeler didn't send those messages or access those sites,' Anderson announced. His smile was a kick to his superior and he was clearly enjoying it.

'We have a witness,' Minshull added, glancing at a visibly shocked Wheeler. 'This was made before DC Wheeler's shift in the garage bay. Every morning for the last three weeks beginning just after six a.m. Oz Synett from the vehicle team can corroborate this.'

DCI Taylor's face flushed with indignation. 'Then who sent the photos?'

'The person who steals my desk every night when he does the night shift in CID,' Wheeler answered, his voice small, resigned.

Anderson's expression darkened. 'We need to bring in DC Bruce Ovenden, Ma'am. Immediately.'

—

Wheeler was quiet as Minshull walked him out to his car, carrying the go-kart. They had left Anderson and DCI Taylor engaged in a staring competition back in the interview room while they waited for a uniform patrol to escort Bruce Ovenden in. Minshull had suggested they go back up to the office, where the team were eagerly awaiting news, but Wheeler declined.

'I just want to get back to my family.'

They reached Wheeler's battered green Volvo parked in its usual space near the end of the car park. Wheeler opened the boot and Minshull carefully slid the wooden vehicle inside.

'It was supposed to be a surprise,' he said flatly. 'For my boys.'

'They'll love it,' Minshull offered, not sure what else to say. 'It looks great.'

'Not made by a racist, misogynistic alt-right supporter, eh?' His red-rimmed stare pinned Minshull to the spot.

'Dave, I never thought…'

'Didn't you? Joel did. Sue Taylor was convinced.'

'Mate, we just needed you to tell us what you were doing. The evidence…'

'…Should have pointed to Ovenden. Without me in the office he could do what he wanted; take advantage of my desk – as you all know too bloody well he does – use my computer to look at that filth…'

'You're right. We should have seen it. But you didn't say anything in there.'

Wheeler slammed the boot lid shut. 'And neither did you.'

'I'm sorry. And for the record, none of the team believed it. They've spent the morning trying to clear your name.'

'More than you and Joel did.' When Minshull tried to answer, he raised his hand. 'No – leave it now. I need to get home and I need to think.'

Minshull nodded. 'Will you be okay?'

Wheeler opened the driver's door, his expression bristling with injustice and pain. 'I don't know.'

Shaken, Minshull watched his colleague drive away.

Chapter Twenty-Four

Anderson

Anderson phoned Wheeler the moment he arrived home from a long and frustrating interview with a defiant Bruce Ovenden. He was racked with guilt and remorse for ever suspecting his friend. Ovenden's unapologetic confirmation of his actions only made it worse. Why hadn't Anderson seen it?

But instead of Dave Wheeler, his incandescent wife Sana answered the call.

'He doesn't have anything to say, Joel. Which is just as well because I have plenty.'

'We made a mistake. I just want to apologise.'

'It'll take more than an apology. You crushed him, you and that bloody Taylor woman. He's in bits. I don't know if he'll recover.'

'Sana, please, tell me how I make this right.'

Her pause made him hang his head in shame. 'You start by not hiding behind a phone line like a coward.'

So Anderson walked the ten-minute journey from his house in the centre of St Just across the village to Wheeler's home, a bottle of his best Balblair eighteen-year-old whisky packed in his rucksack, praying to whoever might hear him that Wheeler wouldn't slam the door in his face.

A grim-faced Sana Wheeler met him on the doorstep and silently ushered him around the side of the house to the garden, where Wheeler's beloved homebuilt shed stood amid flowerbeds and a football-scuffed lawn.

'You've got a nerve,' Wheeler said from his old armchair inside, when Anderson opened the shed door.

'I've also got whisky. Permission to enter?'

Wheeler let out a heavy sigh. 'Better make mine a double, Joel. I figure I'll need it tonight.'

They talked, late into the night and deep into the bottle, Anderson repeating his apologies until Wheeler told him to shut up. It wasn't a complete repair of their friendship by any means, but some stitches were holding. Right now, that was all Anderson could hope for.

–

Next morning, head decidedly sore, he stood in the CID office, hands on hips, scanning the contents of the whiteboard. Behind him the low chatter and insistent click of keyboards edged away as he worked over the various leads in his already crowded mind. It was the stage of any major investigation that Anderson detested: where some progress had been achieved but many more threads lay tangled before them. Every step forward revealed four more potential routes of enquiry.

So far, they knew Oliver O'Sullivan had been killed by a lethal, injected dose of bleach to the neck, the later inflicted head wound an elaborate ruse to disguise the real murder method. They knew he hadn't been seen or heard from by those closest to him for several weeks before he was found. And the location where his body was dumped was a well-known location for a drug gang.

But which drug gang?

Was it linked to the as yet unconfirmed *McGann* that none of Anderson's initial enquiries with neighbouring forces had yet identified? If not, who was responsible for the activity at Abbot's Farm?

They knew O'Sullivan had lied to St Audrey High about his reasons for requesting a sabbatical term. Yet his relationship with his mother suggested a largely loving son who was in frequent communication with her. Why lie about the death of a woman he claimed to love?

There had been one piece of good news, waiting on Anderson's desk when he arrived for work. Brian Hinds had examined the corner of the barn at Abbot's Farm following Cora Lael's unnerving experience there and had found fibres from the T-shirt O'Sullivan was wearing when his body was discovered. As there was no other logical reason why his body would have been in contact with that area of the barn, it could only mean one thing: he had been there. And Cora Lael was right.

Then there were the questions still awaiting any clues: did a drugs gang murder O'Sullivan? If not, who did? Where was his motorbike? How deep into the drug world had he sunk? How much of his life and his freedom had it claimed? Had he lied about losing his mother because he was running from someone within it?

'Guv?'

Anderson glanced to his right, nodding at Bennett. 'Kate. Bloody conundrum this, eh?'

'Just a little.' She handed him a fresh coffee, its aroma immediately soothing. 'I got to the kettle before Dave.'

'An excellent move,' Anderson grinned. 'Super-fast reflexes.'

Bennett's smile became tight. 'Is he okay?'

'He will be. But we tread carefully from now on.'

'Guv! Essex CID on the phone for you,' Evans called.

Anderson frowned. 'Really? Fine, I'll take it in my office.'

Arriving at his desk, he took a slurp of surprisingly good coffee before accepting the call from Evans.

'Putting you through now, Guv.'

'Cheers, Les.' He waited until he heard the click of the connected call. 'DI Anderson?'

'Good morning, I'm DCI Fran Stephens from Essex Police. I head up the drugs task force. I believe you enquired about any McGanns on our radar?'

'That's right. I'm yet to receive a response...'

'...Which is the reason for my call.'

'You've found some for us?'

'Not some. One.'

'Excellent! Send the details over and we'll add it to our list...'

'There's no need. We know who your McGann is. Col McGann.'

Her tone irked Anderson, who felt like a tiresome child being chastised for insolence. 'DCI Stephens, with the greatest of respect, our wider search was one line of enquiry amongst several. We've made

162

the same request to Cambridgeshire, Norfolk, West Midlands and the Met. I really don't think—'

'The McGann you are looking for is Col McGann.'

What was her problem? Sure he didn't have any other McGanns on a list but how could she be so certain the McGann she'd found was the right one? Anderson was about to return fire when he remembered his wife Rosalyn and her stern warning to him that morning about his rising blood pressure.

I know you love your job, Joel, but no element of it is worth paying for with your health, no matter how many tosspots you have to face. I want my husband around to enjoy retirement with at the end of all this...

Breathing out his frustration, Anderson purposefully softened his voice, pushing generous air into every syllable. 'On what basis do you make this judgment, Ma'am?'

'On the *basis* of a fourteen-month undercover operation involving four of my best officers and a team of ten more providing support. We know Col McGann is responsible for bringing some of his operations across the border into Suffolk because my undercover officers helped him do it.'

Anderson caught sight of his wife's knowing smile on the photo he kept on his desk. His blood boiling at the DCI's calm statement, he slowly pushed his coffee mug across to cover her face from view. Ros didn't need to witness his reply to the DCI. Ordinary tosspots he could calm himself into dealing with, but this one was beyond the pale.

'Excuse me? You're telling me you've known of these illegal activities progressing under our noses for *fourteen bloody months* and you didn't think to inform us?'

'I don't like your tone, *DI* Anderson,' she began, but Anderson was just getting started.

'And I don't like your blatant disrespect for a neighbouring force, Ma'am. For *my* team of highly skilled and dedicated officers, currently being *kicked through the mud* by the media for not dealing with the rural drug problem sooner.'

'I'm sorry about that. Truly. But you must stop chasing McGann for now. We are very close to securing enough evidence to permanently take him out of circulation.'

'And he is a major suspect in a murder investigation…'

'At Abbot's Farm?'

Anderson's fingernails dug mercilessly into his palm. 'Yes, at Abbot's Farm. Where a body was found, hence the *murder investigation* I am currently overseeing.'

'That is one of his locations,' the DCI replied, still haughty, but some of the power of her reply had become muted.

'Oh well, that's good to know. Do any of your *best officers* have any information on how Oliver O'Sullivan died? Because I have a grieving mother and a school full of heartbroken kids who would really like to know.'

A pause, then. Anderson would like to have heard a sigh of defeat but none came.

'He didn't kill the teacher.'

'How benevolent of the scumbag—'

'He wasn't in the county on the day Oliver O'Sullivan died. He was operating from his base in Leigh-on-Sea.'

'I want to speak to him,' Anderson growled.

'When we bring him in. Which might not be for a few weeks yet.'

'My team's enquiries are ongoing. If we apprehend Mr McGann in the course of our operation, we will bring him in on suspicion of Oliver O'Sullivan's murder.'

'Absolutely not. I am not throwing aside an operation that has cost Essex Police a considerable amount of money, and cost my officers fourteen months of their lives so that your *rural* force can have its ten minutes of fame.'

'How *dare* you!' Anderson yelled in frustration. 'I expected that kind of prejudiced bullshit from the media but from within our own police family? It's unconscionable! I've a good mind to take this to my superiors…'

Now the sigh he'd wished for sounded. Anderson wanted to slam the phone down but he wasn't about to do that with the imperious DCI thinking she'd got the better of him.

'DI Anderson, I would welcome your co-operation on this…'

'As I and my officers would have welcomed yours, months ago, when being forewarned of the drug activity on *our patch* might have prevented the murder we're currently investigating.'

'We are days away,' DCI Stephens rushed. 'It's on a knife edge as it is. If you can hold fire just for this week, I promise you will be the first to be informed. Then we will ask McGann about your murder victim when he's arrested.'

'Forgive me if I'm not entirely assured by your promises to inform my team of anything. First, I want this pledge in writing, today. Then, when you've got him, you call me and I will attend the interview.'

'I don't appreciate taking orders from a DI.'

'And I don't appreciate my murder investigation being obstructed by a DCI. Yet here we are.'

He pictured the detective pacing her no doubt far better-appointed office than his, knowing she'd crossed a line and lost the higher ground. If Anderson were the kind to push his advantage, he could bring her whole investigation down. But while DCI Stephens clearly thought little of loyalty to her police family, Anderson considered it an immovable point of principle.

'Fine,' she returned, sounding anything but. 'I will be in touch the moment we have him.'

The call ended and Anderson luxuriated back in his seat, the remainder of his really most excellent coffee as sweet a reward as the finest champagne.

It brought him no further to apprehending O'Sullivan's murderer, another frustratingly loose end to add to the many on the investigation board, but ensuring his involvement in the McGann operation felt like a win.

And it proved that Dr Cora Lael had been right.

Perhaps his team had an advantage after all…

Chapter Twenty-Five

Minshull

Why are police harbouring dangerous criminals in Suffolk?
Why are they allowing drug gangs, organised crime and murderers
to operate unhindered? What's in it for them?
Why are criminals, paedophiles and drug lords allowed to terrorise
our beautiful county?
South Suffolk Police don't care about your safety.
Or the safety of your children.
Now is the time for ACTION, not words.
Now is the time for ordinary people to take back what's theirs.
Will you FIGHT to SAVE SUFFOLK?
The BURES BOWMEN won't rest until JUSTICE is SERVED.

'Bloody Nora,' Wheeler said, shaking his head as he and Minshull drove along the coast road. 'When did that go up?'

Minshull scrolled down the Facebook entry. 'Two hours ago. It's had 900 likes already.'

'Maybe we should get them to do our social media gubbins,' Wheeler observed grimly. 'They seem to know what gets clicks.'

'Threats of mob violence and vigilante attacks? Very reassuring.'

'It's sabre-rattling, Minsh. Load of gammon bollocks. I reckon most of their readership couldn't rouse themselves out of their chairs, let alone rouse a rabble.'

The joke was appreciated, but Minshull couldn't shake the sense of dread the wording of the post delivered. 'All the same, we don't need it.'

'I'd be quite happy if I never heard the name of that group again.'

That stung. Minshull glanced at his colleague. 'I'm so sorry, Dave.'

'Yeah, yeah, I know. What ticks me off most is that you and Joel could ever think I agreed with those bastards.'

'We made a huge mistake. You didn't deserve any of it.'

'Yeah, well. It's done now. Is the post signed again?'

Minshull nodded. 'Rhian Butler and Garvey Maitland. Have we found out anything about Maitland yet?'

'He's in his mid-fifties, Suffolk born and bred. Last known address is in Ipswich but he hails from Aldeburgh.' He chuckled. 'Shame. We could've looked him up, seeing as that's where we're heading today.'

'Imagine what could have been, Dave. We could have shouted him an ice cream and gone for a paddle in the sea.' Minshull appreciated the lift in tension. Dave Wheeler was affording him far more grace than he deserved. 'Anything else?'

'Drew said he found links between Maitland and several far right groups about ten years ago, then nothing until this. Reckons our Garvey's come out of retirement.'

'So is he the kingpin, or her?'

'No idea. Either way, their signing it is a warning shot. Usually these idiots only do it if they can hide behind anonymity. No balls, the lot of 'em. Keyboard warriors looking to stir trouble with no direct route back to them if it kicks off.'

'Well let's hope it's just online glory-seeking.' Minshull pocketed his phone. 'We need to keep an eye on them, that's for sure.'

'Another charming bunch to add to the list,' Wheeler grinned. 'Talking of which, why are we going to see this chap?'

'He responded to the appeal for information on the early evening news last night. I spoke to him this morning – he was in the rugby club with O'Sullivan. Says he has information but he needs to tell us in person.'

They rounded a corner and the large expanse of shimmering, grey-green ocean swung into view.

'Very nice of him,' Wheeler said. 'Lovely trip to the seaside is just what we need after all that crap at the weekend.'

It was busy along the beach road in the picture-perfect town, people taking advantage of the warm, breezy day. Minshull liked it here and entertained notions of one day buying a place in the town to renovate. Unlikely on his salary, of course, but dreaming about it cost nothing. Wheeler found a spot on a side road recently vacated by a builder's van and they headed for the apartments one street away from the town's famous beach views. The distant burr of the sea at high tide underpinned all other sound, a rumble so present Minshull half expected to sense it beneath the soles of his shoes.

The young man who met them at the door had the classic build of a rugby prop, tall, broad and blessed with a neck that could bend iron bars. Toby Buchanan also blushed furiously, which made Minshull instantly like him.

'Mr Buchanan? I'm DS Minshull. We spoke earlier. And this is my colleague, DC Wheeler.'

'Thanks for coming over,' he replied, ushering them inside. 'What I have to say needs to be said in person.'

Minshull and Wheeler sat on a low blue linen sofa by a large picture window that offered tantalising glimpses of the sea over the rooftops of the houses opposite. It was a former Victorian four-storey villa that had been divided into four apartments, Toby Buchanan's being on the top floor where servants would have once resided.

Toby fussed over a sleek-looking air press to make coffee for them all and then perched on the edge of a wide blue square-armed chair, his mug brandished like a shield that appeared tiny in his hands.

The coffee was wonderful and Minshull, who liked the look of the gadget that had produced it, was tempted to ask about it further. But time was short and a pile of work awaited him back in CID. He would be lucky to make it home before late evening as it was.

'So, talk to me about Oliver O'Sullivan. How well did you know him?'

'Really well. Been on the team with him for years and we often hung out at the pub after practice on Mondays and Thursdays. I went away with him a few times too, over the years. Lads' weekends, stags, stuff like that.'

'Would you say you were good friends?'

'Yeah. Well, until recently.'

Minshull paused mid-sip of his coffee. 'Recently?'

'That's why I wanted to see you. Three months ago I told him to get lost.'

'Why?'

Toby sighed. 'Things had got out of hand. I couldn't be part of it anymore.'

'What things?'

'Okay, before I say anything else, I just want to say that I made a mistake – a huge mistake – and since I broke ties with him I haven't been involved...'

Instantly, Minshull was paying attention. Caveats like that only appeared before really pertinent information came to light.

'Go on.'

The young man's gaze fell from Minshull's. 'A year ago, he said he could score me some tabs of E for a weekend bash I was having at my parents' house while they were away. I'd never done them before but several of my mates had and they reckoned it would be a laugh. So I bought some. I didn't ask where he got them from – I didn't need to know, I reckoned. And I was pretty certain it wouldn't happen again so I didn't think about it.'

'How many did you buy?' Wheeler asked, careful not to imply any judgment.

'Ten. He brought me fifteen. He said the others were on the house because he figured it would make the party epic. I took them because I thought they were a gift.'

Minshull watched Wheeler taking careful notes, knowing exactly where the conversation was headed. So many 'one-off' interactions were twisted to force more regular purchases and 'freebies' were often the bait used to hook unsuspecting buyers in. 'I take it he used this later to get you to buy more.'

The young man nodded, aghast that Minshull had apparently read his mind.

Oh to be so happily naïve about the world, Minshull thought.

'A few weeks later we were due off on a lads' weekend for our mate's thirtieth. He showed up again, saying he had a special offer. To be honest, I didn't want them. Only a few blokes at my party had tried them and weren't that impressed. I'd flushed the other tabs down the loo. But then he said he'd done me a favour getting hold of them this time – even though I hadn't asked for them. He wouldn't shut up about it, so in the end I gave him the money and binned the tabs.'

Exactly as Minshull had predicted. 'Did he say where he was getting them from?'

'Only that it was *his guy*, like it was someone he bought them from regularly.'

'Did you think he was taking drugs?'

'No.' Toby dared to make eye contact with Minshull. 'I mean, I don't know what that would look like. He was wired a lot of the time, but that was just Dodge. One hundred per cent adrenaline, twenty-four-seven.'

Wheeler glanced at Minshull. 'Dodge?'

'It's what he called himself when he was with us lads. Dodge – Dodger – the Artful Dodger from *Oliver Twist*? It's why he had that tattoo on his arm – a Victorian top hat like the Artful Dodger wore in the film. Reckoned he was more of a wily character than the saintly Oliver Twist his mum named him after.'

One mystery solved, thought Minshull. So if O'Sullivan fancied himself a rogue, had that pushed him into the drug gang's path? Or had he been an unwitting victim of another dealer's games, finding himself recruited to sell drugs on?

'So, what happened then?'

'A few more weeks passed and he was back to his usual self. Said he had a new group of fans at his after-school drama club and we were all ribbing him about only being desirable to fourteen-year-old girls...' He blushed again. 'Not like *that* – I mean, we were saying they would outgrow him quickly when they were the right age to—'

'Probably best to leave it there, sir,' Wheeler cut in, a hint of steel to his advice.

'Yeah, sorry. Dodge just seemed back to normal and then one night he turned up here, late. He was all over the place. Ranting about

170

people letting him down, about people he trusted landing him in it. He wanted me to help him – I mean, I said yes before I found out what he wanted.'

'Which was?'

'He said he had a large bag of cocaine someone had promised to buy but they'd reneged on the deal. He told me I owed him and I had to buy it. I said no immediately. But he wouldn't leave it, just kept insisting I had the money to help him. He was terrified, I mean, scared out of his head.'

Minshull considered his next question before releasing it. 'Did he mention who he was in trouble with if you didn't agree to buy it?'

'Just *his guy* again. I asked who he was; I told him to go to the police about it. But he just went nuts. Grabbed me, threatened to call my company and tell them I'd supplied him with drugs, get me sacked… I wasn't having that. I sent him packing. Told him never to come back and to leave me alone at rugby club, too. That was the last time I saw him.'

'When was this?'

'About three months ago. He didn't show for practice and then one of the guys said he'd lost his mum or something and gone off travelling.' He looked nervously between Minshull and Wheeler. 'That's all I know. I wanted to make sure I wasn't arrested for the tabs. I won't be, will I?'

Wheeler gave a long intake of air, akin to the sound a mechanic makes before presenting a huge bill for car repairs. It was enough to make the imposing figure opposite him shrink back in fear. 'Obviously we can't support drug-buying or taking in any form, sir,' he began, deliberately spinning it out to make his point. 'However, given this was a while ago and you have no evidence of the drugs in question, we won't pursue it.'

Toby Buchanan seemed to melt with relief.

–

'So someone was after him,' Wheeler said, as they drove out of Aldeburgh.

'Looks that way. Question is, how long had he been involved in selling? And how did he get sucked into that as a high school teacher? Were his colleagues at St Audrey's involved?'

At the wheel, Wheeler shrugged. 'Might explain Tom Dillinger's vagueness. Maybe they knew O'Sullivan's mum wasn't dead but found out about the drugs and sent him on a long holiday.'

'We need to ask the question,' Minshull replied, noting it down. He stared at the page as if he could will the missing pieces of the puzzle to appear. Perhaps he could ask Cora to listen for any hint of the drug issue when she was working with her silent teen... He dismissed the thought. Enough that Cora was willing to help them again. He'd been guilty of putting too much pressure on her last time: he wouldn't repeat that mistake.

The beep of the police radio cut across his thoughts.

'*All available units to Abbot's Farm, Semer Road, near Whatfield. Colleagues under fire. Repeat: colleagues under fire.*'

'What the...?' Minshull began.

Checking the rear view mirror, Wheeler slammed on the brakes, steering the pool car into a wide dirt triangle by the entrance to a field, throwing both himself and Minshull forwards, seatbelts jarring tight across their chests. 'We can get there, but not on this road. There's a cut-through about a mile back.'

'Do it,' Minshull said, grasping the edge of his seat as Wheeler threw the car around and floored the accelerator to take them back in the direction they had come.

'Received, Control. DS Minshull and DC Wheeler attending. ETA—' He turned to Wheeler who held up one hand. 'Five minutes.'

'Received, DS Minshull. Take care. Out.'

'Under fire?' Minshull repeated, his colleague gripping the steering wheel with grim determination as they sped along a narrower lane rising over a hill past fields of grazing cattle. 'What the hell does that mean?'

'Steph,' Wheeler replied, through gritted teeth. 'They mean someone's after Steph...'

Chapter Twenty-Six

Wheeler

Hang in there, girl. We're coming…

Dave Wheeler felt sick as he threw the car around the country lanes, racing to help his friend. He had no confirmation PC Steph Lanehan was the colleague under fire – *under fire*, for crying out loud – but he felt it deep in his gut. When he'd seen her on Friday evening for a post-work drink, she'd been bemoaning the fact that her sergeant had kept her stationed at Abbot's Farm despite most of the forensic investigation now being complete.

'He's just got me and the new girl Rilla Davis standing in the mud like right lemons,' she'd complained to him over a pint in the Miller's Arms, their cosy local pub in St Just. '*Collecting intelligence*, he calls it. Code for utter bollocks, more like. Only thing we're collecting is every bleedin' storm blowing over the fields and hypothermia from standing in the freezing cold every shift.'

The familiar warmth of the Miller's seemed an age away now. His dear friend was guarding a murder scene, the favoured location of a drug gang – if what Joel Anderson had relayed from Essex Police was accurate, a drug gang run by Col McGann, one of the most feared drug lords in the South East. What if they'd returned to claim it, believing the police had left, only to find two uniformed coppers on their patch? She was a sitting duck.

'What if the drug gang came back?' he asked, his greatest fears finding a voice.

'I don't know, mate,' Minshull replied, helplessly. 'Just get us there, yeah?'

'I'm *trying*…' The crack in his voice said it all. Wheeler thanked his stars that it was Minshull sitting beside him in the speeding car. Rob knew what Steph meant to Wheeler and his family. Best friend to his wife, surrogate aunt to his boys. Nobody else on the team except Joel Anderson would have understood.

Colleagues under fire… Were they armed? If so, what hope did Steph and her rookie recruit partner have?

His heart crashed against his ribcage as Semer Road came into view, the white sign for Abbot's Farm just up ahead, bright white against a darkening sky. Rain was coming to claim the sun, splitting the sky in two: behind them sparkling sunlight, ahead an angry bank of dark, denim-blue cloud. Wheeler swung the car onto the dirt track leading to the farm – coming face to face with a white Transit van driving at speed towards them, its rear axle swerving wildly as it crashed over the rutted earth.

'Dave!' Minshull yelled, ducking as Wheeler jammed the right lock on the pool car, sending it skidding off the edge of the track and slamming to a halt at a steep angle against the bank leading to a weed-choked field. His head cracked hard against the driver's door window as the engine screamed. Minshull swore and scrambled out of the car, shielding his eyes from the sun as he tried to catch the registration number of the van speeding away to the road.

Wheeler couldn't wait. Grabbing the keys, he rammed the driver's door against the stubborn mud until there was enough space to squeeze out. And then, he was running, slipping on the thick mud and tripping over concealed rocks in the track as Abbot's Farm loomed ahead.

The patrol car was beside the abandoned farmhouse, its windscreen shattered and both headlights smashed. One door hung limply open, its window gone and the roof above it crumpled.

Wheeler skidded up to it, praying nobody was inside. To his relief, his prayer was answered, but his stomach turned at a large slick of scarlet staining the passenger seat, running over the white paintwork and pooling on the ground beneath the car.

'No. *No*…'

The sound of heavy breath and the stab of running feet behind him made him turn. Minshull saw Wheeler's fear before the cause.

'*Shit!* Where are they?'

'I don't know…'

The distant wail of sirens split the air and Wheeler and Minshull looked back to see two squad cars and a support van thundering along Semer Road towards the farm.

'Come on,' Minshull growled, breaking into a run, Wheeler hot on his heels.

The barn where O'Sullivan's body had been discovered had been pocked with missile hits, the edges of the blows splintering the old wood and a mess of broken bottles and rocks lying in the grass where they had landed after being lobbed. The muddy ground between the farmhouse and barn was a mess of footprints as if an army had traversed its width. Angry deep-red streaks marked the open door to the barn, still glistening in the sunlight.

'Steph!' Wheeler yelled, panic strangling his call. 'Rilla!'

'Steph!' Minshull echoed, heading for the open barn.

The wind had begun to pick up now, the encroaching storm loudly announcing its arrival. The first heavy splats of rain began to pepper the ground. Minshull headed inside the barn, calling their colleagues' names. Wheeler was about to follow when a yellow flash near one of the derelict outbuildings caught his eye. Running towards it, he saw familiar silver reflective stripes across the fluorescent yellow – and a dark shape slumped in the mud beneath.

'Minsh!' he yelled, his voice barely audible over the screaming of sirens as the other vehicles reached the farmhouse. '*Minsh!* Over here!'

As he ran, shouts and sirens joined the heavy thudding of his heartbeat in his ears. He was almost at the prone figure when the terrified face of PC Rilla Davis appeared from behind a stack of blue plastic feed barrels.

'Rilla! It's me, Dave Wheeler!'

She let out a cry when she saw him, running into his arms and sobbing. 'They came out of nowhere. We couldn't get away in time… They got Steph. She isn't moving. I didn't know what to do. I thought they were coming back…'

'Shh, it's all right now. We need to check her, okay?'

The terrified new recruit nodded against him, pulling back as Wheeler knelt beside his fallen comrade. 'Lanny... can you hear me, girl?'

Please be alive, he willed her, fighting rising fear as he forced himself to remain calm, aware that Rilla was watching him.

Steph Lanehan was lying on her side, her hat a few feet away and her dark-blonde hair matted with mud. A deep red wound led from her right eyebrow up into her hairline. Gently, Wheeler slid his hand beneath the stiff fabric of her jacket collar and closed his eyes as his fingers found an angry pulse beating against the warm skin of her neck.

'Bloody hell, Lanehan, you nearly gave me heart failure,' he rushed, his vision blurring as he blinked back tears.

She didn't respond but Wheeler heard the quickening of her breath against the ground.

Then they were surrounded, uniformed colleagues patting Wheeler's shoulder and taking care of Rilla as Minshull arrived, kneeling beside Lanehan.

'Ambulance is on its way, Sarge,' one of the uniformed officers said.

'Excellent, thanks,' Minshull replied, a single weary nod communicating solidarity with every watching police officer. Each one understood the terror of a fallen colleague; every one had battled the same all-encompassing fear as they'd raced to the farm.

A murmur from the ground made the assembled officers fall silent. Wheeler leant over Lanehan.

'Don't you dare move, Lanny,' he urged.

'Who invited you?' Lanehan murmured, causing a ripple of relieved laughter among their colleagues.

'Heard you had a party.' Wheeler stabbed at his damp eyes with his jacket sleeve. 'Sorry I was late.'

'Typical,' Lanehan returned, her speech slow and slurred. 'Bet you forgot to bring a bottle.'

'Looks like the gatecrashers brought theirs instead.'

'Should have brought full ones so Rilla and me could get a drink. Bloody cheek... *aaahh*...' She winced as she tried to move.

'No, no, stay where you are, girl.'

'Yes *Mum*…'

'Oi, less of your lip until the paramedics get here,' he replied, promising the Almighty that he owed him for this. 'Just hang tight, okay?'

'Like I have a soddin' choice.'

Wheeler moved back to allow a group of support officers who had fetched blankets from the van to attend to Lanehan. As he stood shakily he saw his stony-faced colleagues solemnly shedding their jackets to gently cover her.

It was too much.

He walked a little way from them, tears arriving too quickly to halt now. Gasping in gulps of air, he reached out to steady himself against the old wooden planks that formed the side of the barn. He hadn't seen a colleague injured since his own days in uniform, over twenty years ago. Back then it had shaken him, but he'd accepted it as a necessary evil. Now, it tore at the core of his being, questioning everything he loved about the job. Everything that had happened yesterday and now this? It wasn't right.

Uncharacteristic anger was coursing through him, too: the hangover of hurt from yesterday's accusations meeting fury that anyone could have attacked two unarmed officers – two female officers – with such ferocity. It was a crime scene where the victim had been a much loved and respected member of the community: what possible motive could Steph and Rilla's attackers have had for targeting the very people working to solve the crime?

He lifted his head as the rain became more insistent, letting it meet his skin like a balm. This time had ended with a rescue, his friend conscious if not unscathed. But if she hadn't been able to radio for help, if they had all been too far away, or if their assailants hadn't fled… He didn't want to think of the consequences.

His emotion beginning to subside at last, he let his gaze travel along the length of the barn. Something had been pinned to the ancient wood, beside the open doorway, its edges dancing in the gusts of rain-peppered wind. Instinctively, Wheeler moved towards it.

A sheet of paper, a single nail piercing the top edge, securing it to the barn wall.

Wheeler's eyes grew wide when he saw what it held.

'Sarge!' he yelled, the heads of the gathered police officers rising as one as Minshull started to run across the farmyard.

'What is it?'

'Our friends left a calling card.'

In the centre of the paper was a woodcut print of a curled dragon with a spear through its heart – the same image used as the profile picture of the Bures Bowmen across its social media platforms and website. Beneath it, scrawled in red ink, the edges of the letters bleeding into the damp paper and streaking down its surface, was a stark message:

JUSTICE SERVED

Chapter Twenty-Seven

Cora

It's okay. You can ask me.

Cora looked at the teenager beside her on the estuary bench. They'd walked for half an hour and discussed several topics, but she had been waiting for the right time to mention the news of Oliver O'Sullivan.

Now, it appeared, it had arrived.

The O'Sullivan murder case had dominated the headlines yesterday, fuelled by news of the attack of two female PCs guarding the crime scene. The nationals had grasped it as a juicy story to break on an otherwise slow news day. Earlier this morning, as she was preparing to drive to Woodsham St Mary, Cora had seen breakfast news programmes on three different channels carrying it as their top story.

The media discussions had quickly switched focus from the potential identity of the teacher's killer and the horrible circumstances of his death to the shock emergence of a violent, previously obscure vigilante group, claiming police incompetency as a reason for taking the law into their own hands. There were unsubstantiated reports of the attack being a warning shot to police, a signal that those responsible for it blamed them for failing to stop drug gangs before an innocent life was lost. An anonymous commenter stated that South Suffolk Police now had O'Sullivan's blood on their hands.

For those who knew the teacher at the heart of the story, it would have been impossible to miss. And for those battling grief over his death, it would have magnified the loss.

Cora's thoughts had strayed to Lottie all weekend, the itch of mystery concerning her reaction on Friday refusing to leave. How did any fifteen-year-old cope with the loss of someone as present and familiar as a teacher? And how much more difficult could it be for a teenager who no longer wished to speak? Yet when she'd arrived, the subject hadn't felt right to broach, too raw and too immediate to launch straight into.

Now she picked her words like pebbles on the beach, selecting and weighing each one before launching it.

'How are you finding the situation with losing your teacher?' Cora asked.

It's hard.

She nodded, feeling the weight of those words. 'Would it help to talk about it?'

You might not like what you hear.

'I'm here to listen. Whatever you want to say is fine.'

Even if it's not what I'm supposed to say?

It was an odd question, reminding Cora again of the strange air that had surrounded Lottie and Esme's conversation last week. 'If it's what you want to say, it's right for you. That's all that matters.'

The teenager released a long sigh that seemed to drift across the quiet estuary like the ghosts of morning mist still floating over the distant fields.

Mum thinks I'm devastated because I loved him. She loved him because everyone did. So she assumes I feel the same. But I don't feel anything.

'Do you think you should?'

Lottie paused before typing. The breaths around her ebbed for a moment.

Everybody else seems to.

'That's not what I asked.'

I feel like it's what people expect. I just want it to go away.

'I understand that.'

Cora had experienced this when her father died – the sudden, unwelcome burden of other people's expectations of how she should grieve. Everybody had an opinion, a ridiculously reductive view of a life experience as unique to each person as their DNA. She should be putting a brave face on for her mother; she should be more visibly upset; she should be shutting herself away from the world to honour his memory; she should get out there and live her life as her father would have wanted… In their awkwardness to talk to someone so raw with grief, these commentators unwittingly piled judgement onto the huge, world-altering burden she already bore. The result being that she wanted to escape all of it – the loss, the words, the reality of life without him.

'You don't have to think or feel anything about it,' she said, her heart going out to the girl. 'Your reactions are true to you. Nobody else can dictate them.'

So you think it's okay?

Cora turned to Lottie and smiled. 'I know it's okay. If you want to talk about it with me, you can. If you want to avoid it completely, do. I'm here to help you develop new ways to express yourself, in whatever way feels right for you.'

Lottie observed her for a moment.

The hidden word began to push through the tide of breath.

Cora steadied her expression as she pushed a little harder with her mind.

G…

…G…

Thanks Cora.

The synthesised voice from the tablet pulled the curtain down over the next part of the word. Reluctantly, Cora abandoned her attempt, muting the repeated breaths as she retreated. It was frustrating, especially when she'd felt so close this time. But frustration would be a barrier to ever retrieving Lottie's concealed word: Cora had to remain calm and be patient.

She'd spoken to Tris Noakes about it yesterday afternoon when he'd called, concerned by the dramatic turn of events in the news. Tris listened as Cora described what she could hear from Lottie: the chorus of sharp inhales, the tantalising glimpses of the single word Lottie guarded so resolutely in her mind, and the near-miss attempts Cora had had as she tried to reach it.

'And you can't get her to pick something up so she can drop it?'

Cora had smiled at his question, which from anyone else would have been impertinent. 'She holds her tablet wherever we go. Her home, as you know, is a highly controlled environment where nothing is left or discarded. There just hasn't been an opportunity for the usual way the voices come to me to happen.'

Tris had considered this. 'I half wonder if Lottie has learned to control her mind like her mother controls their home environment. There is definitely supreme control at work there.'

It was an interesting theory. 'True. I wonder what their house looked like before Lottie stopped speaking. It may be that it was more relaxed before but now Monica over-controls the house because she feels out of control with Lottie.'

'Taking power in the face of a powerless situation? You should be a psychologist, Cora...'

It was well meant and she had laughed. 'Funnily enough...'

'Does she ever put her tablet down? Could you hear anything from it?'

'She carries it everywhere with her. I've been trying to find ways of engineering some kind of touch and discard situation. I even considered suggesting skimming stones down by the estuary to see if I heard anything, but I don't think I could catch the words before the stone hit the water. And actually I don't think any kind of intervention would work with Lottie. This is brand new territory for me, but I believe Lottie is so in control of her mind, so firmly determined to keep everything within, that she wouldn't let stray words leave.'

Tris's sigh of frustration had mirrored her own. 'Then what's the solution?'

'I wait. And listen.'

What are you thinking?

Lottie was staring at Cora, her hazel eyes, flecked with gold, intent on her.

'Nothing, really. My mind was wandering a little. Does that happen to you?'

Since I stopped speaking? No.

Cora tried a different tack. 'Are you conscious of where your mind is, keeping everything in there?'

The hazel eyes widened slightly.

All the time. It's exhausting.

'Are you scared something might escape?'

Sometimes.

'What do you think might happen if it did?'

Why don't you just ask me why I stopped speaking?

Cora concealed her surprise as best she could. Lottie had already proved surprisingly straight-talking but this was not what Cora had expected from the new direction she was steering their conversation in. Deciding to push her luck, she replied, 'Would you tell me if I did?'

Touché.

It had been a gamble, but Cora felt she'd just passed an important test. She grinned at Lottie. 'You tell me whatever you want to tell me, whenever you want to say it. And *don't* tell me whatever you want to keep to yourself. I'm here for as long as you want me to be. I won't outstay my welcome.'

I don't know how to feel about everything.

Her confession hit Cora like a punch to her chest, the sharp constriction she'd experienced during their first meeting returning again. The teenager's eyes flooded and the next thing she knew, Lottie was hugging her. A huge bolt of pain coursed through Cora, as if she were embracing a live wire. She held on despite the intense burning spreading from her chest to her spine, battling to keep her words gentle and steady when she spoke.

'It's okay… It's okay, Lottie… I'm here… You can trust me.'

The staccato breaths rose around them, all glimpses of the word concealed in the teenager's mind obscured by the shock of the pain and the contact.

It was as if Lottie's mind had bypassed words, the power of her emotion assuming physical force. When she finally pulled away, Cora felt bruised.

Sorry.

'Don't apologise.' Cora wanted to nurse her burned torso and distance herself from the teen, but she didn't dare move. Instead, drawing on every last ounce of strength, she held her composure, muting the pain as she did unwanted sound. 'You're facing an unfathomable situation. You have no frame of reference for it and your emotions have nowhere to go but to engulf you. Is that how you feel?'

Trembling, Lottie nodded.

'I don't have answers, Lottie. I wish I did. But I can listen.' She nodded her encouragement as if coaxing a reluctant child out of an emotional meltdown. 'Talk to me.'

Lottie glanced down at her fingers as she began to type. Cora held her body taught against the memory of recent pain.

Everyone at school is talking about him like he's a saint. Nobody is a saint, are they? Even if they die?

'It's what people do. There's superstition about saying anything negative about someone who has died. People confuse respect for someone's memory with accepting their own lived experience of them when they were alive.'

That's what some of my friends are like.

'Do you find that difficult?'

They are entitled to their opinions.

Cora retraced her steps. 'Do you feel that places an expectation on you to be the same?'

Sometimes. More after all the stuff on the news.

'It will pass eventually. I know it doesn't feel like it, but the news only broke six days ago, Lottie. It's still so new.'

Then it's okay to ignore them?

'If it feels easier, yes. You have enough of your own battles to deal with, without assuming theirs, too.'

Thank you.

Cora smiled. 'You're welcome.'

I want to stop talking about this now.

'That's fine.'

Mum made a chocolate cake this morning. Do you want to go back and get some?

Relief flooded Cora, the chance to move and shake off the lingering effects of whatever it was she'd felt from Lottie a welcome reprieve.

They followed the path back along the steadily flooding estuary as the waters of the coming high tide began to wash back inland. Climbing the stile, they emerged on the road, waiting while a tractor made its noisy way past before crossing and ascending the steep drive to Fourwinds.

Nearing the front door, a shout from the side of the building stopped Cora and Lottie.

'Lotts! Over here!'

The teenager rolled her eyes.

It's Dad. He said he wanted to meet you.

'That's fine.'

Cora followed Lottie across the front of her home, skirting the carefully organised flowerbeds edging the gravel driveway and crossing a set of incongruously whimsical stepping stones set into the wide lawn that led to a large, oak-framed building. Cora smiled to herself. It was the kind of home office Tris Noakes dreamed of one day working from. He had countless photographs of similar buildings on his phone ready to show to anyone who took the slightest interest. Cora wondered if he had been granted a view of this one, or if this news would be something she could surprise him with.

'That's a gorgeous building,' Cora remarked.

It's Dad's workshop. He has an office in the loft space above. I use it the most for doing my homework.

'Or escaping?' Cora asked with a smile.

Too right.

The shared joke was a salve to the earlier pain.

A middle-aged man appeared in a doorway at the side of the workshop. He was older than Cora had expected, considering how young Monica Arundel appeared to be. Cora guessed he was in his late forties, possibly fifty, his dark hair flecked with silver around his temples.

Dad, this is Dr Lael, Lottie's tablet announced.

'Trevor Arundel,' the man smiled, offering Cora an oil-smeared hand but withdrawing it at the last moment. 'Ah, sorry. Day off today so I'm tinkering. Let me clean this and we can try again…'

He pulled an old, sage-green rag from the back pocket of his ripped and stained old jeans and began to wipe his hand.

Cora watched as Lottie's eyes followed the movement, then a torrent of breath invaded the space between them. She rocked back a little but neither father nor daughter noticed. The sound increased, so loud Cora couldn't believe that neither of the Arundels could hear it. And then, it began to tear in half, as if both parts were being ripped apart by eager, opposing forces.

At the centre where the separation had begun, a single, agonised word split the air, louder than a scream:

GIL!

Lottie

She understood.

I could feel it.

I don't think Cora realises, but I just told her more than any of the others. I don't know why, or where it came from. I just knew I could trust her.

Why did I hug her, though?

I'm not telling Mum. Or Dad. I've being doing my best to avoid them since Cora left.

It helped, though.

The one thing I've missed through everything is being close to someone. Properly close, not feeling I should be or pretending I am just to find some peace. I feel close to Cora. And I think she feels it, too.

All the same, I have to be careful. Being too open has burned me before. I can't run away with this. I have to be sure.

But Cora understood me today.

For now, that's enough.

Chapter Twenty-Eight

Minshull

'I want them *found*!' Anderson yelled, pacing the CID office like a prowling lion. 'I want them hauled in here and I want them charged with incitement to violence. *Nobody* attacks *my* officers and walks away.'

None of the assembled team were likely to argue. The attack on PC Steph Lanehan and PC Rilla Davis had sickened everyone. Few of them had slept, texts and phone calls traversing Ipswich and the surrounding areas long into the early hours as every member of the team struggled to make sense of the attack.

Minshull felt the aftershocks still reverberating through his team, gathered for the morning briefing now, their eyes as heavy as their hearts.

It just didn't make sense..

Vigilante attacks didn't happen in rural South Suffolk. Officers may be injured occasionally in drunken scuffles or during the course of an arrest, but a gang of thugs rocking up to a crime scene and deliberately launching an assault on two unarmed police officers? That was completely alien here.

Every officer in South Suffolk endured the jibes from family and other forces about their job mostly involving chasing sheep rustlers and solving tractor thefts – and of course it was more than that. But there was comfort in knowing that violent and serious crimes were the exception here, not the rule. This development scared everyone.

The Bures Bowmen were yet to formally claim responsibility and, of course, were very unlikely to. But the unconfirmed reports doing the rounds in the media suggesting O'Sullivan's death was the fault of the police were too horrific to contemplate.

Anderson wasn't done, the fury and fear of the past twenty-four hours rushing out in one molten flood of anger. 'How did they go from posting bollocks on social media to this? Who organised the raid? Who rallied the troops? I want to know. I will not have this set a precedent in South Suffolk. We hunt down everyone involved and we throw the bloody book at them.'

'Absolutely, Guv,' Minshull offered on behalf of the team. 'Drew, was there any mention of the plan on their Facebook and Twitter pages?'

'No, Sarge. The most recent post was about taking back control, but no specifics. We have learned they have a private group on Facebook – it's under a different name, Dragon Army, but our guys tracked it down last night. We should have access by the end of the day.'

'So that's where they may have planned it,' Minshull said. 'Although if they have any sense they'll have deleted those posts before we gain access.'

'They don't have sense!' Anderson spat. 'Mindless thugs don't tend to.'

'With respect, Guv, whoever planned this wasn't mindless,' Bennett said, causing a wave of nods across the team. 'The idiots who attacked Steph and Rilla might have been, but generals do the strategy and then stand well back. They must have been watching Abbot's Farm for a while to know when there was going to be a single squad car there. They planned that attack.'

Anderson frowned. 'You think Maitland and Butler organised this?'

'I do.' Bennett nodded. 'If they're bold enough to sign the public posts, they want it to be known this is their gig.'

The DI's face set like flint. 'Then we bring them in. Today.'

–

News from Ipswich Hospital was better than Minshull had feared. Davis had been treated for wounds to her left forearm and chin caused by flying glass from bottles used as missiles, and had been discharged after a few hours. Lanehan was still under observation, a suspected internal bleed from a rock injury thankfully confirmed as severe bruising upon closer investigation. She had suffered concussion from a blow to the head and had three cracked ribs. The scarlet slick in the squad car and across the entrance to the barn that had so shocked Minshull and Wheeler when they had seen it was revealed to be pig's blood. *The blood of O'Sullivan on the police's hands.* It was a relief that it had not come from the two uniformed officers, but was still a nasty new element of an already horrific attack.

Of all the members of the CID team, Wheeler had taken the attack the hardest. He had been uncharacteristically quiet in the aftermath at Abbot's Farm yesterday and this morning he remained hunched over his computer, avoiding conversation with anyone. With his resolute silence and Bennett's muted response to conversations about anything other than work, the CID office was a strange mix of repressed rage and too-obvious attempts to lighten the mood from Evans and Ellis. Minshull steered an uneasy course between them, while doing his best to keep Anderson from imploding.

What they needed was a breakthrough.

With few leads on the murder investigation, it would have to begin with the arrests of Garvey Maitland and Rhian Butler.

'Right,' he announced, causing the team to raise their heads. 'We have the warrants. Confirmation of addresses in Ipswich for both Maitland and Butler. I have Support preparing to assist. We do this in two teams, with simultaneous arrests. We go in fast and we hit them hard. Who's coming?'

All hands rose.

'Excellent,' Minshull said. 'We'll do this together.'

–

Anderson assumed charge of Team Alpha, driving to an address on Withipoll Street, an end terrace in a road of red-brick Victorian houses that had seen better days. Minshull led Team Beta, heading to an apartment on Coprolite Street, in a new development overlooking the Neptune Marina. As addresses they couldn't be more different.

According to records, Maitland had owned his house since the early 1990s, while Butler had only rented her apartment for five and a half months. Was her property developer boyfriend bankrolling it, Minshull wondered? Ben had said she was 'being taken care of' which implied her living arrangements as well as her legal bills.

Parking a few streets away from the apartment building, Minshull waited for the call from Anderson, who would be getting into position with Wheeler, Evans and one half of the support officer team, ready to approach Maitland's house. They had identified a small driveway at the side of the terrace, leading round to the back yard, so Wheeler and the support officers would head to the rear, blocking any attempt to leave the property.

They had discussed the manoeuvre in minute detail before leaving the CID office and now, despite them operating in two parts of the town, Minshull could picture exactly what Anderson and the others would be doing.

His team plan saw a split team approaching the building, too, but for Team Beta one half headed for the fire escape stairwell while Minshull, Ellis and Bennett followed two support officers straight to Rhian Butler's front door.

'Team Alpha in position,' Anderson's voice hissed in Minshull's ear.

'Team Beta in position,' he replied.

'On my mark... Go, go, go!'

The support officers ran to Rhian Butler's door and pummelled it with heavy knocks.

'Police! Open the door!' Minshull called.

They waited, Minshull counting the seconds. Across the hall another apartment door opened to reveal an anxious face, shutting again quickly when they saw the hallway filled with police.

'Again,' Minshull commanded.

'Police! Open your door!'

On the radio, Minshull could hear Anderson yelling.

One more chance to open this door or my officers will break it down...

Minshull was about to mirror the call when the lead officer raised a black-gloved hand. 'Sarge.'

'Okay, wait everyone.'

A bolt was slid back, the click of a key turning in a lock… and the door opened. Rhian Butler had her hair wrapped in a towel as if she'd just left the shower and was wearing a man's white shirt over black shorts and oatmeal coloured slouch-style socks. She wore a silver half-moon ring in her left nostril and a silver ankh charm on a thin chain around her neck. A small scar traced a pale white line from the right corner of her mouth down to her chin.

'What the *hell* are you doing?' she demanded.

Minshull stepped forward. 'Rhian Butler?'

Her angry blue stare switched from the lead support officer to Minshull, like a pair of sniper sights. 'Who wants to know?'

'I'm DS Minshull from South Suffolk CID. I have reason to believe you are responsible for the attack on two female officers at Abbot's Farm, near Whatfield, yesterday afternoon.'

Butler slowly folded her arms across her body, her chin raised. 'And how do you work that out?'

'You are a self-professed co-leader of the Bures Bowmen, along with Garvey Maitland who is receiving a visit very like this one right now.'

'Really?' Butler gave a hollow laugh. 'Well, I hope your colleagues enjoyed the flight to Spain. He's at his villa in Marbella.'

'We have a no-show here,' Anderson's voice snarled from Minshull's radio. 'Repeat: Mr Maitland is not at this address.'

'We have Miss Butler.' Minshull replied, kicking himself that Butler's story had been verified and that she'd now witnessed their conversation. The mocking smile she wore made it so much worse. Approaching any interview or arrest on the back foot was the worst possible disadvantage and Minshull could tell Rhian Butler was the sort to milk it for all it was worth. 'She informs us Mr Maitland is holidaying in Marbella.'

Anderson's reply was laced with fury. 'Bring her in.'

'I need you to come with us and answer some questions.'

'Do you have a warrant?'

Minshull fixed her with a stare. Clearly she was an old pro at this. 'I do. You can either come with us voluntarily or I will arrest you.'

'What a choice. But I'm afraid I can't speak to you without Mr Maitland here. It's his baby, you see. I just help with the social media side.'

'Then why are you signing the posts?'

'Aw, DS Minshull, have you been reading my hard work? I'm touched. It's so good to have fans...'

That was it. Minshull dropped any semblance of politeness. 'Miss Butler, you're coming with us now.'

Butler laughed. 'Wearing this? Not likely.'

'Then *get changed*.'

'Fine. I'll be five minutes.'

As Butler began to close the door, Bennett stepped forward, her hip preventing it closing. 'I'll help you, shall I?'

Butler appraised Bennett's grey suit jacket, trousers and white blouse with a slow, disdainful sweep. 'I am not taking fashion advice from you, babe.'

Bennett levelled her with a look. 'You are *taking* a pair of trousers, putting them on in exactly *thirty seconds* and coming with us.'

Minshull hid his smile. As he moved to the door with the support officers, he noticed Ellis slip inside the apartment. What was he doing? Groaning, he motioned for the others to stay at the threshold and edged his way in. Butler and Bennett were in the bedroom off to the right of the open-plan space, the door wide open and Kate sternly observing Butler just inside.

He caught sight of Ellis moving over by the large glass window that looked out across the marina. When Ellis looked back, he nodded towards a slim door between the bathroom and second bedroom. Checking the front door was covered, Minshull moved across the polished oak floor to his colleague.

'What is it?' he whispered.

'That door. I think there's someone behind it.'

'Why do you think that?'

Ellis raised a finger to his lips, then pointed down to the thick-piled, expensive-looking rug that ran along the length of the living area. The section nearest the cupboard was pushed up, as if moved by the door recently being opened.

Minshull frowned. The cupboard didn't look wide enough to accommodate anyone. He wasn't even convinced it had space behind it. But Ellis was certain, staring at the narrow door like a police dog finding a scent. Minshull exhaled his frustration, grateful at least that Butler was occupied in the other room. Her knowing they'd failed to find her Bures Bowmen conspirator was bad enough: witnessing two detectives apprehending a stack of towels in an airing cupboard would afford her permanent crowing rights.

'Okay, stand here. I'll open it on three...'

Ellis moved into position. 'Ready.'

'One...' He moved to the door. 'Two...' His fingers closed around the round brass handle. '*Three!*' He yanked open the door – and stopped dead as he came face to face with a pair of black-rimmed glasses, worn by a bald-headed, very surprised-looking man curled up on the slatted shelf of a linen cupboard between stacks of fluffy white towels.

'In here,' Minshull called to the rest of the officers who were in the room in seconds. He turned back to the man. 'Well, I can't say I'm very impressed with your holiday villa, Mr Maitland. Bit pokey, isn't it?'

Garvey Maitland made a lunge for him, but Minshull stepped aside as the two support officers and Ellis grabbed Maitland's arms.

'Right, for that you don't get to choose how you accompany us. Garvey Maitland, I am arresting you on suspicion of incitement to violence. You do not have to say anything. But it may harm your defence if you do not mention when questioned something which you later rely on in court. Anything you do say may be given in evidence. Do you understand?'

Maitland snorted. 'You should be doing a proper job, mate, stopping the scum your lot lets into the county, not hounding members of the public. This is harassment. You're the only criminals here.'

'Thanks for the advice,' Minshull replied, turning his back on Maitland as Ellis and one of the support officers escorted him to the front door.

There was a sudden thud from the bedroom, followed by a yell from Bennett. Minshull and the remaining support officer dashed across the apartment to find Kate gripping Rhian Butler's arms behind her back.

'Get *off* me!'

'Rhian Butler, I am arresting you on suspicion of incitement to violence...'

'*Bitch!*'

'You do not have to say anything,' Bennett continued, through gritted teeth, as Butler continued to struggle. 'But it may harm your defence... keep *still*!'

The support officer grabbed one of Butler's arms and helped steer the hissing, kicking woman out of the apartment, Bennett still grimly reading her rights as they went.

Releasing his breath at last, Minshull radioed Anderson.

'Guv, we found Maitland here, too. We're on our way back...'

Chapter Twenty-Nine

Anderson

Joel Anderson didn't know whether to be happy that both signatories of the Bures Bowmen's incendiary social media posts were currently in custody or remain furious that he should be dealing with this at all while Operation Feldspar had precious few leads. A murder should be enough for anyone.

All the same, it had been a stroke of blessed luck that Drew Ellis had unmasked Maitland's ridiculous hiding place. Once again, the young DC's sharp perception had triumphed. Anderson allowed himself a small moment of self-congratulation for taking a punt on the lanky new detective, when DCI Taylor had disparaged Anderson's choice for the vacant DC position. A year on – and considerably less lanky now – Ellis had already proved his worth ten times over.

Anderson sipped his coffee and looked across the CID office where the team had gathered for an unofficial celebration while Maitland and Butler were meeting with their legal representatives prior to interview. If the arrests and resulting interviews meant a late stay this evening, Anderson resolved to shout them all dinner. He'd had his eye on the new Thai restaurant across the road from South Suffolk Police HQ for a few weeks and had noted with no inconsiderable amount of pleasure that it offered a delivery service. This evening could be the perfect opportunity to sample its delights.

Because it was likely to be a very long evening indeed...

In his heart of hearts, Anderson knew charges wouldn't stick to the two rabble-rousers in the custody suite. Unless the private messages in the Dragon Army group conclusively proved Maitland and Butler had specifically orchestrated the attack at Abbot's Farm, they would likely walk free. They knew it too, of course. Their sort always did. It was a game to them: the arrests, the lack of evidence and the eventual dropping of all charges. Worse, they would return as martyrs, bleating incessantly to their loyal bigot faithful about police harassment of upstanding, concerned citizens while the scum of the criminal underworld were given a free pass.

It was all so predictable. And the police were damned either way.

But while they were here, Anderson wanted to make them as uncomfortable as possible. PCs Lanehan and Davis were the innocent victims of an orchestrated, vicious attack, designed to challenge the authority of the police and vilify them in the public's eyes. He was damned if he was going to allow Maitland and Butler to ride roughshod over his operations.

This time they may well walk free. But the more emboldened they became, the likelier mistakes and missteps would become. And when that happened, Anderson would be waiting…

'Guv?'

Minshull was collecting his notebook and phone from his desk when Anderson looked over.

'They're done.'

'Excellent. You and Bennett take Butler, I'll take Maitland. I'm looking forward to a little chat with our elusive friend. Dave, do you want to join me?'

Wheeler looked up from his screen, his perennial smile worryingly absent. Anderson had hoped Butler and Maitland's arrests might have bolstered him, but the development just seemed to have drained him further. He still worried that Wheeler's wrongful questioning on Sunday had irrevocably stained his colleague's view of the job. 'I have a load of calls to make to O'Sullivan's colleagues and friends for Op Feldspar. They need doing, Guv.'

Anderson acceded. He would leave him be for now.

'No problem. Drew, can you help Dave with that, please?'

'My pleasure, Guv.'

'Okay, Les, you're with me. I reckon our Mr Maitland would like to be properly introduced to you, seeing as he missed meeting you at home today.'

The glee on his colleague's face would ordinarily be enough to make Anderson instantly reconsider his decision, but today a little bit of South Suffolk's dodgiest DC was most definitely in order.

By the doors to Interview Rooms Two and Five at either end of the custody suite corridor, the two teams of detectives paused to acknowledge one another, each officer aware of the gravity of the task at hand. On Anderson's cue, he and Minshull opened the doors and went inside.

Garvey Maitland was seated at the interview desk in a grey hoodie and dark denim jeans, hands folded neatly in front of him. Beside him, a well-dressed man in a suit too expensive to be bought on a duty solicitor's salary made notes in a leather-bound folder.

'Good afternoon, Mr Maitland. I'm DI Joel Anderson. My colleague, DC Les Evans, will be assisting me in this interview.'

Behind the black-rimmed glasses, Maitland's eyes flicked from Anderson to Evans, his expression unchanged.

The solicitor offered a manicured hand for curt handshakes with Anderson and Evans. 'Graham Cairns, Mr Maitland's legal representative.'

'I think we're ready to proceed, if you are?' Anderson assumed the granite exterior of a seasoned interviewer but anger burned, white-hot, within.

Maitland and his solicitor nodded.

He started the recording, calmly stating the time, date and purpose of the interview, listing the names of everyone present. As he did so, he was already lining up his questions as an archer preparing his quiver. He'd half expected Graham Cairns to interrupt immediately with a prepared statement, but none came. Instead, the two men waited for Anderson to begin.

'Mr Maitland, for the purposes of the recording can you please state your name and age?'

'Garvey John Maitland, fifty-four.'

'Thank you. Mr Maitland, you are here because yesterday after-noon, at approximately two fifteen p.m., two of our uniformed officers patrolling a crime scene were subjected to a vicious, sustained and wholly unprovoked attack by a group of persons in a white Transit van. They left the two female officers injured, one seriously. We believe that the online group that you are a co-signatory of, the Bures Bowmen, was directly responsible for provoking that attack. Do you have anything to say to that?'

'No.'

Bastard just smiled when he said it, Anderson seethed. He selected a printed sheet from his folder, sliding it across the desk to Maitland. Cairns leant forward to inspect it.

'For the recording, I am showing Mr Maitland a picture of a woodcut print of a dragon with a spear through its heart. Do you recognise this image, Mr Maitland?'

Maitland deigned to glance at it. 'Yes.'

'What can you tell me about it?'

'It's a medieval woodcut of the Bures Dragon from the legend dating back to 1405. A dragon is said to have terrorised local people in the village until a call across the country brought archers together to kill it.' Maitland sat back, smugly proud of his answer.

'A fascinating story. How does this relate to you?'

'I like the tale...'

No way. He was not going to go through this interview being a clever dick. Anderson changed tack. 'This is the logo used by the Bures Bowmen online group, of which you are a co-founder. Correct?'

'Yes.'

'And you currently run this group with Miss Rhian Butler, correct?'

'Yes again.'

'Given that you recognise this logo and identify it as belonging to your online group, can you explain to me why this was found nailed to the barn where the attack on my uniformed colleagues took place yesterday?'

Maitland shrugged. 'Anyone could have made a copy of that.'

'Okay then, explain to me why the words "justice served" had been written beneath the logo left at the attack site.'

'Again, someone else's idea, I imagine.' He shared a smile with his solicitor.

Anderson let his stare rest between the eyeballs of Garvey Maitland long enough to cause an involuntary twitch in Maitland's hand. Then he calmly looked away, pulling another sheet from his folder.

'For the recording, I am showing Mr Maitland a printout of a Facebook post, posted at five past seven on the morning in question. I quote: *South Suffolk police don't care about your safety. Or the safety of your children. Now is the time for action, not words. Now is the time for ordinary people to take back what's theirs. Will you fight to save Suffolk? The Bures Bowmen won't rest until justice is served.*' He looked up from the paper. '*Justice. Served.* Two words that hours later were written on your group's logo and fixed to the site of a brutal attack on two female police officers. Why is that, Mr Maitland?'

For a moment, Garvey Maitland didn't answer. He maintained a steady expression, but a single crease appeared between his eyebrows. It might as well have been a twenty-one-gun salute for Anderson. He had him.

Graham Cairns' smile tightened just a little.

Anderson waited.

Beside him, Evans remained uncharacteristically still, making quiet notes. Whatever his misgivings about bringing Evans in on the interview, Anderson knew exactly what it would mean to the DC to be here today. The attack yesterday was a line crossed, a threat to the very core of South Suffolk Constabulary. When it came down to it, Les Evans would stand in front of a speeding truck for a colleague, the same as the rest of them. It was why he was still on the team, his considerable list of questionable actions tempered by his commitment to his colleagues.

'Someone's stitching us up,' Maitland offered, finally.

'Why would they do that?'

'Rogue elements. Glory-seekers. They're everywhere these days. Could even be the opposition, dropping us in it. I wouldn't put it past them.'

'You said *the opposition*. What do you mean by that?'

'Antifa.'

Evans's laugh boomed into the interview space. 'Antifa? In Suffolk?'

Maitland glared at him. 'I wouldn't expect your lot to know about it. I mean, you didn't know about the drug gangs but we've been warning about them for months.'

Evans made to reply, but Anderson cut across him. 'That's not what we're here to discuss. I wasn't aware there were *violent vigilantes* ready to attack unarmed officers either until *this post* incited that attack.'

'Maybe you need to ask yourself why—'

'Mr Maitland.'

The solicitor's hand rested on the desk beside the Bures Bowmen's logo – a warning sign. But Garvey Maitland was rattled, any pretence of calm abandoned. He glowered, both arms on the desk now, leaning towards Anderson and Evans.

'We are cleaning up the streets, mate, chasing out the scum trying to poison our young people and abuse our kids. Your lot are more concerned with dragging innocent, law-abiding citizens into pointless custody, while the real criminals – the lot that smashed that teacher's skull in – are still out there.'

'I think now is a good time for a break,' Graham Cairns suggested, but neither his client nor Anderson were listening.

'Know something about that, do you?'

'More than you do.'

'Mr *Maitland*…'

'Because here's the thing, Garvey: I would dearly love to be devoting all my time to finding Oliver O'Sullivan's killer. But yesterday, two of my officers were attacked, incited by language found on *your* Facebook group, leaving *your* logo as a calling card. So all of my team, together with six support officers, had to be diverted this morning to find you and Miss Butler.'

'DI Anderson, I really must insist—'

'A fact you are all too aware of, Garvey, because you weren't at your property, were you? You were hiding in a linen cupboard at the time of Miss Butler's arrest. So here is my question, to which I would be most grateful of an answer: if you are innocent of these charges; if we, as you insist, have made a mistake linking your group to yesterday's attack; why would you hide in a tiny cupboard when police came to your associate's home?'

Maitland didn't reply, slumping back in thunderous silence. His solicitor slammed his expensive folio on the desk to ensure this time he was heard.

'I request time alone with my client to discuss the new evidence presented to him.'

Anderson turned slowly to the solicitor, every polite word edged with steel. 'Of course. Interview suspended at fourteen twenty-three.' They could talk about it all they wanted. His point had been made.

'Call us when you're ready to recommence,' he said, picking up his folder and leaving the room.

Let Garvey Maitland thrash that one out with his counsel.

At least he wasn't smiling now.

Chapter Thirty

Minshull

Ben Minshull was right: as troublemakers went, Rhian Butler was in a different league. While Garvey Maitland fit the stereotype almost to the point of parody – middle-aged, gobby and quick-tempered – Butler was well dressed, calm, eloquent and steel-nerved.

She was smaller than her photo had suggested, the only suggestion of her age a slight crinkle at the corners of her eyes. Butler had the air of someone absolutely at home in her own skin, confident in her own power. She greeted Minshull with a chin held high, her body language betraying no hint of worry or guardedness.

'Good afternoon Miss Butler. I am Detective Sergeant Rob Minshull and assisting me is Detective Constable Kate Bennett.'

Butler looked down her nose. 'We've met.'

Her solicitor stood and offered her hand to Minshull. 'I'm Sylvie Abreo, Miss Butler's legal representative.'

She shook Minshull's hand as if it were a cold damp rag, making a deliberate show of wiping her hand on the edge of her suit jacket as she resumed her seat. *Nice.* Bennett clocked this immediately, her slight shake of the head as she settled in her chair an act of solidarity Minshull appreciated.

'Do you need anything before we begin?'

'We have coffee,' Abreo stated, glancing at her plastic cup with disdain. 'If you can call it that.'

Minshull gave a smile. He might not like her attitude, but she had a point about the state of beverages in the building. 'Unfortunately that's the closest we come to it here.'

The solicitor gave a sniff. 'I do hope you won't detain us long, DS Minshull. My client is keen to leave.'

I'll bet she is.

'As are we all. So let's get started.'

Bennett began the recording and Minshull completed the introductions, Rhian Butler speaking to confirm her name and age, her solicitor making notes from the first word.

'Okay, Miss Butler, let me begin by showing you this.' He slid the copy of the Bures' Bowmen's logo across the desk. 'Do you recognise it?'

'You know that I do.'

'For the benefit of the recording.'

Butler leaned a little towards the recorder. 'Yes, I do.'

'Yesterday afternoon, at approximately two fifteen p.m., two female police officers on duty at a crime scene at Abbot's Farm, near Whatfield, were violently attacked by a group of assailants that arrived in a white Transit van. This,' he tapped the sheet of paper with his index finger, 'was left at the site following the attack. A calling card, one might say.'

'I had nothing to do with that.'

'As the official spokeswoman of the Bures Bowmen group on Facebook, are you responsible for what is posted?'

'I am.'

'Do you write the posts?'

'Sometimes. Sometimes my associate does.'

'Your associate Garvey Maitland?'

'Yes.'

'So who wrote the post that went live yesterday morning at five past seven?'

Butler said nothing, her smirk of a smile designed to goad Minshull.

You picked the wrong detective for that to work.

'I'm aware there have been many posts in the last two weeks, including the one that shared stolen, highly sensitive images from a murder scene.' His words registered with the solicitor if not her client.

It didn't matter to Minshull as long as it landed somewhere on that side of the interview desk.

'If we could just stick to the post in question?' Abreo cut in.

Minshull observed her drily. 'Certainly.' He turned his attention back to Butler. 'I'll refresh your memory, Miss Butler. "*South Suffolk police don't care about your safety. Or the safety of your children. Now is the time for action, not words. Now is the time for ordinary people to take back what's theirs. Will you fight to save Suffolk? The Bures Bowmen won't rest until justice is served.*"'

Before the solicitor could speak, Minshull handed her the print-out of the post. She read it in silence and resumed her note-taking.

'Did you write that?'

'I can't remember.'

'It's signed by you and Mr Maitland.'

'That's a brand thing.'

'A *brand thing*?' Minshull repeated, not quite believing what he'd heard. 'You consider calls for civil disobedience and violence a marketing strategy?'

'It isn't a call for civil disobedience.'

'Isn't it?' He read the words out again, careful to keep his own feelings locked away. The moment he or Bennett revealed any kind of emotion – especially anger – Butler would win. '"*Now is the time for action, not words. Now is the time for ordinary people to take back what's theirs. Will you fight?*" That's a call to arms.'

'So you say.'

'Then what would you call it?'

'Passionate language. We need passionate people to join our cause.'

'Passionate people willing to *take back what's theirs*? Willing to *fight*?'

'It says nothing about attacking police.'

'It did to the thugs in the white Transit van who attacked our officers. Your meaning was crystal clear to them.' Minshull tapped the speared dragon logo again. 'And they left your *brand logo* at the scene. Under which one of them had written: *justice served*.' He pointed at the Facebook post. '"*The Bures Bowmen won't rest until* justice *is* served."' No prizes for guessing where they got that from.'

Butler folded her arms. 'It's a common phrase.'

'You're right. It's also a heck of a coincidence that seven hours after your message was posted the same message was referenced, along with your group's logo, by violent attackers. Pretty perfect outcome for you, Miss Butler, isn't it?'

'I couldn't possibly comment.'

Minshull took a long, slow breath to centre him against the anger writhing inside. 'Where were you at two fifteen p.m. yesterday afternoon?'

'I wasn't in that van.'

'Where were you at two fifteen p.m. yesterday afternoon?'

'I was out.'

Minshull kept his voice low and calm, every syllable an effort to control. 'Out where, exactly?'

Butler glanced at her solicitor, her dramatic eye-roll met by a haughty smirk. 'I was in bed with a friend.'

Minshull saw Bennett's lips fighting a smile. 'Which friend?' he asked.

'Not Garvey, if that's what you're thinking. Not my type.'

'Miss Butler, who can verify your whereabouts at two fifteen p.m. yesterday?'

Her tactic to wrong foot Minshull having failed, Rhian Butler feigned a yawn. 'Seth Naseby. We were at his house in Aldeburgh.'

'The thriller writer?' Bennett asked. When Minshull glanced at her, it was clear she hadn't intended to say it aloud.

'That's right. Read any of his stuff, have you?'

'I have, actually.'

'I would have thought it was too exciting for you, considering.' She gave that same disdainful appraisal of Bennett that Minshull had seen in her apartment earlier. Bennett held her stare.

'So Mr Naseby is your partner?'

'No, I said he's my *friend*. And I don't know why my personal life is so important to you, Detective Minshull.'

She was pushing her luck and she knew it: her solicitor knew it, too.

'If we could just keep to the matter at hand?' she suggested.

Minshull bristled. 'Who organised the attack at Abbot's Farm?'

'I don't know. But it wasn't the Bures Bowmen.'

'Then why leave your logo there? With the words taken directly from your Facebook post?'

'We have no interest in the farm. Or your officers.'

'Your mission statement would disagree with that,' Bennett said, pulling a sheet of paper from her notes.

'How, exactly?'

Bennett kept her eyes on the paper. 'For the benefit of the recording, I am reading Miss Butler the "About" information from her Facebook group's page. "*We stand together, fighting to rid Suffolk of the scourge of drugs, serious crime and paedophiles: elements our police have willingly allowed to grow and thrive. Like our ancient ancestors, we pledge to find these beasts and hunt them down. We will not rest until every last piece of scum is gone.*"'

Butler gave a slow blink. 'So?'

Bennett squared up to her. 'The crime scene your organisation displayed stolen photographs of – which was also the location of the violent attack yesterday on two unarmed female officers – has been widely linked by the media to drugs gangs. Earlier posts on your group's page have focused on drugs gangs crossing the border from Essex to Suffolk. You have stated, not just in your mission statement but also in the Facebook post published yesterday morning, that you consider South Suffolk Constabulary to be ineffectual at stopping the drugs problem. All of these came together in the attack at Abbot's Farm.'

'Doesn't prove I was there. Or Garvey. Or any of our members.'

Bennett glanced at Minshull, to indicate she was done. He accepted the baton.

'We think you intended for that attack to happen. We have requested access to the private group, Dragon Army, linked with the public group page of your organisation. My officers will be going through those posts shortly. Is that where you organised the attack?'

'I wouldn't know. I don't even post in it now.'

'Is that where details were posted of the farm's location, together with information regarding who would be patrolling it?'

'This is insane…'

'So tell me what you think happened, Miss Butler, because it looks damning to me.'

Rhian Butler stared back. 'You have no proof it was us.'

'We have your logo left at the site. We have wording written beneath it that directly quotes the post you wrote yesterday morning. How do you explain that?'

'We're going in circles here,' the solicitor offered.

'Miss Butler is yet to answer the question,' Minshull returned.

'Have you caught any of the people in the van?' Abreo asked.

'We are still looking for them. Do you know who they are, Miss Butler?'

'I don't know anything!' The sudden rise in volume in her reply was a rare chink in the armour.

'My client has stated she doesn't know them. So unless you arrest those responsible for this horrific attack and they tell you Miss Butler arranged it, or confirm that she was in that van, you have nothing but circumstantial evidence.'

'The post you wrote was a call to arms. The attack was in direct response. And your online group, Miss Butler, was referenced by the attackers when they nailed your logo to the barn.'

'We don't care about Abbot's Farm,' Butler shot back, oblivious to the shock of her legal representative. 'Or the body you found there.'

'Rhian—'

'No, Sylvie, if they did their job properly they wouldn't be harassing me or my associate. They would know why none of our followers would care about what happened to that man.'

'Rhian, be very careful what you say.'

Bennett and Minshull exchanged a look. 'What do you mean by that, Miss Butler? What do you know about Oliver O'Sullivan?'

'I know he wasn't the saint you've all made him out to be. Another issue you clearly knew nothing about.'

'We know Mr O'Sullivan was linked to drugs…'

'It's not about the drugs! Is it any wonder that people like me – groups like ours – have to step in to protect the public, when the police are so blatantly unaware of what's happening?'

'I must advise my client to say no more,' Abreo stated. 'I request a break...'

Minshull leaned forwards. 'What do you want to tell me, Rhian?'

Butler had discarded all semblance of calm now, her eyes wild with accusation. 'Find out why Oliver O'Sullivan left his last job in Birmingham. Talk to that school. And then talk to St Audrey's about the complaints they buried. About the two girls suspended from the school while O'Sullivan got a paid holiday.'

A deep sense of dread began to descend on Minshull. 'What complaints?'

'We have to stop the interview *now*...'

Rhian Butler had no intention of stopping. 'The Bures Bowmen will not tolerate paedophiles allowed to operate here, or the establishments that cover up their crimes.'

Minshull sensed Bennett tense beside him as across the desk, the solicitor paled.

'Paedophiles?'

'DS Minshull, this has to stop.'

Heart hammering, Minshull leaned across to the recorder. 'Interview suspended at fourteen twenty-five.' He waited until the machine beeped to indicate the end of the recording and then turned back to Rhian Butler.

'What should we know about Oliver O'Sullivan?'

'You don't have to answer that,' the solicitor warned, placing her hand on Butler's shoulder to guide her from the room.

'Yes I do.' She glared at Minshull. 'Oliver O'Sullivan wasn't a much-loved teacher. He was a monster who preyed on young girls. Nobody in my organisation mourns his loss.'

Instantly, Minshull remembered the comment Toby Buchanan had made yesterday: '*...he had a new group of fans at his after-school drama club and we were all ribbing him about only being desirable to fourteen-year-old girls...*'

'How do you know this?'

'We've been monitoring him for over a year. And there are others. They're operating together. But you wouldn't know that because you're more interested in arresting concerned members of the community who point out your failings...'

His mind skipped to the first news report interviewing people at St Audrey's who had known O'Sullivan – the Head Teacher, the governor, the fellow teacher who broke down during his interview: *'Olly was someone who was a friend to anyone who needed it. Including me.'* Were any of them involved?

'What others?'

'Work it out. But I'll tell you this for starters: the drugs gangs are welcome to O'Sullivan. If they bumped him off, they did the young girls of Suffolk a favour.'

–

'It could be bullshit,' Bennett panted as they raced back upstairs to CID.

'I don't think it is,' Minshull returned.

'She wanted out of the interview. She'd say anything to provoke us.'

'Not this. She lost all control when she told us that. Her solicitor knows more, too.'

At the doorway to the CID office, they stopped.

'This could blow it wide open,' Minshull said, the enormity of Butler's bombshell beginning to dawn.

'I know, Sarge.' Minshull could see his own shock reflected in Kate Bennett's expression. 'What's the plan?'

'Get the team together. We need to get to the bottom of this.'

Chapter Thirty-One

Cora

'Gil?'

Cora nodded, blowing steam from her takeout cup.

Dr Tris Noakes gazed out to sea. 'Friend? Boyfriend?'

'I don't know. But now I've heard it, I think more will follow.'

'What made it break through, do you think?'

Cora watched a pair of seagulls floating motionless as the strong south-easterly wind held them in place over the churning grey waves of the North Sea. 'I think she finally let her guard down. We were chatting to her dad and it suddenly came out.'

'Ah, you met Trevor? You're honoured.'

Cora looked across the bench at him. They had chosen a seat in Sea View Gardens, across the road from Felixstowe promenade. Around them the recently restored garden bloomed, flowers in the borders and the lush green planting thriving in the sea air. It had been Tris's idea to meet here, away from the office. As soon as Cora had confirmed she had uncovered Lottie's locked-in word, he'd insisted he come to her.

'Why honoured?'

'You're the first expert Trevor Arundel has deigned to meet.' Tris sipped his hot chocolate, chuckling self-consciously when Cora pointed out the blob of cream adorning the end of his nose. 'I understand why, in a way. He's a typical devoted dad: wants to make everything all right for his little girl and can't handle it when it's not possible. Monica copes by over-coping; Trevor copes by hiding.'

'In his impressive workshop,' Cora smiled.

The comment had an instant effect on her director. 'Oh my goodness, did you see it?'

'I got the tour.'

'No way! Ah, the dream! I've only seen it from the first floor of the house, looking out of the windows. Original oak frame, everything custom-made from reclaimed timber, the cream of ancient Suffolk craftsmanship being kept alive...' He stopped himself and held up an apologetic hand. 'Sorry. Building geek alert.'

'It's a gorgeous building. Too nice to be covered in oil and bits of engine.'

'He mentioned something about liking to tinker. I can't imagine Monica is happy with him traipsing oil and muck into *that* house.'

'He has a shower built into the back of the workshop,' Cora grinned. 'Oak door, copper fittings, reclaimed Welsh slate tiles...'

'Oh stop! I'll never have any of that on my salary, but a man can dream.' He finished the last bite of his almond croissant and tipped the crumbs from the pink and white striped paper bag onto the ground for a couple of waiting sparrows. 'What did you make of him?'

'He was very relaxed, more than I expected. So different to Monica, but he was in his safe place, I suppose. I'm guessing he's very different when he's in the house.'

'It's like he's under a cloud in there. Lots of passive-aggressive muttering and heavy sighs designed to be heard by everyone.' A thought struck him and he turned to her. 'Didn't you say you heard sighs on the staircase at Fourwinds?'

Cora nodded, impressed again that Tris had listened to what she said. 'I do. It's as if they are in the treads of the staircase and walking disturbs them. Like walking through a meadow in summer dislodges clouds of rising pollen.'

'Could those be Trevor's?'

'Possibly, if you say he's subdued when he's in the house. Maybe it's his emotion from leaving the workshop where he feels free to be himself and walking into the ongoing situation he can't control. Or they could be Monica's. Or Lottie's, after all. Ascending those stairs means walking into a battlefield for all of them: Lottie fighting to hold her silence and her parents fighting to find her voice.'

Tris blew out a frustrated sigh. 'It's just so sad.'

'It is.'

'But we have a word now. That's more than anyone else has managed to get from Lottie. You're doing a fantastic job.'

'Thank you.'

Tris sniffed. 'So what's next?'

'I'm going to press into the place where the word was. Now I know how to get there, I think I can move around.'

'What can I do? I want to help in any way I can.'

Cora considered his question as she finished her coffee. 'When you first assessed Lottie, did you take any family history notes, details of friends, anything where a Gil could be mentioned?'

'We have eleven months of ongoing notes,' Tris replied with a wry grin. 'Each new expert she's seen has demanded another set be made. I'll go through them, see if anything matches.'

'Thanks.'

'One person I think you should meet is Andrew Draycott, Lottie's current form teacher.'

The name was familiar. Cora remembered back to her first walk with Lottie, which seemed a lifetime ago. *Mr Draycott. Andrew, when we're not in the house. He listens to me.* 'He comes to see Lottie sometimes, doesn't he?'

Tris nodded. 'Yeah. He's been great, actually. Checking in on her, getting her out of the house, being a neutral figure between her and her mum. He contacted me quite early on in Lottie's investigations to offer his help. That doesn't happen often, especially in cases where mental health may play a role. Shall I set up a meeting?'

'Sure. Maybe best to do it away from Fourwinds? I'd like to get his sense of how things are with Lottie. And I think we should ask him not to mention it to her when he sees her next.'

'I agree.' Tris glanced at Cora, screwed up his paper bag into a ball and threw it into the litterbin beside their bench.

I can't believe you got to see the workshop it said in his voice as it disappeared inside.

Cora laughed. 'Tris…'

He was unrepentant. 'It's just so cool, Cora.'

Anyone else in Cora's world wouldn't be able to get away with the impertinence, but there was something uniquely endearing about her director's boyish glee about her ability. An adult lifetime of people shrinking back from her when they learned of her emotional synaesthesia had made Cora wary of any interest. Rob Minshull's initial reaction when he'd encountered her ability in action had been disbelief, later grudging respect and then dismissal. While he was working hard to understand it now, making amends for the past, Cora still sensed his wariness around the subject. Tris Noakes had no such qualms. He was a self-confessed fan.

–

Back at the office, Cora gathered all the files of observation notes made by her predecessors who had tried and failed to help Lottie Arundel. Laying them out across her desk she considered the hours invested, the theories disproved. Words of complaint and frustration rose from the handwritten notes as she opened each file, until the office was crowded with loud dissent.

The subject has zero interest in vocal exercises or breathing.

She doesn't even listen to me.

How am I supposed to help the girl when she refuses to even try?

She's goading me now. I can feel it...

Cora let them speak before muting each one.

What they all had in common was that none of their words were directed at Lottie. They were spoken over her head, proclaimed to those around her, not to the vulnerable teen at the centre of it all.

Nobody listens.

There had been such emptiness in those words, such heartfelt abandonment, even when spoken by her tablet. No wonder the other experts had failed to connect.

Cora imagined Lottie Arundel, lost and alone in the middle of them all, clutching the three-lettered name like a single sound of familiarity, as arguments, theories and frustrations yelled around her.

Gil.

Who was Gil? Why had Lottie protected them so fastidiously for all this time?

And now Cora had been allowed to hear the name, what more might she find?

Chapter Thirty-Two

Minshull

It was worse than any of them could have anticipated.

As the CID team gathered to share what they had found after a fractious morning of investigation, the emerging picture of the murdered teacher grew darker by the second.

Rhian Butler had been telling the truth.

'I spoke with the Head of King Edward's Academy in Bournville,' Bennett told them. 'He admitted O'Sullivan had been cautioned on three occasions for unprofessional behaviour, all of which he strenuously denied. Then one of the after-school care team said a year ten girl had made a disclosure to her during an art club. O'Sullivan was sacked immediately and the school dealt with the matter internally.'

'Buried it, then?' Evans asked.

'Ten feet deep,' Bennett replied. 'Police were never involved and the girl's family moved out of the area soon after.'

'Can we contact the girl?' Minshull asked Anderson.

'Tread carefully. She may not be willing to speak to us.'

'Especially if she thinks police didn't care enough to get involved at the time,' Bennett added. 'Kids don't understand why parents choose to avoid the problem. She's probably spent years thinking we abandoned her.'

'Poor kid. Understood.' Minshull made a note of this. 'Butler also mentioned two girls at St Audrey's who made formal complaints of sexual abuse towards O'Sullivan then subsequently left the school prior to him requesting a sabbatical.'

'Is that true, too?'

'That's what Dave and I are going to the school to find out, Guv. Butler didn't give us names, but if she and her organisation found that information, we can locate it, too.'

Anderson sucked air through his teeth as if tasting something offensive. 'So, they buried the accusations but then someone buried O'Sullivan.'

'Exactly, Guv.'

'Do you think that's why he was killed?' Ellis piped up.

'We can't rule it out,' Minshull replied. 'Although we still have the drugs link to investigate. It's possible that's what caused his death, but the allegations caused the death of his jobs.'

'Hardly a fair swap,' Wheeler muttered.

'So, Dave and I are going to St Audrey's. Les, get onto Traffic and see if they've had any joy with vehicles heading to and from Abbot's Farm around the time of O'Sullivan's murder. I know we're unlikely to find anything that far back, but look anyway. I know they're already looking for white vans in the Whatfield area on Monday, so see if anything's come up.'

'Sarge.'

'Kate, can you set up a video meeting with the Head of King Edward's, please? We need everything the school didn't tell police at the time and we can't spare someone to head up to Birmingham to chase it. Later today, if possible. Guv, can you lead that when it happens?'

Anderson saluted with his rolled-up notes. 'Absolutely.'

'Great, thanks. That okay with you, Kate?'

'No problem, Sarge.'

'Good. Drew, keep looking into the membership of the Bures Bowmen. Check follower lists on the page, chase Tech for the transcripts of Dragon Army conversations, make a list of those who have liked and shared the Facebook group's posts. The bastards who attacked Steph and Rilla will be there somewhere, I'm certain. Run any names you find through the system to see if we get matches.'

'Okay, Sarge.'

'Guv, any joy yet with Essex and McGann?'

'Still bloody waiting, but I'll chase again.'

'Great. Thanks everyone. I know all of this is a shock, but we have really strong leads here and we will find the truth.' Minshull looked at Wheeler. 'Dave, are you ready to go?'

'Not particularly.'

Wheeler without his smile was a strange sight. Even though this was the third day Minshull had witnessed it, the change in the DC was hard to accept. With a heavy sigh, he picked up his jacket and headed for the door.

'Then let's get this over with.'

—

This time they made no appointment at St Audrey High, Minshull and Wheeler showing their warrant cards to the startled school secretary who hurried them straight up to the headmaster's office.

Tom Dillinger jumped to his feet as if someone had just connected his desk chair to a live socket, staring at Minshull and Wheeler as the apologetic secretary ushered them in.

'Officers, I don't – did we have a meeting booked?' He consulted the large diary lying open on his glass desk, as if the unexpected arrival of two detectives from a murder investigation might be pencilled in there.

Minshull fixed him with a stare. 'It appears you haven't been entirely honest with us, sir. We need answers.'

Dillinger hastily dismissed the secretary who scurried out, closing the door as she went.

'I really must protest...' he began, but Minshull cut across him immediately.

'Sit down, sir.'

'Did you use the front entrance? There are journalists still at the gate! They will have seen you!' He ran a hand through his hair. 'It will be all over the news, won't it? This is a disaster! If our sponsors see it—'

'Mr Dillinger, *sit down*.'

Minshull's tone caused the head teacher to assume his seat and fall silent. Calmly, he and Wheeler sat, too. 'It has come to our attention that, at his previous post, Oliver O'Sullivan was accused of improper behaviour and one case of actual assault towards young girls between the ages of thirteen and sixteen.'

'I see.'

Any hopes the Head may have entertained of feigning ignorance were dashed already. Tom Dillinger was ghost-white, his gaze flicking between Minshull and Wheeler as it had last time, his hands restless where he placed them on the glass desk. He knew about the allegations: it was impossible to conceal. But how long would he pretend he didn't?

'Were you aware of this when he applied for the job at St Audrey's?'

'Do you think we would have employed him if we'd known?'

'With respect, sir, that doesn't answer my question.'

Dillinger stared at his hands. 'Not when we appointed him, no.'

'Then how soon after?' Wheeler made no attempt to soften the question with a smile.

'You have to understand: Olly is – was – one of our most popular teachers. We saw significant changes in achievement and attendance from the first month he was at St Audrey's. We'd struggled before that. He was wonderful with the kids and everyone loved him. A teacher of his calibre and skill set was exactly what the school needed…' Realising what he'd said, he stopped.

'But a known sex offender on staff wasn't.'

Minshull knew he should rein Wheeler in, but for the moment his colleague's disgust was useful. There was no way Dillinger could laugh the accusations off when faced with Wheeler's rage.

'He strongly denied the accusations at his previous school.'

'And when you received complaints about him here?'

Dillinger stared in disbelief.

The young, affable Head had impressed Minshull when he'd first met him. But all his good impressions crumbled in that moment. 'We know about that, as well. Two girls accused Oliver O'Sullivan of sexual abuse, both fourteen years old at the time. What were their names?'

'I – I would have to check…'

'No you wouldn't,' Wheeler growled. 'You were well aware of them when it happened and you are well aware of them now.'

Beneath the edge of the desk, Minshull lifted one hand. It was enough to send Wheeler back into compliant, brooding silence. 'Why didn't you inform police when these accusations were made?'

'We have policies… due process… We investigate every accusation thoroughly. In-house.'

'Your first duty when a disclosure of abuse is made is to contact police and social services. In the first instance.'

Dillinger was shaking his head, determined to protect his position. 'We need to ascertain whether the accusation is reliable or not before we proceed. That is how we do things here. We need to investigate all claims against members of staff before we act. The only time we would call police and social services first is if a child disclosed they were being abused at home and it would be unsafe to let them return to their parents. In that case social services would of course intervene.'

Minshull couldn't believe what he was hearing. 'That's the correct procedure specified by the education authority, is it? Because if it is, then Suffolk must be the only county in the country that follows alternative protocols. *Every* disclosure reported to us, Mr Dillinger, not just the few you deem worthy.'

'We pride ourselves on—' Dillinger began, but Minshull had heard enough.

'The names of the girls, please.'

The head teacher sagged in defeat. 'Amy Godwit and Bindi Henderson-Aziz.'

'What did they allege?'

'They claimed Olly had marked them out for special attention in his after-school drama club. Gave them extra jobs to do, met with them before the club began and asked them to stay afterwards to help him clear the hall, that kind of thing.' He let out an aggravated sigh. 'They claimed he had tried to touch them on a number of occasions. Amy Godwit alleged he assaulted her in a side room after a dress rehearsal for our production of *The Phantom of the Opera*.'

Minshull heard Wheeler's sharp intake of breath. 'When was this?'

'Fourteen months ago.'

'Did they tell their parents?'

Dillinger nodded, staring out of the window beside his desk. 'Amy's parents were first. They said she'd told them at home after her friends advised her to report Olly.'

'But they didn't go to the police?'

'They didn't want the police involved.'

'And you didn't think to suggest they reconsider, given the gravity of the accusation?'

'It's our duty to follow parental wishes.'

'It's your duty to protect the children in your care,' Minshull countered, the edge in his tone leaving the head teacher in no doubt of his opinion.

'It isn't always as simple as that. Fourteen-year-old girls these days are... well, they're streetwise. Mature. You see how young women dress: it's impossible to know how old they are.'

He was serious, wasn't he?

Aware Wheeler was at the point of self-combustion beside him, Minshull faced Tom Dillinger. 'It's *very easy* to tell a *child's* age in *your* school.'

Every word registered across the desk.

'Bindi thought she was in love with him!' Dillinger spluttered. 'Ridiculous! She thought he wanted to be with her. Fantasies, Detective Minshull. When he spurned her advances she accused him of assault. Don't you see how that might completely blow up? Honestly, if we involved the police every time a student developed romantic notions about their teacher you'd be a permanent fixture in this place. It just looked like a silly, teenage girl's crush that was threatening the career of one of our brightest members of staff.'

'Children being groomed by sexual predators often believe themselves to be in love with their abuser,' Minshull stated, pushing down the urge to slam the principal's head against the glass desk. 'It's an indicator of abuse, not an excuse for it.'

'Well I... We didn't know for sure. We had a duty to investigate...'

'Which I presume you proceeded to do?'

'Of course. As I said…'

'When did you learn of the previous accusations against Oliver O'Sullivan?'

The Head's mouth fastened tight.

The truth dawned on Minshull. 'You knew before.'

'No.'

'Then when did you learn of the previous accusations?'

'Olly mentioned something. Off the record.'

'When?'

'At rugby practice, a few months before. He said the girl's mother had made a play for him and when he said he wasn't interested she got her daughter to accuse him of inappropriate behaviour.'

It was clear, even as he said this, that Tom Dillinger was realising the damning weight of his words.

'He – he said that was why it was never taken to the police. The school agreed to deal with it internally on the understanding that the authorities weren't involved.'

'I see.' Minshull nodded. 'The girl in question left the school shortly after Oliver O'Sullivan's dismissal. Her family moved out of the area. Were you aware of that?'

'Olly didn't mention it…'

'No, I'm guessing he didn't. Interesting, wouldn't you say, that the same outcome happened at St Audrey's? An in-house investigation, a covering up of the damning accusations, and two girls who should have had your protection as a first priority, forced to move to a different school.'

'Nobody forced them…'

'I'll find that out when I speak with them, won't I? I'll also need the names and numbers of everyone responsible for the decision to bury the accusations. Governors, teachers and anyone else involved.'

'Of course.' Tom Dillinger was a man defeated. When he raised his head he appeared on the verge of tears. 'Will you tell the press?'

'We won't inform them, but I can't prevent them finding out. There are people watching your school, Mr Dillinger, people with everything to gain by branding St Audrey's actions as protecting a sex offender. Frankly, I don't blame them.'

'Hang on, you can't say—'

Minshull stood, flanked by Wheeler. 'We'll need details of all meetings, discussions and disciplinary actions taken regarding Oliver O'Sullivan. By the end of today. And there will be further investigations into this.'

'I'll ask Veronica to collate them for you.'

Minshull began to leave, but turned back at the door. 'You knew O'Sullivan hadn't lost his mother, didn't you?'

Dillinger hung his head.

'I thought so. We'll be in touch.'

In the corridor outside, the nervous secretary appeared from a side office, her feet making no sound as she hurried over the thickly woven carpet to meet them.

'I'm preparing the files you requested and I can email you a private link to our school database if that would be easier than collating and printing?'

Minshull smiled. 'That would be great, thanks, Ms...?'

'Veronica,' she reminded him. 'Veronica Sutton. I'll walk you out.'

'There's no need...' Minshull began, but the timid woman stepped into his path.

'I will *walk* you *out*.' She glanced over her shoulder. Was she checking for someone watching her? 'We'll take a different route. The bell is about to go for lunch and you'll never get across the quad when the crowds descend. This way.'

They followed her as she walked back past Tom Dillinger's closed door and turned left into a narrow corridor, a little farther along. Pushing open a single, brass-framed glass door, she led Minshull and Wheeler down a small winding stone staircase, illuminated by arched stained-glass windows that would have looked more at home in the imposing stone walls of Framlingham Castle.

'Sir Eric Moreton, who built the oldest part of St Audrey's, had a bit of a penchant for all things medieval,' Veronica informed them as they descended the stairs. 'He was obsessed with tales of knights and grand castles and *Le Morte d'Arthur*. Hence our completely OTT fire escape.'

'That's fascinating stuff,' Wheeler said, the smallest glimpse of his usual mood appearing. It was such a relief to catch even a moment of it. Minshull wondered if they could second Veronica Sutton to the CID office for the remainder of Op Feldspar, just to keep Dave Wheeler happy with her cheery tales. Maybe her magic would sustain his colleague for the journey back to the office.

Abruptly, Veronica stopped, so suddenly that Minshull and Wheeler skidded on the stone steps to avoid a collision. She was on the fourth step from the ground floor, just where the staircase curved out of view of the glass-panelled door at the bottom. When she twisted back to look at the detectives, her smile had vanished.

'I must leave you here, detectives. That door will take you to the car park.'

'Oh, okay, thank you...'

Suddenly, the secretary grasped Minshull's hand, pressing a folded scrap of paper urgently into his palm. 'You need to talk to Carly.'

'Who?'

'Carly Addison. Her number's on there. I don't have long before they'll miss me upstairs. Call her. Carly knows everything about those poor girls. Things you won't see in any of the files I'm sending.'

Minshull's pulse jumped into action. 'How does she know?'

The shrill ringing of the lunch bell shattered the stillness in the stone stairwell, making Veronica jump and look down towards the door at the end of the staircase. 'I really have to go.'

Minshull folded his hand over hers. 'Veronica, this is so important, thank you.'

'It's the least I could do. The very least...'

'What does Carly know?' Wheeler asked, the shock development bringing the life back to him. 'Is she a student?'

Veronica was already backing up the stone stairs. 'No, she worked here. But she quit because of how badly Amy and Bindi were treated. Talk to her, both of you. She'll tell you the real story.'

Chapter Thirty-Three

Cora

Nothing.

Cora closed the last file and dropped it onto the haphazard pile on the floor beside her sofa. She'd read every note, every observation, muting the frustrations of those who had gone before her as she turned each page. In the lists of friends and acquaintances that had been interviewed six months into Lottie's silence, on the suggestion of the fourth expert sent to work with her, Cora had searched for a mention of a Gil, but found none.

She'd been too hopeful of finding the name in the files, she knew. It would have been a miracle to find it in the first search. Now Lottie had relinquished one word there would be more, she was certain, but part of her wished for the key to all of it to magically appear.

She liked the girl a lot. Despite the horror of being trapped within her own thoughts, Lottie maintained a fierce humour that spoke life and fun through the emotionless tone of her tablet. With her voice restored, Lottie could take over the world.

Cora saw it in Monica's grief, in Trevor's bewilderment: the shadow of their daughter before the silence hanging heavy over every inter-action they shared. She felt it from Lottie, too: the endless sentries of inhaled breath that had masked Gil from view. The presence of mind required to imprison her own voice took not just physical effort but courage, an attitude Cora envied a little. She hadn't had a choice when her voices had arrived as a teenager: Lottie had chosen her silence.

Retrieving Gil from Lottie's thoughts was a significant step forward, but what next? Should she broach the subject directly with Lottie, or wait until more clues were revealed?

She leaned back against a cushion, her mind exhausted from the words she had read late into the night last night and since breakfast this morning, the voices emitting from the files and the unanswered questions each viewpoint raised. As she let her gaze drift around the living room of her apartment, she caught sight of the clock above the mantelpiece.

How was it eleven-thirty a.m. already?

Scrambling to her feet, Cora dashed into her bedroom to change.

—

Tris had arranged for her to meet Lottie's teacher, Andrew Draycott, for lunch in a café in the centre of Woodbridge during his two free periods. It was far enough from the school for them to not be spotted, but near enough for Draycott to return for his final lesson of the day. Lottie was in school today, another reason to meet outside the building; Cora had arranged her next session with the teenager for four-thirty at Fourwinds.

Leaving Felixstowe later than she'd planned put Cora on the back foot, at the mercy of every red traffic light, unexpected tractor and lunchtime traffic snag. By the time she reached the pretty town of Woodbridge all her usual parking spots were gone and she spent a nervous ten minutes driving around to find an alternative.

She arrived at Little Angel's Café at a minute past one after running from her car, and was relieved to see Draycott had yet to arrive. Catching her breath and straightening her jacket, she pushed open the café door. A swell of loud conversation rushed to greet her as a small brass bell chimed overhead. Most of the tables and chairs were empty, but many still had piles of plates, cups and cutlery awaiting collection.

Cora passed the first table, where gossiping ghosts gathered around three floral plates bearing the crumbed remains of scones and smears of jam and cream, a large teapot holding court at the centre. Rosettes of paper napkins resting on each plate carried the juicy morsels of conversation floating up from the table.

I can't believe it.

I knew she was trouble.

He'll leave her now for sure…

Eighteen months ago, the sudden intrusion of sound would have hit Cora as a physical blow, and sent her scurrying to the farthest corners of the room. She smiled to herself now, as she slowly navigated the voices, her well-practised method in play. *Acknowledge each voice, mute it, and move on to the next.*

It had taken the terror of a missing child to bring her method about, to push Cora from the outer peripheries of life to grab hold of her ability and run with it. She wouldn't have chosen the circumstances that had allowed her to finally assume control, but she would forever be grateful that she had.

'Sit anywhere you like,' a flushed-face woman rushed as she hurried from behind the counter to begin clearing the tables. 'Sorry for the mess. We had an early rush this morning and my assistant is at home with flu. The table by the window is lovely if you fancy it.'

'Thanks,' Cora replied, moving over to it. Fragrance drifted in through the open window from pots of lavender outside the café and honeysuckle trailing from hanging baskets across its frontage. Sunlight made the courtyard outside sparkle, bathing everything in a warm glow. Before long the annual tide of tourists would wash into the town, places like this becoming as busy as the lavender pots now buzzing with bees.

The bell over the door chimed again and Cora looked up to see a tall man hurrying in. He was in shirtsleeves, a soft green tie loose at his neck, a messenger bag slung across his chest.

The café owner's head bobbed out of the beaded curtain again. 'Hi, forgive the mess! Take a seat where you like and I'll be over to clear the table.'

'It's okay, I'm meeting someone.' The man raised a tentative hand to Cora and she returned the gesture.

'Oh. Lovely. Be over in five,' the woman grinned, disappearing between the lengths of beads, leaving them swinging in her wake.

'Dr Lael?' the man asked, heading over.

'Hi, Mr Draycott.'

'Andrew, please,' Draycott grimaced as he pulled the bag strap over his head, placing it on the spare chair between them and leaning across the table to shake her hand. 'I like to leave Mr Draycott firmly in his classroom.'

Cora caught the lilt of a Sunderland accent dancing through his words.

'Then call me Cora,' she replied, instantly warming to the pleasant, self-deprecating teacher. 'Dr Lael is a label I'm still learning to carry.'

'Deal.' Draycott flopped onto his chair with a smile, straightening his light-brown-framed glasses on the bridge of his nose. 'What a day! Parking is a nightmare at the moment. Journalists.' He rolled his eyes. 'A lot of them left with the big trucks on Tuesday when someone else's misfortune hit the headlines, but there's a fair few left, holding on for a breaking story.'

'Is it strange, knowing they're in the town?'

'It is. And worse when they're hunting dirt on your pal.'

'You knew Oliver O'Sullivan?'

Draycott's smile dimmed. 'Closest thing to a best mate I've had since I moved to St Audrey's. Thirty-four, man. No time to die.'

'It's awful. Must be hard.'

'The worst. I don't know anyone who'd want to hurt him. I mean, his decisions weren't always the best and he could annoy people some-times. Didn't know when to give it a rest, you know. But murder? It makes no sense to me.' He gave a self-conscious laugh. 'But we aren't here to talk about that. What do you make of our lovely Lottie?'

'I like her.'

'She likes you. She was telling me last week she has a cool new therapist.'

'I'm not really a therapist. Just an observer.'

'You're helping Lottie: that's what matters.'

'Thank you. Lottie tells me you've been visiting her?'

'That's right.' Draycott nodded, picking up the stack of cups and saucers from their table to hand to a very surprised café owner who had just arrived. 'There you go.'

'He's a keeper,' she grinned at Cora. 'Do you hire him out on Saturdays? I could use the help.'

Draycott blushed beneath his fair hair as he grinned back. 'I'm afraid I can only do one table per visit. But I'll bear it in mind.'

The café owner giggled. 'The offer's always open, bor.' She raised a hand to Cora. 'No offence.'

'Um, okay,' Cora replied, not really sure what the comment meant.

'So, what can I get you both? If it's lunch, I have some lovely bacon and asparagus quiche with salad and walnut bread? And a pot of tea? Yes? Good!'

Draycott's grin was wide when the woman left. 'No wonder there's no menus anywhere. I didn't realise we have a psychic tearoom in Woodbridge.'

'Well, it is Little Angel's tearoom. Maybe she's an omniscient being.'

'Not that omniscient, judging by the tables,' Draycott observed, surprised and pleased when Cora laughed.

He felt like an open book, his warm conversation and sense of fun readily at hand. No wonder Lottie liked him. He carried an air of ease that could calm the prickliest of atmospheres.

'I wanted to ask you if Lottie had any friends she might not have told my predecessors about? Best friends, acquaintances, people she wanted to get to know?'

'Not that I know of. None that haven't already been spoken to. All her school friends were asked to do interviews a few months ago because the neurologist was convinced one of them was key to Lottie's silence. But the truth is, all of us are as confused as each other about why she doesn't want to speak anymore.'

'Were you her teacher when she stopped speaking?'

Draycott shook his head. 'No. But I'd started the school newspaper and Lottie was one of my first volunteers, so I got to know her there. She'd been part of the editorial group for about five months when she stopped speaking.'

'Did it happen gradually or all at once?'

'Overnight. One day she was chatting, leading the conversation as she always did; next day, silence. It was so odd. I remember asking her if something had scared her, or if she needed help with anything, but she wouldn't be drawn on it. She'd brought in a notepad to school and insisted on writing everything down and that was that.'

'Had she been upset at that time, or had anything significant to deal with?'

'Not really. She'd mentioned her mam and dad were arguing a few weeks before, but nothing significant. I mean, everything seems like the end of the world when you're fourteen, but no more than it did to any of her friends.' His expression lit up as a thought occurred. 'Actually, two of her friends had moved schools a couple of weeks before. She'd been upset about that.'

'Do you know their names?'

Draycott seemed to hesitate for a moment, his gaze straying to the pots of lavender beyond the glass. Then: 'Bindi and Amy. There'd been some disagreement with the school and the parents had taken them out. We get that sometimes. Lottie had been very vocal about it when it happened. Kept saying it wasn't fair and it was going to "make things worse for everyone" – you know how dramatic teenage girls can be.'

Could her friends leaving have caused Lottie's silence? Cora believed a single event was most likely for Lottie's decision to stop talking, but was it as simple as her friends changing schools? If so, why was it still continuing, eleven months later?

'Has she mentioned Bindi and Amy to you since?'

'Oh they're still in touch and she sees them occasionally. I think that's why we all dismissed them leaving St Audrey's as reason for her silence.'

'Was it mentioned to any of the other experts who have spent time with Lottie?'

Draycott's brow furrowed. 'I don't think so. Like I said, because they're still in touch it's unlikely.'

They enjoyed lunch with easy conversation, Draycott asking Cora more about her doctorate and training and telling her how he'd ended up in Suffolk. A few times, he mentioned the murdered teacher, the light that seemed to surround him naturally dimming each time. When he discarded a sugar packet, Cora caught a woeful whisper, edged with sadness:

He'd have loved this.

'I should be getting back,' he said, finishing the last bite of his quiche. 'But thanks for this.'

'My pleasure. It's been good to meet you.'

Draycott smiled. 'You too. You know it's funny, if Ol was still here he'd be giving me the third degree when I got back to school. Sneaking out for secret lunches with a beautiful woman...' He broke off, horror painting his features. 'Oh, forgive me, I didn't mean...'

A little taken aback, Cora waved away his concern. It was a sweet – if unexpected – thing to say. 'Don't worry. I don't usually get compliments in my line of work.'

'I'm mortified.' He rubbed his chin self-consciously. 'I won't recover from that. I'm so sorry, Cora. Ol was always on at me to get out there again. Dive back into the murky waters of dating. *They're all around you if you open your eyes...* Not when you work in a secondary school, mate, I used to say to him.' There was the dimming of his light again, tangible grief casting a sharp shadow over the teacher. 'I still can't get used to him not being around. He was a cheeky bastard but he made life brighter, you know?'

'Was Lottie close to him?' The question emerged before Cora was aware she was saying it.

'Lots of the girls were. He'd have a little posse of them following him everywhere he went. Like a rock star. Their mams, too. A lot of the male members of staff were jealous of the mam thing. There was a kind of unofficial competition between Ol and Tom Dillinger, the Head, to see how many gushing thank you letters from mams they received at the end of the school year. They had a sweepstake in the staffroom to see who would win.' He grimaced. 'I didn't take part. Bit creepy to be hitting on school mams, I reckon.'

'I'm not sure how I'd feel knowing that was going on,' Cora observed.

'Like I said, Ol could be a bastard. But I don't know, he kind of got away with it because he cared about the kids and the school so much.'

Had O'Sullivan crossed a line with one of the school mums? Could a jealous partner have been responsible for his murder? It sounded extreme but maybe it was a line of enquiry Minshull could use. She would call him later and relay what Draycott had revealed about his friend's questionable idea of fun.

'When are you next seeing Lottie?' Draycott asked.

'Today, at four-thirty. As Dr Noakes discussed with you, it's best we don't tell Lottie we've met. I don't want her thinking we're colluding behind her back.'

'Absolutely.' He stood, fixing his bag over his shoulder. 'Cora, could we do this again? This isn't a hit, I promise – I've just found it a huge help talking about Lottie. I want to do anything I can to help her. She's a great kid and she seems to trust me. But you're the expert and I would really value your opinion.'

It would certainly be useful to find out what Lottie was sharing with her teacher on their walks together – the clues from that may help Cora's own investigations. And it had been a pleasant lunch – awkward compliments aside. 'Yes,' she smiled back, 'I'd like that.'

Back in her car, parked on a side road not far from St Audrey High, Cora sent Minshull a message.

Can we have a quick chat tonight?
I just met Andrew Draycott from St Audrey's.
He told me some things about Oliver O'Sullivan
I think you need to know.
C x

Chapter Thirty-Four

Minshull

There was a strange atmosphere in the CID office today. Minshull half wondered if he'd walked in on the aftermath of an argument. Bennett, Ellis and Evans were hunched over their keyboards, none of the usual jokes or banter passing between them. Wheeler, over by the boiling kettle, shrugged at Minshull when they made eye contact across the eerily quiet office.

Perhaps the weight of the case and the shock of the attack at Abbot's Farm were lying heavy on the team's shoulders. Minshull felt it, too, but his visit to St Audrey's yesterday had galvanised his resolve. Knowing the truth surrounding O'Sullivan's not-so-compassionate leave was a significant step forward.

He'd gone over the files sent to him by Veronica Sutton last night, reading into the early hours. Even in the heavily edited official version of events, the evidence was damning. Two formal complaints had been lodged by the parents of the two young girls, including harrowing handwritten statements by Amy and Bindi regarding O'Sullivan's actions towards them.

Seeing the disgusting details described in the hopeful, expansive handwriting of fourteen-year-old girls was a double injustice: reading them had brought Minshull to tears. Bad enough that it happened, but the school's subsequent action was abuse in itself. The minutes of the governors' meeting revealed the fervour with which those in charge had closed ranks against the girls. An assertion was made – and, tellingly, never countered by anyone present – that the girls' refusal to go to the police was proof they were lying. On the basis of this, it seemed, the decision was made to bury the complaints.

There had been two further letters from the parents to the school, demanding that O'Sullivan be sacked for his actions, then nothing. No copy of a reply from the school, no solicitor's advice, no notes of any disciplinary action taken against O'Sullivan. The final items in the online record were two signed declarations from the parents confirming that both girls were moving to another school.

Today he planned to phone both families. He didn't relish the prospect. But fire burned in his belly: the call of justice in the face of a catalogue of wrongs.

'Tea, Sarge.' Wheeler handed him his Ipswich Town mug. At least he seemed brighter today.

'Take a seat, Dave,' Minshull said. 'Let's have a chat, yeah?'

Wheeler glanced over his shoulder. 'Thought you'd never ask. Place is like a morgue today, only with less chatter.'

He pulled a chair over and sat next to Minshull.

'How are you doing?' Minshull asked, careful to keep his voice at a level the other detectives wouldn't hear over the stab of their keyboards.

'Better,' Wheeler replied. 'I went to see Steph yesterday.'

'How is she?'

'She called me a soppy git for crying when we found her.' He shook his head. 'She's badly shaken up, though. Denying it, of course, but that's Steph.'

'Can she remember anything else about the thugs in the van?'

'Hoods and balaclavas, grey and black clothing, no labels. They knew what they were doing. Two of them carrying buckets of blood, the rest armed with bottles and anything they could grab from the farmyard. She and Rilla were inside the barn when the van pulled up. They thought it was the support van come back to relieve them. Bastards were on them before they had a chance.'

'We'll find them.'

'We might not.' He blew out his frustration. 'What worries me is what comes next. They know they won. Did you hear what Drew said? It's all over their page today: reposts of *The Sentinel's* report with comments disabled, then a post claiming police victimisation.

Maitland and Butler are the heroes of the hour, as we predicted. No mention of the caution we issued them with, though. Funny, that.'

'*Shit!*'

Les Evans's loud voice summoned everyone's attention.

'What?' Minshull was out of his chair, crossing the floor.

'Our friendly neighbourhood fascists just posted this…' He pivoted his monitor so that the fast-gathering members of the CID team could see.

TRUTH UNCOVERED:

Don't mourn Oliver O'Sullivan.

The murdered teacher was a KNOWN PAEDOPHILE, allowed to abuse vulnerable CHILDREN in TWO SCHOOLS.

King Edward's Academy in Birmingham

St Audrey High School in Woodbridge.

The Bures Bowmen believe in TRUTH and JUSTICE.

Spread the word. These schools ALLOWED ABUSE and buried complaints. We believe they are harbouring more paedophiles.

'When was it posted?' Minshull demanded, the office growing darker around him as the team processed the news.

'Thirty minutes ago.'

'Too long. Why is nobody monitoring them? Have the news agencies got it yet?'

Ellis and Bennett were already checking their phones. Minshull saw their faces fall before they replied.

'The *Sentinel's* got it already.'

'No…'

'Sky News is running a breaking news scroll under its live feed.'

Minshull covered his face with his hands. 'Bollocks.'

'Sarge. A Woodbridge community group just named the girls on Facebook. *Daily Call* has mentioned the group's name but not the girls. But anyone clicking through will find it.'

'*What?*'

There was a crash as Anderson's door almost came off its hinges, the DI thundering into the office. 'Take it down!'

'Guv.' Ellis scurried back to his desk, picking up the phone.

Incensed, Anderson turned to Minshull, hands wide. 'How the hell?'

'I don't know, Guv.'

It was Rhian Butler. It had to be. Released with her charges dropped and a caution issued, she had used the one weapon she'd found effective while in custody, to devastating effect. Minshull thought of the phone calls he'd planned to make this morning and felt sick. 'I need to call the families now.'

'Do it. I want all mentions of this taken down from the news sites and social media.' Anderson stabbed at Evans's screen. 'And get those bastards suspended.'

—

They were too late. By the time the post naming the victims had been removed, the revelation had been copied and shared everywhere.

Bindi Henderson-Aziz's number rang out with no reply. Amy Godwit's mother answered her phone on Minshull's fourth attempt, her voice shaking with anger when she spoke. 'You've got a nerve. My phone is ringing off the hook with journalists. I have people outside my house. Amy is stuck at school because they turned up there, too.'

'Mrs Godwit, I can arrange for our uniformed officers to pick Amy up from school...'

'And have her arrive home in a cop car with hundreds of flashes going off? No thanks. Your lot didn't want to get involved in the first place.'

'What? Who told you that?'

'Mr Dillinger. Said the school called it in but the police weren't interested.'

I'm going to nail his nuts to the wall, Minshull vowed. 'Mrs Godwit, it was never passed to us.'

'But he said…' Her voice faded. Beyond it, Minshull could hear muffled shouts from outside her home. 'He said you'd seen the statements and refused to take it further.'

Minshull felt sick. 'The school covered it up. I intend to throw the book at them. But if I could just talk to you and Amy…'

'No.'

'I want to hold them to account. But I need to know exactly what happened.'

'I won't have her going over it again. Not for you or anyone.'

'Amy's testimony would be confidential. It would be safe with us.'

'*Safe?* My daughter hasn't been safe for eighteen months! First *that man* abused her, several times, and then she was accused of lying by that bloody school. Then the police didn't get involved and Amy thought you didn't believe her, either. Even when we moved her to her new school, she blamed herself. My daughter died the day *that man* put his hands on her. And you want to drag it all up again, just 'cos you look bad for not knowing your murdered man was a paedophile? You don't get to play with our lives to look good.'

'Mrs Godwit…'

'Leave us alone!'

Minshull sat back as the line went dead, staring at the receiver. How had the school persuaded Amy and Bindi's parents that the police weren't interested in the crimes committed against them? It made the memory of those two earnest, heart-breaking testimonies, written with all faith that they would be believed and acted upon, even more horrific. South Suffolk CID had failed them without ever having had a chance – all because a head teacher and his co-conspirators at St Audrey High would rather destroy two of its children's lives than dispense with a teacher that might benefit the school.

It was too much. He had to get out.

Grabbing his jacket and phone, head bowed, he made for the door.

'Rob.'

Almost out of the office, Minshull closed his eyes, allowing himself a steadying breath before turning back to face Anderson. 'Guv.'

'The post is gone from the Bures Bowmen's page. From the community page that named those poor girls, too. Takedown notices have been issued for all the media outlets and social sites who linked to it.' His eyes narrowed. 'And you are coming for a walk with me.'

The very last person Minshull wanted a heart-to-heart with was his superior officer. But if he remained in the office any longer, he might lose control completely. It welled within him, anger and injustice, a threatening tide. Nobody in the team needed to see that, especially not today with the heavy air in the room. With no argument left to offer, he simply nodded and followed Anderson out.

They walked in silence down the grey corridor to the stairs, Anderson's glances back as he held doors open for Minshull oddly comforting, although Minshull couldn't say why. They hadn't been the closest of allies, even back when Minshull was still a DC, but the missing child case had changed that. While they would never be friends outside of work, there was an understanding between them. Minshull supposed that was what was at work now.

Instead of heading for the station canteen, as Minshull had expected, Anderson opened a side door and led him outside. They crossed the car park and carried on, walking through the gate and out into Ipswich town centre. It was a mild, cloudy but bright day with the softest whisper of a breeze that met them between the buildings as they moved through the streets.

Minshull followed the DI, bewildered but unwilling to stop.

'Where are we going?' he asked, at last, when they had walked several streets with no sign of Anderson stopping.

'For a walk,' Anderson replied, as if impromptu tours of the town were common CID behaviour. 'As I said.'

'Guv...'

'Shut up and walk.'

Did all Caledonian-born coppers stride like that? Minshull considered himself fit, but keeping in step with his superior was proving a struggle.

'Okay, am I in trouble?'

They had drawn level with a former Methodist chapel, its windows boarded with builder's screens and a large banner draped across its front announcing the imminent availability of luxury apartments. Anderson groaned and stopped abruptly by its front steps and pillared entrance.

'Why would you assume you were? Come on, Rob, you know me better than that.'

All he had wanted was ten minutes in the silence of his car, a chance to make some sense of what he'd heard and channel his horror into action. High-speed walks and cryptic conversations with his boss wouldn't help him do either.

'I just needed some air,' he said.

'I saw your face, son. You needed more than that.'

He could deny it. Assure his boss he was fine and head back to the station. But Anderson knew. What was the point in pretending he was wrong?

'The school lied to Amy Godwit and Bindi Henderson-Aziz. They made them put their allegations in writing, told them they were speaking to us on their behalf and left them waiting a week while they worked out a plan to bury the story. Then they told the girls and their parents that the police didn't believe the allegations and wouldn't investigate.'

'What the—Why?'

Minshull slumped against a stone pillar. 'Because if the families believed the police weren't interested they wouldn't try to report it themselves. It was an insurance policy. The school abused trust – on *every* level...' Hot tears welled and Minshull didn't stop them. 'They made us complicit in their lie. And we became abusers by association. It's... It's evil.'

Anderson's frown deepened as he witnessed Minshull's struggle. He hesitated, then reached out to clamp a firm hand on his shoulder. 'We'll get them for this.'

'It doesn't help those kids. Or the others...'

'Others?'

Minshull stabbed at his eyes with the sleeve of his jacket. 'Rhian Butler said they were watching other teachers at the school. The Bures Bowmen's post today said it, too.'

'What do you think?'

'At this point, I don't know.' He took a full, shuddering breath, the swell of emotion beginning to ebb.

Anderson fell silent beside him, the two men watching a cloud of starlings bobbing and weaving above them, following the line of the street. Minshull could have kicked himself for granting his superior a glimpse behind the careful mask he always wore at work.

'If you need some time...'

'No.'

'I'm just saying.'

'I need to be here.'

Anderson nodded. 'Just keep talking, okay? To me, to Cora.' When Minshull looked at him, the DI offered a smile. 'I know what she means to you.'

'It isn't...'

'Not my business either way. But keep talking, Rob. Silence damages. You know I know what I'm talking about.'

'Guv.'

'Whatever you need on Feldspar, you've got it. Anything. I'll square it with Sue Taylor.'

An unexpected sparkle of mischief presented itself to Minshull. 'Don't you mean *Detective Chief Inspector* Sue Taylor, Guv?'

Anderson gave a wry smile that took years off him. 'Trust me, kid, when we're out of the station she's *just* Sue Taylor.'

Minshull laughed despite the heaviness in his body. 'If word ever gets out...'

'Then we're quits.' He held out his hand.

Minshull shook it. 'Apparently so.'

Chapter Thirty-Five

Cora

> Hey you
> If you're going to see Lottie this afternoon, check the news first.
> Let me know if Lottie's seen it and what her reaction is.
> Anything she mentions could be important.
> OK to call you around ten p.m. tonight? Going to be a LONG one here.
> Let me know. Rob

Sitting in her car on the drive outside Fourwinds, Cora thanked her stars that she'd thought to check her phone before going in to see Lottie. She clicked on a news website and her hand flew to her mouth.

It was the lead story, the lurid details piling up with her growing horror, the implications for Lottie, her friends and the school unfathomably dark.

Amy Godwit and Bindi Henderson-Aziz had been mentioned in the initial list of Lottie's friends compiled by Tris Noakes when Lottie was first referred ten months ago, but weren't included in the round of interviews of her closest friends six months into the investigations. Someone had pencilled *No longer at school* next to their names. Now it made sense.

Cora had arrived at Fourwinds thinking she had a clearer picture of her young charge. Meeting her teacher had seemed an important forward step, an significant ally secured for her investigations. But the damning revelations scrolling on her phone screen cast doubt on everything. Did Andrew Draycott know about Oliver O'Sullivan's history, or his association with young female students they had both taught?

Everything Draycott had told her in the bright and welcoming café a few hours ago had suggested he was unaware. But what if he knew and still supported O'Sullivan? If the school had buried reports of abuse as the news story suggested, had Draycott been part of the conspiracy?

While she tried to formulate a plan of action, Cora sent a reply back to Minshull.

> Hi Rob
> I've just seen it. Amy and Bindi were mentioned in Lottie's notes as her friends but they were listed as having moved schools.
> I don't know how much she knows, if anything. I'll let you know.
> Ten p.m. is fine. Don't think I'll be sleeping much tonight.

Cora paused, her finger hovering above the screen. Should she ask? She thought of the detective sergeant faced with the unfolding horrors, arriving fast on the heels of the terrible attack on his colleagues. Typing quickly, she added:

> Are you okay? If you want to talk, I'm here.
> C x

Heart thudding, she pressed *Send* and stuffed her phone into her bag.

Monica Arundel seemed unaware of the scandal breaking over South Suffolk as she welcomed Cora in. She was calmer than Cora had seen her before, talking all the way upstairs and across the room to her daughter.

'Lotts, Cora's here.'

One moment.

She was holding her phone in both hands, her fingers moving furiously over the keypad. Her tablet rested on her knees where she sat cross-legged in the middle of the white set of sofas. A curtain of dark hair fell around her hands as she typed.

'Phone away, please,' Monica began but Cora stopped her, an idea forming. Monica would hear the news sooner or later, and her reaction could make or break the progress Cora had made with Lottie. If Cora told her first, she had a hope of managing Monica's response.

'Actually, I couldn't trouble you for a drink, could I?' she offered. 'I haven't stopped all day.'

Monica glanced at her daughter, then smiled. 'Of course. We have regular tea or I have some new herbal teas a friend recommended?'

'Tell you what, why don't you show me?'

'Oh. Okay. Lottie, I'm just taking Cora to choose a new tea.'

They taste like dust and despair.

Cora smiled over at the teenager, glad of a moment of lightness in the face of what was coming. 'Thanks for the warning. I'll take my chances.'

In the kitchen, Monica pulled a wooden box with a glass lid down from an overhead cupboard. Inside, colourfully wrapped tea bags lined up in neat rows within nine square compartments.

Of course they did, Cora thought to herself, wondering what Tris Noakes would make of this new height of organisational control. Even the teabags obediently fell into line under Monica Arundel's hand.

How would the chaos of the news be received in her ordered world?

Cora waited until the mugs were filled, colour bleeding from the chosen teabags into the freshly boiled water. Steeling herself, she lowered her voice, turning her back on the living area and Lottie.

'There's been a development.'

'With Lottie?'

Cora kicked herself for the hope in Monica's eyes. 'No, not with Lottie, although I met her teacher today and we've worked out a strategy moving forward.'

'Then what?'

'It appears… There are allegations in the news. They're saying Oliver O'Sullivan had a history of inappropriate behaviour towards students. Specifically, teenage girls.'

Monica gripped the edge of the white marble island. 'Who's saying this?'

'A Facebook group broke the story—'

'Oh well, *Facebook*…'

'—and the school has admitted complaints were made. I'm so sorry to bring this to you but I thought you should hear it from me.'

Lottie's mother was frowning. 'What has this to do with us?'

'The two girls who made allegations – and subsequently left the school – were Lottie's friends. Amy and Bindi?'

'But they were… No, they've got it wrong. Bindi's mother said they were moving because her husband got a new job. Her new school was closer. Kids move all the time. The girls were about to start their GCSEs; it was the last time they could feasibly move before that work kicked in…' She was piling up caveats and contingencies in the face of the speeding train of realisation, her eyes already comprehending the truth that her mouth was so busy denying.

Cora placed her hand gently on Monica's, talking slowly and carefully to her as if she were a child. 'It's important you know so that we can be there to support Lottie when she finds out. In her vulnerable state, a shock like this could undo everything we've worked to achieve.'

'Is it true? Did Oliver hurt those girls?'

'I don't know for sure. But it looks possible. There was a previous allegation at his last school.'

Monica's eyes closed. 'What do we do? How do we tell her?'

Cora looked back at the teenager who was still stabbing at her phone screen. 'If her friends are hearing the news now, it's possible she already knows. The important thing is that we let her process the news in her own way. I'm here, you're here, so she knows she's not alone. But we have to give her license to find her own response. Whatever she does, we go with it, okay?'

'I can't…' She breathed, leaning heavily against the kitchen island. 'Not this. Not now, on top of everything…'

'I know. I understand. You're not alone, either, Monica. I am here as much for you as I am for Lottie.'

Monica blinked at her. 'You are?'

'Of course.'

'That means a lot.' She took a deep, shuddering breath. 'So what do we...?'

Cora picked up the mugs and handed one to Monica. 'We have our tea, we chat, and we take it from there. If Lottie wants to go out, I'll take her; if she needs company, we'll both stay close in here.'

Monica nodded, gripping her mug with both hands. 'I'm glad you're here, Cora.'

Lottie looked up when her mother and Cora sat down. Her expression was difficult to read: had she heard the news? Was it a shock or did she already know O'Sullivan's secret?

'Busy day?' Cora asked, nodding at the phone in Lottie's hands.

I saw the news. Everyone's seen it.

'Oh my darling.' Monica's face crumpled and she reached out to her daughter, her hand not quite making contact.

I'm okay.

'Do you want to talk about it?' Cora asked.

The breaths swelled around Lottie in a protective cloud of air.

If you want to talk about it I don't mind.

'Did you know?' Monica asked, fear filling her question. 'I mean, were there rumours?'

I heard stuff, early on. I thought it was lies.

Lottie let her gaze travel from her mother to Cora.

I can't believe they named Amy and Bindi. Why would they do that?

'They don't care about people,' Cora replied. 'They just want to break the news before anyone else.'

It's not on there now. But everyone knows.

Cora decided to push her luck. 'Have you heard from your friends?'

A shake of Lottie's head.

They're offline.

'Not surprising, really. Those poor girls...' Monica's eyes welled and she looked down at her tea. 'Look, Lotts, unless you need me to

246

stay, I think it best you talk to Cora about this. I won't be much help, I'm afraid.'

Her daughter slid her hand across the white linen sofa to curl around her mother's.

That's fine. Why don't you go for a walk? It might help.

Monica smiled as she wiped her eyes. 'That's what I'm supposed to say to you.'

I learned from the best.

Cora watched regard pass between them before Monica left. When they were alone, she took a breath and faced Lottie.

'I'm going to be completely straight with you. I know the detective who is going to be investigating this. If your friends want to talk to someone, in complete confidence, I can give you his details to pass on.'

You know a detective?

'I do.'

Do you fancy him?

Cora laughed with surprise. 'Lottie!'

A slow smile became visible behind the dark veil of hair.

Men in uniform. I hear it's a thing.

'Not my thing. And he doesn't wear a uniform.'

So you do fancy him.

'You're impossible.'

You like me for it.

'You're right, I do.'

Lottie flicked a handful of hair over the top of her head, revealing her face. Red blotches edged the lower lids of her eyes as if she had recently been crying.

Why do men do that? Go for kids?

The question hit like a rock. 'I don't know. I'm not sure I want to know. It's control, it's a sexual urge… And unfortunately it's been hidden and ignored by society for a long time. Plus the men doing it can often believe it's reciprocated, when it isn't and could never be. They can be charming, excellent at their jobs, good at drawing people in. That's why it's such a battle for survivors to find justice.'

It's messed up.

'It is.' Cora observed Lottie, picking her next words with utmost care. 'Did Amy or Bindi talk to you when it was happening?'

Lottie stared back. Her fingers remained still beside the tablet.

'You don't have to tell me.'

I thought I could trust him.

Cora's heart went out to her. 'You should have been able to.'

I wish…

Cora waited but Lottie had stopped typing. 'What do you wish?'

The teenager bit her lip, eyes trained on Cora.

'What do you wish, sweetheart?'

The breath sentries returned, surrounding Lottie, weaving layer upon layer around her, binding her words. Cora waited, heart in mouth, not wanting to break the moment in case something more arrived. Then Lottie sagged, her head turning to the window, the tablet slipping from her knee onto the sofa.

I wish… the words repeated. But this time a human voice spoke them. Lottie's voice.

Cora looked at the teenager's lips but they weren't moving. Heart pounding, she switched her focus to the tablet, lying untouched by Lottie for the first time. Cora willed volume into the voice attached, tuning her mind to its frequency.

I wish… it said again.

Cora pressed in.

I wish… Gil…

Gil. The sudden arrival of the word Lottie had withheld rocked Cora.

'What do you wish, Lottie?' she asked again, willing her to respond. Breath held, she watched the teenager's fingers reach for the tablet, lift it back onto her lap and start to move.

It wasn't just Bindi and Amy.

'What?'

There were others. Things you don't know.

Was Lottie saying she was one of them?

'You can tell me, if you want to,' Cora said, being careful to speak softly.

There's so much you don't know.

'So tell me. I can help.'

It's not my story to tell.

What did any of it mean? Was Gil another of O'Sullivan's victims? Had they all sworn Lottie to secrecy?

Cora edged closer, her mind gently calling to the space where Gil's name had been. 'You don't have to carry this alone. I'm here for you.'

Lottie turned from the window.

Nobody understands.

'I'm trying to. Let me help you.'

Trust is hard for me. I want to trust, but I'm scared.

'I'm not going anywhere, Lottie. I'm here, for as long as you need me.'

I need to think about this.

It was a rapidly closing door, but Cora pressed on. 'Take all the time you need. I'm here whenever you want to talk.'

Thank you. For not being shocked.

Cora felt the moment leave; relieved, for now, that it had passed. 'I can't say I wasn't shocked to hear about what your teacher had done. But you are entitled to your response, Lottie. Whatever it is, it's right for you. You have my support all the way.'

—

As soon as she left Fourwinds she called Tris to inform him of Lottie's revelation. From now on, they would both monitor any further information the teenager offered. Without specifics it was impossible to move on it, but every word noted would add to the evidence they could bring. It was frustrating, but they had to wait until Lottie or one of her friends disclosed more.

It was still heavy on Cora's mind later that evening as she wrote up her notes. Lunch and Andrew Draycott seemed a lifetime away as she recalled their meeting. Everything he'd talked about that had seemed so positive nine hours ago was tainted now with suspicion

249

and unanswered questions. He'd mentioned Lottie's friends Bindi and Amy, dismissing Lottie's anger about their leaving school as the words of an overdramatic teen. She recalled his observation about O'Sullivan having '*a little posse*' of girls '*following him everywhere he went. Like a rock star*'. And worst of all, O'Sullivan's remark that Draycott had relayed about potential love interests – '*They're all around you if you open your eyes*' – became a sinister mandate for O'Sullivan's actions.

It all indicated a man operating without boundaries, laughed with and egged on by envious male colleagues, while his victims were joked about, talked over and dismissed.

And there were more girls, the secrets of whom Lottie had seemingly appointed herself sole silent keeper.

Was Gil one of them?

Was Lottie?

Cora didn't want to consider the possibility, but a sudden change in character, the withdrawing, the silence – all were classic indicators of abuse.

Had Oliver O'Sullivan stolen Lottie's voice when he abused her trust?

Hating the growing evidence on her laptop screen, she pushed it away and left the table to go into the kitchen.

She was just filling a glass with water when her mobile rang. Abandoning her drink, she hurried back into the living room to answer the call.

'I haven't woken you, have I?' Minshull asked. He sounded tired, his voice low and the words requiring effort.

'No. I'm still working.'

'That makes two of us.'

'You're still at the office?'

'No.' She could hear a yawn and imagined Minshull's weary stretch. 'I brought it home with a takeaway but I'm not making much progress on either.'

Cora looked at her abandoned bowl of pasta, cold and congealing next to her laptop. 'Ditto. How's it going?'

'Apart from a murder victim being a monster, a school covering up abuse, vigilantes attacking my colleagues and the media gunning for us on all counts, pretty well.'

'It's horrible.'

'Yeah, it is. I'd say occupational hazard, but all this at once is – it's something else.'

'I can't imagine what that's like.' Cora moved to her favourite armchair by the window. The moon was rising over the ink-black waters of North Beach, a silvery trail dancing from horizon to shore. An oncoming wind rattled at her windows as if impatient to get inside. She drew a blanket over her knees. 'How's everyone in the team?'

'Angry. Scared. Dave's veering between trying to joke and sinking into brooding silence. Kate and Drew are both quiet. Even Les is lying low.'

'And Joel?'

She heard the brush of a laugh from Minshull's side of the call. 'Joel is remarkably upbeat, considering.'

'And you?' It felt a risk to ask, as it had when she'd sent the message earlier.

There was a pause. Cora immediately wished she hadn't asked him.

'Honestly? Not good. I'll get there, but I need someone to be straight with me to kick off the process. How did it go with Andrew Draycott? You said he mentioned something I should know?'

Cora gazed out at the moon. 'He was talking about Oliver O'Sullivan. They were great friends and Andrew idolised him a bit, I think. He was saying O'Sullivan always had a posse of teenage girls around him and that the mums loved him, too. He sounds like he was charismatic, using charm to draw people to him.'

'Classic signs of an abuser.'

'I don't want to think that, but you're right. Andrew said some of the staff ran an unofficial sweepstake at the end of each school year to guess which male teacher would receive the most glowing thank you letters from school mums.'

'What? That's horrible!'

'I know. But if there was a culture like that openly accepted in St Audrey's, it makes you wonder what was tolerated in private. And the news story today just seems to confirm it.'

'What did you make of Draycott? Do you think he was part of it?'

It was a question that had bitten at Cora all day. 'He seemed genuinely embarrassed about the sweepstake thing and O'Sullivan's cavalier attitude to women. Before I found out the other stuff I thought he was nice. Open, friendly; he cares about Lottie a great deal and he's determined to help her... I liked him. I *want* to like him...'

'But?'

'I just don't know.' She braced herself for what had to be said next. 'Lottie knows Bindi and Amy.'

She could almost hear Minshull sitting to attention. 'She does?'

'They are listed in her early notes as close friends, although once they left the school they don't feature in her files. But she's still in touch. I told Lottie I know you and. if the girls wanted to talk, you would be there for them. I hope that was okay?'

'I appreciate that, thanks. Not that it'll do any good. The families don't want anything to do with it, quite rightly. Did Lottie say anything about O'Sullivan?'

The wind had picked up beyond the window, the approaching storm sending its first angry splats of rain to pepper the glass. Cora closed her eyes, remembering the first words she'd heard in Lottie's voice.

'She knew about Bindi and Amy. She said there were others.'

'She said that?'

'Yes. While I've been working with her I haven't been able to hear her voices from her belongings as I usually would. Just intakes of breath. And there was a word I sensed at the centre of it. It's taken a while to retrieve it. When it appeared, it was a name: Gil. When I was with her today I heard it again, and then Lottie said it wasn't just Bindi and Amy. There were others.'

'Gil?'

'That's right. So I was wondering, is there anyone in Lottie's class, or maybe a year above or below, who might have been known as Gil?'

'Wait a minute…'

Cora heard the soft bursts of Minshull's breath against her ear as he stood and moved across his apartment. 'I have a list of student names the school sent across…' The sound of a zip being drawn back, sheets of paper rustling. 'Hang on, here it is. Gil… Gil… *Shit.*'

'What is it?'

'Laura Gilchrist, same year as Lottie, different form.'

'Would she have been taught by O'Sullivan?'

'She isn't listed in any of his English classes…' Minshull was breathless on the other end of the call, as more paper flicked near the receiver. Cora imagined the knot at the centre of his brows that appeared whenever he was concentrating. She pictured the swift motion of his hands; that drive he could tap into at will sending his body in motion. Then a long, slow exhale. 'She's on the list of his after-school theatre clubs. Dance captain.'

Dance captain. A position of authority within the club. Someone considered to be closer to O'Sullivan. Someone he might conceivably spend extra time with…

Cora turned cold. 'It fits.'

Minshull groaned. '*More of them.* That's what the leader of the vigilante group claimed when we arrested her on Tuesday.'

'Arrested? So you got the people who attacked Steph?'

'No. Not yet. She's more of a general, keeping her hands clean, way back behind the frontline. We had to release her. But the post today on their Facebook page alleged the same thing.'

'More kids.'

'More kids. It stinks.'

'It does. If O'Sullivan had carte blanche to operate, it could mean countless more girls were harmed. He got away with it at his former school and he was allowed to get away with it at St Audrey's. He must have thought he was invincible.'

'And egged on by Draycott and the male teachers.'

'I don't think Andrew knew,' Cora countered, not really sure why she wanted Andrew Draycott to be innocent.

'He must have seen stuff, even if he didn't agree with it. And he should have said something.'

'You're right.'

'Are you seeing him again?'

'I said I would, but now…'

'No, carry on. He's obviously close to Lottie and he might tell you things he wouldn't tell us if he feels protective of the kid.'

Cora didn't know how to feel about this. But she could see how spending more time with Andrew could help both Lottie and Minshull, and maybe give her the answers she was seeking. 'Okay. I'll keep you posted.'

'Thanks, that's brilliant. It means a lot that you're helping… It means a lot to me.'

'Thank you.' She felt suddenly awkward, the silence between them packed with questions neither were prepared to address. 'I should probably let you go.'

'Yeah. I should let you get back to it, too. Who knows, if we crack on we stand a chance of being in bed by midnight. Ah, I-I mean…'

'Sleep would be good,' she replied, a smile accompanying her rescue of him.

'Yes it would. Listen, I hate to ask, but if there were other girls abused…' Cora heard the pause; hated that she knew what was coming. '…could Lottie be one of them?'

Fear gripped her chest. It was the unspoken, unavoidable question she had wrestled since her visit to Fourwinds.

'I don't want to believe it. But I think she might be.'

Chapter Thirty-Six

Anderson

Anderson had just stepped out of the shower when he heard the shrill bark of his phone from the bedroom.

'Damn it,' he muttered, flinging a towel about himself and dripping water and soap suds across the bathroom tiles and over the bedroom carpet.

'You're in demand this morning.'

Rosalyn Anderson was holding his phone in bed, wearing nothing but a smile. Bloody hell, she was stunning… Tempted to switch off his phone and steal another ten minutes with his wife, Anderson accepted it, his good humour vaporising when he saw the caller ID.

'I have to take this,' he apologised, cursing the universe that the call he'd waited days for should choose to arrive now.

'It can wait,' Ros chuckled, pulling the duvet back around her. She had been married to a policeman long enough to know the deal. 'Question is, can you?'

Grinning at her, Anderson answered the call.

'DI Anderson? DCI Stephens from Essex Police. Good morning.'

It would be, Anderson grumbled to himself, *if you hadn't picked now to call*. 'Ma'am, hello. Do you have news?'

'He's in. But time is not our friend. Is there any way you can get to us today? Preferably before twelve?'

Anderson ran through his options. It was almost seven a.m. A train journey would mean at least two changes, the line notorious for delays and replacement buses. It could take two hours, or four. Driving would be quicker: around an hour and a half if he was lucky.

'I can do that,' he replied.

'Excellent. As soon as you can, please. We have eighteen hours to interview him and a lot to get through besides your questions. I'll have one of my officers meet you at the front desk.'

'Thank you. I'm on my way.'

—

After a journey made more nail-biting by roadworks on the road out of St Just and a diversion off the A12, Anderson arrived at the imposing headquarters of Essex Police in Chelmsford.

There had been an opportunity, fifteen years ago, that might have seen him move here, which would have meant an early promotion to DI from his then DS rank. He'd aced the interview and even taken Ros on a drive around the Essex countryside scouting for potential areas to live. Maldon had been a favourite, with its pretty high street rising from the River Blackwater and impressive, red-sailed Thames Barges moored up by the quay. But his then superior – Rob Minshull's father, celebrated hero of South Suffolk Constabulary and all-round nasty scrote – had insisted he stay in Ipswich, promising him career opportunities that never materialised until the old sod retired.

Arriving back, after so many years, Anderson realised this was the only thing he would ever be grateful to John Minshull for. Essex would have been a good challenge, but Suffolk had his heart. Years after leaving his birthplace of Motherwell, southeast of Glasgow, the village of St Just and the police HQ in Ipswich were where he felt most at home.

How different his life might have been, he mused as he waited at the front desk for the officer from Fran Stephens' team to fetch him. Would he have thrived here?

'DI Anderson?'

A smartly dressed young woman was at his side, hand outstretched.

'Hello,' he said, rising to greet her.

'I'm DC Ellen Wright. I'll take you up to the team.'

They walked quickly across the building to the suite of rooms that belonged to the drugs task force. Anderson imagined his team's faces if they could see the brand new monitors, state of the art interactive whiteboards and gleaming new workstations with lower-back-friendly chairs. You could still smell fresh paint and newly laid carpet, for crying out loud. The only time the carpets in South Suffolk Police HQ were ever changed was when the splits in them became too wide for gaffer tape to hold them together.

'DI Anderson to see you, Ma'am,' Wright called around a frosted glass door and blessed Anderson with a brief smile as she walked back to her section. The outline of the DCI appeared in the glass moments before she emerged.

'Joel – welcome.' Fran Stephens said, extending her hand.

'Thanks for the call, Ma'am,' he replied, just about remembering his manners.

DCI Stephens was taller than he'd expected. Younger, too, but everyone seemed younger than him these days. In person she was far less intimidating than she had been on the phone, a smile even making an appearance now and again. Everything about her was polished, from her impeccable trouser suit and heels to the glossy chignon she wore her hair in. Anderson wasn't sure if the slick new police unit was an extension of her, or if she'd been specifically chosen to fit it. He, on the other hand, suspected he messed the place up just by standing there.

Quickly, it became apparent why Fran Stephens was kinder in person. She'd seen the news.

'How are your officers?' she asked, as they walked to the custody suite, which appeared to be accessed via a labyrinth of corridors. 'That attack was horrific.'

'Both on the mend, thankfully.'

'Vigilante groups in Suffolk,' Stephens said, shaking her head. 'And I thought our patch had it all.'

'Right now I don't know whether I prefer the drugs gangs.'

'I hear you. I heard the latest about our friend the teacher, too.'

Our friend.

The lurid details being reported by every news agency this morning made Anderson's blood boil. That man should never be *friends* with anyone.

'It's shaken everyone,' he admitted, as they came to a halt beside a wide grey door. 'As you know, we don't expect this kind of stuff on my patch.'

Stephens gave a nod of apology. 'About my comments initially...'

'Nothing I haven't heard before, Ma'am,' Anderson grinned. 'Give me tractor thieves any day. Is he in there?'

'He is. Honestly, I'm expecting No Comments but we have a little over thirteen hours left and I intend to ask him about every piece of evidence we have. My second is in with him now, going over the first round of allegations. You're up next, before we hit him with the undercover stuff.'

Anderson recognised her weariness, the result of long unblinking hours of work and waiting surrounding the arrest of a major criminal. 'It's good you got him,' he offered. 'So much work will come to fruition today.'

Stephens observed him for a moment, as if seeing Anderson afresh. 'Fourteen months is a long time when you count every minute. I'll just be pleased if we get him on any of the charges. He's been famously slippery before.'

'Best of British, Ma'am.'

'Appreciate that.'

The grey door opened and a young man peered out into the corridor. 'Ready when you are, Ma'am.'

Stephens nodded and Anderson followed her into the interview room.

Col McGann watched them enter, his tired-looking legal representative studying their every move with suspicion. No handshakes in this interview; the mood was very much established already, several hours of questioning having already been completed.

McGann appeared surprisingly fresh for a man pulled from his bed before midnight, incarcerated and questioned for hours. He was a short man, with a full head of hair and a silvering Cavalier beard at odds with the pale grey hoodie and tracksuit trousers he wore. Anderson guessed his age to be the darker side of his forties but these days it was difficult to tell. The silver greys might have been summoned prematurely, given the pressures of his current occupation.

258

Stephens nodded at the mirrored glass wall for the recording to resume and a red light came on over the interview desk. 'DCI Fran Stephens has just entered the room, DI Joel Anderson from South Suffolk Constabulary attending. DI Anderson is here, Mr McGann, to ask you specific questions relating to an unexplained death at a location we understand your operation uses.'

McGann's solicitor's head snapped up. His client made no response.

'We weren't made aware of this,' the legal representative countered.

'It's in the briefing notes you were given prior to interview,' Stephens returned, coolly. 'Page thirty-two, paragraph four.'

The solicitor scrabbled to maintain his dignity as he flicked through the notes to find the page.

Stephens waited. Anderson watched the power play with amusement.

'All good now?'

'Yes. But keep your questions relevant, DI Anderson.'

Cheeky git.

Stephens nodded for Anderson to begin. He rested his hands on his notes, not needing to read them now. He'd spent so long preparing while waiting for McGann to be arrested that he probably recited them to Ros in his sleep.

'Thank you, Ma'am.' He fixed his eye on Col McGann. 'Mr McGann, do you know this man?' He passed a photo of Oliver O'Sullivan to McGann and his solicitor.

'Sorry, no.'

'Take a closer look. This is Oliver O'Sullivan. A high school teacher, although I'm guessing neither you nor your associates would have known that. It appears he kept that information close to his chest, along with a lot of other things...' He offered the drug lord a smile. 'Not your problem, though. You'll notice from that photograph that O'Sullivan had a distinctive tattoo on his left arm. A brown velvet top hat: he liked to refer to himself as Dodge – as in, the Artful Dodger, a reference to the book his first name was inspired by. Do you recognise that?'

McGann's eyes narrowed and then he pushed the photograph back. 'No.'

'Mr O'Sullivan was involved in drug activity. We have witnesses who he tried to supply with drugs. He was murdered in an old barn at Abbot's Farm near Whatfield, Suffolk. Middle of nowhere, old abandoned farm, you get the idea. We are aware that a drug gang had been using this as a location for quite some time. What can you tell me about that?'

'No comment.'

Anderson had seen it coming, but a tiny sliver of hope had remained that McGann might do the decent thing and offer information. Right now, the two sides of Oliver O'Sullivan's life didn't quite connect. The abuse allegations had, quite rightly, eclipsed the original investigation, but what of his association with drugs? Had he kept it separate from his other illegal activities? Or would they discover drugs had played a part in his school life, too?

He pressed on regardless. He'd been granted thirty minutes and he would make the most of every one of them. 'He was found dead in the barn. He'd been injected with bleach and the back of his head was shattered by a heavy blow after he'd died. An execution, you might say. It was punishment, designed to create maximum suffering before death. We suspect he was familiar with that location. We suspect he went there to pick up a supply of drugs to sell. Why was he murdered, Mr McGann?'

'No comment.'

'What you might not know about Mr O'Sullivan is that he's currently hit the headlines for a second time in as many weeks, only this time because it's alleged he abused young girls in his care at two schools. We have the names of three victims; we believe there to be more.'

Anderson caught a flicker in McGann's expression. He pressed his advantage.

'Fourteen-year-old girls, subjected to a catalogue of sustained abuse. And then, to add insult, silenced by their school and forced to leave. Disbelieved. Discarded.'

McGann's head turned a little, his eyes seeking counsel from his shocked solicitor.

Anderson went for broke. 'I want justice for those kids as much as I want to find his killer. But unless I know more about Oliver O'Sullivan, those victims may well be failed again.'

Was it enough? McGann had much more to lose if he co-operated because to confirm his operation had control of Abbot's Farm would be to confirm the testimony of the undercover officers who'd hidden in his gang for over a year.

Anderson waited, Stephens silent beside him.

McGann reached for his plastic cup of water and took a long, slow sip. He placed it back, Anderson spotting the merest hint of a tremble in his little finger.

'I'm not saying I knew him,' he began, nodding at his surprised solicitor. 'But I heard things.'

'Mr McGann, are you certain…?'

'On this, George. Not the rest.' He looked at Anderson. 'I will deny the rest because the charges are plainly wrong, but I won't go down for that scum.'

'Talk to me.'

McGann chewed his tongue for a moment, getting the measure of the DI. 'He was a liability. Got in too deep and thought he was a kingpin. I heard he kept asking for Rohypnol – well, I don't condone that. And neither do my associates. I have kids myself, DI Anderson. Two girls. I worry for them.'

Odd to have morals on one drug but none on everything else, Anderson mused, but he'd seen it many times during his police career. The gentlemen's agreements, the code of ethics – such as it was – that seasoned criminals often observed.

'But he was dealing?'

'So I heard. But pretty soon his handler told him to get lost. That was months ago, I believe.'

'We have witnesses saying he was trying to palm off large quantities of cocaine on anyone he thought might have the means to buy.'

McGann shrugged. 'That's what happens, I hear.'

'What happens?'

'I've heard that bastards like him take out a big order, think they can shift it, fail to find buyers but still owe for what they bought. Interest, too. Like with any transaction of goods, I assume.'

'How much did he owe?'

'I didn't deal with him, so I don't know.'

'But it would be significant?'

McGann shrugged again.

Stephens looked pointedly at the wall clock. Anderson would have to cut to the chase or risk running out of time.

'Did you kill Oliver O'Sullivan?'

'No.'

'Did one of your associates kill him?'

'No.'

'Then why was he there?'

'Bottom line is, he shouldn't have been. I hear that operations at that location had moved on, months ago. Not that they were my responsibility,' he added, careful to cover his back. 'But I am not having his murder dropped at my door. I did not murder that man. I did not order his execution. But I would shake the hand of the man who did.'

'That's our time,' DCI Stephens announced, nodding at the glass. 'Interview paused at twelve-thirty p.m. Mr Rovira, do you require a recess before we start again?'

'I think that would be wise,' the solicitor said, hurriedly gathering his notes together.

'Thank you, sir,' Anderson said, meaning it.

McGann gave a nod. 'You nail the bastards that let him get away.'

Anderson never expected to find common ground with Col McGann, but there it was. 'I intend to, Mr McGann. You have my word on that.'

–

Fran Stephens walked Anderson to the exit, pausing at the door. 'Look, Joel, I apologise again for our first conversation. I feel we didn't make the best of starts.'

'That's okay, Ma'am. Easily done.'

'You were excellent in there,' she offered, her smile genuinely warm. 'We have him on record linking himself to the location and the operation, which is far more than we had previously and we haven't even hit him with the evidence of our undercover team yet.'

'Consider it my gift to thank you for getting me in there. Although if you have any future intelligence regarding my patch...'

'You have my assurance I'll pass it on as a priority.'

'Thank you.'

Stephens smiled and pulled a card from her jacket pocket. 'We're in the process of setting up a new unit dealing with rural crime. I've been asked to head it up. And I'll be looking to appoint.'

Anderson was aware he was staring. 'Ma'am.'

'I would be open for further conversations, if you would be interested?'

'It's very generous of you...'

'Think about it. You would be an asset here, Joel.'

Anderson chuckled all the way back to his car.

He was about to start the engine when his phone rang. 'How's it going, Guv?'

'McGann knew him but said he'd been kicked out. He shouldn't have even been at Abbot's Farm. But he talked – a lot. I think we gave the Essex lot enough to build a case. What do you have for me?'

'I spoke to Cora last night. The young girl she's working with who is a student at St Audrey High was best friends with Amy Godwit and Bindi Henderson-Aziz. She indicated more girls were involved.'

'She told Cora this?'

'In a manner of speaking. She's electively mute.'

'What?'

'Cora heard a word from one of the girl's belongings. A name: Gil. I checked the student lists and there's a Laura Gilchrist in the same year, dance captain of O'Sullivan's after-school theatre club.'

'Shit.'

'Exactly. I'm on my way to see the woman whose name I was passed by the secretary at St Audrey's – Carly Addison? She worked at the school but left because of the way Amy and Bindi's complaints were buried. I'm going to ask her about Laura, see what I can find out.'

'And Cora's client?'

He heard a rush of a sigh from Minshull. Poor kid was doing his best, but his reaction yesterday worried Anderson. Rob Minshull was famously level-headed in the face of every investigation. But tears in the street? He needed to keep a closer eye on him. He knew only too well how the job tried to destroy you.

'She stopped speaking eleven months ago. Two weeks after Amy and Bindi left St Audrey's. It's possible O'Sullivan is the cause.'

Anderson paused as he took this in. 'Find out all you can. We need to know every victim. No child left behind, Rob.'

'No child, Guv.'

Lottie

They're not answering my messages.

They must be so scared.

I hate watching it on the news. The reporters are picking over every detail like it's a freak show. Like they enjoy it. They don't care who they hurt.

Just like he didn't.

I don't think they've tracked down the girl from the Birmingham school yet, but if they found Amy and Bindi's names and addresses that easily, how long can she stay hidden?

I can't escape it.

We turned the TV off but then it kept coming up on my tablet as breaking news. It's being posted on all my socials, Facebook is full of it and it's all anyone wants to talk about in the group chat.

I can't escape *him*. Even though he's dead.

Maybe now the school will do something. Maybe Mr Dillinger and his cronies will get sacked and replaced. They should, for what they did.

I wish the girls would answer their messages. I don't know how they'll cope this time. Amy's only just started eating well again and Bindi's got a new counsellor. I want to know they're okay.

Esme is terrified. Her mum's kept her off school because she thinks the situation is getting to her. She doesn't know the half of it.

Dad was raging again last night. All the rubbish I've heard before – he's going to take me out of St Audrey's, he's going to get me home school tutors… He won't. Mum doesn't want me at home as much as I am already and Dad can't cope with either of us here.

At least now they know the truth about him. How he wasn't the hero everyone made him out to be. I just wish the news channels didn't have to drag Amy and Bindi through it all again. Like they were to blame for making him the way he was.

And that's just the names they know.

What if they find out about the others?

What if they find out about me?

Lunchtime News Report

'A murder investigation in rural Suffolk has taken a sinister turn this week. High school teacher, Oliver O'Sullivan, whose body was discovered on an abandoned farm near Whatfield in the south of the county, has now been revealed as a dangerous sex offender who preyed on young girls in two schools. Emma Jane Lambert has the latest.'

'This is Woodbridge, a pretty market town in the picturesque county of Suffolk. A favourite destination of holidaymakers in the summer, today it is a town in crisis. A teacher from this school, St Audrey High, was found murdered last week in what was suspected to be a drugs-related incident. Horrific enough, but new, shocking revelations have emerged regarding the victim, Oliver O'Sullivan, and historic child abuse offences that have rocked this town to its foundations.

'The story broke on Facebook yesterday. Local pressure group, The Bures Bowmen, posted damning accusations about Mr O'Sullivan's behaviour toward vulnerable teenage girls. Within hours those girls had been named, later retracted at the insistence of police. The school is yet to comment on the individual cases, but said this morning in a statement:

St Audrey High School is gravely concerned by the allegations posted online and in the media. The safety of our pupils is our number one priority and we will not tolerate any proven instances of abuse. The historic cases in question are under police investigation and as such would be inappropriate for us to comment upon at this time. We would like to reassure students and parents that St Audrey High School is a safe place for all.

'South Suffolk Police have confirmed that they are investigating the allegations and will be seeking prosecutions if it is found that St Audrey High covered up complaints of abuse from the two students who are no longer at the school. But the police themselves have come under fire, with two of their officers attacked at the murder scene on Monday afternoon and allegations of the force's mishandling of the serious issues of child abuse and drug gangs, to which Mr O'Sullivan is now rumoured to have also belonged.

'And this morning, a further twist: these flyers, posted across the town and in neighbouring villages, bearing the logo of the Bures Bowmen. Two words are printed underneath: SEEK JUSTICE. A spokesperson from the group was unavailable for comment today.

'One man's death has opened a Pandora's box of horrors that nobody in this tight-knit community can comprehend. And as anger grows – and vigilante action is feared – the town today is cowed beneath the threat this volatile atmosphere brings.

'Emma Jane Lambert, Lunchtime News, Woodbridge in Suffolk.'

Chapter Thirty-Seven

Minshull

'Flyers? What flyers?'

Bennett sounded tired as she read the news report on her phone. 'They look like the one left at Abbot's Farm after the attack.'

Minshull kept his eyes on the road, looking for the sign to Evernam. 'What the hell are Maitland and Butler playing at? They know we'll trace this back to them.'

'It's not specific, though. They aren't saying *against police* or *against drug gangs*. Just *seek justice*.'

'One look at their page and you know what they mean.'

Bennett rubbed her eyes. 'But they're not actually saying it. And if you ask them, they'll say it's someone piggy-backing on their logo.'

'Their *brand logo*,' Minshull replied, teeth gritted at the memory of Rhian Butler's term.

'Thugs, bigots and vigilantes. Nice brand. Where are we going again?'

'Evernam. That's where Ellis lives now, isn't it?'

Bennett seemed to bristle in the seat beside him. 'I think so.'

Minshull cast a glance at her. 'Everything all right with you two?'

'Yes. Why?'

'It's just you've been a bit off…'

'I'm tired, Sarge. And worried about all this. Me and Ellis are okay. It's just playing on everyone's mind.'

'Not sleeping well?' Minshull risked.

'Not particularly. You?'

He gave a weary smile. 'Same.' He glanced at her. 'This chat today could get heavy. I think Ms Addison might know about more kids than just Amy and Bindi.'

'I'm ready for that.'

Minshull gazed out across the tree-lined fields. 'I'm glad one of us is.'

Carly Addison lived in a converted former stable on her parents' farm on the outskirts of the large village of Evernam. The farm managed a herd of milking cows but most of its income came from the newly built creamery making traditional cheeses and ice cream. Many of the original outbuildings had been developed into holiday cottages and the site had the kind of carefree vibe so beloved of property supplements in Sunday papers, the sunny images masking the huge amount of work required to keep it all going.

She was waiting at the open stable door, watching out for their arrival. Her smile was bright, her expression anxious as she greeted them.

'Thank you for seeing us,' Minshull said, as she led them inside.

'I'm just so glad you called,' she replied, inviting them to sit on a rose-patterned sofa beside an open fireplace with a woodburner at its heart. 'I've been trying to muster the courage to contact you since the news broke.'

'Anything you can tell us will be treated in the strictest confidence,' Minshull reassured her. 'And it really will help us.'

'Okay. What do you want to know?'

Minshull and Wheeler settled, notebooks ready, a plan they had agreed during the journey over: *find out what she knows, and then ask about the others*. Specifically, Laura Gilchrist and Lottie Arundel.

'How long did you work at St Audrey's?'

'Just under five years. I started as a graduate trainee teacher and then took on a history specialism. I also assisted in the after-school programme.'

'Were you working with Oliver O'Sullivan in his after-school club?'

Carly picked at a loose thread on the sleeve of her Breton-striped shirt. 'Not initially. I was working with Mrs Doig who Oliver took over from. She retired not long after.'

'Did you get on with him?' Bennett asked.

'Yes, in the beginning. He was charming, self-deprecating; he could make you smile on a bad day. And the kids loved him immediately, I mean, that was evident from day one. He had so much energy, you know? He wasn't afraid to be silly, where Mrs Doig had always been a bit staid and took a back seat instead of getting involved.'

'You sound like you were impressed by him?' Minshull hated the question for the connotations later parts of the story might bring, but it was important to establish whether Carly Addison was telling the truth or had an agenda to push. It would be the first question a cross-examining lawyer would ask. And while it was unlikely this would ever come to court, Minshull didn't want to take any chances.

'Are you asking if I fancied him?' The question was flat and instantly made Minshull feel worse than he already did. 'Maybe, at first. Everyone did. I think it was his presence I liked more than him. There was always a discrepancy between his persona when people were looking and if you caught sight of him on his own. Like those Wild West towns where the buildings have elaborate façades but nothing much behind them. Of course, it's easy to see it now, knowing what I know.'

'When were you first aware that something was wrong?'

Carly gave a long sigh. 'It was maybe six or seven months into him running the after-school clubs. There was this big joke in the staff room about him being St Audrey's answer to Harry Styles, trailed everywhere by crowds of adoring fans. You hear that stuff all the time. Teachers are the worst for it – mercilessly ribbing each other. But with Oliver it was different. It had an edge to it. Something nasty.'

'What worried you?' Bennett asked.

'It was always girls – thirteen, fourteen years old. I'd hear them chattering when they were waiting for the clubs to start. Working out what they were going to do to make him notice them. Giddy when he did. Within a few months there was a distinct group of about six girls who would be in before the others, stay closest to him during the sessions and help him tidy the room at the end. They would be there until they turned fifteen and then they'd be replaced by younger girls.'

Replaced. It was an interesting term to use.

'Can you remember any of their names?'

Carly nodded, twisting the edge of her sleeve around her fingers. 'In the last group, before I left, there was Amy Godwit, Bindi Henderson-Aziz, Esme Richards, Sammy-Jo Lacey, Lottie Arundel – um…'

'Laura Gilchrist?' Minshull prompted, kicking himself when Carly frowned. He shouldn't have led her.

'No, not Laura. Did someone say she had been?'

'She was mentioned as a possible member of the group,' Minshull said, knowing full well the mention came from him. 'Because of her being dance captain.'

'No. Laura didn't get on with the clique culture. She called them "the desperates" – I remember a big row breaking out after that. Anyway, she may have been listed as dance captain but only because they couldn't find anyone else to fill the role. She left the theatre club soon after the row and joined the swimming team instead. Typical that St Audrey's didn't bother to update the list.'

Minshull stuffed his frustration away. If Cora's client had been protecting Laura Gilchrist it could have provided a clear link between O'Sullivan and the girls closest to him. He was torn: as a human being it was a relief to find that Laura hadn't been involved – one less life left potentially damaged by the teacher; as a detective it was a dead-end he didn't need. Cora may have been wrong about this but she had already more than proved her importance to the case by identifying McGann. He would tell her as soon as he could – not least to let her know that her own investigations into the *Gil* she'd sensed in Lottie's mind were far from over.

'So, you saw an unhealthy culture amongst the girls in the theatre club. Did you mention it to anyone?'

'I told Tom Dillinger.' Carly's cheeks reddened. 'He said it was being monitored.'

'And was it?'

Her face reddened. 'It was a lie. Like the lie they told those poor girls about the police not wanting to investigate.'

'How did you discover it was a lie?'

'Because I watched the Oliver O'Sullivan clique get worse. And then I got chatting to one of the girls, Sammy-Jo, one Wednesday late afternoon before theatre club started. She'd had to go for a dental appointment and had missed *the trip*, as she called it.'

'A school trip?'

'That was what I thought. In a school that size there were always trips going on, so I figured it was one I hadn't heard about. When I asked her, Sammy-Jo thought it was hilarious. She said it was a special event; a private trip Oliver had arranged for his favourites.' The twists of her sleeve left great white lines across her index finger now, knuckles whitening with the pressure.

Minshull's stomach knotted in time with the twisting fabric. 'Where had they gone?'

Carly shook her head. 'There's a former field studies centre out on the mudflats near the estuary mouth. One of the other teachers had been fundraising to renovate it for the school and community groups to use. There's a bird hide, a small kitchen – a bit like the kind of wooden bothies you find in the Highlands for hikers. Oliver had the keys and booked one of the school minibuses to take his chosen girls out there.'

When Minshull looked at Bennett, he saw she had paled.

'And the school sanctioned this?'

'I don't know. He'd called it a drama club orientation for his "peer group leaders" so they probably thought it was a new extension of his precious after-school programme that was supposed to bring all these big investors in to support the school.'

Minshull made a note, his mind spinning. What was next with this case? Every time one thread untangled, four more knotted in its place. 'Okay. Did Sammy-Jo tell you what they were doing there?'

'She was rather vague about it, probably because it was the first trip and she hadn't been able to go. But then she told me Oliver had called them his "inner circle" and said that the field centre was "their reward". I think he sold it as a kind of common room especially for his girls.' She shuddered, her eyes welling. 'I'm sorry.'

'Take your time, Carly,' Bennett soothed. 'You're doing great.'

'There's no rush,' Minshull added, taking a box of tissues from the low oak coffee table and passing it to the distressed former teacher. 'Do you need a break?'

Carly dabbed her eyes and nose, giving a defiant shake of her head. 'No. I want to do this. Just give me a minute.' She blew out a series of long exhales as she fought to regain control, finally nodding. 'Okay. I raised my concern with the teacher who was looking after the renovation fund for the field centre but he assured me the girls were going there with Oliver as a work party to help prepare the building for the contractors. So I left it. Until Lottie Arundel came to see me.'

Lottie – Cora's client. Minshull's every nerve stood to attention. 'What did she say?'

'She told me one of her friends had been propositioned by Oliver out at the field centre on another of the trips. He'd made some jokey suggestive comment and when she didn't know how to respond, he'd said being in his inner circle was a privilege that carried certain… *responsibilities*. He'd indicated that he would ask his "best girls" to assist him in a "special way".'

Bennett swore under her breath and instantly raised her hands. 'Forgive me.'

Minshull should have reprimanded her but today it was justified. That horror needed a voice at the moment it arrived. 'Did he make her do anything?'

'Not that time. I told Lottie to ask her friend to come and see me, but she never did. Judging by the statements the two girls made, I think that was Amy.' She wiped her eyes again. 'And I haven't forgiven myself because if I'd made her bring Amy to me, I could have spoken up before it got out of hand.'

274

Bennett's hand was on her arm immediately, protocol forgotten in a moment of compassion. 'You were there for them. That was what mattered. You cared enough to ask.'

Carly observed Bennett through tears. 'You're kind. But it was my responsibility to act. I knew it was wrong,' she stabbed a hand to her stomach, 'in *here*. I knew as a teacher, as a woman… But without actual testimony from the girls all I could do was monitor the situation.'

'The teacher you spoke to, the one managing the field centre restoration project, who was that?'

Carly sniffed. 'Andrew Draycott. He's still at the school. Oliver was his big chum, you know. He couldn't see anything but good in him.' She gave a derisory snort. 'Easy to do when you're a man and not in danger – no offence to you, DS Minshull.'

'You're right.' Minshull conceded the point, the mention of the teacher now helping Lottie – and talking to Cora – making him uneasy. 'Do you think Draycott was involved?'

Carly considered this for a moment. 'I can't see it. He was just in thrall to his friend. I reckon he was an ego boost for Oliver, validation for him to continue. Even if he'd seen anything questionable, I doubt he'd have spoken up.'

Should Cora be allowing Draycott to spend time with Lottie? Minshull regretted his advice to her on the phone last night to keep talking to the teacher. Should he tell her? Or ask her to find out more about the field centre project?

'So when did you first hear of Amy and Bindi's allegations?'

'When their parents formally approached the school. But I'd seen the signs – Bindi was withdrawn, going off into huddles with Amy during break times and at lunch, and neither of them seemed themselves. I know Lottie tried to help them and they all stopped coming to theatre club. But they didn't come to me again and refused to say anything when I asked how they were.'

'Do you think the abuse was continuing?'

'I don't know. The production of *Phantom of the Opera* was the last thing the girls did with the theatre club and they had moved away from the clique by then. I've always wondered if the assault Oliver subjected Amy to was in retaliation for that.'

'O'Sullivan proving he still had power over her.' Bennett looked sick.

'Yes. I don't want to think that. But I just don't know.'

'So when the complaints were made, what then?'

'Well, that was why I left. They put those two girls through absolute hell: not only having to tell their parents but also reliving it on paper for all the senior leadership of the school to see: deputy head, heads of year, school governors – many of whom were parents of kids at the school. It was mishandled from the start. No anonymity. No outside advice sought. No mention to social services. Then they lied to the parents about the police not thinking the case credible enough to investigate. I tried to talk to Tom Dillinger about it, but he insisted the matter was closed. I tendered my resignation the next day.'

'That lie about police has disgusted all of us in South Suffolk Constabulary,' Minshull admitted. 'We investigate every allegation of abuse, of minors particularly. We feel the injustice keenly. And all of us want justice now.'

'Not like those idiots posting *Seek Justice* flyers everywhere,' Carly said, taking Minshull by surprise. 'It was on the news this morning and Mum said they've been posted to every shop in Evernam. Where were they when Oliver O'Sullivan was attacking those young girls?'

Minshull closed his notebook. He had heard enough. Andrew Draycott must be next on his list to talk to. And then, when they had enough to make a case, he would deal with Tom Dillinger. 'This has been incredibly helpful, Carly. Thank you for your honesty and your bravery.'

'It will make a difference to the case,' Bennett assured her. 'We're determined to bring the Head and governance of St Audrey's to account for their actions.'

They stood together, Minshull bruised by the encounter. By the look of his colleague, Bennett felt the same. It was going to be an interesting drive back to police HQ. Maybe they would stop on the way, find somewhere to walk a little and let everything settle before rejoining the team. There was a little mobile snack van in a lay-by on the outskirts of Ipswich beside a footpath leading to a small wooded area near the river. It was quiet and, during the week, deserted. A moment of calm was definitely in order.

'Thanks again,' he smiled by the front door. 'I'll be in touch.'

'Thank you. I want them to have to answer for their actions.' She shook her head. 'I just can't get away from the evil of it. The way those children were coerced into surrendering their safety, their freedom, their peace of mind and personal privacy, just to be one of Gil's Girls...'

On the doorstep, Minshull froze. 'What did you call them?'

'Sorry?'

'Just now. What was the inner circle called?'

'Gil's Girls? I-I thought you knew...'

Minshull's shoulders prickled. 'Who is Gil?'

'Gil *O'Sullivan*. It was a nickname Oliver liked to use, something he said his friends in drama club at his school used to call him – like Gilbert and Sullivan? He liked his inner circle to call him Gil when they were away from school. It was a badge of honour to use the name and Sammy-Jo said the girls would brag to the younger kids in the theatre club about it. That was the insidious thing: all of them had heard the same from older girls before they moved on. Oliver made it something to aspire to.'

Minshull was reeling as he and Bennett returned to the pool car.

'Are you okay, Sarge?'

He didn't reply, his thoughts in a million places at once. Gil was Oliver O'Sullivan's secret nickname, only shared with his inner circle of underage girls. Carly Addison had named Lottie Arundel as one of Gil's Girls. Cora said Lottie had guarded the name Gil; that it had taken hours of careful work to coax it from her. Lottie had stopped speaking two weeks after Amy Godwit and Bindi Henderson-Aziz quit the school. What if the 'friend' she had gone to Carly to talk about was herself? What if she had been a victim of O'Sullivan before her friends?

'Minsh. Talk to me.'

When he blinked, Bennett was standing beside him in the farmyard, her hand resting on his arm.

'I need to talk to Cora.'

Lottie

Lotts
I saw you were online
Are you OK?

Bindi
Can't talk now

Lotts
Just tell me you're OK

Bindi
I'm not OK.
It's everywhere.
Now everyone at my new school knows

Lotts
They'll forget soon

Bindi
They won't.
I got called SLUT today
Like I chose him

Lotts
They're idiots

Bindi
They were supposed to be my friends
Now I have nobody

Lotts
I'm your friend
You have me, B

Bindi
I have to go.
Mum doesn't want me messaging
in case the papers have bugged me

Lotts
Have you heard from Amy?

Bindi
No
You?

Lotts
She hasn't answered my messages.

Bindi
You made it worse for her

Lotts
Don't say that.
I was trying to help

Bindi
You went to Ms Addison.
She went to Mr Dillinger.
He told Gil.
Amy paid the price.

Lotts
Don't say that
It wasn't my fault

Bindi
...
...
...

Lotts
B – listen to me
It wasn't my fault

Bindi
...
...
...

Bindi has left the conversation

Chapter Thirty-Eight

Cora

'Everything okay, Lottie?'

Cora peered at the teen, who had been glaring at her phone for twenty minutes as they walked along the estuary path.

I'm fine.

'How are your friends?'

None of your business.

The words hit Cora like a slap. She stopped walking. Lottie powered ahead, walking ten yards before she realised Cora was no longer matching her steps.

Cora stuffed her hands into the pockets of her hooded jacket and waited. There had been a shroud over Lottie since she'd arrived at the house and it was getting too heavy to escort. It didn't help that she knew Minshull was meeting with the teacher who had quit St Audrey's in the wake of the child abuse allegations. If she named Lottie as one of Oliver O'Sullivan's victims, it would answer so many questions and present a clear way forward.

Tris Noakes certainly seemed convinced that abuse – or some deep betrayal of trust – was the root cause of Lottie's silence.

'I think you need to prepare yourself,' he'd advised that morning when she'd called him from a side road at the north end of Woodsham St Mary, suddenly needing reassurance before approaching Fourwinds. 'Given what happened to her friends and what's being revealed about the teacher, it seems the most obvious explanation.'

'But I don't know anything about accepting disclosures of abuse,' Cora had argued. 'And if she tells me via the text-speech software, is it permissible evidence in court?'

'You're thinking too far ahead. Your responsibility in the first instance is just to listen. Don't promise confidentiality, don't ask leading questions, let Lottie talk – in whatever manner she wishes – then, as soon as you can, make notes when you leave the house, write down everything you can remember, including your side of the conversation. Report it to me and I'll handle it from there.'

It was so much to remember, so much pressure to get it right. Around her, screaming from every newspaper and television bulletin, were the consequences of getting it wrong. She wouldn't fail Lottie as St Audrey High had failed her friends.

We're lost – a voice sounded from her feet.

She looked down to find a ripped page from an Ordnance Survey map of the Suffolk coast trapped in the long yellow grass, blown inland and now resting against her boot.

She bent down to pick it up, the grumpy male voice repeating in her hands. So immediate. So easy.

Why can't you be like this? The thought broke into the sound, surprising her. Her own voice. And there it was: the reason she'd felt so at sea with this case, the itch of frustration no amount of progress with Lottie's trapped voices could satisfy.

For the first time, her ability wasn't serving her. In the missing child case over a year ago and during the work she had done with Tris Noakes's department since returning to Suffolk, the emotional echoes attached to objects like fingerprints had been her guiding light. While the significance of those secret voices took longer to discern, the starting point was always the same: the voice.

With Lottie there was no peripheral sound, no trapped emotion begging to be heard. The waves of breath and the imprisoned name didn't respond to Cora's mind like the object voices did. She felt adrift because the anchor was missing – the anchor of the voices only she could hear.

Lottie hadn't chosen silence because it was easy, or on a whim. The sheer effort it required to imprison her voice and hold every emotion captive had to come from a place of abject fear. And that could only come from a singular experience so cataclysmic, so world-altering, that silence was the only option.

But without the usual tools at her disposal, was Cora the right person to press into that silence?

Why did you stop walking?

Stung, Cora faced the teenager. 'You told me to mind my own business.'

The teenager's frown darkened the shadows around her eyes. *You're supposed to be helping me. That's your job.*

Oh, so a fight was in order, was it?

'I'm supposed to be listening to you. *That's* my job. But you don't want to do that today. You don't want to do anything. Apart from be obnoxious.'

Now her own fear was talking: fear of being in a situation she had no gauge for, fear of what might lie at the root of Lottie's silence, fear of being othered by the very person she was trying to help.

Her old insecurities might have been put to bed when she started to push the boundaries of her ability, but they had yet to be fully laid to rest.

You can go if you don't like it. Nothing's keeping you here.

Cora wasn't going to achieve anything by arguing the toss. If they had reached an impasse, there was no point prolonging their session.

'You're right. See you, Lottie.'

Heart thudding, she turned her back on the teenager and began to stalk away. Tris would be shocked. Monica might never forgive her. But there was too much battling in her own mind for her to be of any use to Lottie today.

She had almost reached the stile by the road when the electronic voice sounded, close behind her.

Are you my friend?

Cora stopped walking but didn't turn back.

Are you my friend, Dr Lael?

'I want to help you.'

What if I don't need another therapist? What if I need a friend?

'Why do you need a friend, Lottie?'

Because I'm totally alone.

Slowly, Cora turned. Lottie was a pace away, head bowed, hazel eyes peering beneath dark brows, staring intently at her. She seemed diminished, a fragile child reaching out.

'You have your friends.'

They won't talk to me.

'It's hard right now with all the stuff in the news.'

They blame me.

It was so unlike the Lottie she had come to know. Stripped of the shield of humour and the confidence despite the silence, she was small, vulnerable and scared.

'It isn't your fault.'

I tried to help. I thought I did the right thing. But Amy got hurt…

GIL

The name punched through the air between them.

Cora fixed her mind on it. 'Who hurt Amy?'

Lottie shook her head, fingers stabbing the screen. *I can't say.*

GIL

How could Cora leave now?

'Amy wasn't hurt because of you,' she began, careful to hold the knowledge of the voice betraying Lottie's secret as closely as Lottie did. 'She was hurt because someone she trusted abused that trust.'

She blames me. Bindi blames me. I only wanted to make things better.

Tris Noakes's words came back to Cora: 'Don't promise confidentiality, don't ask leading questions, let Lottie talk…'

'Lottie, we can make this better. I can help you.'

I made a promise to help them.

'Then we'll do it together.'

Lottie blinked.

Cora's ears screamed with the tension that fizzed and pulsed around them. Lottie had unwittingly revealed the key to all of this: her testimony against Oliver O'Sullivan would be the final nail in the coffin for Tom Dillinger and the decision-makers of St Audrey's that had so catastrophically failed their students.

Her *spoken* testimony.

In her own voice.

Cora knew what she had to do.

284

Chapter Thirty-Nine

Minshull

She wasn't answering her phone.

Minshull stared at the screen of his own, the five missed calls logged there underlining his frustration. Had she worked it out? Or would the news be a blindsiding blow?

She might be with Lottie Arundel now. From their last conversation he got the impression Cora already suspected that the teenager was one of O'Sullivan's victims. The lines of connection were there: it stood to reason that Lottie might have suffered the same fate as her friends. O'Sullivan operated a small group each year and Lottie was one of the six when Amy Godwit and Bindi Henderson-Aziz were assaulted.

He needed to warn her about Andrew Draycott's involvement too. Whether the teacher had been fatally blinkered to O'Sullivan's motives or well aware and complicit by his silence, the fact remained that giving O'Sullivan keys to the field centre had facilitated the abuse of children. Cora should be aware of all of it.

He considered sending a text, but this information should be delivered in person at best or during a call at the very least. Instead, he left a voicemail message on his sixth unsuccessful attempt to call her.

'Hi Cora, it's Rob. I really need to talk to you. Give me a ring as soon as you can, even if it's late.'

It wasn't ideal, but it would have to do.

'Sarge.' Across the CID office, Les Evans had his hand raised.

'What have you got?' Minshull pocketed his phone and headed over.

'Two of the male teachers at St Audrey High just had pig's blood thrown over their cars.'

'What?'

'They went out at lunch break and found them. It's just been called in. Bures Bowmen flyers pinned under the wipers.'

'Does the school have CCTV in the staff car park?'

Les grimaced. 'They *did*. But the security team found a fault yesterday and were in the process of getting the camera fixed.'

'Oh great.'

'I'm afraid there's more.'

Minshull sighed, the weariness of the week slamming back down on his shoulders. 'Go on.'

'The Head, Tom Dillinger, just received this.'

Evans turned his monitor to reveal the photograph of a blood-splattered flyer, identical to those that had been reportedly distributed across the area, the story widely covered with morbid glee by every news agency during the past few hours. *SEEK JUSTICE* was just visible beneath the angry streaks of red.

'Was this at school?'

'No. He's working from home today. But his video doorbell caught this image.'

He clicked on a video file and a grainy black and white image of a wide, brick-paved drive filled the screen. A white Transit van pulled up beside a Range Rover and a hooded figure jumped out, running up to the doorstep to push an envelope through the letterbox.

'Stop it there,' Minshull directed, leaning closer to the screen to try to make out facial features. The face was in shadow, with what looked like a mask pulled over the lower half. Minshull groaned, but then noticed the van behind the intruder, bright white in the monochrome film. 'Hang on, can you read that number plate? Is that a three and a five?'

'I can't make it out. Oi, Drew!'

Ellis looked up. 'What?'

'Bring your annoyingly fresh eyes over here.'

'All right, Grandpa.'

Ellis joined them, shooting Evans a wry look. The ribbing between the two of them had become worse in recent months, but had faded to almost nothing during the stress of the past week. In a strange way, it was comforting to see it return.

'Can you read that plate?'

Ellis leaned in. 'That's an eight, not a three. Look, you can see the shadow of the other side. It looks like it's been scuffed with something.' He tore a sheet from the reporter's notepad on his colleague's desk, grabbed a pen and wrote down the full registration number. 'There.'

'You bloody genius, Drew! I could kiss you!'

'Please don't, Les.'

'I saw a five and an eight when the Transit drove us off the road at Abbot's Farm,' Minshull said, the sharp image suddenly returning to his mind. 'Could that be the same van?'

'Suffolk's not exactly short of white Transits, but it's possible.'

'Possible is good enough for me. Drew, get on to Traffic. Put out an all-unit search on that reg. If we're lucky it'll still be driving round.'

'Yes, Sarge.'

The phones on Bennett's desk and Minshull's desk began to ring simultaneously. Bennett answered hers before Minshull reached his.

'Where? Okay, thanks.' She put her hand over the receiver. 'Sarge, one of the governors of the school just received a threat from someone claiming to be part of the Seek Justice movement.'

'What on earth? Dave can you answer that?' Minshull called, leaving his desk phone ringing and moving to Bennett's side.

'On it,' Wheeler replied, crossing paths with Minshull halfway.

'Okay, I'll take it.' He accepted the receiver from Bennett. 'Hi, this is DS Minshull, how can I help?'

'Hello. I'm Bill Mayhew, head of governors at St Audrey High School. My wife just had a call from a man who told her there would be an attack on one of my developments today. I'm in London, I can't get back. My wife is on her own. I don't know what to do.'

'When was the call, sir?'

'Fifteen minutes ago. She called me in tears, terrified they'll target the house, too.'

'Did the caller say who was planning the attacks?'

'He said the Seek Justice movement. It's those idiots posting the damned dragon leaflets everywhere, isn't it? He told her any business that hid paedophiles deserved tearing down. I have three developments in Suffolk, but two aren't widely known yet. I think they're going to target Silverfields.'

'What kind of development is it?'

'We're renovating and repurposing some former barge warehouses on the banks of the River Deben, near Woodbridge. Four warehouses on the site, used for freight by sea from the 1890s until the 1950s. The buildings themselves are largely in good condition, which is how we've managed to turn the project around so quickly. If they are damaged now, the cost could be prohibitive to rectify.'

'We'll get someone over straight away. In the meantime, does your wife have somewhere safe she can go? The house of a friend or family member, perhaps?'

'Her sister lives in St Just. I'll tell her to go there.'

'Excellent. As soon as you can sir, please, just to be sure.'

'Understood. Thank you, detective. It's those bloody vigilantes isn't it? The ones that attacked your officers? They're terrorising the school already.'

'Leave them to us,' Minshull said, aware of the stares of the room on him, fear already setting in. He ended the call and faced the team.

'I need two of you to go over to the Silverfields development site by the River Deben near Woodbridge. I'm asking for volunteers.'

Silence met his request.

He didn't want to choose. They had been through enough already and there could only be more in store. But someone had to check the site and he was due to meet Anderson and DCI Sue Taylor for a progress report in ten minutes.

'If this is the same gang that attacked Steph and Rilla we have a chance to catch them in the act. If they're using the van from that attack, we've got them. I don't want to demand anyone go, but...'

'I'll do it, Sarge.'

Bennett raised her hand.

'Okay. Thank you, Kate.'

'Then I'll go too.'

'Cheers, Drew.'

'I can do it by myself,' Bennett countered.

'Not alone, you can't. I'm coming.'

'Are you calling me incapable?'

'No, it's a two-person job.'

Minshull watched Ellis and Bennett regard each other for a moment. So be it. Perhaps investigating this would give them a chance to work out their grievances.

'Excellent. Thanks, both of you. Park the car where it can't be seen and just observe, okay? Don't put yourselves in danger. If the van or anyone else shows up, call it in. Don't be heroes, yeah?'

Bennett and Ellis collected their things and left, pointedly avoiding one another in the doorway.

'Targeted campaign?' Evans asked, summoning Minshull's attention back to the office.

'It looks that way. Get onto the Tech bods, would you? Chase them about the transcripts from the Dragon Army closed group they're compiling for us. If Butler, Maitland or anyone connected to the Bowmen has put out a call on there, we have them.'

'Sure, Sarge.'

'Ah a contented CID, this is what I like to see,' DCI Sue Taylor's voice boomed into the office as she strode in, gracing Wheeler and Evans with cursory nods as she passed. Their pointed stares back at her went unnoticed. 'Rob, shall we?'

Collecting his notes, a deep sense of unease taking residency in his gut, Minshull followed her into Anderson's office.

Chapter Forty

Ellis

'I don't know why you're here.'

Ellis sagged in his seat behind the wheel. The hour since they'd arrived had been spent in stony silence, the half hour journey before it peppered with his own failed attempts to engage Bennett in conversation. He'd been willing her to speak: now he wished he hadn't bothered. A silent Kate Bennett was preferable to this. What was going on with her? She'd been quiet before but Ellis thought they'd worked through the earlier weirdness after their visit to O'Sullivan's former partner. In recent days they had seemed closer than ever. Why had she bitten his head off in the office? And why was she being arsey now?

'I am here because it's a two-person job and nobody else volunteered.'

'Oh well, don't do me any favours...'

'I give up.'

'Didn't take you long.'

He twisted in his seat. 'Okay, what's your problem?'

'I have a problem now, do I?'

'Apparently so.'

'I don't appreciate being rescued.'

Was she serious? '*Excuse* me?'

'*Then I'll go too*, you said – as if it wouldn't have been a consideration if Dave or Les had volunteered instead.'

'You got that from what I said?'

She had a glare that could cut steel, he reckoned. Why was she aiming her Bond-villain skill at him?

'How would you have felt if it was the other way around? If I'd volunteered because you did?'

'I would have been happy to have you with me,' he shot back, aware of how pathetic it sounded. 'Not assumed you were patronising me.'

Her arms folded across her body and she turned her killer stare to the passenger door window. In frustration, Ellis turned his head to the driver's side.

They had found a small dirt bay to park in, beneath the cover of a twisted birch tree growing at an angle from a grass-covered bank. Beyond it lay an overgrown field. The bay was set back a little way from the construction site, meaning that the dark blue pool car wouldn't be easy to spot from the road or the former warehouses.

The Silverfields development was deserted. No sign of any vehicles besides theirs, the lengths of temporary Heras fencing around the perimeter undisturbed. Dust on the concrete road leading to the site held no recent footprints and the glassless windows of the warehouses revealed no signs of movement within.

It was a hoax. It had to be.

There had obviously been some kind of orchestrated effort to terrorise the staff, head and governors of St Audrey's – and it had worked. The message had been sent that they were being held responsible for the ill treatment and abuse of the two girls, regardless of whether or not they ever faced prosecution for their actions.

SEEK JUSTICE.

It chilled his blood.

If someone had told him when he'd joined up that vigilante groups would even exist in Suffolk, let alone be active to the point of officers being attacked, he would have laughed them out of the room. His family called him PC Plod even though he'd been a DC for over a year now, and every family get-together inevitably included jokes about hunting stolen tractors and chasing down sheep rustlers. It wasn't supposed to be a patch where vigilantes might set about you with bottles and rocks and buckets of blood. That was the stuff of TV thriller writers' wild imaginations, not the reality of rural policing.

He loved being part of the team. He could even tolerate Les Evans's constant jibes about him being the kid in the office. Most of all, he loved surprising them. He was damn good at his job and he liked them seeing it. But he wanted to do more than just fit in now. He had a point to prove. He'd started pushing himself, physically and mentally, working out to improve his strength and stamina and putting himself forward for jobs he might have shied away from in the past.

Jobs like this one.

Why was it so hard for Bennett to see that? Hadn't she done the same when she'd first joined CID?

Or was that why she was being off with him now?

'I don't think anyone's coming,' she said, the shock of her voice in the silence making him look back. 'They were just trying to put the wind up the bloke. Hit him where it hurts, without ever doing anything.'

'They turned up at Abbot's Farm,' Ellis countered. 'They turned up at St Audrey's. The instances are clearly linked.'

'Or it's idiots piggy-backing on a not very original idea.'

Why did that feel like a personal attack?

That was it: he was done sitting in here, the sole target for whatever crap Kate Bennett was mired in.

'I'm going over there,' he said, pocketing his radio and reaching for the door handle.

'What? No!'

'Sitting here tells us nothing. I'm going to have a look, see if there are any signs someone's been there.'

'Minsh told us to stay in the car.'

'Minsh isn't here, is he?' he grinned back, opening the door. Her glower was his reward. He wasn't rescuing her now, was he?

He was vaguely aware of Bennett's continuing protestations from her open window as he crossed the narrow country lane and jogged over to the fence barring the concrete road. It was the kind of fencing beloved of music festivals and building sites: silver mesh panels secured by heavy concrete blocks at the base. Ellis followed the line for a few panels until he found one that hadn't been fitted properly, one edge resting on the top of the concrete base block rather than fitting into the deep slot within it. He grinned. There was always one. Gripping the metal edge near the bottom, he shouldered it, lifting it up enough to pivot the panel away from the block.

Growing up on a farm had its advantages. Like getting into places your grandad and uncles thought they'd fenced off…

He risked a cheeky thumbs-up in the direction of the pool car and slipped through the gap he'd created.

Moments later he heard the slam of a car door and the pounding of running feet. Smiling to himself, he carried on walking towards the warehouses.

'We're not supposed to be in here,' Bennett puffed, pulling level with him.

'Hey, if you don't feel up to it, Granny…' he began, a jibe which would have earned him a playful cuff and a wry laugh six months ago but now sent a jab of disgust through him.

'If anyone turns up we're screwed,' she shot back. 'No back-up, unarmed, totally on our own.'

Ellis jabbed his thumb over his shoulder. 'Nobody is going to come in through that fence quickly. And if they have a van it'll take even longer. We can be out of the other side by the time they've moved the panels.'

'I don't like it,' Bennett groaned but she didn't stop walking.

'Then go back to the car.'

'Drew!'

He started to prepare another volley to counter hers when something caught his eye. 'Hang on – over there.'

'What?' The sight of Kate Bennett stuffing away her anger was almost as rewarding as the flash of white he'd seen tucked between the two warehouses on the right of the site.

He was pretty certain of what he'd seen, but as he neared it, his suspicions were confirmed. As they rounded the nearest warehouse, it came into view.

'Is that…?' Bennett began, passing Ellis to reach the vehicle first.

A white Transit van, its sides caked with dried sprays of mud as if it had driven along a muddy dirt track not too long ago.

'Check the reg,' Ellis said, the thrill blasting away every other thought. He followed her to the rear of the vehicle.

It was the van from the doorbell cam video, the eight in its registration number half-obscured by a thick smear of mud.

'Bloody hell,' Bennett said, looking along the side of the van. Her smile was completely unexpected and for a moment she and Ellis just grinned at each other.

It wasn't a ceasefire, but a glimpse of the team they had been.

'You need to call Minsh,' he said, suddenly remembering where he was.

'So, call it in,' Bennett said. 'Your idea to come in here. You found it.'

'Cheers.'

She offered a brief smile. 'I'm going to check the rest.'

Ellis watched her walk away for a second, then turned back to make the call.

Chapter Forty-One

Bennett

Kate Bennett kicked against the old concrete as she powered across the warehouse site.

What was happening to her?

It had begun as a defence mechanism, a determination to prevent any of the problems in her private life from slipping out to the team. As the only woman in the department it was hard enough to maintain equal terms with the others: any hint of domestic problems and she would be right back battling to be seen as the same as them. In the force, relationship problems were considered women's problems that only women should have to deal with.

Private life problems. She'd never expected to have them and was furious that she hadn't seen them coming.

She'd deliberately kept her head down, avoiding the usual banter and chats that might coax the truth out of her. If the team thought her unusually quiet or standoffish, so be it. Better to be allowed to throw herself into work than be constantly reminded of what awaited her at home. Or who wasn't waiting any more.

Why was she so incensed by Drew Ellis volunteering to join her?

He was a good kid. He worked hard. He didn't take the piss like Evans or bark like Anderson. He was fun to be on a job with and his powers of observation were second to none. Of all the members of South Suffolk CID team, it should have been a relief to be paired with him today.

She reached the doorway of the farthest warehouse, the door long since gone. Its cavernous interior reached four storeys up from dusty floor to rusted rafters, shafts of light from the upper windows traversing the space, pooling down across the floor. She slipped inside, her footsteps echoing in the empty building. A sudden beating of wings caused her to jump and look up to see a startled pigeon making a bid for freedom through one of the high glassless windows. The developer had said they'd done a lot of the restoration work already: judging by the state of this warehouse they had a long way yet to go.

What would it be, anyway? The warehouses were too far from the nearest towns and infrastructure to be housing, too large to be industrial units. The air was heavy with the scent of dust and rust, the stone floors were rutted where large machinery had once lived and the space had a claustrophobic air, despite its walls rising high up from the ground. Bennett couldn't imagine anyone feeling at home here.

A sound from outside made her think of Ellis, calling the office to report their lucky find. Regret followed soon after. She had been completely unreasonable with him today.

Why?

The answer arrived with sudden clarity. He'd changed. That was his sole offence.

She closed her eyes as realisation finally dawned.

While the whole team undoubtedly felt the weight and the worry brought by Operation Feldspar and the growing threat of the Bures Bowmen – or those acting in their name – everybody else had retained their familiar characteristics. Wheeler, the oil on troubled waters; Evans, the tightrope-walker teetering on the right side of the law; Minshull the brooding but fair leader; Anderson the passionate superior who protected them all with the fun and ferocity of a mother bear.

Ellis was supposed to be the kid. The lanky, awkward one. The one who blushed on cue every single time. The one who viewed each case with the wide-eyed wonder of a brand new recruit.

But he hadn't been that for months now, had he? He was self-assured, his observation razor-sharp, his physical presence suddenly not that of a kid. And his instinct to fight back growing every day.

He was pushing himself, changing his approach, changing who he was as a copper and as a person.

She wasn't doing any of that at work. Because deep down, Bennett didn't want change. Not now.

She needed work to stay the same: the sole certainty in the swirling maelstrom of the rest of her life where everything was breaking apart.

She didn't even have a home yet – not since Russ Bennett had dropped the bombshell of his *other* family and announced he was ditching their home along with their five-year marriage. Camping out in a rented house that felt like a soulless cell was not Bennett's home. The CID office was home: where she could breathe, where she knew who she was. Where *nobody changed*.

That was the truth. That was why her anger had flared at the sight of someone embracing change, daring to be different.

She had no business being angry with Ellis.

He deserved an apology.

Guilt burning her stomach, she hurried out into the light. As she did, she thought she heard someone yell…

Chapter Forty-Two

Bennett

The rock came out of nowhere.

By the time Bennett was aware of its trajectory, it had glanced her shoulder, throwing her off-balance. She called out, but the sound was little more than a garbled cry, causing Ellis to turn around in shock as another heavy missile knocked her from her feet.

'Kate!'

'Find cover!' she managed, folding into a ball on the floor, hands raised over her head. More stinging blows registered on her arms and legs, smaller pebbles striking her body in a hot shower. 'Run, Drew!'

Shouts ricocheted around them; it was impossible to gauge the number and position of their assailants by the sharp sound reverberating around the empty buildings. From somewhere nearby, Bennett thought she could hear running feet as Ellis yelled into his radio for back-up.

A bottle smashed close to her head – too close – enough to jerk her body upright, survival instinct overriding the burning pain across her body. From the shards of green glass vivid scarlet liquid oozed out, staining the ground an angry red.

Pig's blood.

Yells and obscenities rained around her, distorted by the loud buzz in her ears and the pumping of blood at her temples as she struggled to move away.

And then, strong arms were hauling her to her feet, dragging her up from her position amid the debris. In panic, Bennett lashed out, kicking and scratching as hot breath swore at her neck, but her blows only served to tighten her assailant's grip.

This was *not* happening. She wasn't going to be attacked like Steph and Rilla had been. They hadn't been able to fight back. But she would.

Dizzy from effort, the iron scent of blood in her nostrils, Bennett felt herself being pulled through a narrow doorway into the shadowy depths of one of the warehouse spaces. In a last ditch attempt to free herself, she twisted in the grip, her elbow making one final, defiant contact with her attacker's stomach. She felt the air leave them, the grip loosening momentarily – it was enough for her to deliver a second blow and kick her way free.

'It's *me*,' a winded voice rasped behind her.

Bennett stopped running and turned back.

Drew Ellis was slumped in a heap on the dust-covered floor, one arm nursing his ribs, his face flushed and contorted by pain.

'*Shit*, Drew…'

'I was trying to get you out of there, idiot!' He winced, supporting his body on an ancient empty cable reel. 'You bloody hurt me.'

'I didn't know it was you…' Bennett took a few steps towards him, then glanced back to the small doorway he'd dragged her through. Moving as quickly as her aching frame would allow, she edged to the opening and hauled the iron door shut. Beyond the ancient brick walls, shouts and general confusion were muted but still too close for comfort. 'We should find somewhere else until back-up arrives. I don't trust this building as a hiding place.'

'Best we've got,' Ellis returned. 'And I wasn't exactly spoiled for choice when I grabbed you.'

'I thought someone else had me. One of them. I didn't expect… You're *strong*,' Bennett said, before she could think better of it. Her words registered as blows to Ellis, the hurt in his expression impossible not to see.

'I *am* strong.'

'Dave said you've been working out, but…'

'I told you that months ago.' He grimaced as he pulled his body upright. 'Not that you ever listen to me. None of you do. I'm stronger than you think.'

'I never said—'

'You didn't have to.' He shook his head. 'I'm just The Kid, aren't I? Lanky streak of piss that knows nothing. That's all you lot see.'

In the half-light of the space he appeared older suddenly, hollows carved beneath his cheekbones by dark shadow. It was striking, alien. Bennett felt her stomach twist. She had once been the butt of jokes in the CID team as the youngest member. She'd hated it then, but how was she any better than her colleagues had been now?

'I'm sorry.'

'Whatever.' His radio crackled and he turned away to answer. The move felt like a snub. 'Ellis.'

'Where are you?'

'We're in a warehouse on the east side of the lot.'

'And the gang?'

'I don't know, Sarge. They don't sound as near as they were.'

'Okay, hang tight. We've got two cars a minute away. Is Kate with you?'

Ellis closed his eyes. Bennett shrank back into the shadows.

'Yes. She's hurt.'

'I'm *fine*…' Bennett began, but a sharp pain in her skull begged to differ.

'Keep her close. Stay hidden as best you can.'

The call ended, the warehouse left to uncertain echoes and the cry of gulls overhead. Bennett leaned against the damp wall and wished herself anywhere but there. If their assailants were looking for them, they hadn't chosen the right building to search yet. It was little comfort: if the gang arrived before the squad cars she and Ellis would have nowhere to go in this empty, dead-end place.

She closed her eyes as another wave of pain claimed her head.

'Shift up.'

A grunt of effort sounded as a body dropped next to hers. In the deep shadow of her corner of the derelict warehouse, Bennett couldn't make out his features, but as least Ellis was there.

'They came out of nowhere,' she said, still reeling from the attack.

'I know.'

300

'Who the hell were they?'

'I'll give you one guess.'

'The Bowmen? How did they know we were here?'

'They set the trap, didn't they? Told Mr Mayhew they were attacking his development. Waited for us to turn up...'

'Was the van being here a set-up, too?'

Ellis didn't answer, resting the back of his head against the wall. One arm still cradled his injured ribs. Bennett didn't want to think about the bruises she might have caused there – or worse. The whole experience clung uneasily to her.

'Drew, I...'

'Don't.'

Something had shifted in the air between them. Bennett couldn't place what it was. She opened her mouth to speak – just as a flood of sirens and blue lights shattered the stillness.

—

They didn't speak in the squad car that spirited them back to Ipswich. Bennett kept her head turned to the darkening sky beyond the car window, the first lights of the town firing into life beneath. Above them a single strip of angry flame split the sky, one last gasp of the sun before the night. She felt cold, shock setting in from her injury and something else, something as dark as the encroaching charcoal clouds, seeping into the back seat between her and her colleague.

She didn't argue as she might have done when her uniformed colleagues ushered her into A&E. She followed in step with Ellis through the brightly lit corridor, entering adjacent bays without a glance. An inexplicable heaviness seemed to hang over them both despite the surrounding noise and activity.

Was it embarrassment at being rescued? Guilt for attacking Ellis? Neither would have given her a moment's thought before this.

She thought of the empty house awaiting her at home. The echoing rooms nobody in the CID team knew she haunted. The boxes she couldn't bear to unpack after a shift at work. The bottle of wine in the fridge she didn't dare drink for fear of not being able to stop. And the pitiful answer to the question of whether there was anyone she wanted to call.

There was no one waiting at home.

There wouldn't ever be again.

In Bay Twelve of Ipswich General A&E, aloneness hit Kate Bennett full on.

Later she would dismiss it as a symptom of shock, a sudden release of emotion caused by her injuries. The tired doctor held respectful vigil beside her examination bed, one hand resting gently on the blue paper sheet close enough to signify his support, while silent sobs shook Bennett's body.

Five hours later, her head wound dressed, shoulder bandaged and painkillers administered for the pain, Bennett stepped out into the night chill to find a familiar figure standing next to a dusty, dented green Volvo where she'd expected a taxi to be.

'You look like crap,' Dave Wheeler smiled, opening the passenger door. 'Dread to think what the other guy looked like. Ride home, ma'am?'

'What are you doing here?'

'Minsh told me they were letting you out. Are you okay?'

'Did they get them?' she asked, deflecting the question with one of her own.

'Some of them. The rest drove off before we could stop them.' Wheeler's smile fell. 'I'm sorry.'

Then no, Bennett thought, climbing into the car. *I'm not okay at all.*

—

She was quiet on the drive to St Just, lost in thought while surrounded by pain from her head, shoulder and the cuts and bruises over her body. Wheeler's deliberately light chatter became a soothing burr she could sink into. But as the lights of the village appeared on the horizon, panic forced her to attention.

'Reynard Street, isn't it?' Wheeler asked.

'That's right,' she answered, hating the charade that was necessary to protect her privacy.

'Oh now, remind me of the number. Forty-eight, is it?'

Bennett bristled. 'Forty-six.'

'That's right. Been so long since I last visited your gaff. We should do dinner one weekend. Sana would love to see you. And Russ, of course.'

'Sure.' She hated lying to Dave but the thought of the alternative was beyond what she could handle.

The sight of her former home sent stabbing needles through her heart. All she had to do was stand and wave until Wheeler left and then the ordeal would be over.

The night air had a chill that turned her skin to gooseflesh, the bruises and cuts on her body stinging as she smiled at her colleague.

'You get yourself in now,' he said, leaning across the car and grinning at her from the passenger window.

'I just need to find my keys,' she replied, holding up the clear plastic bag containing her belongings from the CID office that had been dropped off at the hospital for her. 'You get home. Thanks for the lift. Say hi to Sana for me.'

'I will. Rest up now,' Wheeler said, revving the engine.

'Yes *Dad*.' The skin cracked at the corners of her lips when she smiled but she did it anyway, relief flooding her frame as Wheeler turned the car around and drove away.

Bennett waited until the red rear lights of Wheeler's car disappeared from view before she let the smile slip from her face. The effort of maintaining it had left her dog-tired. With a last glance at the house beside her, she set off slowly down the street.

The walk to reach her new address would only take five minutes, but tonight every step felt lead-heavy. When she got back she would collapse into the nearest chair and pull the duvet over her, since the bed she should be crawling into was still in pieces upstairs in the bedroom.

She finally rounded the corner at the end of her former street – and stopped.

A familiar vehicle was parked beside the curb, Wheeler out on the pavement leaning against the Volvo.

'Now, how about I take you back to your actual home?'

Hot tears pricked her eyes. 'Dave, I—'

'I heard some talk about it in the Miller's. I didn't want to say anything until you did.'

'How long have you known?'

'Couple of weeks.'

'Who else knows?'

'No-one at work. Russ is a bastard, Kate. You don't deserve his crap.'

'Then why do I feel like I'm the one being punished?'

Tears brimmed and fell despite all her willpower demanding them to stay. Without a word, Wheeler moved to her and wrapped her in his arms, his embrace both a soothing blanket and a stark reminder that she'd failed. She'd failed to hide what had happened, failed to carry on as if Russ Bennett never existed and had never smashed her heart with his betrayal.

Wheeler led her to the passenger side and helped her into the seat, fussing over her in a manner only he could get away with. And when they pulled up outside the rented house she still couldn't call home, she didn't protest when he escorted her inside.

She didn't want to invite him in, but the fight had left her. In pain from her injuries and her aching heart, she allowed him to help her onto the sofa, watching wearily as he headed into the kitchen to find a glass of brandy and a huge pile of toast that must have been all the bread she owned.

'You need help unpacking?' he asked, when they were sitting together, the television chattering away to itself in the corner of the living room for the comfort of its noise.

'I'll get round to it.'

'Sana's taking the kids to her sister's over the weekend. I could pop over Sunday, help you shift this stuff? Drew's off that morning, too. We could call it his weightlifting practice.'

'No,' Bennett replied, harder than she'd intended. The memory of the strangeness between her and Ellis earlier refused to leave. 'You're kind but it's fine.'

'Are you thinking Russ'll ask for you back?' He held up his hands when she stared at him. 'It's just I know that game. Before Sana I had the same happen to me. First wife. Left me for a bloke with three kiddies. She left the door open just a little bit, the carrot dangled at me whenever she wanted something. Kept me hanging for nine months. My flat had boxes all that time.'

The very last person Bennett would have expected to share a life experience with was Dave Wheeler. He always seemed so steady, so happy in his life. 'I didn't know that. Sorry.'

'See, you're not the only one who can hide stuff,' he grinned kindly. 'People go, "Oh, it's just Dave Wheeler, Mr-I'm-All right-Jack, he doesn't have any problems". But they know bollocks. All of us are hiding, Kate, just some of us more in plain sight.'

'Don't tell anyone,' she pleaded.

'On one condition.' Wheeler took a sip of the tea he'd made himself. 'Me and you sort these boxes on Sunday.'

How could you stay irritated with Dave Wheeler? Accepting defeat, Bennett rolled her eyes. 'Yeah, okay. But no mocking my interior design style.'

'Best perk of the job, that. Regular Laurence Llewellyn-Bowen, I am.' His wide smile softened. 'You'll be good, kid. Your Uncle Dave's going to make sure you are.'

Chapter Forty-Three

Cora

'Oh my goodness, are they okay?' Cora stared across the wooden picnic table beside the breakfast food van as Minshull handed her a wrapped sandwich.

'They're pretty shaken up,' he replied, munching on a steaming bacon roll. 'Kate has concussion and took a knock to her shoulder; Drew has several bruised ribs. They suffered glass cuts from the missiles, too.'

'Did you arrest anyone?'

'We caught three. The rest escaped in the van. But we think it's the one used in the attack on Steph and Rilla, so uniform are out looking for it.'

'Bloody hell, Rob.'

'I know.'

Cora watched the market traders setting up their stalls in the shadow of Ipswich Town Hall. The market in Princes Street was a particular favourite of her mother's. She smiled, thinking of her once timid mum, who had spent years locked in her home, off exploring her world and currently hiking Lake District mountains this week with a group of ladies from St Just WI. She'd spoken to her on the phone last night, amazed again by the confidence she could hear in Sheila Lael's excited recounting of their adventures.

'Maureen split her walking trousers halfway up Helvellyn, would you believe it? But then this very hunky National Park ranger gave her his jacket to cover her modesty. We all think she did it on purpose. We took him for a pint when we got back down.'

'Sounds like fun.'

'It was. It is. Next time you should come with us, love. The girls are a hoot. They can pretty much drink everyone under the table, too. I don't think I've had so much wine since your dad and I were at college.'

'Dad would be proud.'

'He would be proud of you, too. How are you, sweetheart? We caught a bit of the news last night.'

'I'm okay. Just hoping I can help the young girl get through it.'

'If anyone can, it's you. Just be careful, okay? And tell that lovely detective of yours to be careful, too.'

That lovely detective of mine. Cora smiled into her breakfast roll now.

'You need to be careful,' she told him. 'My mum says so.'

Minshull raised his eyebrows. 'Sheila keeping tabs on me, is she?'

'Your goose is cooked in that department. Lucky for you she's in the Lakes this week.'

'That's sweet. Tell her not to worry.'

Cora felt the subtle shift in tone and broached the subject they had both carefully avoided since meeting for breakfast. 'So, why did you want to see me?'

Minshull rested his roll back in its silver foil wrapper. 'We spoke to Carly Addison yesterday, the former teacher who knew Amy and Bindi? She knew Lottie, too.' He fixed her with a stare. 'Okay, there's no easy way to say this, so I'm just going to tell you: I know who Gil is.'

The breath left Cora's body. She steadied herself in her seat. 'Laura Gilchrist? The dance captain on the theatre club list?'

As soon as she said it, she knew it wasn't. Minshull's expression couldn't hide the horror of what was coming.

'Gil is the nickname Oliver O'Sullivan used with his inner circle.'

Cora's hand went to her mouth, the cry that threatened to split the calm of the market muffled against her palm.

'He said his school friends used to call him Gil because of his surname and the link with musical theatre. Gilbert and Sullivan. The girls he kept closest – the children he abused – were known as Gil's Girls. Amy and Bindi were in that group. And so was Lottie.'

'Rob…'

'I know. I had to tell you face to face. I couldn't bear to say it on the phone last night.' He looked up at the yellow striped awning over the service hatch of the food van. 'I hate this. I hate the whole thing. The more we discover, the worse it is.'

'It all adds up. Lottie said Amy and Bindi aren't talking to her because they blame her. She went to a teacher…'

'…Ms Addison.'

'Okay. And the teacher went to Mr Dillinger, who told Gil. They believe Amy was assaulted as a punishment for talking about the abuse.'

Minshull swore loudly, apologising to the food van owner who was setting out tables next to them. He leaned closer to Cora, his voice hushed but anger punching through every word. 'So Dillinger not only lied to the girls and their parents about us, but he also facilitated Amy's assault by passing on confidential disclosure details to a suspected abuser. And he still defended O'Sullivan, even when we shoved the evidence under his nose. The man is a monster.'

'People protect abuse. They don't want to believe it, they think it doesn't happen, or they just don't want to deal with it. Doesn't make it right. But it happens all the time.' She saw the flicker in Minshull's expression, her heart sinking further. 'There's more, isn't there? What aren't you telling me?'

'Someone else facilitated the abuse – whether he was aware of it remains to be seen.'

'Who?'

'Andrew Draycott.'

'No…' Cora bowed her head. She'd wanted to believe her doubts about the teacher were unfounded, but her gut had served her better than her head.

'I'm sorry. He allowed O'Sullivan to bring Gil's Girls to the field centre out on the estuary that he was raising money to renovate.'

'He must have known what was going on, mustn't he? Even if he was in denial about everything else, he must have heard the rumours. I can't talk to him now, not after this.'

Minshull hesitated, smoothing out the folds of the silver foil as if preparing an even path for his words. 'No, I think you should. I'm asking you to. And I know it's a huge ask but Cora, you have an advantage over the team and me: you might hear something from him.'

Was he really asking her to do this? She'd felt conflicted enough about the teacher before this latest revelation but spending time with him now, pretending she didn't know, while scrutinising his unconscious thoughts for the worst possible information? How was she meant to do it?

'I really don't think I can.'

He was on the edge of his seat now, eyes fixed on her, hand reaching for hers. 'I need you to do this. I need to know how much Draycott knew – and if he was involved himself. Because O'Sullivan may be beyond prosecution, but his accomplices aren't.'

'You can't ask me to do this…'

'I'm not asking. I *need* you to do this for me. If there were other girls – if there *are* other girls – I need to know. We couldn't stop O'Sullivan harming those children, but I am damned if I let someone else continue his legacy.'

Cora stared back. 'Is Andrew a suspect?'

'He could be.' He paused, eyes fixed on her. 'For both offences.'

'You think he killed O'Sullivan? Why do you think that?'

'What if he saw what was happening, knew who O'Sullivan was – the drugs, Gil's Girls, his seeming invincibility – and wanted to stop him? I kept going over it last night after the attack. It's possible.'

Cora couldn't believe what he was suggesting. 'No. No, he's devastated. Still talking about O'Sullivan like he lost his biggest hero. Why would he do that if he'd murdered him?'

Minshull let out a long groan. 'I don't know. I don't know about any of this. But if Draycott was in thrall to O'Sullivan and saw him as a role model, what might it have done to him to see his hero fall? What if Draycott killed him to stop the abuse?'

'Then why would he mourn him?'

'Because he was mourning the hero he thought O'Sullivan was.'

'And if he didn't kill him, but he'd become part of the abuse?'

'One of the leaders of the Bures Bowmen said they were watching another teacher at St Audrey's. She didn't name him, but she said she had sources close to the school who had confirmed he was in collusion with O'Sullivan.'

'So Andrew could have been in on everything? And he's mourning O'Sullivan because Oliver got Andrew involved and was no longer there?'

'It's plausible. If he aspired to be like O'Sullivan in every way – charming, popular with the opposite sex, able to get away with behaviour others couldn't – might he have become involved in the abuse because he thought he could get away with it, too?'

'But he's spending time with Lottie. Alone. They go for walks…' Her stomach twisted. '…along the estuary path. How far is the field centre from Woodsham St Mary?'

Minshull paled. 'It's right at the end of the estuary, a mile or so out towards the coast.'

'Walkable in an hour?'

'Easily.'

Cora rocked back in her seat, her hand sliding away from Minshull's. 'So he's abusing Lottie?'

'I don't know.'

What if I need a friend?

The memory of Lottie's words returned, a new, sinister edge to their meaning.

Because I'm totally alone.

It couldn't be Draycott, could it?

'He said he wanted to help her. He wants her to speak again.'

'What if he's checking what she knows? She stopped speaking two weeks after Amy and Bindi left the school. She was part of O'Sullivan's inner circle. She told a teacher about his advances to Amy but then watched her friend suffer a horrific ordeal because Gil found out, and then have to leave the school. What if the knowledge she held terrified her into silence? What if Lottie holds the key evidence to all of this?'

It chimed with Cora's own revelation about the teenager's testimony. 'I'm changing tack with her now. She was very vulnerable last time I saw her and I think she's looking for someone to tell. If I can persuade her to speak again, I believe she will tell us things that bring the leadership of St Audrey's down. I think she wants to speak.'

'Then you have to listen. And you have to find out what Draycott knows and what his motives are.'

It was unavoidable, the two dovetailing together. If Lottie Arundel was the key to everything – and Andrew Draycott saw Cora as an ally – she had to put herself between them.

'I'm scared,' she said, shocked that she'd admitted it out loud.

Minshull took her hand again and this time he held it tight. 'So am I. But this is the best shot we've got. I'm here for you, whatever you need. Will you help me?'

Cora felt the strength where their hands met. 'Yes.'

Lottie

> **Lotts**
> Why haven't you been over?
> I haven't seen you for ages

> **Es**
> Mum was keeping me at home.
> And I didn't know what to do

> **Lotts**
> ?

> **Es**
> Bindi called me.
> She told me to stop talking to you

> **Lotts**
> Why?

> **Es**
> She said you were the reason Gil hurt Amy.
> It's so messed up

Lotts
It wasn't my fault.
I was trying to make it stop

Es
I know

Lotts
What did you say to B?

Es
I'm not going to stop talking to you.
You're my best friend

Lotts
Thanks E.
I'd do anything for you

Es
And me for you.
But I'm scared

Lotts
I know you are.
But I've got a plan.
Cora is going to help me

Es
What have you told her?

Lotts

Nothing yet. I wanted to be sure.

But she's cool, E.

She said she'll help me

Es

Does A know?

Has he met Cora?

Lotts

I think they met last week.

But he doesn't know what she said to me

Es

I have a bad feeling about this

Lotts

Gil told you to stay quiet.

A was his friend.

We won't let A silence you, too

Es

Can you really trust Cora?

What if she takes A's side?

Adults stick together

Lotts

Cora isn't like the others.

I think she's the friend I've been waiting for.

I think she can help us stop this

Es
I hope you're right.
I hate being scared all the time

Lotts
Me too

Chapter Forty-Four

Cora

You're quiet today.

Cora quickly assumed a smile and turned to Lottie. 'I'm a little tired. Sorry. I should have had more coffee this morning.'

We don't have to make these if you don't want to.

'No, I think it's a great idea. I'll concentrate hard.'

Lottie shot her a wry grin.

Make sure you do. These are important.

Between them the glass table was covered with embroidery skeins in every colour imaginable. They were piled up, a complete muddle of shades, and Cora wondered if this was Lottie's rebellion against Monica's military-tight organisation. She'd seen Lottie's mother's disdain whenever Monica had passed near the dining area, hurrying quickly away as if scared the disorganisation might affect her or spread further into her carefully controlled home.

It had been years since Cora had made a friendship bracelet. She remembered a few summers as a teen sitting with Liz Allis in the back garden of her childhood home, twisting and weaving the rainbow-hued threads into rope-style bands they wore until time and use frayed them beyond repair. When her brother had gone off travelling he'd taken handfuls of the bracelets – by then forgotten by his sister as she started her university career – stuffing them into his rucksack as offerings for travellers he might meet along the way.

She thought of Charlie now, seemingly settled in Melbourne after years wandering the globe. At least he was in regular contact with their mother these days. Sheila had become adept at FaceTime and

Zoom, swapping her once near-obsession with online auctions for an avid pursuance of her son wherever in the world he happened to be.

Her family's newfound stability had been a great help to Cora. She wondered how she might have coped with this case had the old problems still been present to summon her time and energy. Knowing Charlie was finding peace and Sheila was bravely striking out into the world gave Cora the mind space to focus on the job at hand.

She needed that. Her tiredness today followed two nights without sleep as questions about Draycott, Lottie and the malevolent spectre of O'Sullivan danced never-ending circles around her mind.

Had she been so wrong in her initial impression of Andrew Draycott? It wouldn't be the first time she'd been mistaken, nor would it be the last, but she had been so comfortable in his company, so confident of his character.

Had he hurt Lottie? Was he planning to? Cora couldn't imagine it. Had he known what O'Sullivan was doing? That was harder to determine. Did he hand his friend the keys to the remote field centre knowing O'Sullivan's sins, or was he completely unaware? And how could she move forward with Minshull's request to get to know Draycott to discern his motives with all the other questions yet to be answered?

You've got a knot.

Cora inspected the bracelet between her fingers. 'Ah. That's a big one.'

Just weave it in.

'Won't it leave a bump?'

Call it a design feature. Mistakes make them more interesting.

'Great life theory,' Cora laughed.

You can have that one for free. The next one will cost you.

'I'll bear that in mind.'

After Lottie's broodiness the last time they had met, her cheeky jokes were a welcome change. She seemed happier today. Calmer. Cora watched her for a while, the teen's head bowed over her work, her hair twisted into a high top-knot that danced as she inspected the growing bracelet in her hands.

If Cora was to discover what Lottie knew, now was as good a time as any to begin.

'Have you seen Andrew lately?' She caught Monica's stare from the seating area and quickly corrected her mistake. 'Sorry: Mr Draycott.'

We went for a walk at lunchtime. He had a free period this afternoon so he had enough time to visit.

Cora nodded, the story familiar from her own experience of him. 'Where did you walk?'

Just up the path a bit. He tried to show me how to skim stones. Only he was rubbish at it.

Was that an excuse to get close to her? Sickened, Cora packed away the thought. She couldn't think like that if she was going to make herself talk to him again.

'What do you think of him?'

He's okay.

'Just okay?'

Lottie shook her head as she typed.

Why, do you fancy him?

'No.'

I forgot. You have the hunky detective.

'Behave. You know what I mean.'

Why does it matter?

How could she explain it without rousing Lottie's suspicion? Cora kept her attention on the twisting threads as she spoke, examining the progress of each word as she watched the loops and passes of embroidery silk.

'It's important to me to keep an eye on all the aspects of your life to see how they might affect your communication needs. We might need to make adjustments for different occasions, or certain friendships might require new methods so that they feel more natural for you.'

If you have to think like that about everything no wonder you're tired.

She had a point.

'Okay, how about this: do you see Mr Draycott as a friend for now, helping you find a way through this? Or could you see your friendship still being around in five years, ten years, or longer?'

Lottie considered this, her rainbow-woven fingers paused above the glass table.

He's a just for now friend.

'Why do you think that?'

Because he feels sorry for me. If my voice comes back, he'll leave.

'And how do you feel about that?'

It's necessary. Some people are necessary in your life. Until they're not.

It was a surprisingly adult thing for Lottie to say. Cora wished she'd had that level of insight at her age.

'That's very wise.'

Sometimes I surprise myself.

'Funny. Okay. How about… Esme?'

Friend for life.

'Straight in there, no hesitation.'

Lottie beamed.

She is. I love her to bits. I would do anything for her.

'She's lucky to have you as a friend.'

I'm lucky to have her.

'So you're going to grow old together?'

One hundred per cent. We'll be the two old biddies in the corner, nattering away.

It was a telling comment. 'When you picture that – you and Esme in your nineties, putting the world to rights, do you picture your voice being there?'

Over on the white sofas, Monica Arundel's design magazine lowered a little.

Lottie raised her eyes to meet Cora's careful stare.

Yes.

Cora offered an encouraging smile. 'That's good.'

The teenager appeared to falter momentarily. As she did, the half-woven bracelet slipped from her fingers. When it landed on the table, Lottie's voice appeared from it, crystal clear:

The danger will be over by then.

Chapter Forty-Five

Anderson

"*The Essex Police Drug Task Force has today secured a total of fifteen charges against Col McGann. This covers the full range of his illegal activities, from supplying Class A drugs to masterminding seven significant drug gangs spread out across the country including Suffolk, Cambridgeshire, Northamptonshire, Sussex and Essex. He is currently on remand and will face a trial in the coming months. I would like to pay tribute to my incredible team, including our undercover officers, surveillance teams and analysts. And I would also like to take this opportunity to thank Detective Inspector Joel Anderson and his team from South Suffolk Constabulary, whose insight and assistance played a major role in today's outcome.*"

DCI Fran Stephens smiled on screen as camera flashes rained down. It was the happiest Anderson had seen her. He thought of her business card, nestled in the dusty depths of his wallet, and the unexpected opportunity Essex had offered him for a second time. He wouldn't accept. He was fairly certain of that. But the knowledge of its presence when he'd spoken to DCI Sue Taylor yesterday had been a tonic to his spirit.

I am a man in demand, Sue. Belittle me at your peril...

Turning from the screen, Anderson grinned at the two people sitting opposite him at his desk.

'That includes you, Dr Lael.'

'Thank you.' Cora blushed beside Minshull, who was watching her with pride. Partly because he knew what was coming next and partly, Anderson suspected, because his detective sergeant was more than a little invested in the remarkable young woman seated next to him.

'What you heard at Abbot's Farm helped take Col McGann out of circulation. It gave me an opportunity to glean information about O'Sullivan from him that steered the investigation in a way we might have missed. And what he disclosed during that part of the interview provided evidence our colleagues there could use to secure charges from the CPS.'

'I'm glad it helped.'

'It's more than that. You heard O'Sullivan too, and that corroborated the theory that he'd been conscious when he was murdered.' He paused, knowing his next words were necessary – and long overdue. 'And the case last year…'

'It was my pleasure.'

Anderson wondered how true that was. None of it had been easy. 'Cora, I asked you to come in this morning because I have a proposition for you.'

Cora glanced at Minshull, who kept his eyes fixed on Anderson.

'I spoke with Detective Chief Inspector Sue Taylor yesterday and she agreed: we want you on our team. Permanently.'

'But I have a job…'

'As a consultant expert,' Minshull said. 'We would bring you in as we do legal advisors, tech specialists, profilers. So it wouldn't be every case, but when we need answers that regular evidence isn't providing.'

Cora didn't reply. Minshull's smile tightened a little. Anderson waited. After an uncomfortable pause, she spoke.

'I'd like to think about it.'

'Of course. I realise this is a lot to take in.'

Anderson watched the doctor regroup, packing her surprise away behind careful words. 'Thank you. I promise I'll consider it.'

Anderson held up his hands. 'That's all I ask. You're an asset to this team. It's taken some members longer to realise it than others, but what you've done for us hasn't gone unnoticed.'

'I appreciate that.'

'Excellent. I will await your reply. Rob, I've asked Tom Dillinger at St Audrey's to call a meeting of senior staff and governors so we can advise them on next steps while the security threat remains high. It's been arranged for two p.m.'

'So when they need protection we jump?'

He had guessed Minshull's reaction before it arrived. Nobody in the team was keen to do any favours for the leadership at the school, but with threats continuing against those who had collectively failed Amy Godwit and Bindi Henderson-Aziz, it was a necessary evil. 'The threats are too close to the children at the school to ignore. And there are other members of staff who have been dragged into this by association. They deserve our attention. You know the drill.'

Minshull gave a grudging nod. 'Guv.'

'In the meantime, why don't you take a couple of hours off? It's very early and I'm guessing neither you nor Cora have had breakfast yet. I don't need you back here until eleven.'

Surprise from the other side of his desk was all the reward he'd hoped for. He had ulterior motives for his suggestion, of course. The revelations of Operation Feldspar and the aftermath of the attack on Ellis and Bennett continued to rock the team and he suspected Minshull was bearing much of the burden on their behalf. Cora looked exhausted, too: working with one of the suspected victims of Oliver O'Sullivan must require every ounce of emotional strength. Anderson was surprised by how protective he had become of these two: perhaps if they were able to support one another he could stop worrying quite so much about the toll it was taking on them both.

Besides, neither of them would request any time for themselves. In that respect, they were equal.

'There's a place near the river that does a great breakfast roll,' Minshull suggested, looking between Anderson and Cora, as if seeking assurance from them both. 'We could drive out there and have a walk, maybe?'

'Great idea,' Anderson said, his plan succeeding. 'Off you go.'

Watching them leave, Anderson caught sight of his wife's wise smile in the framed photograph on his desk. She would be proud of him, if she knew. Not that he was likely to tell her. That knowledge in the hands of Ros Anderson would be a dangerous thing indeed…

The morning passed in a steady burr of activity and conversation. Both Ellis and Bennett were back at their desks, their presence much welcomed by their colleagues, who were rightly fussing over them. There was still an odd air between them. Anderson noticed it but resolved not to interfere. One intervention this morning was more than enough.

'Guv, you should see this.' Wheeler was at his door, stern-faced.

Anderson left his seat and followed Wheeler into the main CID office, nodding his acknowledgement of the team. At Wheeler's desk he leant down to look at a document on screen.

'What am I looking at?'

'Tech just sent this over. They've had a right old game making sense of transcripts and user information for Dragon Army, the private group linked with the Bures Bowmen's main Facebook account. This is the list the guys have compiled of all active members, with conversations listed chronologically, most recent at the top. They've traced all the users now and are going through the content to see if action was suggested, supported or planned there. But this is what I wanted you to see.'

He tapped the screen halfway down, where a run of five conversation threads was grouped together, the same two users' names appearing.

Anderson blinked and leant closer. 'Wait, is that…?'

Wheeler looked up at him, the reason for his absent smile now clear. 'Rhian Butler. And Lottie Arundel.'

'What were they talking about?'

'We're still gathering all the details. But it seems young Lottie was asking for advice.'

'Advice from Rhian Butler? In a private group she must have been invited into? What advice would a fifteen-year-old girl need from the leader of a vigilante action group?'

Wheeler's expression darkened. 'Advice on how to unmask an active paedophile.'

'*Shit…*'

'Guv!' Evans was on his feet, a phone receiver in his hand. 'Traffic just found Oliver O'Sullivan's motorbike.'

Anderson snapped to attention. 'Where?'

'It passed a speed trap on the estuary road near Woodsham St Mary twenty minutes ago.'

'What?'

'They're bringing the driver in.' Evans's eyes were wide with the revelation. 'It's Trevor Arundel. Lottie Arundel's father.'

Chapter Forty-Six

Wheeler

'I told you, I was just taking it for a run.'

The man at the interview desk looked ready to throw up. Wheeler kept his head down as the thinly concealed fury of Joel Anderson raged beside him.

'And it's a lovely day for a ride, Mr Arundel, I am not disputing that fact. What I want to know is why you were riding *that* bike.'

'I had a free morning and the weather was good. I wasn't aware that it was against the law.'

'Don't be smart with me, sunshine.' Anderson caught the sharp stare of the duty solicitor seated beside Trevor Arundel and reeled himself back in. 'Why do you have that bike?'

'I've been repairing it.'

'For how long, exactly?'

'I don't know, a couple of months?'

'And where did you get it from?'

'From my workshop...'

Wheeler winced. If the arrested motorcyclist thought his answer was good, he was in for a nasty shock.

'Very good answer. Very clever. Let's try that again, shall we: where did you get that motorcycle from?'

As Anderson rounded on Arundel, Wheeler studied the man. Was he being deliberately obtuse or did Trevor Arundel really not know whose bike he was riding? Did the comebacks cover his fear of being found out or his utter incomprehension of the trouble he was in?

The links were scarily easy to make. Oliver O'Sullivan's bike was missing from his home, believed to be his means of transport to Abbot's Farm, where he was murdered. Trevor Arundel's daughter Lottie was a student of O'Sullivan's, also lately confirmed as one of his notorious inner circle, Gil's Girls. Two of her best friends had been abused, leading to their leaving the school, the abuse buried. Lottie Arundel had stopped talking two weeks after the girls moved.

What if Lottie had been assaulted? And what if she'd told her father?

Could Trevor Arundel have tracked O'Sullivan to the remote barn and murdered him?

The threads met but somehow felt wrong. If he was concealing the motorbike as evidence, why take it out for a ride where there was every chance he'd be seen? Wheeler could see Anderson's brain making the links: would he sense the danger too?

'Mr Arundel, where did you get the motorbike from?'

Trevor Arundel stared back with righteous indignation. 'I don't see how that's relevant.'

Wheeler mentally ducked.

'It is relevant, sir, because we have been looking for that bike for the last fourteen days. That is why my uniformed colleagues at the speed trap flagged the bike's registration when you drove past.'

'Why have you been looking for it?'

'Why do you think?'

'I have no idea! I don't know why I am here, I don't know why you're asking me the same, incessant questions over and over again and I don't know what you want me to say that I haven't already.'

Wheeler heard the hiss of a slowly released breath through Anderson's gritted teeth. 'DC Wheeler, would you care to inform Mr Arundel of the particular history of the motorcycle he is in possession of?'

'My pleasure,' Wheeler answered, glad of the opportunity to diffuse the dangerously volatile atmosphere in the small interview room. He consulted his notes, the pause giving him a moment to breathe. 'The registered keeper of your vehicle is a Mr Oliver O'Sullivan from Woodbridge. His bike went missing around nine weeks ago, around the same time we believe he went missing.'

'What?'

Wheeler didn't raise his head as he read, but he could already feel the effect his words were having on the man on the other side of the interview desk.

'Mr O'Sullivan was a teacher at St Audrey High School in Wood-bridge, a popular member of staff and a favourite of his students...'

Wheeler's gut turned at the words. Everyone knew what O'Sullivan really was. He swallowed hard to dislodge the ball of emotion at his throat, and continued: 'Mr O'Sullivan was found dead in a barn at Abbot's Farm on Semer Road, near Whatfield on Wednesday 19th April. He was murdered. His motorcycle was missing.'

Now he lifted his head, staring directly at the visibly shaken man opposite.

Joel Anderson rested a hand gently on the edge of the desk – a sign that Wheeler had said enough. Relief flooded Wheeler's body.

'Did you know Oliver O'Sullivan?'

'He's my daughter's teacher, so yes.'

'Did Mr O'Sullivan sell you his motorbike?'

'No.'

'Did he ask you to take care of it?'

'No, why would he?'

Anderson didn't blink. 'Did you take it from him?'

'No.'

'Did your daughter have concerns about her teacher?'

'What does that have to do with—?'

'He assaulted two of her closest friends. Did she tell you he had harmed her in any way?'

'I can't believe you're asking me this.'

'Did he hurt Lottie? Were you horrified when you found out?'

Wheeler couldn't look. He knew the questions were valid, but that didn't make them any easier to hear.

'No. *No!*'

'Did you lure Oliver O'Sullivan to the barn at Abbot's Farm on Semer Road near Whatfield?'

'*What?*'

'Maybe you just wanted to confront him, to scare him. Maybe you didn't intend to hurt him. Maybe things escalated...'

'I – I—'

The duty solicitor coughed.

Anderson afforded her the slightest glance. 'And when he was dead, you shoved his body into the piles of clothes at one end of the barn...'

Hang on... Wheeler was suddenly alert. What about the real murder method? O'Sullivan died from a large dose of bleach, injected into his neck, not the theatrical smashed skull his killer had hoped police would be fooled by. Had Anderson overlooked it? Forgotten? Or was he about to round back on himself to ask?

'Guv,' he said, as low as he could.

'...and then you took his motorcycle home, hiding it in your garage.'

'Absolutely not!' Arundel glared at the solicitor. 'Aren't you going to stop him?'

'You don't have to answer.' The solicitor's calm was impressive given the anger playing out all around her.

'But he's saying I murdered Lottie's teacher! That O'Sullivan *touched her*...' His voice broke as emotion overwhelmed him.

'Guv...'

'Did he touch her, Mr Arundel?' Anderson demanded, unrepentant, his question pressing salt into a gaping wound. 'Is that why your daughter is no longer speaking?'

'*I don't know!*' Arundel collapsed, his sobs shuddering through his body as he covered his eyes.

In that moment, Wheeler wished himself as far as he could get from Interview Room Three. He didn't want to hear any more.

'DI Anderson,' the solicitor began, but Joel Anderson had finally seen sense and had fallen silent.

They observed the broken man for some minutes, the only sound being recorded by the machine on the desk: the desperate sobs of a man completely out of his depth.

Then Wheeler stepped in. This had to stop. It was getting them nowhere. If Anderson minded, he didn't let on, rod-straight in his seat, eyes trained on Arundel, lips firmly shut.

'Where did you get the bike from, sir?'

'A friend… I was fixing it for a friend…'

Wheeler rested his arm on the desk, praying Anderson kept quiet. 'Which friend, Mr Arundel?'

Trevor Arundel pushed a hand over his eyes, wiping the tears away. 'A friend of Lottie's. Rhian Butler.'

Chapter Forty-Seven

Cora

The small patch of woodland beside the river was a haven of dew-soaked green. Cora breathed in the rare air that stung her lungs with its freshness. It was beautiful here and yet so well concealed from the main road snaking its way into Ipswich. How many times had she sped past on her way to work and missed it?

Minshull was right about the food van, too. The breakfast roll was almost too much to eat: piping hot bacon, sausage, the softest poached egg and sweetest mushrooms, with a hash brown fixed to the top of the bun by a wooden skewer.

Now, they were walking slowly along the wooded path, carefully stepping over moss-swathed rocks and twisted ancient roots that wove a rich texture beneath the trees.

She needed this.

They needed this.

The past week had been a relentless assault on both of them. Cora could see the toll it was taking on Minshull, usually so immovable and calm in the face of whatever his job threw at him. Should she ask him about it? She felt unsure. Their friendship, such as it was, had no defined boundaries yet. The fluid nature of their association suggested a wealth of possibilities but also proved tricky to navigate when it came to more personal subjects.

Was that what Joel Anderson was trying to set up by sending them out of the office? It seemed unlike him, but Cora had witnessed the detective inspector paying closer attention to Minshull than he had before. They had been through a lot together, but that was no indicator of how close they should be.

'This is just what I need,' she said, smiling at Minshull when he drew level with her.

'Me too.'

'It's gorgeous here. I can't believe I've passed the food van in the lay-by so many times and never known this was behind it.'

The sun had just begun to push through the pale clouds above them, dappled light filling the woodland and passing across Minshull's shoulder. He was quiet, but Cora didn't mind. It was good to be in the moment, with no intrusion of the pressing matters surrounding them.

'How did you find this place?' she asked, after a while. They had reached a sand and shale patch at the edge of the river. Minshull hopped down the bank and offered his hand to help her down. She took it, mirroring his smile as he steadied her.

'An ex introduced me, actually.'

'Oh.'

One boundary found...

'Yeah, sorry. Awkward, much?' His grin put Cora at ease. This was clearly a situation they both found odd. 'A couple of years ago. She worked for the Wildlife Trust and they did some restoration work on the path farther down from here.'

It was strange to think of Minshull having a life beyond the CID office. Even though Cora saw him outside of work hours, he always seemed connected to it, whether they were running along the coast path or enjoying a meal out.

'Well I am grateful to your ex,' Cora said, laughing at her own words. 'This is not the conversation I thought we'd be having today.'

'Makes a change from murders and vigilantes,' he replied, swatting a fly that was buzzing about his head. 'So while we're both reeling from that... Have you dated since...?'

He didn't need to finish that sentence. Cora grimaced. 'No. Can't say I miss it.'

'Or him.'

He was wearing a gentle smile when she looked at him.

'That too.'

'He was a tosser. I can say that now.'

'He thought you were after me.'

'Shows what he knows.'

Cora didn't reply. It was fun but that was the moment to stop. She bent down to pick up a handful of river-smoothed pebbles, turning them over in her palm. 'So, do you come here often?'

Minshull's laugh dislodged a wood pigeon from the branches above them. It blundered through leaves and branches in its panicked escape.

'Now who's propositioning who?'

'That's not what I meant and you know it.'

'When I can,' Minshull replied, the mischief still playing in his expression. 'Kind of good to have it on standby, you know.'

'Thank you for bringing me here.'

'Any time.'

Cora smiled and looked down, turning one hand over and carefully balancing four smooth pebbles, one on each of the knuckles at the base of her fingers. It was a meditative act, something her father had shown her how to do on the beach at Felixstowe when she was tiny.

'What are you doing?'

'Pebble-flip. My dad's favourite game. He'd set up a contest – him, my brother Charlie and me. So you balance the pebbles here and then—' she flicked her hand, setting the stones flying, quickly turning her hand over to catch them in her palm, '—you catch as many as you can.'

'Okay.' Minshull leaned closer, watching. 'And then what?'

'This.' Cora flicked her hand again, the pebbles landing and skidding off the back of her hand leaving only three where they started. 'The winner is the one with the most pebbles on the back on their hand after two pairs of rotations.'

'Got it.' Minshull scooped up a handful of pebbles, looking up at her, a wide grin spreading. 'Prepare to lose.'

'Oh, it's on! Ready?'

'Ready.'

Giggling, they began to play.

'Okay... Flip!'

'Ah! I lost one!'

'You still have three. I've got all of mine though.'

'Yeah okay, rub it in.'

'You're still learning. Ready to flip back? This is the tricky one, remember? And... flip!'

'Oh yes!' Minshull caught all of his remaining pebbles, punching his free hand in the air. 'How about you?'

Cora offered her hand with only two pebbles precariously balanced on her knuckles.

'Denied! The master loses to the apprentice...'

'You are so competitive!'

'You're only complaining because I won.'

'One round. You won one round. There's still another...'

'Well, if you need another round...'

'It's the rules!'

'Hmm.'

Amused, Minshull observed her. The change in him was startling – so markedly different from recent days. So welcome. Here, he was fun; free, as if he had shrugged off the darkness he'd carried like a heavy rucksack and left it far up the bank, concealed in the dank shadows at the woodland's edge.

Cora felt the air settle between them, the river hush. She let her gaze travel to their outstretched hands now inches apart, pebbles still balanced there.

As Minshull followed her line of sight, his phone began to ring.

'I've got to...'

'Of course.'

He flipped his hand, catching one pebble as the others clattered back to the river beach, pocketing it as he answered.

'What? When?' He looked back at Cora, the darkness returned. 'Are you bringing her in?'

Cora didn't wait to discover what was happening: his expression said it all. She scrambled back up the bank onto the woodland footpath and started to hurry back towards the car, Minshull hot on her heels.

Within five minutes they were back inside the vehicle, the wheels skidding on the uneven ground of the lay-by beside the food van as Minshull floored the accelerator and they sped away.

'They arrested Trevor Arundel,' he said, frowning at the road ahead.

'When?'

'Traffic picked him up about half an hour after we left the office. He was riding O'Sullivan's motorbike.'

Cora remembered her first conversation with Trevor Arundel by his beautiful workshop, Lottie's sudden relinquishing of *GIL* seeming to come from nowhere... No – wait: his hands! Trevor was wiping oil from his hands just before *GIL* appeared... Did Lottie know the missing motorbike was in there all along?

Had her father murdered O'Sullivan for his crimes against her and sworn his daughter to secrecy? Was that the reason for Lottie's silence?

'I need to call Lottie. If she's seen her father arrested...'

'Wait: there's more. Lottie has been talking to Rhian Butler – one of the leaders of the Bures Bowmen.'

'No! No, you're wrong.'

'They talked in a private Facebook group – Dragon Army. It's hosted by Rhian Butler and her co-conspirator, Garvey Maitland.'

'What were they talking about?'

'How to reveal a paedophile in public.' He shook his head. 'We're waiting for the full transcripts. But what if Lottie went to them because she was scared of someone else getting hurt if she told a teacher? Like what happened with Amy? Lottie told Carly Addison, who told the head teacher. He told O'Sullivan – and shortly after that Amy Godwit was assaulted.'

Minshull slowed the car to turn into a much narrower lane that passed over a hill flanked by fields. He was driving a criss-cross route in an effort to beat the building midday traffic into Ipswich. The car bounced and butted its way over the uneven, pothole-scarred lane.

Could she believe this? Cora considered the revelation, but none of it fit. 'How would Lottie even know where to find a vigilante group? Let alone get herself invited to the private chat room of one?'

'The Bowmen have been mouthing off online for months. Yelling about keeping our towns and villages safe from the threat of child molesters and drugs gangs and their incessant call for ordinary people to seek justice. On a cesspit social media site they would have been easy enough to find… Oh!' He slapped a hand to his forehead. 'I am so stupid!'

Cora twisted in her seat. 'What is it?'

'When we arrested Rhian Butler she told us she had a source watching teachers at St Audrey's. Why didn't I think it was one of the students?'

'Lottie was spying on her teachers? Why?'

Minshull was still castigating himself for his mistake. 'These groups, they pull people in. People on the peripheries, people who feel the police don't care about them. People who've been hurt…' He looked at Cora, eyes wide. 'Survivors of abuse.'

'If O'Sullivan abused Lottie as one of Gil's Girls—' she began.

'—she might have thought the police wouldn't care, like they hadn't with her friends.'

Because I'm totally alone.

The sickening realisation hit Cora, winding her. 'What if Gil abused Lottie because she challenged him about Amy and Bindi leaving school…?'

What if it isn't what you want to hear?

She breathed hard against the ball of pain that formed at her chest, the thought of the terror Lottie might have endured too much to bear. Terror so great that it forced Lottie to bury her own voice – and Gil's name – far out of reach. 'What if O'Sullivan is the cause of all of this? What if he stole her voice?'

'Shit, Cora…'

'I have to check she's okay.'

'Do it. We need to know what she knows. If he told her not to speak…'

'I know.' Cora was already finding Lottie's home phone number, her fingers clumsy across the phone screen. 'I'll call her mother.'

The car sped through the Suffolk countryside, Minshull muttering under his breath as he swung them around the tight corners where the narrow country lanes edged wide fields.

On the fifth ring, Monica Arundel answered. 'Yes?'

'Mrs Arundel – Monica – it's Cora. I just heard about Trevor. Are you okay?'

A sob sounded close to her ear. 'I don't know what's happening. I called Ipswich police station but nobody will talk to me.'

'I'm with DS Minshull now. Everything is okay, Trevor's at the station and they're getting to the bottom of it.'

'I can't believe he took that bike out! He promised me...'

Cora placed a hand on her collarbone, fighting her breath for control. 'Monica, did you know where the motorbike came from?'

'What? No! Some friend of a friend asked him to tinker with it. My brother died in a motorcycle crash, nine years ago. Trevor knows I won't have anyone I love near one of those death traps. I only agreed to him having it in the workshop if he promised he'd never ride it.'

'What's she saying?' Minshull hissed beside her.

Cora lifted her hand to ask him to wait. 'How's Lottie? I wanted to check she's okay. A shock like that could—'

'She's not back yet.'

'Not back?' Cora's heart contracted. 'Where is she?'

'Andrew came over this morning. He was doing some work at that field centre he's renovating and he asked Lottie to go and help him.'

'No!'

'What's wrong?'

'Monica, where is the field centre? Can you reach it by road?'

At Cora's mention of the location, Minshull gripped the wheel.

'There's a track... Just past the village hall. It's signposted as a bridleway to Silver Edge, but it's driveable. Why?'

'I'm going to go there now.'

'Will you fetch her home? I don't know what's going to happen.'

'Of course I will. If she gets back in the meantime, keep her there and call me straight away, okay?'

'Is she in danger?'

Cora battled to keep her reply steady. If what Minshull had intimated about Draycott was true, how safe was a vulnerable fifteen-year-old with him, alone, far out on the estuary? 'We're on our way. Try not to worry.'

'She's with Draycott?'

'It looks like it. We have to get there.'

'Where?'

'We can reach it on a dirt track from Woodsham St Mary.'

'Okay. Hold on!'

Cora braced herself between the dashboard and the passenger door as Minshull slammed his foot on the brake. The car lurched to a sudden stop on the country lane, their seatbelts jamming taut and cutting into their chests. As Minshull quickly reversed up the lane towards the entrance to a farm, Cora's phone beeped.

It was a text. From Lottie Arundel.

> Cora
> You said my voice matters.
> I'm ready to TALK about Mr O'Sullivan.
> I need you here.

'What is it?' Minshull demanded from behind the wheel.

Tears burned Cora's eyes. 'Lottie says she's ready to talk. TALK is in capitals. Rob, I think she wants to speak…'

Lottie

She's coming. Like I knew she would.

I told Esme we could trust her.

What will it be like when I speak, after all this time? Will my voice even work?

Cora asked me, right at the beginning, if I'd ever tested my voice since I stopped speaking. I never have, not even when I've been out on the estuary path by myself and there was nobody to hear me.

I made a promise.

A vow.

I can't break it until it's time.

My hands are shaking. I wasn't expecting that. I should probably sit down when I tell Cora – my legs feel strange, like they'll fail the moment the sound leaves me. I want to be strong when I release the truth. I want it to be right.

Rhian said I'd done the right thing, telling her. She said it would stop other girls getting hurt. She was there for me when nobody else was: she understood.

But Rhian isn't replying to the message I sent.

I wanted her to be here for this, because without her it wouldn't be happening.

I've checked the message again and there's no tick beside it to say she's read it. Yesterday in Dragon Army she told me she'd be at home all day today if I needed her. Where is she?

Chapter Forty-Eight

Anderson

'No comment.'

She knew she was in trouble. Anderson had seen her brought in the first time after the raid on her home that had also yielded Garvey Maitland as a bald-headed bonus prize. She was cocky, then, mouthing off to anyone who would give her the attention she so clearly craved.

What a difference a week made.

Bennett sat beside him in Interview Three, her face as stony and immoveable as an Easter Island head, no doubt a white-hot molten floe concealed behind it. It was scary, made more so by the furious red scars that peppered her face, the still-healing legacies of the attack she'd suffered in the name of the Bures Bowmen.

'You could help us out, Rhian. You could clear this up and we could end this pointless game.'

'No comment.'

'Why were you in possession of Oliver O'Sullivan's motorcycle?'

'No comment.'

'Why did you ask Trevor Arundel to hide it for you?'

Did she just yawn?

'No comment.'

'Did Trevor Arundel murder Oliver O'Sullivan?'

'No comment.'

'Did you assist him?'

Butler's eyes narrowed. 'No comment.'

'What is Trevor Arundel to you? Friend? Father of a friend? Lover?'

A snort from Butler, a look of derision.

'I don't think he's her type, Guv,' Bennett replied, her tone flat, stare boring into her prey.

'Oh?'

'She was very vocal about her sexual preferences the last time she was here. Prefers her partners more *thrilling*, if you get my meaning.'

'I fail to see how this is relevant or a professional manner in which to conduct an interview,' Sylvie Abreo snapped, making another note. The solicitor had been noting a lot of things since Anderson began questioning her client.

'And I fail to see why your client refuses her right to talk to us about this serious matter. So, again, Miss Butler: why were you in possession of Oliver O'Sullivan's motorcycle, days after he disappeared? And why did you ask Trevor Arundel to take care of it?'

Thunder rumbled beneath Butler's brows. 'No comment.'

Anderson had heard enough. He was done treading carefully. Baby steps had never been his style.

'Okay, let's try this: you murdered Oliver O'Sullivan.'

Sylvie Abreo's head jolted up from her self-righteous notes.

Though horror paled her expression, Butler didn't reply. It didn't matter: her shock was all Anderson needed to know.

He pressed on. 'We know you talked to Lottie Arundel. We know she sought you out on your Facebook page, that you subsequently invited her to join the private group, Dragon Army. It would have had to be you, as you're listed as host. Garvey too, of course, but while he seems a nice kind of thug, he's hardly one to check friend requests. Sounding plausible so far?'

Butler and her solicitor said nothing; their bookend glowers rather gratifying to see.

'We suspect Lottie Arundel was a victim of Oliver O'Sullivan. That he abused her, as he did her friends in his horrific inner circle. We think she came to you because she believed the Bures Bowmen would stand up for her. She came to you because she thought her teachers, her school, maybe even her family wouldn't believe her. She'd watched her friends betrayed by the very people who should have kept them safe. And she was determined to give them a voice.'

'If you suspect all this, why bother asking my client?' The solicitor asked pointedly.

'Because we believe your client also abused Lottie Arundel's trust.'

'How, exactly?'

'Excellent question. How did you do it, Rhian? Did you promise her the matter would be taken care of? That you'd send your questionable membership to go and sort O'Sullivan out? Did you take Lottie's pain, her fear, her experience, and use them to further your cause?'

'No!'

'You don't have to answer, Rhian.'

'I won't have him say that!'

'Oh I don't know, Miss Butler, I would've thought you'd be eager to take the credit. One less predator to prey on Suffolk's children. *Justice served.*'

'Absolutely not!' Butler's whole demeanour had changed, the first suggestions of fear gritted between her teeth and pulling at her jaw.

Anderson had her now. Even if the mental picture didn't quite fit. Rhian Butler was a scrapper, of that there was no doubt; but O'Sullivan had been well over six feet tall, with a rugby player's frame – how had Butler overpowered him? How had she smashed his skull and lobbed his body halfway into the wall of refuse sacks? Then, inspiration dawned.

'Garvey helped you, didn't he? You administered the bleach...'

'Bleach? What are you talking about?'

'Oh please, you thought the head injury would fool us? My colleague, Dr Amara, loves a good puzzle. She knew immediately that the broken skull wasn't the way Oliver died.'

Butler paled further.

'So, you administered the bleach into his neck – perhaps when he was sitting? And you watched him die a long, drawn out, undeniably painful death. A suitable punishment for his crimes. There are many people out there who wouldn't blame you. More, when the revelations are finally out at St Audrey's. But you needed to cover your tracks. So Garvey came to help with a bit of brute force and a handy blunt object. Then he disposed of the body.' Anderson leaned as far across the table as he dared. 'How am I doing, Miss Butler?'

'You're trying to pin this on me.'

'Lottie came to you. O'Sullivan wound up dead at Abbot's Farm. You asked Trevor Arundel to hide the motorbike for you. I'd say the evidence is compelling, Rhian.'

'It's circumstantial,' Abreo shot back.

Anderson folded his arms, letting the back of the uncomfortable grey plastic chair slowly take his weight. 'You murdered Oliver O'Sullivan because of what he was. Because Lottie Arundel sought your help when nobody else was interested.'

'No.'

'That's what I want to charge you with. And Mr Maitland, too. My colleagues DC Evans and DC Wheeler are talking to him right now.'

'No. I won't have it!' Butler was on her feet. 'I won't let you do this!'

As he watched the solicitor persuade Rhian Butler back to her seat, Anderson took the opportunity to regroup. The motorbike bothered him. Why give it to the one person who could link Butler with Lottie? If it hadn't been a premeditated killing – if a confrontation had simply got out of hand and O'Sullivan had somehow sustained a head injury, why hide the motorbike at all?

And then there was the matter of the bleach… Nobody took a large amount of bleach and the equipment required to administer it on the off-chance it might be useful in a confrontation. It required research, thought, planning and strategy – skills Rhian Butler had in spades.

But why make Lottie's father complicit in the murder, which would naturally point back to the girl?

Unless…

It came to him in a glorious flash of clarity. 'An insurance policy.'

'What?'

Bennett was watching him too; now, a deep frown making the healing glass scars across her forehead shift and dance.

Anderson could kick himself. It was so simple.

'You told Lottie Arundel that O'Sullivan's bike would need to come to her house. You persuaded her to sell the lie to Trevor that it was an old bike in need of some TLC. Knowing how much he enjoyed

342

tinkering with machines, it made sense. It was also convenient that his workshop was large enough – and the house remote enough – for it to be concealed for a long time. You set it up. And then, you threatened the girl.'

'No!'

'You told her to hold her tongue. You said if she told anybody – if she even spoke a word – the police would be tipped off that a dead man's motorbike was in her father's workshop, and that he would be arrested for murder...'

'No, you've got it wrong...'

'I don't believe I have. You stole Lottie's trust and then you robbed her of her voice.'

'That's *not* how it happened...'

Anderson wasn't stopping now. The pieces clicked into place as smoothly as if they'd been oiled, every duck lining up. It rarely happened these days, but when it did, it reminded him why he loved being a copper.

'And you kept her silent, by making her watch her teacher, Andrew Draycott. You told her where there was one paedophile, there were more. You singled him out as O'Sullivan's best friend, and insinuated that they shared all the same interests. Did you intend to murder him too?'

'Are you *listening* to me? That's *not* how it happened!' She really was desperate now, her face streaked with tears, her hands balled into indignant fists. 'I didn't want to be involved! I didn't ask for this!'

The solicitor put down her pen, closing her eyes.

Bennett stopped writing.

Anderson waited, his flow suddenly cut.

'It wasn't me!'

Chapter Forty-Nine

Minshull

'What if we're wrong about Draycott?' Cora asked, as the car crested a hill, the river estuary sparkling into view ahead.

'In what way?'

'What if he's gained her trust so that she can testify about O'Sullivan?'

Minshull's brow knotted. 'Convoluted way to go about it.'

'Think about it: Draycott saw what was going on, but also how St Audrey's was closing ranks against the girls. He didn't want to be seen as disloyal – for one thing, he didn't want to end up unemployed like Carly Addison. So, he decides to tackle the issue from the inside, while everyone's attention is focused on burying Amy and Bindi's accusations.'

'He turns to the silent girl who knows all of them...'

'...and works with her to uncover everything she can't say.'

Minshull glanced at her. Was she wanting Draycott to be innocent because the alternative was too awful to consider, or was there another reason?

'It matters to you, doesn't it?'

'What?'

'Draycott not being a monster.'

He felt the heat of her stare as he resolutely kept his eyes on the road.

'There are too many monsters in this case, that's all. I'd like to think someone has the power to surprise us.'

'Do you want me to come in when you see Lottie?'

'I don't think so. She doesn't know you. If she really is about to speak, she needs to be surrounded by people she already trusts.'

It was as he'd expected. 'I'll stay in the car, just outside. If you need me, yell.'

'Thanks.'

Minshull took a right at the next junction and the first houses of Woodsham St Mary came into view. Ahead lay the village hall, a short, squat single-storey 1930s building with a faded grey roof and yellowing paintwork. It sat on a small triangle of grass at the meeting of three narrow roads.

'That one.' Cora pointed to the right hand lane, a blue bridleway sign pointing down it beside a red telephone box.

Minshull steered the car down the lane. A row of whitewashed cottages edged one side, a large blackthorn hedge on the other. At the end of the houses the tarmac road came to a halt, a large wooden gate separating the road from the dirt track beyond.

Cora jumped out and wrestled with the stiff metal latch, swinging the gate open for Minshull to drive through. The wind had picked up: this close to the wider estuary it blew in straight from the coast. It whipped the ends of Cora's auburn bob around her face, the strands obscuring her features as she closed the gate and hurried back to the car.

'It's going to be rough from here,' Minshull advised her, bracing himself for the journey ahead and wishing the pool car had been a sturdy four-by-four and not a battered Ford with its best days behind it. 'Hold on.'

They set off, rolling and bumping over the rutted track. Minshull's shoulders ached within seconds as he fought to keep the car in the middle of the bridleway. Wind-bent hawthorns stood as twisted sentries for the first couple of hundred yards and then they parted, the wide, flat estuary spreading out into view. Sandy mudbanks rolled into patches of shimmering white water, the strengthening coastal breeze blowing rippled lines across them. To the right, the shape of a wooden building came into view, silhouetted dark against the bright sky.

'That must be it,' Minshull said, avoiding a large pothole before steering the car onto a hardstanding path that cut through a grass-topped sandbank, raised a little from the rest of the estuary land.

'I can see a car beside it,' Cora said. 'That must be Draycott's.'

Was she keen to prove Minshull wrong regarding the teacher? The thought sat uneasily within him. Everything pointed to Draycott being involved, including the loan of this dilapidated building for Gil to take his 'girls' to. How had he justified it to himself? At the very least he must have questioned why a man in his thirties would be taking five fourteen-year-old girls to a remote spot all by himself. You would know if your mate was doing something dodgy, wouldn't you?

Wouldn't you?

And yet, Cora remained determined to give Andrew Draycott the benefit of the doubt. It made no sense to Minshull, but the text message from Lottie did appear to suggest she had reached some decision regarding what she knew about O'Sullivan. Had Draycott invested time in gaining her trust to reach this point?

'What are you going to tell Lottie to do?' he asked her.

Cora hunched down in her seat. 'She already knows that you and I are friends. I haven't worked it all out yet, but I think I have to encourage her to speak – physically or using her tablet – and then suggest we come out to talk to you.'

'Do you think she'll trust me?' The question was more vulnerable than Minshull had intended and carried a far deeper meaning than he wished to reveal. *Like Draycott*, the words finished in his mind. *Will Lottie trust me as much as she trusts him?*

It was going to be purgatory waiting in the car, deliberately not party to the conversation Cora would be having with her young client. Minshull hated being on the outside of anything, a position he'd been forced into many times over the years, especially when colleagues suspected his career progression was down to being the son of a celebrated former DCI. But today it was a necessary evil: Lottie Arundel held the key to the whole of Operation Feldspar. Her testimony about O'Sullivan, Rhian Butler and the blinkered leadership of St Audrey High could pave the way for justice to finally be done.

Not the kind of justice trolled out by the Bures Bowmen, drip-fed like poison by Rhian Butler and Garvey Maitland, but *Minshull's* kind of justice. It was too late to make Oliver O'Sullivan pay for his crimes. It wasn't too late for the others to answer for theirs.

Nearing the field centre, Minshull spotted one side of the building that had no windows. He could park alongside it and be concealed from view of anybody looking out. Carefully, he slowed the car to a crawl and steered parallel with the wooden cabin. Killing the engine, he turned to Cora, the sudden silence rushing into the car like an eager tide.

'This is it. Are you ready?'

Everything in Cora's expression screamed that she wasn't. She forced a smile over the evidence to the contrary.

'As I'll ever be.'

Before he knew what he was doing, Minshull's hand was on her arm, her shock at its presence there as sudden as his. 'I'm here for you.'

Cora's hand rested gently on his, the warmth surprising. 'Thank you.'

'Don't take any risks, okay? Yell for me and I'm there.'

She nodded, taking a breath as if drawing strength from him.

And then she was out of the car, running towards the steps of the field centre.

Lottie

I just heard a car.

Cora's here.

I'm scared and excited, but mostly relieved that this is nearly over. I'm tired of holding it inside. I've carried the truth for too long. Now, at last, I'm ready to release it.

I have Andrew to thank for that. I'm so glad he brought me here; that this doesn't have to happen at home. He was right: this is easier done away from everyone else. I'm sick of being watched, of people picking over every damn detail without my consent.

I just want to live now, on my own terms.

I'm done with hiding.

There's a sound by the entrance. My heart skips.

She's here.

And it's time to find my voice.

Chapter Fifty

Cora

At the top step of the field centre building, Cora paused. She lifted her gaze to the weather-beaten roof, the rusted nails and flecks of paint that might once have been green revealing the sorry state it was in. From the track approaching, it had appeared in a much better state of repair: up close the extent of its problems was plain to see.

Should she knock?

Cora had sent a text back as she and Minshull had raced here, assuring Lottie that she was on her way. Beyond this door, the teenager was waiting. Cora prayed Lottie really was ready to speak. Pushing the handle, the door creaked open, forty-year-old hinges protesting her intrusion.

And there she was. Standing holding her tablet, in the middle of what once had been a classroom, its wide, single window framing the beauty of the estuary.

'Lottie. Are you okay?'

I am now you're here.

The breaths around the teenager that had faded in recent days were noticeably louder here. Cora felt the constriction in her airway as she had before. But that could be nerves, or the immensity of the occasion. Cora pushed it all aside: what mattered now was finding Lottie's voice.

'Are you ready to try and talk?'

The teenager's smile vanished as she bit her lower lip.

I want to speak so badly.

Cora took a step closer, her hand outstretched. 'I know you're scared. But this is the right thing to do. I believe in you, Lottie. I know you can do this.'

Then help me.

'I'm here,' Cora urged. 'Talk to me. You can tell me anything.'

The teenager's fingers moved across the tablet screen.

Even if it's not what you want to hear?

That phrase again: the exact words Lottie had spoken at the beginning.

'I want to hear whatever you want to tell me. I want to hear you speak. It's time.'

Lottie's hands were shaking as she reached for the power switch. Cora didn't dare breathe. Lottie could still change her mind. She could still back out. Cora watched, acutely aware of her own heartbeat, which sounded louder in this old, mostly forgotten place, as Lottie laid the tablet down on the windowsill.

I just want to speak, her voice shivered up from it.

Cora reached out her hand and Lottie took it, her chilled fingers gripping it like a life raft.

They had arrived – at last – at the moment Cora had feared she might never see. A wave of strong emotion threatened to sweep her away, but she held her ground.

'There's no rush,' she began, keeping her voice low. 'Take your time. Whatever you want to tell me is okay. I'm here for you. You know you can trust me.'

Lottie smiled, tears burgeoning in her eyes. Slowly, deliberately, she opened her mouth.

There was a moment then when everything paused. Cora heard Lottie's shuddering intake of breath, saw the fear in her eyes before they closed. And then—

'Will... will you help me?'

The sound was cracked, the edges grating as if they had rusted over time. But to Cora, it was the most wonderful sound.

Imprisoned for so long, kept captive behind an iron will, but now released, it was everything Cora had hoped for during the hours she'd worked alongside the teenager. All of that work, that encouragement, that belief... Her heart swelled with pride that Lottie had dared to find her voice again.

It was stunning to witness.

The intake of breaths that had guarded Lottie ebbed away, leaving only the sound of her true voice and the distant sounds of the estuary outside.

Cora didn't hide her emotion now. 'Of course I'll help you. I'll do anything.'

Lottie seemed to hesitate, her lips moving as if rehearsing lines. Was she having second thoughts? Was the comfort of the silence she had surrounded herself with calling her back?

Determined not to lose this moment, Cora pressed in. 'Whatever you need. We're in this together, aren't we? I'm here. And I'm not leaving.'

The most beautiful smile broke across Lottie's face. It was hope and triumph: a monster defeated, a dragon slain. Still holding Cora's hand, she led her across the room to a large hatch cut into the horizontal lines of timber. With her free hand, she pointed through the gap.

'He's in there.'

Chapter Fifty-One

Anderson

'Then who was it?'

Anderson rounded on Rhian Butler. None of this made sense. Was she about to throw Garvey Maitland under the bus?

'I knew he was going to be there, I will admit that. I arranged with Lottie to get him there. We worked it all out. But it wasn't to kill him. That was never the plan.'

'Then what was?' Bennett's question cut through the noise in Anderson's head.

Rhian Butler put her head in her hands, all semblance of bravado and smugness gone. 'We were just going to scare him. Garvey and I were going to threaten to blow his whole operation open: tell the school everything. The girls, the drugs, the lies he'd told, all of it. And then Garvey was going to give him a minute to decide: leave Suffolk immediately or face the consequences.'

'This is a pack of lies, Ms Barker. I think you colluded with a vulnerable teenager to get her there as insurance. And then you made her watch while you executed her abuser...'

'No! O'Sullivan never abused her.'

The interview room fell silent. Anderson was reeling, unable to gain his bearings. He struggled to reply, but Bennett succeeded.

'Then why did she seek you out, specifically requesting help with unmasking a paedophile?'

'Because of her friends. O'Sullivan propositioned her once. Or tried to. Lottie pushed him away and told him she was going to tell the school what he'd done. So he abused Amy and threatened Lottie

352

that if she told anybody else, Bindi would be next. Then her other friends in Gil's Girls.'

'Evil bastard...' Bennett breathed, clasping a hand to her mouth too late to stop the words escaping.

Butler stared at Anderson, her eyes begging him to trust her. It made him shrink back, the request unfamiliar in this room, where so often the person on the other side of the desk was pushing you as far away as possible. 'Please, DI Anderson, you have to believe me. We got him there to scare him away. That was all.'

'How did you get him there?'

'I told Lottie to start being nice to him. I'm not proud of that. I told her to get him on her side, to think his threats had made her compliant...'

'Compliant to his abuse?'

'No! I would never ask that! She'd let slip that he was a huge fan of Seth Naseby, the thriller writer. He's my—' She broke off, avoiding Anderson's stare. 'We have an arrangement. An intimate one... I told Lottie to say her friend knew Seth really well. The story was that he was researching his next book and was scouting locations he might include. We already knew Abbot's Farm was somewhere O'Sullivan frequented and he'd made mention of drugs to Lottie at one of the visits to field centre. Lottie just fed him the idea.'

Anderson could barely catch the threads being tossed around him. 'So O'Sullivan gets to meet his hero if he takes him to a great location for his book?'

'To a rural drug den. Yes.'

'And is Mr Naseby aware of any of this?'

Butler shook her head. 'It was just a story to get O'Sullivan there.'

Already, it was too much to take in. But it was only half the story.

'So what happened?'

'Lottie told her mum she was going to hang out with her friend Esme at her house in Woodsham St Mary. But instead, she met O'Sullivan on his motorbike by the village hall and he drove them over. Lottie's mum has a thing about motorbikes: she'd never let her kid ride one. Garvey and I went over in his van. The plan was for us to drop Lottie back in the village once we'd given O'Sullivan his marching orders and scared him out of town.'

'So what went wrong?'

Butler glanced at her solicitor, who waved her on, the evidence so great against her client now that it was better for Butler to tell the truth 'We got lost. I don't know what happened, we missed a turn or something. We had to turn around, retrace our steps until we found someone we could ask for directions. By the time we found the farm, we were forty minutes late.'

She coughed and swallowed hard, reaching for the plastic cup on the desk for a long sip of water.

'And when you arrived?'

'Lottie met us in the farmyard. She was in a state, a really bad way. I mean, she didn't know whether to laugh or cry. I figured it was nerves getting the better of her. I wish it had been… She led us into the barn. And that's when we saw him. His eyes were open. His face… He was slumped in a corner of the barn. Lottie said she'd thought we weren't coming, so she'd sorted the problem.'

It was preposterous, the whole story. Anderson had heard enough. 'This is a pack of lies. How did a fifteen-year-old girl overcome a fully grown, six-foot-tall man, all by herself?'

'I don't know! He was dead when we got there. I thought she'd found some drugs, he'd overindulged himself – I don't know! The first I knew about bleach and injections was in here – today. When you told me.'

The details of O'Sullivan's murder had not been disclosed to the press. The leaked crime scene photographs had shown a devastating head injury: there had been no need to disabuse the media of that as the means of murder. Anderson lined up the evidence again: the plan, the delay, the teenager's response…

And then, the cold, sickening possibility hit him. Was Butler telling the truth?

He didn't want to believe it. He pressed on. 'So how did O'Sullivan receive the head injury?'

'We argued about it for a long time. A couple of hours, going over and over it. And then Garvey said we should leave the body for your lot to find. Not hide it or try to pretend O'Sullivan went missing. He wanted people to know the man O'Sullivan was. And the truth would come out – like it did.'

'Like *you* announced on your page.'

'You lot weren't getting it. The school had buried the other girls' allegations. If it weren't for us, O'Sullivan would have been mourned and fawned over, not served the justice he deserved.'

'The justice you manipulated a fifteen-year-old girl to help you mete out?'

'That was her plan, not mine!'

Lottie's plan. Lottie's response. Everything within Anderson tried to push the accusation aside.

'Where did you hit O'Sullivan?'

Butler's gaze dropped to her hands. 'Garvey did it in his van. He had a plastic sheet he put down first. Then he used a sledgehammer...' She swallowed hard. 'There wasn't as much blood as he expected but he still wouldn't let me see inside the van afterwards.'

'I'm guessing he cleaned away the evidence?'

Butler nodded.

'So what about the other teacher? You said there was another teacher at St Audrey's who was a child abuser.' Bennett held Butler with her stare.

'I – I made it up. But statistically...'

'You lied.'

'Lottie told me about Andrew Draycott. She said he'd been O'Sullivan's best mate, that he'd given him the keys to the field centre so O'Sullivan could take the girls there. He was hardly innocent.'

'He isn't a paedophile.'

'No. I don't think he is. Lottie said he was devastated by O'Sullivan's death. He thought she was too because he'd seen her getting close to him while she was setting up our plan and he assumed she'd loved him like he did. When Lottie stopped speaking, he'd offered to help.' She ran a hand through her hair, watching the two detectives, gauging their response. 'It wasn't a stretch to suggest Draycott was the same as O'Sullivan in every way.'

'Why? Why do that to an already traumatised child?'

'We needed information. Lottie was the only person we could send into St Audrey's. She was happy to do it...'

A sharp rap at the interview room door made Anderson jump to attention. 'Kate, can you continue?'

'Guv.' She leaned to the recorder. 'DI Anderson is leaving the room.'

Anderson opened the door, grateful for the reprieve. He needed to think, to make some sense of the horror building within him.

Ellis was waiting for him in the corridor. 'Sorry to interrupt, Guv. The Sarge just called. He's at the field centre on the estuary with Dr Lael. Lottie Arundel and Andrew Draycott are inside, Cora's just gone in.'

Anderson went cold. 'What are they doing there?'

'Lottie asked Cora to go. She says she's ready to talk about O'Sullivan.'

'Oh holy— *no!*' Anderson wrenched the interview room door open.

'DI Anderson has just re-entered the room...' Bennett rushed, but Anderson was already facing a startled Rhian Butler.

'Did you tell Lottie you lied?'

'What?'

'Did you tell Lottie you'd lied about Andrew Draycott?'

'No – I didn't. Why would I?'

Suddenly the world around Anderson began to crumble. He stormed back into the corridor, Drew jumping in surprise when he reappeared.

'Call Minshull back. Tell him to get Draycott out of there. Now.'

'Why, Guv?'

Anderson's breath was ragged as he started to run towards the stairs, the horrific truth finally taking root. 'Because Lottie Arundel is going to kill him.'

Lottie

She's shocked. I thought she would be.

But she needed to know the monster he was.

The way she was talking about Andrew the other day, I knew she liked him. She said she didn't, but you know when someone is that invested in someone. Like Amy was. Like Esme was – until Gil threatened her.

They all show their true colours sooner or later.

'Lottie, what happened?' she asks, edging into the old kitchen. I think she's scared to touch him. But it's okay: he can't hurt her now.

'He was like Gil,' I say. It's strange to be speaking again, like I've stolen someone else's voice and lodged it in my throat.

'That doesn't answer my question…'

Is she going to touch him? Ugh, she is. Why can't she just leave him alone?

'He's dead,' I say, like it's the most obvious thing and Cora won't see it.

'How?' She's kneeling beside him, her hand at his neck. 'How did this happen?'

I pick up the syringe that's lying on the cracked blue vinyl worktop and wiggle it at her. It's much bigger than the ones you have your vaccinations with, but then it needs to be. Esme's mum has a bunch of them in her vet's bag that she leaves in the hall when she gets in from work. It was the easiest thing to steal. I don't think she even noticed it was missing.

'What was in the syringe?' Cora's voice is flat, no character in it at all. Like the voice from my tablet.

'Bleach,' I tell her. Because, honestly, it's brilliant. One of the people in Dragon Army shared a link to this really dark site that showed all different household things that could hurt people. Rhian took it down, of course, but I bookmarked it.

Nobody looks for bleach. That's what the website said.

'We have to call an ambulance…'

'No. You have to help me hit him.'

She stares at me like I have three heads. I expected more from her. She said she'd be in this together with me. Did she mean that, or not?

'Cora, you said you'd help me…'

'To talk, Lottie! I said I would help you *talk*. Not murder someone…'

'You don't have to murder Andrew. He's dead already.'

She's standing now, pacing the floor and muttering to herself. I thought it might take her a moment to get her head around it, but this is taking too long.

'You need to hit him so it looks like he fell. That's what Garvey did.'

'I can't hear this. Do you realise what you've done?'

What kind of a question is that? 'I've kept my promise. And I've got my voice back.'

She's stopped walking now. 'What promise?'

Ah. That's my mistake. I forgot Cora couldn't see it. She just seemed to know me so well, as if we were connected. Sometimes it even felt like she was inside my head, like she could see it all there.

She came here when I asked. The least I owe her is the truth.

We move back into the old classroom. I don't think she wants to be near the body. That's fine by me. I don't like looking at it either.

'Bindi told me first. They'd been acting really weird, not getting involved with the Girls, missing drama practice. It made Gil angry – and that was bad for everyone. So I went round to Bindi's and Amy was there. Bindi told me he'd asked her to do stuff – horrible stuff. She pushed him away, but she thought it was just her he'd done it to. She was really upset. Then Amy started crying and said it had happened to her, too. So I said they should tell someone at school. Ms Addison had been asking questions at the club for a few weeks, about the Girls and that. So I said I'd talk to her on their behalf. But Ms Addison told Mr Dillinger and he told Gil. And then…'

My voice stops working. It cracks and squeaks and I have to swallow a few times to stop myself crying.

Cora's crying now. I thought she might. She reaches for my hand and everything is okay again because I know she's going to help me. She promised she would.

'What was the promise?'

'Gil stole my best friend's voices. He made it so they had to leave school – so they were punished for telling the truth. They were asked to write it all down, everything, and then they were told they couldn't talk about it anymore. And Gil was just there, carrying on, saying whatever disgusting thing he wanted to us, lying about who he was, because he could. Two weeks after my friends left the school, Bindi tried to slit her wrists. I found her.'

My last three words come out like a whisper.

I don't want to remember what that looked like.

'Oh Lottie…'

'She begged me not to tell anyone. Then I found out about Esme.' I wipe my eyes on my sleeve. 'She saw Gil assaulting Amy in the changing room. She told him she was going to the police but he said if she did, one of her friends would get hurt. Her best friend. Me. And that's when I made the promise.'

Cora is watching me, her face wet with tears. I can't tell what she's thinking. But I carry on.

'Gil stole Amy's voice. He stole Bindi's voice. He robbed Esme of hers, too. So I made a vow: I wouldn't use my voice again until I stole his.'

She stares at me for a moment, taking this in.

'But after he died…'

'By then I knew about Andrew. Rhian said men like them always hunt in packs. She said to look for the person that was grieving him the most. And he was pathetic. Crying on that news report, coming to spend time with me because he thought I'd loved Gil, too. And he has the keys to this place. Where Gil brought the Girls. Where he asked for things in return that none of us should ever have been asked for. There's no way Andrew didn't know the truth. He didn't deserve to have a voice. So my promise became about him, too.'

'And now they're both dead and you can speak again.'

I smile – because finally she understands.

'So, how do I do this?'

'You need something heavy. Garvey used a sledgehammer but there's nothing like that here. A big rock would do it.'

Cora looks around. There are only paint pots in here and they're half empty. She turns back. 'There are some big rocks at the edge of where I parked,' she says – and I almost laugh out loud because this is too perfect.

'Let's get one!' I say, but Cora steps in front of the door.

'No – you need to stay with Andrew. Just to make sure.'

She's right. He seemed to go too quickly but Gil took ages to die. What if Andrew isn't quite gone yet? Cora is such a good friend. I knew she was the one.

'You go and get it,' I say, heading for the kitchen. 'But hurry.'

Chapter Fifty-Two

Minshull

They were taking a long time.

Minshull checked his watch. Thirty-five minutes.

If Lottie was gathering courage to use her voice, it might take hours. But with Draycott there, Minshull had hoped the process might be quicker.

Should he go in?

No – Cora had been clear on that.

He let out a long sigh that fogged the driver's door window. Here he was, on the outside of the action, just as he'd expected. Anderson would have Rhian Butler in custody now. He would be finding the truth of what happened at Abbot's Farm. Minshull kicked himself for being so easily persuaded to leave the office. He might have known the biggest break in Op Feldspar would happen the moment he wasn't there.

He caught sight of his pained expression in the rear view mirror and laughed at himself. How much of a diva was he?

He would have chosen Cora over Rhian Butler every time. He wanted to be here for her. She had worked with that poor kid for hours to achieve what he hoped was now happening inside the old, battered field centre. Did it help her, knowing he was just outside?

The car creaked as billows of wind buffeted its sides. Man, it was bleak here. No wonder people had stopped using this place. It had all the cosy charms of a graveyard.

He hunkered down in the seat, pushing his hands into his trouser pockets. Finding an object in the left pocket, he pulled it out. A smooth grey pebble, the sole surviving playing piece from the game Cora had showed him by the river. It was warm in his palm, and he was instantly reminded of Cora's hand on his just before she went into the field centre...

The sharp tone of his mobile split the moment. Minshull scrambled to pocket the pebble and answer the call.

'Sarge?'

'Hi Drew. What's happening?'

'Is Draycott there?'

'He's inside the field centre building with Cora and Lottie Arundel.'

'Is he alive?'

'Sorry?'

'You have to get Cora and Draycott out of there.'

'Whoa, whoa, back up. What's going on?'

Ellis sounded breathless. 'Rhian Butler says Lottie killed O'Sullivan. She injected him with bleach. And Butler lied to her about Draycott. Lottie thinks he's a paedophile, too. Minsh, you have to get them out.'

'Get back-up,' Minshull yelled, already halfway out of the door, fighting against the oncoming wind to push it open. 'And an ambulance.'

'On their way. I called them before I called you. Be careful, Sarge.'

The kid was the murderer? Minshull couldn't believe it. But all he could think about was getting into the building to reach Draycott before Lottie Arundel did.

And getting Cora out.

Chapter Fifty-Three

Cora

It took all of Cora's strength to walk calmly to the door. Lottie was watching: one hint of the terror raging within her would give the game away.

All around her, the screams of Andrew Draycott played out on an endless, sickening loop, Lottie's real, hissed first words rising from the syringe abandoned near him.

You're a monster. You're going to die like he did.

The hesitant words she'd witnessed Lottie forming had been a show for her benefit. Lottie had regained the right to her own voice the moment she'd stabbed Draycott with the syringe.

Cora wanted to stuff her hands into her ears to deaden the voices, but she forced her body to stay tall, her steps unhurried. If she could get out, she could reach Minshull and they could call for help. The door was close now, the handle within reach…

'Don't be long,'

Cora swallowed the bile in her throat that Lottie's call summoned. 'I won't be.'

She reached for the handle…

The door burst open.

Cora fell back in shock, her shoulder slamming against a stack of classroom tables against the opposite wall. Minshull skidded to a halt, staring down in horror.

'Cora!'

'Get out!' she yelled over the cacophony of voices, the trapped sounds of Draycott's murder now rising like a furious tide. 'Get help!'

But Minshull was already on his knees, his arm around her waist, trying to help her stand.

'No…' Cora moaned, desperate to stop him, but the voices were too powerful to find her own within them.

'Let her go!'

Lottie Arundel's voice cut through the haze of sound like a banshee. Minshull looked back and raised his arm – then yelped in pain. As Cora kicked against the weight of the voices to struggle to her feet, she saw it: the syringe, embedded deep in Minshull's bicep. She reached for it, but Lottie was already pulling it from his arm and raising it high to strike again.

'Lottie, no!'

'He was attacking you!'

'He was coming to help us! Put the syringe down!'

'No!'

Minshull cried out again as the needle crashed into his shoulder. He made to grab Lottie's wrist but she slipped free, taking the needle again. He grasped his arm, blood seeping into the fabric of his shirt, the stain growing beneath his fingers.

The screams rose again, the pressure within Cora's mind unbearable. As fast as she muted one, another would rise in its place. It was no use. She had to stop Lottie and get Minshull out. It was too late to save Draycott. She'd thought she felt the faintest pulse, but that was too long ago. What mattered now was saving Rob.

With every ounce of strength she could summon, Cora pushed her body up from the floor and launched herself at the furious teen.

'Stop this!' she yelled into Lottie's stunned face, as they fell back against a pile of tools, dustsheets and paint tins against the wall leading to the kitchen. There was a jolt as Lottie's head cracked against a toolbox, her scream of pain joining Draycott's repeated final scream in the room.

You're a monster…

Lottie's thought-voice bobbed in the waves of sound and Cora saw the syringe fall from her hand. She rolled off the teenager's crumpled body and made a grab for it, struggling to her feet and stumbling to the window in the back of the kitchen, syringe in hand. She leaned over the wooden carcass that had once held a sink, but the window latch was inches further than her fingers could reach. Glancing down, she saw Draycott's body.

She had no choice.

She raised her foot, gently resting it on the fallen teacher's shoulder.

'I'm sorry,' she whispered, as she pushed her weight against it.

The body sagged beneath her, but Cora surged forward, casting back the latch and throwing the syringe as far as she could.

She dropped back to the floor, not daring to look at Draycott as she hurried back into the classroom. The pile of decorating tools had toppled across the floor and Minshull was staring at the door, hand still clasped to his arm.

Cora turned – and lost her breath…

Lottie

They're quiet now.

I empty the bottle of paintbrush cleaner over the rolled dustsheet across the door. I like the feeling it gives me – them watching and me making the decisions. Rhian says that taking back power is what makes her get out of bed in the morning. That's justice: taking back what's been taken from you.

I reach beneath the small shelf just beside the doorframe and it's still there.

Gil's lighter.

When the Girls came out here, he used to give them cigarettes. Hand-rolled, all kinds of weird stuff inside. It amused him, fourteen-year-olds getting off their heads.

Cora and her detective watch in horror as I raise it up. I flick the top and the flame appears.

I'm not going to drop it. I'm not stupid. I haven't gone through all this just to chuck my life away. My revenge on Gil and Andrew and everyone at school who tried to stop the truth getting out will be to *live*. For as long as I can.

And to seek justice, like Rhian does.

'Put that down, Lottie!' Cora has her hand on the detective's shoulder and I don't know if she's protecting him or holding him back.

'It's over,' he hisses, through gritted teeth. Is he in pain? He must be by now.

'You have to promise that you'll take me home,' I say. Because I'm not stupid. I know the police will be interested in me now. But while I have their attention, I want to make myself heard.

'We all need to get out safely,' Cora says. I wonder if she hurt herself when we fell because she keeps wincing like someone's playing music too loud in her ears. 'Put the lighter down and we can go. Rob's got his car. It's only ten minutes' drive to your house.'

I glance at the detective. He looks scared now. 'Will you take me home?'

'Of course.'

I look back to Cora. 'Can I trust him?'

'You can.'

'Do you trust him?'

'With my life.' There's no hesitation. She's definitely in love with him.

It's enough. I'm tired now.

I lower my hand and move to snap the lighter closed. But the brush cleaner bottle was sticky when I opened it and now my fingers slip.

I watch it fall. It takes so long, but I can't move.

And then everything is burning.

Chapter Fifty-Four

Cora

'Put it out!'

Flames shot across the rolled sheet, the old wood of the door beginning to smoulder immediately. Thick, dark smoke billowed into the space, the acrid smell of burning catching the back of Cora's throat.

But Lottie didn't move.

'Move out of the way!' Minshull yelled, grabbing hold of the table stack to haul his body upright. The bloodstain on his sleeve was still growing, vivid red against the white. He staggered across the room and started kicking at the flaming dustsheet, swearing and yelling as flames licked at his heels. With one final effort, he kicked it aside – but the door was already alight.

Then Cora remembered the window in the kitchen over Draycott's body, still wide open from where she'd thrown the syringe.

Grabbing Lottie, she hauled her away from the door, pushing her to the far side of the room.

'The window's open in the kitchen,' she yelled. 'It's fanning the flames!'

'Can we get out through it?'

'It's too small but I need to close it.'

'No! There's no time.' He kicked at the paint tins, so perilously close to the remains of the burning dustsheet, to get them out of the path of the fire, then looked over at the large viewing window looking out to the estuary. 'We go through there.'

Cora grabbed a table from the stack and hauled it over.

A thud behind her made her turn, in time to see a half-empty paint tin roll straight into the path of the flames.

'It's burning...' Lottie murmured, her gaze fixed on the burning side of the field centre building.

'Grab the table with me!' Minshull was lifting one side of the table with his good arm. Cora caught the other, and together they pushed it straight through the glass.

She ducked from the flying splinters of glass as the window shattered, reaching over to grab Lottie. 'Move,' she urged the stunned girl. 'We have to go.'

Another thud sounded, followed by a crack as more tins began to burn. Not waiting any longer, Cora grabbed Lottie and bundled her towards the window.

'I can't...' Lottie began, but Cora wasn't listening. The screams rose and exploded as the whole building filled with flame. Cora pulled her to the window, kicking at the few remaining shards still in place. Then she lifted her up and rolled her out.

Lottie landed on the grass-covered sand as the screams of the building merged with the screech of approaching sirens.

Minshull had slumped against the window, his face grey with pain.

'I'll follow,' he said, swaying a little as the heat surged around them.

Cora flung her arm around his waist and brought his body close to hers. 'Not likely,' she said as she gave one last pull and they fell from the window.

Then there were voices on the wind, their approach finally pushing back the screams of the burning field centre. Cora held Minshull to her, their foreheads pressed together.

Feeling the reassuring warmth of his breath on her face, Cora closed her eyes.

Two Weeks Later

Fifty-Five

Cora

'Ready?'

'You have an unfair advantage here,' Minshull complained, nodding at the sling cradling his right arm.

'You only need one hand to play,' Cora returned, the pebbles balanced perfectly on the back of hers. 'Stop moaning.'

'Don't I even get a sympathy vote? May I remind you that my arm was fractured when you fell on it?'

Was he ever going to let her forget? 'I was saving you, remember?'

'Is that what you call it?'

Cora groaned. 'I'll give you best of three. I can't say fairer than that.'

Minshull grinned, shifting position on the beach to better support himself. 'Then prepare to lose *three times*...'

Cora laughed as their game began, the sound of the ocean and delighted children racing along the shore the only sounds she cared to hear.

It had been a long fortnight since they'd escaped from the field centre. Lottie was being cared for at a specialist facility while around her the arguments raged over how best to proceed with her prosecution. Tris knew the details, but Cora didn't ask. She didn't need to know. She had succeeded in her part of Lottie's story – bringing the teenager out from her self-appointed silence and finding the root cause. It was too painful to think of the rest.

At least those in power at St Audrey's were finally facing the consequences of their actions. Tom Dillinger had been relieved of his post, as had Bill Mayhew, the Head of Governors, both now under investigation for malpractice and severe breaches of child protection. Rhian Butler and Garvey Maitland awaited sentencing after pleading guilty to all charges. Last week, following a lengthy battle, Facebook finally took down the Bures Bowmen's page and the Dragon Army private group.

Minshull had relayed all of this to Cora with little celebration. The entire team had felt the gut punch of Operation Feldspar: for some, the job would never quite be the same.

'Two, one!' Minshull exclaimed, annoyingly adept at pebble-flip despite his injuries from which he was still recovering. 'You're buying the ice-creams.'

'You are such a kid.'

Minshull rested back against the rocks between the beach and the promenade. 'A kid who trounces you at pebble-flipping and really deserves a triple scoop.' His smile softened a little. 'You given any more thought to Joel's offer?'

Cora let her gaze travel out to the horizon. 'Maybe.'

'Maybe – is that a yes?'

'It's a maybe.'

'I think it would be good for you.'

Surprised, Cora turned to look at him. 'Why?'

'Because you need us.' He let the pebbles fall from his fingers, sending them bouncing and spinning across the sand and shingle. 'And we need you.'

'I don't know, Rob.'

Minshull followed the progress of a happy, sea-damp collie chasing a ball across the beach towards the shadow of the pier.

'I need you.'

Cora looked back at the sea, a hundred questions dancing across the waves.

'Maybe.'

A letter from MJ White

Dear Reader,

This is a story about the right to be heard.

When I first imagined Lottie Arundel and her silent world, I knew hers would be a story that might break my heart. Nobody should ever feel their voice is unimportant. But I wasn't prepared for how deeply her story would affect me.

While I was writing this book, the right of women to have autonomy over their own bodies was making headline news in America, with implications for the whole of the world. At the same time, allegations of abuse were coming to light from the very highest seats of power: in politics, in the film and TV industry and in countless other areas of society. The constant silencing of the truth by those responsible was abhorrent to me and I wanted *The Silent Child* to address this.

Parts of this story deal with very dark subjects. I wanted to highlight the effect that such cases have – and continue to have – on those who are forced to endure abuse, and how society's propensity for denial and disbelief damages voices that should always have been heard. As someone with personal experience of abuse, I wanted to show utmost respect to survivors and express the anger that so many are denied their right to voice.

The story takes place a year on from the events of the first book in this series, *The Secret Voices*, the aftershocks of that case still resonant with Dr Cora Lael, DS Rob Minshull and the South Suffolk CID team. Cora is pressing into her ability, choosing to see the possibilities of her emotional synaesthesia instead of being isolated by it. Emotional synaesthesia doesn't exist, but it is inspired by the lived experience of people with real-life, sensory-based synaesthesia.

If you enjoy *The Silent Child*, let me know! You can get in touch via Twitter, Instagram, CounterSocial, Facebook and YouTube and also on my weekly Facebook Live show, *Fab Night In Chatty Thing* – it takes place every Wednesday night at 8pm and I'd love to see you there. My viewers are the reason you are reading this book and series. And if you fancy leaving a review or, better still, telling other people about this book, I would be very chuffed indeed!

Thank you for coming with me on this second adventure for Cora and the gang. I hope you enjoy it – I wrote it for you.

Brightest wishes

Miranda x

Twitter: @wurdsmyth and @MJWhite13
Instagram: @wurdsmyth
CounterSocial: @wurdsmyth
Facebook: MirandaDickinsonAuthor
YouTube: mirandawurdy

If you have been affected by the themes in this book, help is available:
Women's Aid: www.womensaid.org.uk
Rape Crisis: www.rapecrisis.org.uk
National Male Survivor Helpline and Online Support – Safeline: www.safeline.org.uk
LGBT+ support – Galop: www.galop.org.uk
Children and young people aged 18 and under – Childline: www.childline.org.uk
If you are concerned for a child or young person's safety: www.nspcc.org.uk
If you think a child or young person is at immediate risk of harm, **call the Police** on **999**.

Acknowledgments

The second book for any author is tricky to write. The second book in your first ever crime series is daunting to say the least! But I am beyond lucky to have an amazing team of cheerleaders, experts, wise word-wranglers, emergency chocolate-and-tea providers and eager readers, who have made the writing of *The Silent Child* a total joy.

Thanks as ever to my fabulous agent, Hannah Ferguson, for her faith in me, and fierce support of my writing. Thank you to the incredible team at Hera Books whose passion, insight and huge enthusiasm for this story have encouraged me and pushed me towards even more darkly devious twistiness. Huge thanks to my editor, the amazing Keshini Naidoo, whose fervour for the story and utter glee at discovering this book begins with a body were precious gifts in themselves. Thanks to my brilliant copyeditor Jennie Ayres, for wise, insightful advice and the best reaction comments throughout the copyedit! Thanks also to my proofreader, Andrew Bridgmont.

Thanks to the wonderful PC Steve Franklin for his expert advice and insight into life as a police officer. Any mistakes in police procedure are mine alone.

As ever, massive thanks to my gorgeous audience for my weekly Facebook Live show, *Fab Night In Chatty Thing*, for their excitement about the series and huge love of Cora, Minshull, Anderson and the team. Also to my wonderful followers on Twitter and Instagram, including Emma Jane Lambert, who appears in the book as the Lunchtime News reporter. I hope you all enjoy this story!

Huge thanks to the wonderful crime writing community for making me feel so welcome. Special thanks go to CL Taylor, Mari Hannah, Dorothy Koomson, Emma Kavanagh, Julia Chapman, Louise

Beech, Rob Parker, Neil Lancaster, Steve Cavanagh, Simon Toyne, Adam Simcox and Chris McDonald for their kind words, endless encouragement and general awesomeness. (All their books are amazing – read them!) Thanks also to gorgeous writers Rachael Lucas, Kim Curran, Craig Hallam, Phillipa Ashley, Sarah Morgan, Fionnuala Kearney, Ian Wilfred, Andy Jones, Lynsey James, Josie Silver, Kim Nash and Emma Cooper, for cheering me on and keeping me going.

Thank you to Claire Smith and AG Smith, the Mints and the Dreamers, together with my Mum and fantastic in-laws Phil and Jo White, for always believing in me. As always, all my love and thanks to my lovely Bob and fabulous Flo – I love you to the moon and back and twice around the stars xx

Cora's second case is about finding your voice and using it when it matters. Thank you for allowing me to continue telling Cora's story.

Miranda x

Book Soundtrack Playlist

For every novel I write, I compile a music playlist that captures the emotion and atmosphere of the story I want to create. I play it every time I work on the novel, from first draft to finished book, and it helps me to maintain the mood and experience I want readers to have reading my story. Here is my book soundtrack playlist for *The Silent Child* – enjoy!

Main theme:

FORCES OF DESTINY (No Choir) – Two Steps from Hell & Nick Phoenix – *Legend Anthology*
SALTWATER – Chicane – *Best of Chicane*
THE SUN'S GONNA RISE – Sam Ryder – *The Sun's Gonna Rise EP*
FLEE – Paper Aeroplanes – *Forgotten Songs, Pt 1 (EP)*
GIVE ME THE FUTURE – Bastille – *Give Me The Future*
ERASER – Ed Sheeran – *÷*
LITTLE WHITE LIES – Florrie – *Little White Lies*
LET GO FOR TONIGHT – Foxes – *Let Go For Tonight*
EVERYTHING BUT YOU (ft. A7S) – Clean Bandit – *Everything But You (single)*
RED RIBBON – Madilyn – *Red Ribbon – Single*
I KNOW A PLACE – MUNA – *About U*
FLOYD TO KE ANLONG/PEEL PIER FEAR/THE WRANGLER (ft Ross Ainslie) – RURA – *Our Voices Echo EP*
AIR FÀIR AN LÀ (ft. Sian) – Niteworks – *Air Fàir an Là*
SAUDADE, SAUDADE – Maro – *Festival Da Canção 2022*